Deborah Carr, *USA Today*-bestselling author of *The Poppy Field* and *An Island at War*, lives on the island of Jersey in the Channel Islands with her husband and three rescue dogs.

Her Mrs Boots series is inspired by another Jersey woman, Florence Boot, the woman behind the Boots (Walgreens Boots Alliance) empire. Her debut First World War romance, *Broken Faces*, was runner-up in the 2012 Good Housekeeping Novel Writing Competition and *Good Housekeeping* magazine described her as 'one to watch'.

Keep up to date with Deborah's books by subscribing to her newsletter: deborahcarr.org/newsletter.

www.deborahcarr.org

 x.com/DebsCarr
facebook.com/DeborahCarrAuthor
instagram.com/ofbooksandbeaches
pinterest.com/deborahcarr
bookbub.com/profile/deborah-carr

T0200800

Also by Deborah Carr

NEIGHBORS AT WAR

DEBORAH CARR

One More Chapter
a division of HarperCollins*Publishers* Ltd
1 London Bridge Street
London SE1 9GF
www.harpercollins.co.uk
HarperCollins*Publishers*
Macken House, 39/40 Mayor Street Upper,
Dublin 1, D01 C9W8, Ireland

This paperback edition 2024
1
First published in Great Britain in ebook format
by HarperCollins*Publishers* 2024
Copyright © Deborah Carr 2024
Deborah Carr asserts the moral right to be identified
as the author of this work

A catalogue record of this book is available from the British Library

ISBN: 978-0-00-870723-1

Printed and bound in the United States

For my darling husband, Robert Carr who I miss every single day.

1962 – 2023

After the War Cabinet advised that the island of Jersey had been demilitarised, a second telegram was sent to the Lieutenant Governor of Jersey, Major General Harrison, on 19 June 1940, days before the invasion of the Channel Islands.

'The Channel Islands will not, repeat not, be defended against external invasion by sea or air.'

Prologue

9 MAY 1945

Helen heard another footstep on the stairs leading to the attic and covered her little boy's mouth with her hand. She forced a smile. 'Remember, Bobby,' she whispered, 'we mustn't make a sound.'

His small hand moved hers away. 'Because the Nasties are in the house?'

Helen nodded, her heart breaking to think that hiding in an attic from the Nazi officers who were billeted next door was part of his daily life. 'That's right.'

'We're safe in our fort though, aren't we, Mummy?'

She raised a finger to her lips, hearing heavy soles slowly making their way to their tiny hiding place, behind the secret cupboard under the eaves.

Seeing he was about to speak, she covered his mouth again and pulled a silly face. 'We are safe in here, but we must shush now,' she said, hearing an unmistakable creak on the floorboards directly outside their attic room, followed by a squeak as the door opened.

Desperate to clasp Bobby tightly against her, Helen resisted, aware that to do so might alert him to the seriousness of what was happening. He looked up at her, his large blue eyes so like his father's, and for the first time Helen saw fear.

Chapter One

June 1941

Helen heard her aunt coughing as she carried Bobby down the stairs to join her for breakfast. Anxiety gnawed in her stomach. This had been going on for weeks now, probably even months, and she wished her aunt would do as she asked and see a doctor.

'Morning, Helen.'

Helen tried to smile but failed. She manoeuvred her six-month-old son into his highchair and handed him a toy to keep him busy while she prepared his porridge.

'Morning, Aunt Sylvia.'

Her aunt looked up from pouring out two cups of tea. 'You seem a little cross.'

Not wishing to be unkind, but needing to impress the urgency of her aunt's condition on her, if that was what it would take to make her see sense, Helen tilted her head to one side. 'I know you keep trying to reassure me about your cough, but I think we both know it's been getting worse, Aunty. Won't you go to see the doctor? If not for yourself, then for Bobby?'

Her aunt drew back one of the chairs for Helen to sit on. She caught a fleeting expression on her aunt's face and tensed as it dawned on her she was about to hear bad news.

'You have seen him, haven't you?' She closed her eyes, wishing she had said nothing. She wasn't ready for this. Her aunt was the only relative she had left who cared for her and Bobby.

Sylvia placed a cup of tea in front of her before doing the same with her own, then sat down. She sighed heavily. 'I'm sorry, Helen. I should have told you before now, but I couldn't find the words.'

Bracing herself for what was to come, Helen clasped her hands in her lap. 'Tell me.'

Her aunt's attention was taken by two German soldiers talking angrily outside their front door.

'Have a look and see if you can work out what that's about?' her aunt said, pointing down the hallway.

Helen ran to the living room and looked outside, slinking backwards when one of the uniformed men turned to her. She wished she understood German like her close friend and neighbour, Peggy Hamel. Seeing one of the men indicate the houses opposite theirs, Helen understood what the fuss was about and returned to her aunt.

'It seems that someone has painted a V on the front doors of two houses across the road,' she said, unsure whether to be excited or concerned about any repercussions.

'There's been quite a bit of that going on around the place, I gather,' her aunt said thoughtfully. She gave a wry grin. 'I wish I had the courage to do something similar.'

She began coughing again and Helen winced to hear the rasping. 'I'm glad you don't. I—' A loud bang on the front door made her jump. 'I think we're about to be asked about the vandalism across the road.'

Bobby began to cry. 'It's all right, poppet,' Helen soothed, hugging him.

Another loud bang was joined by an order to open the door. Sylvia began to get up but Helen stopped her. 'No. You stay here with Bobby. I'll speak to them.'

Her heart pounded heavily in her chest and she swallowed the nausea threatening to reach her throat as she opened the door with a shaky hand. 'Yes?'

A sharp-featured officer of about thirty-five glared down at her. 'You are the inhabitant of this house?'

'Yes. I live here with my aunt and son.' She tried not to look at the deep scar running from one side of his mouth almost to his ear and wondered what might have caused it.

'We will speak to them.' Without waiting for Helen to say anything, he stepped into the hallway, forcing her to move backwards out of his way. 'They are where?'

Speaking loudly to warn her aunt, Helen indicated the kitchen. 'We're through here. If you'll follow me.'

She heard the front door being closed and the heavy jackboots as the two uniformed men followed her through the house. Helen widened her eyes at her aunt, who seemed far calmer than she was at that moment. Bobby stared up at the men, seeming too astonished at them to cry.

'What is your reason for forcing your way into my home?' Sylvia snapped.

Helen went to stand next to her aunt, shocked by her attitude to the soldiers.

'I am Hauptmann Wilhelm Schneider and this is Leutnant Klaus Müller. We wish you to tell us if you saw the traitor who painted the Vs on the doors opposite your house.'

Helen didn't dare look at her aunt, but immediately insisted she had seen nothing.

'I didn't notice it last evening,' Sylvia said, only a slight quaver in her voice. 'I therefore presume it must have been done under cover of darkness.'

'And we were in bed by ten o'clock last night,' Helen added. 'I only noticed it this morning when I heard you both outside and went to see what the fuss was about.'

'Fuss?' The taller of the two officers glared at her, causing Helen to shiver. 'The person will be caught.' His certainty made her fear for whoever had done it. 'And they will be treated accordingly.'

Seemingly satisfied with their enquiry, they turned on their heels and left the house.

Helen ran after them, closed the front door and locked it. She went back to the kitchen and sat heavily, breathless from shock at having the hated officers in her home.

'Well, that was rather frightening,' Sylvia said in a playful voice as she smiled at Bobby. 'Wasn't it, poppet?'

Helen watched the concern fade from her little boy's face and was grateful to her aunt for her reaction. She drank a mouthful of her cooling tea and recalled what they were talking about before they had been interrupted by the Wehrmacht. 'Don't think I've forgotten about our earlier conversation.'

Her aunt smiled. 'I had hoped you might have done.' She sighed. 'You'll be pleased to know that I have been to the doctor. A few times in fact.' She picked up her cup, blew on the tea, then, changing her mind, lowered it again. Raised voices filtered into the room from outside before they heard banging on the Hamels' door at number 3. Sylvia scowled.

'What did the doctor say, Aunty?'

'He's done tests and it's not TB, thankfully, but he prescribed some medicine and said I need to take things a little easier.'

Helen wanted to believe what she was being told but she was aware her aunt played things down and doubted she was hearing the full story. 'Is that it, or is there more?' She took another sip of tea. Her voice wavered. 'I want to be able to support you but I can only do that if I know exactly what's wrong.'

Her aunt stared at her for a moment. 'I suppose you should know,' she admitted. 'He did say that the virus has weakened my heart and that although I seem fine now, I do need to be careful and that it will get worse over time.'

Did that mean her aunt was going to die? Helen tried not to show her panic. 'How much time?'

'He couldn't say. He did say I need to be careful not to catch any winter colds, if possible. Eat as well as I can. Rest. That sort of thing.'

Helen listened intently, trying to work out how she could help. 'We'll just have to ensure you take things easier, then, won't we?' She swallowed the lump in her throat. 'You've been so good taking Bobby and me in without any questions or—'

'Enough of that.' Her aunt smiled. 'I'm fine. There's no need to concern yourself about me. And having the pair of you here has been a joy. It's given me a new lease of life, despite everything going on around us.' She held out her hands and looked around the room. If you hadn't arrived on my doorstep last year, I would have had to face all this nastiness on my own now, wouldn't I?'

Helen supposed she was right, but that didn't stop her feeling grateful that her aunt had simply opened the door and welcomed her inside her home when she had arrived that June morning straight from the ferry, pregnant, heartbroken and terrified about what she should do next.

'Maybe you'll be able to rest this afternoon?' she suggested as a German shouted at someone outside.

Helen wondered if it might be easier living further away from town but pushed the thought aside, aware that her aunt had lived at 2 Tynemouth Terrace on St Aubin's Road since moving to Jersey with her husband in the twenties. She knew Aunt Sylvia would rather lose sleep than let Nazis force her from her home.

'Not much chance of that,' Sylvia replied, resting a hand on Helen's shoulder. She nodded in Bobby's direction. 'You don't want to be late for work at the villa now, do you?'

'The villa' was Villa Millbrook, a beautiful Arts and Crafts style house owned by Lady Trent, the woman behind the Boots empire. As far as Helen was aware, the elderly lady had been persuaded by concerned relatives to spend the war at a family home in Scotland. Helen was glad she wasn't there to see her beloved home being lived in by Nazi officers since it had been requisitioned at the beginning of the Occupation.

Helen had been working there for a few months now, thanks to her aunt knowing the housekeeper, Mrs Edwards, and arranging for her to have an interview. She didn't mind her job assisting Mrs Jeune, the cook, even though it meant waiting on German soldiers in the dining room. And she was grateful that her aunt loved looking after Bobby.

'You're right. I should be going. I'll just give him this last mouthful then I'll tidy up first.'

Her aunt waited patiently for her to finish feeding him, then took the empty bowl and spoon from Helen's hands. 'Off you go.'

Helen watched enviously as her aunt picked up a cloth and wiped Bobby's cherubic face. She wished she could be the one to stay with him.

'Go on, then. This little one will be fine with me.'

'I know he will,' Helen said, standing and kissing her aunt briefly on the top of her head. She felt a familiar tightening in her throat, thinking of her aunt's unconditional love, which had given Helen back the confidence she had lost. Aunt Sylvia had only suggested once, just before the occupation, that Helen contact her parents to see if they would welcome her home again. Helen had refused, mortified to have fallen pregnant without having a wedding ring on her finger. She thought of Richard, the man who had crushed her dreams as well as her heart when she'd discovered that he already had a fiancée, and wondered what he would think of their bonny six-month-old son.

'Helen, I can see you're thinking about what happened again.' Her aunt gave her a sympathetic smile. 'You must think ahead, dear. There's no point in longing for the past. I know, I've done it for years since losing my darling Malcolm.'

Helen opened her mouth to deny what she was doing but was silenced by her aunt's knowing look.

'It won't do you or this little one any good to ponder on what might have been,' Sylvia added. 'And as far as being good to you both, I only did what any other relative of yours might have done.'

They both knew that wasn't true. Most families would have done the opposite and turned Helen away in disgrace.

Sylvia waved her out of the room. 'Now, get a move on or you'll be looking for another job.' She spilled some of Bobby's food from the spoon and tutted to herself as she went to fetch a damp cloth to clear it up.

Helen watched Sylvia walk through to the scullery and then kissed Bobby's forehead. 'You be a good boy for your great-aunt Sylvia while Mummy is away.'

Hearing footsteps, she straightened up.

'Are you still here?' Sylvia came back in with a scowl before shooing her away. 'Go. Now.'

Helen set off on her half-hour walk to work contemplating how much she loved living on this beautiful island, where she, her parents and her older brother had come to stay with their aunt every summer holiday when she was younger. The island was different now, with German road signs, Occupation Reichsmarks as the currency and the hated grey-green German uniforms on every street. She loathed the red-and-black banners hanging from buildings. Even their clocks had been put forward one hour to coincide with the Continent.

'Good morning,' she said, smiling at Ida Hamel next door, who was coming out of her house. Helen liked their neighbour. There was something sad about her – probably, Helen thought, because she had been widowed only eighteen months before – but she didn't seem to judge Helen in any way, nor did her daughters Peggy and Babs, and for that Helen was grateful.

Helen went to cross the road, stopping when a black car with familiar insignia flying from the aerial blasted its horn. She was shocked that she had nearly been run over. Although she mostly remembered to look left instead of right before crossing the street, she knew that sometimes she still automatically looked right first.

She quickened her pace along the pavement, cheered at the thought of Bobby, who had recently begun crawling, causing her and Aunt Sylvia to move all the ornaments in the living room up on shelves out of his reach.

Something caught Helen's eye, and she hesitated in front of a shopfront, where a placard was affixed, stating, 'Jewish Undertaking'. She stared at the sign, her good mood vanishing, and clenched her fists, enraged to think people were being put into categories. Hearing heavy footsteps, she noticed a uniformed soldier walking in her direction and immediately moved on.

How must the shop's proprietor feel about that sign? What was the world coming to when this sort of thing became a way of life?

Several minutes later Helen passed another shop but this time the placard read, 'Under an Aryan administrator'. Helen fought the urge to turn around and run back to her aunt's home, wanting to blot out what she had seen. Poor Bobby – what had she done, bringing him into a world this cruel?

She decided there was little she could do but make the best of things. She was here now, and so was Bobby. She just needed to put one foot in front of the other and make the best of what was coming to her. She forced a smile and kept walking.

Chapter Two

PEGGY

Peggy finished typing the last of the transcripts she had been working on that morning, checked the document for errors and took the paper from her typewriter. She read through what she had done and couldn't help thinking that although her work for the government was vital, as far as she was concerned coming into contact with the Nazi officers at work tainted her somehow. If it hadn't been for her boss, Advocate Clarry Le Gresley, a well-respected local lawyer, persuading her that she could help the islanders by translating orders received by the Superior Council from the German authorities, she would have had as little to do with them as possible.

It was strange to think she had been doing this work for almost a year now but it still unnerved her to be in the same room as one of them. If it wasn't for this part-time role that she fitted in with her secretarial work for the Advocate, she would love working at the legal firm much more.

Peggy set the translation on top of the mounting pile on her desk. Her boss was a kind man who had taken her on soon after she returned to Jersey having spent twelve months studying in Hamburg. She recalled how he had finally persuaded her to take on the role. 'Even if we only have a couple of days' notice about new regulations before they're announced to the islanders it still gives us time to warn those who will be affected,' he had explained.

The worst thing for Peggy was that she had sworn not to discuss her work with anyone. But she reasoned that although this might be a small act of resistance on her part, if it saved someone then she was willing to do it.

She mostly succeeded in dismissing her concerns about possible repercussions should she be caught, but occasionally her worries got the better of her. 'It would break my mother's heart if I was to go to prison,' she'd told the Advocate. 'Or, worse, be sent away to one of the camps.'

The Advocate had assured her he would never let that happen, as had his son Tony, junior lawyer and Peggy's boyfriend. Peggy doubted either of them had any power to protect her, but eventually reasoned that as her boss was one of the most highly regarded lawyers on the island, having him looking out for her could only be a good thing.

She stretched her arms and flexed her fingers. She might only be twenty-one but she felt as if she had aged a lot in the previous twelve months, since the unthinkable had happened and the Nazis had invaded the island. She supposed most people felt the same way with the stress of living under Nazi rule.

'Peggy, is everything all right?'

Startled by her boss's voice, she tried to gather herself. 'Yes, Advocate Le Gresley. Sorry, I was thinking.'

He gave her a knowing smile. 'If you've finished typing up those letters I dictated earlier then please bring them through, would you?'

She stood, turned the top page of the work she had finished transcribing facedown, and, picking up the letters along with her notepad and pencil, followed him into his office next door. She watched as he read the first letter.

'You're a conscientious girl, Peggy.' He picked up his fountain pen and signed the letter in his neat, swirling handwriting. Then, picking up the small blotter on his desk, he rolled it over the wet ink. He looked up at her. 'I hope the translations aren't worrying you as much as they once did.'

They did but she wanted to reassure him, sensing his concern came mostly from a feeling of responsibility for being the one to involve her in the first place. 'Not as much.'

'You don't find it too difficult dealing with these people?'

Peggy didn't like to lie. 'Sometimes, but I'm getting used to it.'

'I'm relieved.' He pushed the signed letter towards her to fold and slip into the relevant addressed envelope and drew the next one towards him. 'If you do ever find it's becoming too much, I want you to tell me.' He pointed at one of the letters. 'That one will need to be delivered by hand; today, please.'

She looked at the address, happy to see it was on the Esplanade and only a short walk away.

When the letters were signed, Peggy thanked him and left. As she closed his office door behind her, she turned and slammed into someone. Hands grabbed her as she toppled backwards and stopped her from landing in a heap on the tiled hallway floor.

'For pity's sake,' she grumbled through clenched teeth as she bent to retrieve the envelopes scattered around her feet. 'Look where you're going next time.'

'Here, let me.'

Hearing the deep voice of the man she had begun seeing two months before, Peggy blushed. 'What are you doing on this floor?' she asked, surprised to see him, sensing something was wrong.

He smiled down at her. She was almost five-foot-eight tall but he still towered above her. Unable to help herself, Peggy ran her fingers through his almost black hair, brushing it back from his forehead where it had fallen forward as he bent to collect her dropped papers.

'I came to speak to my father about something.' His mouth stretched in a grin and Peggy felt her breath catch in her throat, still unable to believe this man who so often kept to himself had shown such an interest in her. 'But mostly I was hoping to see you.'

'You were?' she asked, wishing she didn't feel slightly shy with him now. He wasn't her first boyfriend, but he was different from any of the boys she had ever come in contact with. Maybe it was because of the time they were living in that he seemed more grown up, or simply because he had been to law school and was a few years older than her. Mostly, she supposed, it was because she was falling in love with him.

'Yes, why?' he asked, a twinkle in his dark blue eyes. 'Don't you believe me?'

Hearing heels clattering down the stairs, Peggy cocked her head to one side. 'You're going to get caught down here if you're not careful.'

He didn't seem to care and shrugged, bending down and

kissing her quickly. 'I'd better go. We don't want one of the secretaries catching me with you and starting rumours.'

Peggy grinned. 'They can't be rumours if they're true, though, can they?'

'I suppose not, but you know how my father insists that any personal relationships are kept out of working hours.' He winked at her. 'And he'd be especially cross if he thought I was interrupting his golden girl's work.'

She pushed his shoulder. 'Then what are you doing here now?' she teased. Hearing the footsteps coming closer, she took his wrist and pulled him into her office.

'You may as well come in for a moment and tell me how your meeting went.'

He shrugged. 'All bad news, as usual. My father is concerned that the officers we're getting here now are less gentlemanly, and that it's only going to get worse as time goes on.'

Peggy realised she had noticed a subtle change in the manners of the soldiers walking the streets. Her aunt had thought it was because the original ones who'd come to the island had been career soldiers and used to the way of life. They had now been transferred elsewhere and gradually their replacements had been conscripted soldiers who, she supposed, resented being forced to leave their families almost as much as she and the islanders resented them being here.

'It's a frightening time for us all,' Tony continued. 'Cut off from family, friends, not being able to fight with the rest of the world.' A shadow crossed his face and for a moment he stared down at the desk, seeing something only visible to him.

'You wish you were fighting, don't you?'

'Of course I do,' he sighed miserably. Peggy decided now

was the time to ask why he hadn't left the island before the invasion, while he still had the chance.

'I hadn't expected to be stuck here but my appendix decided to almost rupture just before I was supposed to leave. So, to my eternal frustration, I was recuperating in hospital after an appendectomy, knowing my contemporaries from college were proudly serving our country while I was stuck at a desk doing nothing useful.'

So that's why he's still on the island, she thought, sad that he had missed out on doing as he had hoped. She began to try and reassure him, but he closed his eyes and shook his head. Opening them again, he gave her a gentle smile.

'Ignore me. I forgot myself for a moment.'

'It's fine.'

'No. I mean it, Peggy. I get resentful sometimes. If I had left when I expected I would never have met you.' He smiled and took her into his arms, pressing his lips softly against hers before pulling away. 'Sometimes fate has plans for us we don't see coming.'

Wasn't that the truth, she mused.

Chapter Three

HELEN

Helen stood at the entrance of the large house with its stone pillars topped with griffins on each side and waited for the soldier on duty to come out, check her papers and let her enter the property. Looking up at the imposing stone house, she knew she should be grateful for her job. And she was – she would just rather not have to work so close to Nazi officers.

A grumpy-looking sentry walked up to her, and Helen waited silently as he inspected her Occupation Identity card, before opening the metal gates further to allow her into the grounds.

'Is everything all right?' Mrs Jeune, the cook, asked as Helen entered the large kitchen at the back of the building, having made her way along the labyrinth of corridors to get there.

'It's fine.'

'Your aunt any better today?'

Ordinarily Helen wouldn't have shared her aunt's personal

information, but the cook and Aunt Sylvia were friends, and Helen liked Mrs Jeune despite her stern ways.

'Not really,' she admitted miserably. She removed her coat and hat, walked through to the small room next door to hang them up and collect a clean apron. She slipped the apron straps over her head and returned to the kitchen, tying them behind her back. 'She's a bit worse, to be honest, but she has finally been to see a doctor.'

Cook focused on turning over a large joint of meat, basted it, replaced it on the metal tray it was lying in and put it back into the enormous stove. 'That's good news. I'm sure Sylvia will do what she thinks best in the end.'

Helen wasn't sure what she meant but knew Cook didn't like to be questioned so said nothing. 'Where would you like me to start?' she asked, aware Cook expected everyone to help ensure all the meals were served on time.

'Dulcie's in the scullery. See if she needs any help then come back here and start cutting up the mushrooms and tomatoes for their breakfast.'

'Good morning, Dulcie,' Helen said, smiling at the slim girl. Dulcie was sixteen, three years younger than Helen, but she appeared older – perhaps, Helen guessed, because she had a difficult life. The girl could be tetchy at times and had taken a few months to get used to Helen working there, but mostly she was kind and Helen always liked to help her whenever she could.

'Morning.'

The sulky reply wasn't unexpected, and Helen went to stand next to her. 'Cook thought I might be able to help you with a few things.'

Dulcie cocked her head to one side to indicate several pans

drying on the draining board. Helen picked up a tea-towel and one of the pans, then noticed Dulcie glance at the doorway and put a wet finger up to her lips. 'Cook was called in earlier to prepare something for a load of 'em. They've been 'ere most of the night chatting about something,' she whispered.

Helen frowned. 'Poor thing.' She knew Cook already worked long hours, without being made to come in any earlier. She was always there when Helen arrived, and when she left. Helen wondered how she kept going. 'She can't have much time at home.'

They heard the kitchen door open and the sound of Mrs Edwards' heeled shoes upon the tiled floor. The housekeeper was insistent on everything she overlooked being impeccable. Helen liked her, but sometimes found the woman's high standards a little difficult to keep up with.

She finished wiping the final pan and set it down on the side. 'I'd better get out there and start that chopping.'

'Ah, there you are, Helen,' Mrs Edwards said, when Helen entered the kitchen. 'You and Dulcie will be serving lunch today.'

Dulcie? Helen was used to occasionally having to wait on the officers with other girls, but never with Dulcie. She knew without seeing her face that she would be horrified to hear this.

'What about the other girls who serve in the dining room?' As soon as the words were out of her mouth, she knew she should have kept her thoughts to herself. Mrs Edwards' frowned. 'That is to say...'

Mrs Edwards' gaze fell on her and then she turned to Cook and gave her a pointed look before addressing Helen. 'Since you seem so curious, dear. Marie and Jeanette are both unwell and won't be returning until tomorrow or the next day.'

Helen hated to think she had upset the woman who had given her work. 'I'm sorry for speaking out of turn, Mrs Edwards. It won't happen again.'

Mrs Edwards' expression softened. 'I'm sure it won't.'

The back door opened and an untidy man Helen recognised as the gardener walked in. He immediately removed his cap and it was clear from the look of concern on his ruddy face that something was dreadfully wrong.

'What's the matter, Tommy?' Mrs Jeune asked, going over to him closely followed by Mrs Edwards.

He looked at Helen and Dulcie, who had joined them, then, seeming satisfied, puffed out his cheeks and closed the door behind him. 'We have a problem and I'm not sure what to do about it.'

'Helen, fetch Tommy a cup of strong tea,' Cook ordered. 'Er, Dulcie, I'm not sure why you're hovering when you've got pots to wash. Get back to that scullery.'

Helen went over to the kettle and did as she asked.

'It's the silver, Mrs Edwards.' His voice was low but Helen could still hear what he was saying. She wondered why the gardener was interested in the silver.

'I thought it was safely put away.'

Helen realised by the tone in the housekeeper's voice that she didn't mean the silver was in a cupboard but hidden somewhere. Aware she needed to hurry up with the tea, she poured in a little milk and gave it a stir.

'It is, but that's the problem. Him in the office called me in earlier and questioned me about hidin' things. I'm sure he could tell I was fibbin' when I said I knew nothin' about any treasures.'

'I'm not sure what the problem is, though,' Cook said.

Helen carried his tea over to him and put it down on the table, then returned to the worktop and pretended not to be listening as she continued tidying up.

He groaned. 'He's ordered me to have the veg patch dug up. By tomorrow first thing.'

Helen heard one of the women gasp.

'We need to do something.' It was Mrs Edwards' voice and she sounded unusually flustered.

'I know but there's a lot of stuff to move and I can't do it all by myself. What if I'm seen? I don't want to be sent away to one of those camps in Germany.'

Upset to hear the man's desperation, Helen went over to the table. 'Maybe I know someone who can help,' she said, thinking of Peggy's boyfriend Tony. She didn't know him well but had overheard him reassuring Peggy one night outside their homes and suspected he was involved in acts of sabotage that had been happening on the island.

Three surprised faces turned to her, and she realised she was about to be told off for interrupting.

The day passed quickly and as Helen hurried home with Peggy's younger sister, Babs, who had kindly waited for her after dropping off some knitting to a friend of her mother's in Millbrook, she tried to think how to approach Tony.

Worried she might be seen as being rude, she said, 'It's not often I see you out this way.' She knew that she and Babs went in different directions to get to their places of work.

'I only had a half day at Boots today,' Babs explained. 'Naturally, Mum took that to mean she could keep me busy with jobs for her.'

As Babs moaned, Helen waved the sides of her coat to try and cool down as they walked. Her skin was sticky with perspiration after the long day working in the kitchen and her nervousness at serving the German soldiers. She hated having to go into the dining room when they were there. She wished she had a thinner coat to wear on such a hot June day. Working in the kitchen had been bad enough but now they were walking quickly in the bright sunshine it somehow seemed even worse. Tomorrow she would go without a coat and simply wear her best cardigan.

As they chatted, Helen couldn't help thinking how much nicer it must be serving at one of the counters in Boots like Babs. Most importantly though, she was relieved to have someone to talk to and take her mind off having committed herself to speaking to Tony about the issue at the villa.

'Isn't it funny?' Babs said in her usual bubbly way. 'I work at Boots and you work for the lady who helped run it for years.'

Helen wasn't sure that was correct, but didn't like to argue. 'I'm sorry I haven't been able to meet her,' she admitted. 'She seems to have achieved a lot in her almost eighty years.' She tried to picture herself at Lady Trent's age and reflected that all she would like to have achieved by then was to be happily settled in a home of her own, with Bobby married and bringing up his own children. The thought made her smile.

'What are you thinking?' Babs asked, nudging her and interrupting her thoughts.

'I was only wondering what I might be like at eighty.'

Babs giggled. 'You've got a long way to go before then, and a lot of living to do in that time.'

Helen wondered if those years would be spent here stuck on the island. As much as she loved it she hoped to have the freedom to choose whether to stay or leave. If the Nazis won the war then she doubted that choice would be given to her.

They reached their respective homes and Helen was relieved to see Peggy chatting to Tony. She had known Peggy and her sister for a year now but was always struck by how different their appearances were: Babs, the younger sister, was blonde and bubbly, while Peggy was tall and dark. It made Helen think of her own brother, Stephen. Her mood dipped at the thought of how he might have reacted to her running away without saying goodbye to him. She pushed away the upsetting thought.

Babs waved at her sister and Tony before giving Helen a brief hug. 'I'd better go and let Mum know I've dropped off the knitting.'

Peggy gave Helen a questioning look. 'Is everything all right?'

'Not really,' Helen admitted quietly. She looked around and, seeing several people walking by, indicated her front door. 'Would you and Tony come inside for a moment?'

They followed her in and, after Helen had been through to see her aunt and give Bobby a kiss, she returned to join them in the living room.

'I was hoping to see you, Tony,' she said keeping her voice down so as not to alert her aunt to what was happening. She quickly explained the situation at work and how she was hoping he might know what to do. 'Whatever it is must be done this evening, I'm afraid, because the veg patch is being dug up first thing tomorrow. I've been trying to think how to move it all somewhere safe but I haven't any ideas so far.'

She noticed that, instead of looking concerned, Tony seemed delighted to be involved.

He thought for a moment, then raised a finger. 'I know exactly what to do.'

'Already?' Helen and Peggy asked in unison.

He laughed. 'Yes, I've heard of someone else doing exactly what I'm going to suggest.' He narrowed his eyes. 'But we're going to have to go back there around dusk so it can be done this evening.'

'We'll be cutting it fine if we want to be home again before curfew,' Peggy said thoughtfully. 'These summer nights don't get dark until ten sometimes.'

Helen agreed. 'I'll need to go spend some time with Aunt Sylvia and Bobby before I can go back.'

Tony frowned. 'What makes you think I'll take either of you with me? This could be dangerous.'

Helen swapped glances with Peggy before addressing him. 'I'm the one with the pass. I'll need to get access to the house on some pretext, then I'll be able to go and let you in through a hidden door in the garden wall.'

Peggy nodded. 'Yes, and you'll need me to help move everything.'

'No.' He shook his head. 'I agree I need Helen's help, but not yours, Peggy. I'll not let you risk getting into trouble.'

Helen grimaced, knowing that her friend wasn't going to be told what to do.

'I don't think that's for you to decide, Tony,' Peggy said before giving Helen a triumphant look. 'Right, then, what time shall we meet outside?'

They arranged to meet up at nine-thirty.

'Suits me,' Tony said. 'I can go home for supper and will be back here so we can make our way there slowly and gauge how soon the sun will be setting.'

'Yes, I'd better get home now, too.' Peggy rubbed Helen's upper arm. 'I'm looking forward to doing this tonight.'

'It does feel good to know you're fighting back somehow,' Tony said. 'Even if most of the time the Jerries are oblivious to what's happening under their noses.'

Peggy sighed. 'As long as it stays that way we'll be fine.'

Helen heard the fear in her friend's voice and felt the same way. 'Thank you both so much. I know Tommy and Mrs Edwards will be very relieved to know we're going to help them.' Although nervous to be actively taking part in a blatant act of resistance, Helen did her best to hide her anticipation. 'I'd better go and see how Bobby's been for Aunt Sylvia today. I'll see you both later.'

Chapter Four

PEGGY

P eggy held Tony's hand as they walked along St Aubin's Road on their way back to Villa Millbrook. Discussing hiding the silver was one thing, but physically digging a hole while trying not to alert the guards was going to be difficult. Her nerves increased with every step she took closer to Villa Millbrook. She was beginning to wish she hadn't been so quick to volunteer to help.

'You're trembling,' Tony whispered. 'If you want to change your mind, just say so. I'm sure I'll be fine doing this with Tommy and Helen.'

Feeling guilty for allowing her concerns to be obvious, she gave his hand a gentle squeeze. 'No,' she said, determined to see it through. 'I'm just a little nervous, that's all. I'll be fine and I know I'll be glad I've done something to help '

He leant over and kissed her lightly on the cheek. 'You're a brave girl, Peggy, and that's partly why I love you so much.

He had told her he loved her. She gave him a gentle nudge

27

as she tried to recover from the surprise. 'The feeling's mutual,' she admitted happily.

'You two still fine to do this?' Helen asked, slowing and turning to them.

'We are,' Peggy reassured her, now more determined than ever to see it through.

'Absolutely ready,' Tony said. 'The housekeeper and gardener don't know we're coming, I assume?'

Helen shook her head. 'I considered telephoning the house but didn't want to alert the officers in any way. I've never phoned before so it might look suspicious. I'm just hoping Mrs Edwards will still be there.'

'What about Tommy, though?' Peggy asked, doubting the gardener would still be at work that late in the evening.

'It's fine,' Helen said. 'He lives in a cottage across the road from the park. I'll point it out to you, Tony, so you two can go and speak to him and tell him our plans while I go into the house and speak to Mrs Edwards.' She had a thought. 'In fact, he'll be able to let you into the garden. He rarely comes into the kitchen and never the house, so he must have a shortcut from his cottage.'

Tony nodded. 'Then we'll do that and wait for you in the garden whenever you're ready.'

They reached the corner where St Aubin's Road veered off to La Rue de Haut and watched Helen walk towards the entrance of the imposing house where she worked, before continuing down the main road towards Tommy's cottage. At the first of three cottages they stopped and, opening the iron gate, walked up the short pathway and into the porch. Tony knocked on the front door. Peggy marvelled at the vivid red shards of light streaked across both their bodies by the setting sun shining through the coloured glass in the porch.

The door opened after a few seconds and a wizened man with a suspicious look on his face glared at them. 'Yes?'

'May we come inside for a moment, please?' Tony asked. 'We have a message from Helen, er, Miss Bowman. She's with Mrs Edwards as we speak.'

'You'd better come this way.' Tommy frowned and stepped back to let them in. 'I'm not sure what this is about,' he said, softening slightly towards them.

Tony explained about their plan. Tommy brightened and within a few minutes was leading them along a through way to the side of his cottage. 'This is the best way to get into the garden without being seen,' he said keeping his voice low. 'But we need to be careful. They're crafty buggers, those Jerries.' He stopped and peered past Tony to Peggy. 'Sorry about the language, Miss.'

'Please don't worry,' Peggy said, liking the man and relieved she had offered to help him.

'You're very good to help us out like this,' Tommy continued. 'I'm not sure what her ladyship would think if we didn't manage to keep her precious things safe for her. She's always been very good to me. She's nearly eighty, you know.'

Peggy thought of Florence Boot and how she and her husband had always been so generous to the people of the island. She was glad to think the elderly lady didn't have to witness all that was happening to the island and its people that she loved so much.

They reached the garden and once inside crept silently along the border among the trees to the vegetable patch.

Tommy stopped once and pointed up at a balcony stretching the width of the house and overlooking the long, immaculate lawn to their right.

'They go out there for a sneaky ciggie sometimes,' he warned. 'There's others at the entrances to the house and at the front. There'll also be a couple patrolling the garden every hour, so we don't have time to waste.'

'What about spades?' Tony asked when they reached the vegetable patch and were standing in the shadows next to a carefully trimmed hedge that blocked anyone's view of them from the property.

'I'll fetch them now.'

Tony slipped his arms around Peggy while they waited. 'How are you holding up?'

Her legs were like jelly and she wasn't sure they were strong enough to keep her from falling over, but she had no intention of letting him know how terrified she was. 'I'm fine,' she lied, forcing a smile. 'I'm glad we're doing this together.'

He pulled a face. 'I can't say I am. I'd feel much happier knowing you were safe at home.' He kissed her lightly. 'But I have a sense that we'll remember this night for the rest of our lives and it's something we can bore our grandchildren with during family gatherings.'

'You think we'll have grandchildren?' she asked, delighted to think he saw a future for the pair of them.

'Don't you?'

She slipped her arms around his waist and rested her head on his chest. 'I do now.'

Hearing footsteps, they broke apart and Peggy held her breath, terrified in case they were about to be discovered.

Tommy stepped out between two bushes holding two spades, closely followed by Helen carrying two more.

'I found Miss Bowman waiting for me at my toolshed.' He cocked his head towards a bed of spinach. 'It's under there.'

'And where's the bonfire?' Tony asked.

'Over that way.' Tommy pointed to the right of where they were standing. 'The ground will be harder there, so I reckon the ladies should probably dig up the spinach here, while we tackle the bonfire and dig that hole. We're going to need to be careful to keep the ash and bits of burnt wood and stuff away from the soil so that we can put it back on top of the stash when we've covered it up.'

'Good idea.' Tony nodded, then addressed Peggy and Helen. 'Will you two be all right to dig up the silver? We'll come back to help you move it as soon as we're done.'

'Of course,' Helen whispered. 'Mrs Edwards has called them into the dining room for a tasting of some bottles of sloe gin she's been keeping in the cupboard for a special occasion. She's going to pretend that she's only just discovered it and do her best to keep them away from the west of the house, where we are.'

'That's clever of her,' Peggy said. 'Right, let's get on with it.'

Peggy watched Tony leave with Tommy and took a spade from Helen. 'I hope you're feeling strong,'

Helen grinned. 'So do I.'

It was a warm evening and Peggy was perspiring after fifteen minutes' digging. She and Helen had carefully placed the spinach they had dug up to one side, away from the mound of soil that now stood next to the hole. 'Look, that's one of the bags,' she said spotting a khaki canvas bag. 'Help me lift it out, will you?'

She hoped the silver was well wrapped to dull any sound as they lifted the first three bags they discovered.

'Shush,' Helen said, grabbing Peggy's right wrist tightly.

Peggy immediately stilled, horrified to hear heavy boots walking somewhere nearby. She stared into Helen's eyes, wide with fear. Neither of them dared to lower the heavy bag in case they made a sound. Hearing another voice, then laughter, Peggy willed them to go somewhere else. Where were they? she wondered. Following the voices, she spotted a red glow through the bush behind them. They were having a cigarette on the balcony, just like Tommy had warned.

She grimaced, desperate to lower the bag, and saw that Helen was struggling, too. There was no sound coming from where she had heard the men digging earlier and for the first time Peggy realised how dark it was. The only light was coming from the full moon.

'Would you gentlemen like a top-up?' she heard a lady ask.

'Mrs Edwards,' Helen mouthed, relief on her face, when the men's voices receded into the house and they heard the balcony door closing. 'Thank heavens for that,' she murmured, lowering the bag next to the mound where the other two were placed.

'Right,' Tony said, joining them with Tommy. 'We'll take these bags and bury them while you two refill that hole.'

'You'd better replant the spinach as best you can,' Tommy said. 'Don't worry too much, I'll straighten them out when you've gone.'

Peggy was relieved that refilling the hole was much easier and quicker than digging it had been. As soon as they had replaced the spinach, they hurried to join the men and help them at the bonfire site.

'This is such a good idea.' Tommy said, clearly impressed. 'No one will ever think of looking under this lot.'

The moonlight lit the patch where they were stamping on the soil to harden it before scattering debris and ash on top. It was incredible, she thought, and couldn't help smiling.

'I'm impressed. You'd never know this had been moved.'

'You wouldn't,' Tommy agreed, holding out his hand for the spades. 'I'll be out here first thing to set another fire, so that even if they do fancy coming this way with their search they'd be put off by the smoke and flames.'

'We'll go the way we came in,' Tony said, patting Tommy on the back. 'Good luck tomorrow, and don't forget to let me know if you need help with anything else.'

'I will, lad,' he said, giving Tony a smile, displaying more gaps than yellowed teeth. 'You're a goodun and no mistake.'

'I'm glad you think so.'

Peggy followed Tony and Helen through the shrubbery and back to Tommy's cottage. They wiped soil from their shoes before brushing it from their hands and straightening their hair and clothes.

'We'll have to do,' Peggy said, aware that if they weren't careful they'd wouldn't be home before curfew. 'We need to get going.'

She and Helen left Tony to make his way home and walked the last part together.

'That was frightening,' Peggy admitted. 'But now it's done I can't help feeling exhilarated, don't you?'

'I do,' Helen agreed. 'I'm so glad we were able to help them out of this sticky situation.' She sighed. 'I feel as if I've really done something worthwhile tonight.'

'Me, too,' Peggy agreed as they reached the bottom of their front steps. 'See you tomorrow then.'

'Yes,' Helen said. 'And thank you again.'

'There's no need to thank me. What are neighbours for if not to step in when needed?' She gave Helen a wink and ran up the steps and into number 3, feeling more alive than she had done in a year.

Chapter Five

PEGGY

Peggy's exhilaration was short-lived. The following morning, as she was walking down Castle Street towards the Esplanade on her way to hand-deliver a letter for Advocate Le Gresley, she heard harsher voices than usual barking orders. Her stomach clenched in fear. Why did she have to deliver something right where there was a commotion? Aware the letter must be important for her to have to take it straight away, she forced herself to keep walking.

At the top of Castle Street she noticed islanders grouped on either side of the road. Wondering what was happening, she manoeuvred herself to the front, horrified to come across a scene straight from one of the Gothic novels she and Babs had read to each other growing up.

'These poor people,' a woman next to her sobbed.

Peggy didn't want to look at the dreadful spectacle of exhausted men and women but was unable to tear her eyes away when she realised some were little more than children. Skin and bone, their poor battered bodies wearing clothes that were as good as rags, they hobbled along, their legs manacled, as guards screamed orders.

She knew they were among many now being brought to the island from camps on the Continent, to be put to work on the concrete fortifications that were blighting more and more of the island.

The woman next to her shook her head slowly. 'They don't look as if they have enough strength to do much more than walk, poor souls.'

Peggy wished she had something to give them. One of the women tripped and several in the crowd surged forward automatically to help her but were screamed at to get back, just as another soldier hit the fallen woman hard on the side of her head.

'Stop it!' Peggy screamed, wanting to snatch the rifle from him and hit him in retaliation. She stepped forward, taking a breath to shout again, when someone pulled her back. She grabbed at the muscular arms around her waist and kicked, desperate to be released. The person put her down, took her by the shoulders and turned her roughly to face him.

'Tony? Why did you do that? Didn't you see what he was doing to that poor defenceless woman?'

He took her by the wrist and led her further away without speaking.

Furious with him, she tried to snatch her arm from his grip.

'Stop it, Peggy,' he said his voice gentle. 'I'm as incensed as you by what happened, but you're not helping her by antagonising those guards. Most of them look as if they're enjoying abusing those poor people.'

She was about to argue but realised he was right. 'But we can't just stand by and do nothing.'

He looked past her for a second. 'I agree, but now is not the time for bravado.'

'Then, when?'

He didn't speak for a moment. 'I'm sorry if I was rough with you just then, but I saw that guard looking in your direction and needed to remove you immediately.'

'It's fine,' she said, aware she might have hurt him. 'I wouldn't have kicked if I'd known it was you.'

'That's good to know.' He pulled an envelope from his pocket. 'You dropped this as you pushed your way through the crowd.'

Peggy grimaced. 'Thank you. Your father would be furious if I lost it.'

'Maybe you should deliver it now.'

Shocked to have been careless, Peggy nodded. 'I'll do it straight away.' She gave him a grateful smile and hurried to the address on the envelope, looking over her shoulder a couple of times when she heard screaming. She was sickened by what she had witnessed.

As she reached the correct address it occurred to her that Tony hadn't answered her question about when they might find a way to help the forced workers.

Chapter Six

HELEN

Helen made her way downstairs after a sleepless night. The stress and adrenalin rush from helping Tommy at Villa Millbrook were tiring and she had expected to sleep fitfully, but hearing her aunt coughing through the night had upset her and she couldn't help being frightened at the thought of her aunt's prognosis. Why had she waited until it was too late for treatment? Her aunt had always appeared to be strong yet now her heart was weakened. Helen couldn't imagine life without her beloved aunt. She took a steadying breath. It was her support Sylvia needed now, not someone falling apart.

Helen made them both a cup of tea. When her aunt didn't appear ten minutes later, Helen tried to suppress the nagging sense of unease she had felt since waking. Hoping her aunt was having a lie-in after their emotional discussion the night before, she decided not to disturb her. Aunt Sylvia would be down in time for when she had to leave for work, so she fed

Bobby as usual and made herself a bit of toast and a second cup of weak tea while she waited.

It was odd eating breakfast alone. Aunt Sylvia always joined her and mostly rose earlier than she did. Helen's heart ached as it dawned on her that this would be her future if her aunt succumbed to her illness. Her throat tightened and, not wishing to be caught crying when she was supposed to be strong, she wiped away her tears with the heel of her hand. She glanced at the clock and realised she was going to be late if she didn't get a move on. Placing two wooden building blocks on Bobby's highchair tray to keep him entertained, Helen ran upstairs to check on her aunt.

She knocked lightly on the bedroom door. 'Aunt Sylvia? May I come in?'

Hearing a faint groan, Helen gently turned the handle and pushed the door open. She peeked inside, noisily clearing her throat to alert her aunt to her presence.

The curtains were still closed and the room dark. 'Aunt Sylvia?' Still hearing no reply, she pushed the door wider and walked in, gasping in horror at seeing her aunt lying grey-faced in her bed. Helen ran to the bedside. Why the hell had she not come up sooner?

'Aunt Sylvia? Can you hear me?'

Sylvia turned her head slowly towards her and murmured something. Helen couldn't miss the faint sheen of perspiration on her aunt's face.

'I'm not sure,' she said eventually, her voice croaky. 'My head hurts dreadfully. I'm sorry, Helen, but I don't think I'm well enough to take care of Bobby today.'

'Don't worry about that,' Helen said. It took every ounce of her strength to hide her panic. 'I'll fetch you a cool flannel and some water, then I'll run next door and ask Ida or Babs to look after him while I fetch the doctor.'

Sylvia raised a limp hand. 'No need.'

'I don't think we have much choice, Aunty.'

She ran to the bathroom, took a clean flannel from the small cupboard, rinsed it in cool water, wrung it out and returned to her aunt's bedroom. She folded it and rested it lightly on her aunt's forehead.

'Better?'

'Yes,' she croaked. 'Thank you, dear.'

'I promise I won't be long.' Not wishing to waste a moment, Helen hurried downstairs. She scooped Bobby into her arms and ran next door to number 3.

'I'm sorry, Mrs Hamel,' Helen said, hating to disturb them so early. 'But my aunt is extremely unwell, and I need to fetch a doctor. Would you mind if I leave Bobby here with you while I phone his surgery?'

'Sylvia, unwell?' She pulled her cardigan tightly around her, folded her arms across her chest and scowled. 'What's wrong with her?'

Helen swallowed tears. 'I think she's dying.' It pained her to say the words but she knew it was something she needed to face.

Seeing shock register on her neighbour's face made her wish she had been a little more sensitive, but it was too late now, and she had no time to waste. 'May I leave Bobby with you while I run to the telephone box?'

Ida nodded. 'Pass him over.'

'Thank you,' Helen said relieved. 'I promise I'll be as quick as I can.'

'Hospital, you say?' Ida asked, her eyes wide with surprise, forty-five minutes later.

'The doctor drove her there himself a few minutes ago.'

'You never said what's wrong with her exactly. She's always seemed so strong.'

Helen explained, making sure to be gentler this time.

Ida's hand flew to her chest. 'Poor Sylvia.'

Helen noticed the time on Ida's mantel clock. She was late for work and now her aunt had been hospitalised she needed to bring in her wage more than ever. She hoped Cook wouldn't mind her taking Bobby in with her. 'I'm sorry, but I must leave for work. I'm already dreadfully late.' She went to carry Bobby out of the kitchen but Ida reached out to stop her.

'Hold on a moment. Don't you work at that smart house at Millbrook?' She narrowed her eyes. 'With all those Nazis?'

Helen wished Mrs Hamel didn't make what she did sound unsavoury. She wondered how she knew where she worked. She doubted that it had come from Babs. Her expression must have shown her thoughts.

Ida shrugged. 'I've heard people talking at the greengrocers, as you do. Anyway, you can't surely be taking this little one to that place?'

'I'm sure it'll be fine,' Helen fibbed.

Ida looked aghast. 'What? This little mite, spending the day among those brutes? What can you be thinking?'

'What choice do I have?' Helen asked, close to tears.

'I would keep him,' Ida said. 'But I need to go out this morning.'

'It's fine. He's my responsibility.'

Babs had left while Helen was helping the doctor take her aunt to his car, and with no one else to ask, Helen thanked Mrs Hamel and left. After fetching Bobby's pram and his bag, with everything he might need for the day, she set off towards Millbrook, grateful that the old-fashioned deep pram her aunt had obtained for her soon after Bobby's birth was still big enough for him.

She pictured her aunt's gaunt face as she was driven away by the doctor. Overwhelmed by the sudden change in her situation, Helen had to stop and take a few deep breaths to steady herself. She needed to be strong, for Sylvia's and Bobby's sake. She pushed back her shoulders and raised her chin. She could do this.

By the time she reached the kitchen, Helen felt perspiration running down her back.

'Where the devil have you been?' Cook scolded as she watched the pram being pushed into her kitchen. 'And what on earth do you think you're doing, bringing that baby into this house?'

Helen didn't have a chance to answer before Dulcie ran from the scullery, a dripping saucepan in one hand and cloth in the other, her mouth open.

Helen tried to ignore the girl's shock. Cook knew about her circumstances, but now Dulcie would, too. She would rather her situation not be common knowledge, but it was too late to worry about that now.

'I'm very sorry, Mrs Jeune,' she said, just as Bobby began wailing. 'Aunt Sylvia has been taken to Overdale Hospital this morning and our neighbour has errands to run. I wasn't sure what else to do so I brought him with me.'

Cook wiped her hands on her apron and walked over to

close the kitchen door. Then, going to the pram, she peered at the screaming child. 'There's an orphanage at Sacre Coeur, not too far from here,' she said matter-of-factly. 'You could make arrangements for him to be taken in there.'

Helen couldn't speak. How could Mrs Jeune think her capable of abandoning her baby? 'Why would you even suggest such a thing?' She hadn't meant to be rude but had to say something even if it meant her losing her job.

Cook glared at her. 'You can wipe that indignant look off your face for a start. I only mentioned Sacre Coeur because they also have a nursery for little ones whose mothers work.'

Mortified to have misunderstood, Helen lowered her eyes. 'Sorry. I thought you meant—'

'I'm well aware what you thought.' She indicated Bobby, who was now puce in the face from screaming. 'If you want to keep him here you'll need to keep him quiet. We can't afford to let the Kommandant hear this racket, or you'll be out of a job and I'm too busy to lose you.'

Helen sensed that, despite the harsh tone, Cook was looking out for her and Bobby.

'I'm sorry, I shouldn't have brought him here, but I don't know many people and didn't know who to ask. I don't want to get anyone into trouble, not when you and Mrs Edwards have been so kind to me.'

'Mrs Edwards knows you have a baby?' Dulcie asked, reminding them both she was there.

Cook spun round and pointed to the scullery. 'Get that dripping pot back into the basin, then come back and make us both a cup of tea.' She jabbed her stubby finger at Dulcie's chest and Helen immediately felt sorry for the girl, who was only being curious.

'Yes, Cook.'

Helen watched as Dulcie slunk out of the room.

'Right, madam,' Cook said, turning her attention back to Helen. 'Comfort that baby before the entire Wehrmacht come running to this kitchen.'

Helen picked him up and cuddled him, but when he didn't quieten and she had checked his nappy was clean, she wondered if maybe she should try feeding him. Unsure what to do, she tried to think how to broach the subject.

Cook gave her a knowing look. 'Dulcie, whatever are you doing in there? Get out here now and make us that tea.'

The girl returned to the kitchen. Mrs Jeune immediately picked up one of the chairs and carried it to the scullery, placing it down near a small table. 'There. You look after Bobby and come out when you're ready.'

Helen thanked her, grateful for the privacy to feed him. As soon as Bobby had latched onto her breast, she began to relax, relieved to have a few minutes alone with him to gather her thoughts.

As she stroked his downy hair Helen thought how the events of the morning had shown how precarious her position was on the island. She lived in her aunt's home and Aunt Sylvia was the only person close to her. She missed her parents and even her brother, with whom she had mostly squabbled. Even Richard. Especially Richard, she realised, despite how their relationship had ended.

She heard plates clattering and wondered how long she could expect to keep her job if she didn't find someone to care for Bobby. If only she hadn't been so hasty running away from home and taking the ferry to Jersey without even giving her parents the chance to allow her to stay. The shock of discovering that she was pregnant and then, on the same day, that Richard wasn't free to marry her had been shattering.

Bobby made a contented sound and Helen knew that despite her predicament she wouldn't swap him for anything or anyone.

'You all right in there?' Mrs Jeune asked from the other side of the scullery door.

'Yes, thank you.' Helen wished she could have remained in the peaceful room for a bit longer but had pushed her luck more than enough already. 'Coming now.'

She rearranged her clothes with her free hand, glad she had become more adept at doing so as the months passed. She wondered how long she would keep producing milk and hoped it would be for a while yet. At least her milk was free. She kissed her sleeping baby's forehead, relieved he was calm now.

Helen opened the door and joined Cook and Dulcie in the kitchen. She ignored Dulcie's judging glare and settled Bobby in his pram before returning to the scullery to fetch the chair and return it to the kitchen.

'Sit down and drink this,' Cook said, pushing a cup and saucer towards her. Dulcie mumbled something under her breath. 'I don't know what you just said, my girl,' Cook snapped. 'But whatever it is, keep it out of my kitchen. Now, bring a plate with a few of those biscuits I baked yesterday. I think we could all do with one.'

Brightening instantly, Dulcie did as Cook asked and came back to sit with them.

Helen waited for the women to take a biscuit each. She knew she needed to address her situation with Dulcie.

'I know me having a baby is a bit of a shock for you, Dulcie.'

Dulcie opened her mouth to reply, but caught Cook's warning glare and picked up her teacup instead.

Helen was grateful for the support but felt the need to explain herself. 'I think Dulcie deserves an explanation if I'm to stay working here.' She hoped Cook wouldn't disagree.

'If you like.' Cook took a sip from her cup.

'Thank you.' Helen tried to work out exactly what to say.

'I thought you was a nice girl,' Dulcie said.

'That's enough of that, Dulcie.' Cook snapped.

'I'm aware what people think of me, Mrs Jeune, and that's fine,' Helen said in Dulcie's defence.

'It is not fine,' Cook argued. 'I will not have people judging others in my kitchen. If Mrs Edwards approves of you working in this house and I'm happy for you to assist in my kitchen, then that's all Dulcie needs to know.'

Mrs Jeune was far more understanding than most. Helen wondered if maybe something similar happened to someone close to her, or was she simply a very accepting person?

'I appreciate your kindness, I really do, but I want Dulcie to understand that I had expected to marry Bobby's father, but it wasn't to be.'

Dulcie's face softened slightly. 'Did he die?'

Cook slammed her cup onto her saucer so hard Helen was surprised it didn't smash the porcelain. 'Dulcie. You've been told more than you needed to hear, and I'll thank you to keep whatever questions you might have to yourself. Do you understand?'

Dulcie's eyes lowered. 'Yes, Cook. Sorry, Helen. I didn't mean to offend.'

'It's fine,' Helen said hoping to defuse the situation.

The day passed slowly and Helen only needed to interrupt her work a couple of times to take care of Bobby before the day finally ended. It was a relief to be able to go home.

She fetched her coat. 'Thank you for your understanding today, Mrs Jeune.'

'No need for thanks, Helen. If your aunt is still at Overdale tomorrow, I don't mind you bringing the little un back here. He's been no trouble today, not really. I wouldn't do it every day, mind. And he's getting bigger and will soon want to move around. But for the time being you may bring him with you if you have no alternative.'

Helen couldn't believe her luck. 'That's very kind of you. Thank you.'

She walked home feeling less panicky about the following day. As she passed First Tower and neared Tynemouth Terrace her thoughts returned to her aunt and what she would soon have to face. Helen took a deep breath, desperate not to cry in public.

It had been devastating having to face a future without Richard, but losing her aunt was unimaginable. She didn't know if she had the strength to deal with it.

Chapter Seven

PEGGY

July 1941

I t was the following afternoon – another hot day – and although the small window in her office was open, little fresh air was coming into the room. As Peggy typed, she couldn't dismiss the notion that maybe Helen's work serving high-ranking officers could be of some use. She wasn't sure she was right to involve her in subterfuge, but she reasoned that since Helen had taken part in the hiding of the Villa Millbrook silver, she was more than willing to do her bit for the greater good of the islanders. She should at least give her the option.

She studied her translation, realising how much information she had gleaned from her work already. Seeing so many documents helped her to work out the mindset of the individuals behind the new edicts. Helen, through her waiting on the officers, must surely hear all sorts of conversations. The information the pair of them could gather could be useful and would no doubt be welcomed by Advocate Le Gresley's underground group.

There was a knock on her office door, snapping her out of her thoughts. Peggy sat up a little straighter as the door opened and a fair-haired messenger entered.

'Good morning.'

He gave a nod, his face serious. 'Good morning.' She waited while he placed in her in-tray an envelope she knew would contain documents needing translation. He left without saying another word and Peggy stared at the buff envelope. From its bulk she guessed there was quite a lot of work needing her attention today.

———————

Peggy was almost home when she spotted Helen hurrying along the opposite side of the road. Checking it was clear, she ran over to join her. 'Helen, slow down a minute, will you?'

Helen stopped walking and turned to her, a smile lighting up her face. 'Peggy. How are you?'

Peggy was worried that she was about to approach her friend on a matter that could go very wrong. 'Do you mind if I have a quick chat with you before you go to see Mum and fetch Bobby?'

Helen frowned. 'Is everything all right?'

Peggy nodded. 'Yes, fine. There's something I need to ask you, that's all.'

'Go ahead.' She waited patiently while Peggy gathered her thoughts.

'I've been thinking about your work at Villa Millbrook.' She kept her voice low and stopped talking as two women walked past. 'It occurred to me that with you working in close proximity to German officers, you could be in an excellent position to pick up snippets of information that could prove useful.'

'I see.'

Peggy saw the alarm on Helen's face and wanted to reassure her. 'It's just a thought. I've not shared it with anyone else. Please don't feel you have to do anything that'll make you uncomfortable.'

'It's not that,' Helen said quietly. 'I'm touched you're trusting me, but I don't see how I can help.'

'Why not?' Peggy asked, unable to hide her disappointment.

Helen cringed. 'I would love to, but they speak in German and if I don't understand what they're saying I'm not sure what use I'll be to you.'

Why hadn't she thought of that, Peggy wondered, irritated with herself for missing the obvious. 'Of course they do,' she said almost to herself. 'I forget that most people don't speak the language.'

Helen touched Peggy's arm. 'It was a good idea, though. And I will do my best to find anything out for you. You never know, maybe I will discover something useful.' She smiled.

Relieved, Peggy relaxed. 'Thank you. I'm glad you didn't mind me asking.'

'Don't be silly. I'm delighted you asked me.'

Peggy grinned. 'I suppose we should go and fetch your adorable little boy now.'

Chapter Eight

HELEN

August 1941

I t had been three weeks and still her aunt was confined to bed in hospital. Further tests for consumption, or, as the doctor had referred to it, tuberculosis, had proved she didn't have it and Helen was enormously relieved.

'But she needs to remain at Overdale to recuperate as much as possible,' he had told her. He explained further about the virus that had severely affected her aunt's heart. Helen was relieved to hear that if Sylvia took things easy, ate better and rested more, her death wasn't as imminent as they had both supposed. She looked forward to having her aunt back home the following week.

She couldn't imagine how they expected Aunt Sylvia to eat better, though, with the restrictions on food that were constantly being tightened. Mrs Hamel had been generous with her help, taking Bobby while Helen worked, but she wasn't free today and Helen hoped he would be calm when she took him to the villa.

She was pushing his pram down the corridor to the kitchen when a severe-looking officer startled her by stepping out of a room and stopping in front of her. Helen held her breath, wishing she could turn and run back the way she had come. It was one thing Cook and Mrs Edwards knowing Bobby was there, but another entirely when a member of the Wehrmacht found out.

'And who do we have here?' he asked in passable English. He walked around the pram to peer inside. 'He is your baby?'

Unable to speak or even look up at his face, Helen stared down at Bobby, watching the man push the hood of the pram down so that the light from a nearby window lit up her son's face.

'He is a fine boy.'

'Er, thank you.'

'I have seen you here,' the officer said. 'You serve in the dining room.'

'I do.' Surprised, she looked up at him. He had a severe, untanned face, unlike most of the other soldiers she had come across. And a deep scar ran from the right side of his mouth to his ear. With a jolt, she remembered him as one of the soldiers who had come to Aunt Sylvia's about the V signs. She wished he would move out of her way and let her get to work before Mrs Jeune assumed she wasn't coming.

'My apologies,' he said in near-perfect English. 'I should introduce myself. I am Hauptmann Wilhelm Schneider of the Wehrmacht.' He studied her and Helen struggled to keep from shivering under his sharp gaze. 'Your name?'

'Helen. Um, Helen Bowman.'

'Good morning, Frau Bowman. He held his finger over the pram and Bobby gripped it firmly. She wanted to snatch her son's hand away. 'He is a strong baby.'

'He is.'

'You have enough food to feed him?'

She looked up at him, unsure what he was implying. Forgetting who she was addressing, Helen snapped. 'My baby is perfectly well taken care of, thank you.'

He stepped back looking stunned.

Cringing at her stupidity, she tried to defend herself. 'That is to say—'

He raised a hand and shook his head. 'I was not insulting you. I only ask because I am aware mothers must cope with less now.'

'I see,' she said, feeling a little appeased. 'I should go, or I will be late for work.'

He stepped back from the pram and held one arm out, indicating that she should pass. 'It was pleasant talking to you, Frau Bowman.'

Helen didn't dare hesitate and pushed the pram towards the kitchen, eager to get away from him and into the safety of Cook's domain. She shuddered as she closed the door behind her and leant against it.

'What's happened?' Mrs Jeune narrowed her eyes.

'I was stopped in the hallway by an officer,' she said, her voice trembling. 'He wanted to know about Bobby.'

The cook folded her arms across her ample chest. 'Did he now? And what did he say?'

Helen repeated what had happened. 'He seemed friendly enough,' she admitted, hoping she hadn't read the man's intentions incorrectly. 'But there was something in his expression that unnerved me.'

'Maybe he's a father and missing his own kiddies?' Cook said, picking up a ladle and scooping what looked like a meat and vegetable stew into a serving dish. 'We tend to forget they're people sometimes. I imagine most of them would rather be back home than stuck here.'

The thought hadn't occurred to Helen, and it calmed her slightly. She hoped she wouldn't be needed to serve in the dining room. One conversation with the Hauptmann had been more than enough for one day.

It was a busy but peaceful morning in the kitchen with the usual chopping of vegetables, stirring of sauces and running back and forth at Cook's will. Relaxing into her day, Helen realised there was only half an hour until lunch was ready to be served. Cook had told her not to worry about helping in the dining room, which was a relief.

She pushed Bobby's pram to Coronation Gardens, the park across the road from Villa Millbrook, where she sat in the shade of the pavilion looking out over the sea. She thought back to her only other visit to the park, with her aunt, just before the war, and the relaxing afternoon they had spent walking past the beautiful rose gardens and watching children paddling in the large shallow pool. Aunt Sylvia had explained how Lady Trent had the park designed and built at the beginning of the Thirties to commemorate her late husband. She had brought the renowned French designer, René Lalique, to the island to install his famous crystal in the windows, baptismal font, altar and light fittings of St Matthew's Church, next to the park.

As she ate her sandwich, looking out at the array of trees

and flowers in the gardens, Helen felt nostalgic for those seemingly innocent times three years before the Nazis had invaded, and mourned the unforeseen changes everyone had faced since the opening of the gardens, which Lady Trent had timed to celebrate the coronation of the King.

She was returning to the kitchen, having taken through a pile of used bowls to Dulcie, when she saw Mrs Edwards leaving, a furious scowl on her face.

'What's happened?' Helen asked as soon as the door closed behind the housekeeper.

Mrs Jeune grimaced. 'Mrs Edwards has discovered that last evening one of the officers pushed a lit cigar into Lord Trent's portrait and damaged it.'

Helen felt a pang of sadness. 'No, but that's such a beautiful painting. Why would they do that?'

'I've no idea. What I do know is that there's a right ruckus going on about it because no one has owned up yet.' She glanced towards the door and lowered her voice. 'Mrs Edwards is dreadfully upset. I think mostly because she feels responsible for keeping everything shipshape while her ladyship is away.' She sighed heavily. 'Her poor ladyship. She'll be devastated when she sees what they've done.'

'Rotten sods,' Dulcie said.

Hearing the cursing, Mrs Jeune turned to her. 'What are you doing eavesdropping when you should be working? And don't dare use that language in my kitchen again, do you hear me?'

'Sorry, Cook.'

Helen watched Dulcie skulk back to the scullery and took the opportunity to push Bobby's pram out of the way. Having spent almost an hour playing in the gardens, he was now fast asleep and Helen hoped he'd stay that way for a while yet.'

'Dratted girl,' Cook mumbled. Then, turning to Helen, she said, 'Better smarten yourself up. I'm told you're needed in the dining room after all, and we don't want to increase Mrs Edwards' anger by you being late.' She shot a look at Bobby. 'I'll watch over the little one.'

Helen had little choice but to comply. What other employers would allow her to bring her baby to work, after all?

'Better go and put a brush through your hair and fetch a cap and clean apron.'

Helen ran from the kitchen to the side room to change into the correct outfit.

'Who is this then?' a fair-haired officer she hadn't seen before asked when she carried the tray into the dining room.

Helen didn't reply and willed her hands to stop shaking. She doubted she would ever get used to this part of her work.

The officer she had spoken to that morning stared at her, but Helen pretended not to notice, doing her best not to interact with them while still being respectful. It was a bit of a struggle. As she collected the crockery from the officers' first course, she noticed two of them whispering. The younger one, who had commented on her when she walked in, reddened when she caught his eye.

Eager to leave the room, Helen quickly pushed in front of the other waitress and took the tray carrying the soup tureen and bowls from the dining room.

'What's the matter now?' Mrs Jeune asked as she passed her on her way to the scullery. 'If you're worried about little un, there's no need. He's been as good as gold.'

Not wishing to be thought of as ungrateful, Helen shook her head. 'I'm fine,' she fibbed.

'Good. Then hurry up and take this meat through.'

As Helen carried in the heavy joint of meat she recalled her conversation with Peggy. She needed to stop feeling frightened of these men and focus on finding out useful information for her friend. Feeling emboldened, she quickened her step towards the dining room.

Chapter Nine

PEGGY

A couple of days later, Peggy was working through her last few pages of dictation when there was a familiar knock on her office door. 'Come in,' she called, aware it was Tony. Losing her concentration, she misspelled a word. 'Blast it.'

'Sorry, I didn't mean to distract you.'

'It's fine,' she said, not wanting him to think it was his fault. 'It's good to see you.'

'You seem out of sorts,' he said, his head on one side. 'Something troubling you?'

She explained about Helen not understanding German. 'I don't know why I ever assumed she might,' Peggy admitted miserably. 'Now I have a feeling I've made her feel inadequate in some way. I wish now I'd never said anything about her listening for snippets of information when she's serving the officers.'

He frowned. 'Could you teach her a few German words or phrases she can listen out for?'

'Like what?' she asked, intrigued.

'Things that would alert your suspicions which we can then investigate, or look out for. Words for "prisoners" or "secret". He hesitated. 'I hate the word, but maybe "slave" too, although they're probably more likely to call the poor souls they bring over "sub-human".'

'Urgh, this lot really are despicable,' Peggy said, more determined with each passing moment to do as he suggested. 'Good idea, I'll do that. I sense Helen really wants to help in some way. I think doing so will help her justify working so close to them. Thanks, Tony.' Realising he hadn't mentioned his reason for stopping by her office, she asked, 'Was there something you wanted to speak to me about?'

'I nearly forgot. Babs is waiting outside for you.' He glanced at the work she still had to do. 'Shall I go and let her know you'll be with her as soon as you can?'

'Yes, please.'

He kissed her. After he had left Peggy thought about his suggestion to come up with a list of words or phrases for Helen. The idea was a good one and would give Helen something to work with. Remembering her work and the typo she needed to correct, Peggy forced herself to focus on the job. As soon as she had finished, she slipped the typed documents into a folder and placed them in her desk drawer, ready to be taken through to her boss's office first thing in the morning.

Her coat on, she hurried outside to find Babs laughing and chatting happily with Tony.

Tony spotted her. 'Here she is.'

Babs beamed at her and gave Peggy a hug. 'We were wondering when you were coming.'

'Sorry for making you wait.'

'It's fine,' Babs said, linking her arm through Peggy's. 'Thanks for keeping me company, Tony.'

'Let's get a move on then,' Peggy said, her grumbling stomach reminding her she hadn't eaten anything since breakfast. 'I'm starving. I hope Mum's managed to buy something decent for supper.'

'Me, too,' Babs said.

Peggy's thoughts turned to Helen. She felt sorry for her, being alone. 'Maybe we should pop in to see how Helen's coping without her aunt?'

'That's a good idea. Mum said they're hoping Sylvia will be coming home soon.'

Peggy spotted a woman pushing a pram further ahead on the other side of the road. 'Look,' she said, pointing. 'I think that's Helen. If we hurry, we'll catch up with her and be able to help her lift the pram into her house.'

Once inside Helen's home, Peggy held Bobby while Helen washed her hands and put the kettle on the stove to boil. 'Looking after a baby by yourself and working must be exhausting.'

'It is a bit. Do you two have time for a cuppa?' Helen asked, looking less troubled than she had when they first caught up with her.

Peggy shook her head. She didn't want to use any of Helen's rations. 'No, it's all right. We just wanted to see how you were coping being here alone.

'Aunt Sylvia sent a message to me at work letting me know she's being discharged tomorrow. She insists she's feeling much better.' Helen stroked Bobby's head. 'It's a huge relief, I can tell you. I can't wait for her to be back home with us again.'

Peggy could imagine it. It was bad enough for her, trying to cope with the changes in her own life even with family around her. She also knew lots of people, whereas Helen barely knew a soul. The thought made her glad she and Babs had called in to see her.

'I'm sure it is,' Babs said. 'If you like I can ask Mum if you can join us for supper.'

'That's kind of you,' Helen said thoughtfully. 'But I should make sure everything is ready for my aunt. She'll probably arrive home when I'm still at work, so I'll need to prepare everything tonight.'

'How are you finding your job?' Peggy asked, wondering if that was what Helen had been mulling over when she spotted her earlier.

'It's not too bad.' She shrugged. 'I know I'm lucky to have it.' She glanced at Bobby. 'Cook is a bit scary, but kind, and Mrs Edwards is fine, not that I've seen much of her day to day.'

'What about the officers? It can't be much fun working around them?' Babs asked, tickling Bobby and making him almost wriggle out of Peggy's arms.

'I don't have much to do with them, which is a relief. Although one did stop and chat to me the other day. He unnerved me, if I'm honest. Although it wasn't anything I can put my finger on.'

'Our mum says to always trust your instincts,' Peggy said.

Helen took the kettle off the stove. 'My aunt always says the same thing.'

'We'd better get going now, Peggy,' Babs said.

'I suppose we should,' Peggy said, noticing Helen looking thoughtful as she made tea. 'You go ahead, Babs. I want to cuddle this little one for another couple of minutes.'

'Don't be too long, will you?' Babs said, chucking Bobby under his chin and leaving.

As soon as the front door closed Helen looked at her. 'Is there something you want to speak to me about?'

Peggy was impressed she had noticed. 'You're very perceptive. Even my own sister didn't pick up on that.' She arched an eyebrow. 'There is.'

Helen listened in fascination as Peggy suggested teaching her a few specific German words.

'What do you think?' Peggy asked, hoping Helen wouldn't feel overwhelmed. 'I don't want you to feel you have to, but if you are still willing to help, this might be a way of doing it.' She watched as Helen briefly mulled over her suggestion.

'I definitely want to help and I think this could be a perfect solution.'

Peggy didn't want to alarm Helen by mentioning Tony's part in it. She beamed. 'That's settled then. I'll come up with a list of words and phrases for you to learn and if you hear any of them you can let me know. Taking note of the tone of their voices will also help for context.'

She saw Helen's shoulders straighten and a smile cross her face and knew she had done the right thing in sharing Tony's suggestion.

'I'm nervous about doing it,' Helen said. 'But I'm excited to put your idea into action.'

'Great, then I'll get that list to you as soon as I can.'

Chapter Ten

HELEN

Helen was grateful to Mrs Hamel for offering to look after Bobby again for the day. She was lucky to have such caring neighbours, and for the first time she felt that she was becoming accepted as one of their own. She thought back to Peggy's idea. It was a brilliant one and gave her back a tiny speck of power, knowing she was doing something, however small, to help defy these overconfident men.

The tips of her fingers touched the small piece of paper in her pocket. On it were a few words Peggy had slipped to her that morning when they met outside their front doors. She had spent her thirty-minute walk to work learning the words – including 'prisoner', 'spy', 'informer' and 'arrest' – by heart as Peggy had requested. Now she was eager to burn the paper as soon as she had the opportunity. Helen hadn't felt this excited for a long time and looked forward to doing something useful.

Arriving at the entrance to the house, Helen waited for the barrier to be raised. The officer waved her through. She thought of the Hauptmann with the deep scar on his cheek and how uncomfortable he had made her. She was glad she hadn't seen him recently. Maybe he had been billeted elsewhere, she thought hopefully.

Relieved to reach the kitchen without being stopped, Helen hung up her coat and, taking the slip of paper from her pocket, put on her apron.

'You're looking chirpy this morning,' Cook said, indicating a pan of eggs in water Helen needed to keep an eye on. 'Your aunt back home now, then?'

'Later today, hopefully. I don't think she'll be able to look after Bobby for a while, though.' Helen smiled; her aunt might have her own ideas about that. 'But my neighbour has offered to babysit again tomorrow.'

'I'm glad you have good neighbours,' Cook said pointedly. 'We all need them, especially now.

'We do.' Helen watched the older woman go to the meat safe, open it and look inside. Whilst Cook's attention was distracted, Helen moved the pan and dropped the piece of paper into the flames underneath.

'Those should be ready now,' Cook said, making Helen jump. She was going to need to calm her nerves if she was to be any use to Peggy. 'Peel them, then they can go into a serving bowl. Put a lid on and take them through to the dining room with those cold cuts of meat on that tray. I've no idea why they requested boiled eggs today, but who am I to question these people?' She took a large pan from a hook to her right. 'One of the girls has already taken through the bread, butter and coffee, so you'd better hurry along.'

Helen changed her apron to a pinny and put on a lace cap, irritated to have to serve in the dining room.

'Ahh, here is the little mother,' one of them said as she

entered, carrying the heavy tray over to the oak sideboard. She didn't recognise his voice and supposed one of the others must have been talking about her. Probably that Hauptmann, she thought, suppressing a shiver.

The other waitress, Mabel, gave her a sympathetic look before taking a tray of empty bowls from the room. Why did she leave her alone? Helen wondered, noticing there were three soldiers sitting at the dining-room table.

Mrs Edwards entered the room as Helen was putting the food onto plates ready to serve. 'Hauptmann Schneider, there is a telephone call for you.'

The man stood and left the room with Mrs Edwards.

Helen served the others, anxious to return to the kitchen as quickly as possible. Leutnant Müller usually said hello. He seemed shy and was pleasant-looking in a fresh-faced way, with his pink cheeks, fair hair and blue eyes, but he had a way of staring at her that was a little unnerving.

'How is your little boy today?' an officer she had seen a few times asked. 'He is here?'

They must have been talking about her, she realised, the thought making her feel unsettled. She would much rather they left her alone to do her job rather than insist on speaking to her. Surely they knew how uncomfortable it made her having to converse with them? Maybe it hadn't occurred to them, or could it simply be that her feelings were irrelevant to them?

'No, he's not here today. He is well, though.' She fetched the coffee pot and held it up. 'Would you like more coffee?'

Hauptmann Schneider returned to the room and raised his cup without speaking, waiting as she poured the dark, steaming liquid into his cup. Leutnant Müller, unlike his superior officer, didn't often look her in the eye, or make her feel anxious. There was something cruel in the Hauptmann's leer that made her skin crawl. His small, dark eyes had no softness in them. She didn't think she was imagining things, but supposed it could be something to do with her natural suspicion of men wearing the Wehrmacht uniform.

She left them to eat, relieved to return to the kitchen. She realised she hadn't picked up any information for Peggy, and was disappointed to have let her down. It was early days, though, she reminded herself, assuming there would be plenty more opportunities for her to overhear something useful.

'You really don't like serving them, do you?' Cook asked, grinning at her. 'Not that I blame you. I'd much rather be shut away in here.'

Helen puffed out her cheeks. 'I'll probably learn not to mind so much.'

'Good girl.' Cook indicated the kettle. 'That's about to boil. As soon as it does, you, Dulcie and I can take a moment to eat a bite of something before it's time to clear their dirty plates.'

Helen walked over to the kettle and removed it from the heat when it started whistling. She spooned tea leaves into a pot and added the water. There was no time to heat the pot first, not if they were only having a quick break.

'Butter us a slice of bread each,' Cook said, shooting an impatient look at Dulcie. 'I'll cut us a small slice of this ham I've kept back to eat with it. We'll need to be quick so that none of them catch us eating their food. There'll be hell to pay if they do.'

Helen enjoyed watching her boss misbehaving; it cheered her up. She took the pot, cups and saucers and a small jug of creamy Jersey milk over to the table and sat with her two workmates.

Taking a bite of her bread and ham, Helen closed her eyes, relishing the delicious sweet taste. 'This is heavenly,' she said, trying to recall the last time she had eaten anything so perfect, especially now that rationing was becoming stricter a year into the occupation.

'This is such a treat,' she whispered. 'Thank you.'

Cook tapped the side of her nose. 'I'm sure we all know to keep this to ourselves, don't we, Dulcie?' She raised her eyebrows and stared at the girl who, Helen realised, had been enjoying her unexpected breakfast too much to listen to what was being said.

'Pardon?'

'We're to keep this a secret between the three of us,' Helen repeated.

Dulcie looked from Helen to Cook, an indignant expression on her face. 'I won't tell no one, you can be sure of that. Cross my heart and hope to die.'

Cook laughed. 'There's no need to go that far.'

Helen ate the last mouthful, relishing every morsel.

Mabel entered the kitchen and called out from the doorway, 'They've finished eating.'

Helen stood and straightened her apron. 'I'm coming.' She accompanied Mabel to the dining room and was relieved to see that Leutnant Müller was the only one still there. After Mabel had left the room, Helen picked up the tray of crockery she had just finished loading and lifted it ready to carry it out of the room, but before she reached the door, the leutnant stepped in front of her, blocking her exit.

Helen's breath caught in her throat and she almost dropped the tray. Had he noticed her listening to them talking earlier?

'Please, let me pass. I don't want to get into trouble.'

He raised both hands in the air. 'I do not wish to frighten you.'

'You're not,' Helen lied, sticking out her chin and trying her best to sound brave.

He reached into his pocket. Helen stepped back, nervous about what he was about to do, and was stunned when he pulled out one of the boiled eggs she had brought to the dining room earlier. 'I kept this for you.'

Unsure what to say, she shook her head. 'I can't take anything from you, you must know that.'

He looked down at his feet, then back at her. 'I only wish to help you.'

She still wasn't certain where this was going. 'I should be taking these things to be washed.'

'Take the egg.' His cheeks reddened. 'It is only one egg.' He held it out and Helen stared at it. She would love to take it. What a treat it would be for her aunt later. Eggs were so scarce these days, especially for those like her and Aunt Sylvia who lived near town and had nowhere to keep poultry.

'For your little boy,' the leutnant added. 'He would like it, no?'

Seeing her opportunity, she decided not to tell him that eggs made Bobby unwell but, after hesitating, nodded. 'Um, thank you. Will you hold the tray for a moment?' she said, not liking the idea of asking him to put the egg in her skirt pocket.

He did as she asked and as soon as it was hidden in her pocket, Helen retrieved the tray. 'I must go now,' she said quietly, wishing she didn't feel as if she had done something terribly wrong.

As she walked home that evening, Helen played the incident over and over in her mind. Had she done the right thing accepting the egg? Was it a gift? Surely not. She gasped, causing a woman walking towards her to look at her oddly. Not wanting to attract unwarranted attention, Helen winced and reached down to rub her ankle, pretending to have twisted it.

'You hurt, dear?'

'I'm fine, thank you.' Relieved when the woman walked on, Helen fell to wondering again. By accepting the egg had she collaborated with the Germans? Had she? She felt sick at the idea and forced the thought from her mind. It was too late to worry about it now. Anyway, was taking something that small for someone dear to her such a terrible thing? Helen decided it wasn't and determined to focus on her aunt's reaction to having something tasty and nourishing to eat.

As she neared the terrace, Helen noticed Mrs Hamel waving off the doctor. Helen broke into a run. Had he dropped her aunt home, or was he there delivering bad news?

'Mrs Hamel,' she shouted to get her attention before she went into her home. 'Mrs Hamel!'

Ida stopped on her doorstep and waved for Helen to slow down. 'Nothing to panic about, my dear,' she soothed. 'The doctor brought Sylvia home a short while ago and I've just settled her in your living room with the little un and a cup of tea.'

Relief flooded through Helen. 'Thank you. That's such a relief.'

'Bobby's sleeping so shouldn't bother either of you for a

bit,' she said. Then, folding her arms across her chest, she cocked her head towards the front door and lowered her voice. 'She's still weak but doing well, so the doctor says. We have the same doctor, Sylvia and me. I've known him since he was in nappies, so he knows he can trust me, and that Sylvia and I go a long way back.'

Desperate to see for herself how her aunt was, Helen smiled. 'It's very kind of you and thanks for looking after Bobby for me again today. I'd better see if there's anything my aunt needs.'

'You do that, love. I can have Bobby again tomorrow, so there's no need for you to fret about that.'

Helen doubted her aunt would be happy with the arrangement but she couldn't leave him with her for an entire day, not yet anyway.

'I'm very grateful for your help.'

Ida waved her comment away. 'No need. He's a little love and I enjoy spending time with him.'

'Well, it makes all the difference to me. You must let me know if there's anything I can do for you.'

'Just drop him off, any time after eight.'

'I will, thank you.'

Ida rested a hand on Helen's arm. 'Right, I'd better get in and cook something for our tea. My girls are always peckish when they get home of a nighttime.'

Once inside, Helen heard Bobby chattering away to himself. Happy to see him awake, she picked him up. 'Let's go and find Aunty Sylvia, shall we?'

She laughed when Bobby babbled a reply and walked through to the living room.

Her aunt seemed smaller somehow, but her eyes were

brighter than they had been for a while and her pallor seemed to have faded since the previous week when Helen had been able to visit her.

'You look well,' Helen said, going over to her, bending and kissing her forehead.

'I feel much better now I'm back home.' She opened her arms. 'Let me give my great-nephew a cuddle.'

'Are you sure you're ready to hold this pudding?' Helen wasn't worried for Bobby – she knew her aunt would never ask to hold him if she lacked the strength – but didn't want her to exert herself so soon after being discharged from Overdale.

'I've waited far too long already.'

Helen saw her aunt's smile widen when Bobby reached out towards her. 'You see? He's missed me as much as I've missed him.'

Helen knew she needed to tell Sylvia about Bobby being looked after by Mrs Hamel.

'Why?' Aunt Sylvia grumbled.

'Because you must take things easy.'

Her aunt scowled. 'Nonsense, I've been looking forward to having him to myself.'

Helen sat down on one of the chairs. 'I understand how you feel but I won't change my mind. Maybe by Monday you'll be stronger. You can have him then.'

The look of disappointment on her aunt's face tugged at Helen's heart. Bobby reached out and touched her lower lip with his finger, giggling when she pretended to bite it. 'I suppose you're right.'

Helen recalled the boiled egg in her pocket. She took it out and held it up. 'Look what I've brought you.'

Sylvia frowned. 'How did you manage to stop it from breaking?'

'It's hard-boiled.'

She watched as her aunt's eyes narrowed suspiciously. 'I hope you didn't take this without asking. You don't want to be caught stealing from the Wehrmacht, it would be a dreadful offence.'

'Aunty,' Helen said, shocked her aunt assumed she would do such a thing. 'I'd never steal.'

'Then how did you get it?'

'One of the soldiers saved it for me from his breakfast.'

Sylvia puffed out her cheeks and sat up slightly, handing Bobby back to Helen's arms. 'Lovey, I'm not sure if that's not equally dangerous.'

Helen's earlier anguish resurfaced. 'Please don't say that. It was all perfectly innocent, I can assure you.'

'I don't doubt it, as far as you were concerned.' She frowned. 'I'm not so sure the soldier felt the same way, though.'

'I believe he did,' Helen assured her, beginning to wonder whether she was right.

'Tell me exactly what happened, and I can make up my own mind.'

Helen explained about Hauptmann Schneider and how he made her feel. 'I wouldn't accept anything from him, but Leutnant Müller seems very different. He's shy and not at all sure of himself.'

Her aunt stared at her thoughtfully. 'Being shy doesn't mean he's trustworthy.' She hesitated. 'I don't wish to upset you, dear,' she began. 'You might have a child but you're still naïve in the ways of the world. Some men might not be as gentlemanly as you suppose.'

Helen stared at her, trying to understand what she meant. Then it dawned on her, and she felt as if her aunt had slapped her. 'You mean how I misjudged my relationship with Bobby's dad, Richard?'

'Sorry, love, but yes, that's exactly what I mean. You thought him trustworthy, didn't you? And you knew him far longer than you have this chap.'

Helen got to her feet. 'All I did was accept a boiled egg and I only took that because he intended it for Bobby. It wasn't even a gift for me.'

'Do sit down and try not to overreact. Let me try to explain a bit better.'

'I'd rather you didn't. This is nothing at all like what happened between me and Richard.' She winced, recalling her hurt at his betrayal, still so raw. 'I don't know how much contact you've had with officers of the Wehrmacht, Aunty, but it's not as easy as you might think to refuse an offer from them.' Realising how that sounded, she added, 'Although, naturally I would refuse anything I felt might be untoward.'

'Helen, love. That's not what I meant, and I hope you know that.'

Helen did. She realised she was upsetting her aunt by her reaction and forced herself to calm down. She sat. 'I'm sorry,' she said lowering her voice. 'I didn't mean to be rude, but I couldn't bear for you, of all people, to think badly of me.' She swallowed the lump in her throat.

Sylvia reached out to take her arm 'My dearest girl, I would never think that of you. The circumstances with Bobby's father were heartbreaking. All I want for both of you,' she said, stroking Bobby's head, 'is to be safe here, with me. I only meant to advise you.'

Guilt swept through Helen and once again tears threatened to overwhelm her. 'I know and I feel badly for overreacting. I promise I'll never do anything to compromise my welfare, or Bobby's.'

'I know you won't, sweetheart.' Her aunt smiled. 'Let's agree to forget this conversation. Shall we go to the kitchen? We could slice a piece of bread each and cut this egg in half. I think we both deserve a tasty treat before our supper, don't you?'

Chapter Eleven

HELEN

Helen entered the dining room to clear up after breakfast was finished, stopping suddenly when she realised two soldiers were still there, whispering frantically by a far corner. She tried to tidy as quietly as possible and not clatter the crockery or cutlery, hoping they wouldn't notice her. They were clearly cross about something.

She strained her ears to try and pick up any of the words Peggy had given her. She heard Hauptmann Schneider say *'Hohlgangsanlage acht.'* It meant nothing to her and she continued tidying. Then she heard him hiss a word she did recognise from the list Peggy had given her, *'Untermenschen.'*

Helen gasped in surprise to hear the word for 'subhuman'. Peggy had explained that it was how the Nazis saw the Russian enforced workers whom they had brought to the island to work for Organisation Todt building fortifications.

The men stopped talking and without thinking Helen looked over her shoulder at them to see the one she didn't recognise glare pointedly at Hauptmann Schneider. Helen immediately turned away, tensing.

'You, there. What are you doing?'

She clenched her teeth, furious with herself for making such a careless mistake. 'I'm sorry, I caught my fingernail on the edge of the tray,' she lied. 'I didn't mean to interrupt you. She saw a look of confusion on the Hauptmann's face and hoped he believed her. 'Would you rather I finish clearing up later?' she asked in the most innocent voice she could muster.

Hauptmann Schneider shook his head after a moment's hesitation. '*Nein*. We leave now.'

She waited for them to go. Listening to their footsteps as they went down the corridor Helen turned back to the messy dresser laden with plates of half-eaten food, her mouth watering at the sight of a piece of bacon that remained on one of the serving dishes. She picked it up and ate it, savouring every salty mouthful as she hurriedly tidied up. She didn't want to be caught eating their food but was aware that although they still had food coming into the island from France, not much of it reached the locals and hardly anything had much taste anymore.

As she chewed Helen mulled over what she had heard of their furtive conversation. Excited, she realised she finally had something to share with Peggy.

Chapter Twelve

RICHARD

R ichard took a deep breath to try and control his anxiety as he stood across the road from Helen's family home. He had walked her to the Grove Street terrace of Victorian houses many times when they were seeing each other. He wondered how she would react, seeing him on her doorstep after all this time?

He recalled the last time he had seen her in the summer of 1940 and was embarrassed by his immaturity back then. They had spent a blissful day walking on Black Heath before going to Greenwich Park and enjoying a picnic, lazily snoozing in the sunshine for a couple of hours before making their way back to her home.

How was he to know they would bump into his fiancée Felicity as they walked to the Underground station? Not that he should have been surprised when Felicity – who he knew had a malicious streak – had taken off her cotton glove and shown off her engagement ring to Helen before leaning forward and kissing Richard on his cheek. He had been too dumbfounded to speak and simply watched as Felicity linked arms with her friend and strolled away, giving him and Helen a wave over her shoulder.

'You're engaged?' Helen exclaimed, her beautiful grey eyes filling with unshed tears. 'Richard, how could you? I thought you loved me,' she said, talking over him as he tried to explain. 'I assumed we would be getting married.' She pointed in the direction of the park. 'I stupidly expected you were leading up to proposing today.'

She had marched off, insisting he didn't follow her. Not that he had listened, initially. His heart ached as he recalled catching up with her and taking her arm, only for her to snatch it away. 'Please, let me explain.'

The look of disappointment and deep hurt in her eyes was something he had never been able to dispel. 'What is there to explain?' she had asked with a bitter laugh. 'You are engaged to be married, and not to me. You have lied to me, Richard. And to her.' She had frowned. 'Not that she seemed very upset.' A thought had occurred to her. 'Or surprised, for that matter.' She pulled away from him. 'Why is that, I wonder?'

'Helen, please,' he said, desperate to make her understand how much he loved her. 'It's not as it seems.' His hand went to his chest where she had pushed him away from her. 'Give me time to resolve this. Please. I promise you I will.'

'No.' She had turned her back on him.

'But Helen, I love you.'

She had turned to him, then, tears running down her pretty face, causing his heart to break for the hurt he had caused her. 'But she is the one wearing your ring, and I'm the one…'

'I know,' he had said when she hesitated. He was grateful

for the chance to speak again. 'You're the one who's been let down and I never meant that to happen.'

She glared at him, then, with a look of pure fury before bursting into tears. 'Oh, just leave me alone, will you. You've done enough damage.'

He had been so stunned by having to face the truth of his stupidity that when she ran off, he lost her in a crowd. By the time he had gathered his senses and followed her she was gone.

If only he hadn't decided to give her time to calm down before going to her home and trying to reason with her. If only he had gone straight after Helen and explained that he and Felicity had been childhood sweethearts but he already knew their relationship was over, from that first day he met Helen waiting for her friend outside the cinema. He should have explained right then that he had told Felicity months before that he couldn't marry her.

Everything would have been fine if he had refused to give Felicity time to come to terms with the end of their engagement, but he had felt too guilty about feeling more deeply for Helen in that first meeting than he had ever done for his fiancée.

He had come to Helen's house several times after that, only to have the door slammed in his face by her brother or one of her parents and told never to come back. He had written to her time and again since that horrible day but hadn't received any replies. And then he had joined up.

At least now his leave had finally been granted, and this time he was determined to speak to her, to explain about his engagement with Felicity and that it had finally been ended that day. He exhaled sharply, straightened his cap and crossed the road with as much confidence as he could muster.

His shoulders back, he took a steadying breath and rang the doorbell. He had met her parents and brother a few times and had always got along well with them before he and Helen had fallen out. He couldn't blame them for being angry on her behalf at the misunderstanding.

The door opened and Helen's mother stared at him in disbelief. Richard opened his mouth to speak but her expression darkened and she shouted over her shoulder to her husband, 'Eric, come here, will you.'

'Mrs Bowman, I'm—'

She raised a hand to stop him. 'Eric, now.'

This wasn't going the way he had hoped. They were still angry even after all this time. Disturbed by her reaction, Richard tried to think what to do. 'Mrs Bowman, I—'

She shook her head and pushed the door to. It wasn't completely closed, and he heard her footsteps hurrying down the hallway. Unsure whether to leave or wait, his decision was taken from him when the door was flung open and Stephen, Helen's older brother, stood glaring at him.

'Is your mother all right?'

'No, she bloody isn't.' He glared with such hatred in his eyes that Richard took a step back. 'How dare you show your face here? After what you've done to my sister.'

'I was hoping to explain everything to Helen.'

'What, about you having a fiancée while you were seeing my sister?'

Richard hated confrontation but he had no intention of being put off from seeing Helen this time. 'I wrote to Helen several times about that,' he said. 'and explained that I had broken things off.' He forced a smile. 'There's nothing stopping us being together.'

'You should have finished things before you started courting my sister.' Stephen narrowed his eyes. 'Anyway you're far too late for explanations.' Stephen's eyes slid to Richard's right sleeve. 'Sergeant, I see. Well, bully for you.'

Richard felt sick. 'What do you mean, "too late"? What's happened?'

Stephen shook his head slowly and looked as if he wanted to throttle him. 'What happened, Sergeant, is that my younger sister ran off that night, caught the ferry and has been living with our aunt since last summer.'

Richard tried to make sense of what he was being told. A boat? Nausea coursed through him as it dawned on him that the only aunt Helen had ever mentioned was Sylvia and she lived in Jersey.

He grabbed hold of the wall to steady himself. 'No,' he whispered, barely able to comprehend the repercussions of what he had done. He swallowed to gain some control. 'You mean she's in Jersey?'

Stephen gave a slow clap. 'The penny's dropped, I see. Yes, unfortunately that's exactly where she is. Living on a damn island surrounded by bloody Nazis.'

Richard struggled to contain his senses. What had he done. No wonder Helen's family had been so angry with him. He tried to think clearly. 'Do you have her address?'

Stephen shook his head. 'You really are something else, do you know that?' Scowling, he added, 'You can't just post a letter there, you know.'

'What about a telegram?' He tried to calm down before

losing control of his emotions as the full impact of her situation and his part in it dawned on him.

'All I know is that if you don't leave this property in the next three seconds,' Stephen sneered, poking Richard in his uniformed chest, 'I won't be responsible for my actions.'

'Has he gone yet, Stephen?'

Richard heard Mrs Bowman's tearful voice and knew he had done enough damage to this family. 'I'm going,' he said. 'Please apologise to your parents for me, Stephen. I really am sorry for everything I've done.'

'Just go.'

Crushed, Richard saw how angry Stephen was and turned to leave. He immediately heard the door slam shut behind him.

If only he had gone after her that afternoon. But he hadn't, and now the woman he loved was living under Nazi rule. He had no idea if there was anything he could do to rectify all that he had done. He had caused her to run away straight into a situation neither of them could have imagined. He decided that he wouldn't stop searching until he found a way of helping her, somehow.

Chapter Thirteen

HELEN

'How's your Aunt Sylvia's health these days?' Cook asked when they sat down for their morning break between serving breakfast and preparing lunch.

Helen cupped her mug of tea in her hands despite the heat in the kitchen, soothed by the warmth of the drink. 'She's not doing too well, I'm afraid.' She didn't like to add that each morning when she went downstairs for breakfast, and each evening when she returned to the house after work, she was anxious that something might have happened to her aunt in her absence. She would give a lot for reassurance that her aunt's health had fully returned, but she couldn't fool herself; the reality was that her aunt was much slower these days, even though she did her best to hide it.

'I can see by your face how worried you are about her,' Cook said, her voice gentle.

Helen had worried about her aunt many times but hadn't expected Mrs Jeune to have noticed her concerns, since she was always so busy cooking. 'It probably doesn't help that there's little healthy food available. The doctor said she needs more protein, preferably red meat to help her iron levels, but where are we supposed to find good meat nowadays?'

She heard the panic in her voice and smiled to soften her tone. Her aunt wouldn't thank her for sharing their private matters with someone who wasn't family.

'Can I help?' Cook asked before being distracted by something at the kitchen door.

Helen turned to see Leutnant Müller standing in the doorway looking sheepish.

'My apologies. It is nothing.' He gave a curt nod before leaving and closing the door quietly behind him.

'Well, that was odd,' Mrs Jeune mused. 'Then again, some of them can be very strange.'

'They can,' Helen said, embarrassed in case he had caught any of their conversation. 'I shouldn't go on about Aunty Sylvia.'

The older woman stared at her sagely. 'It's perfectly natural you should worry. You had a dreadful shock when she was taken ill and, let's face it, she is your only relative here.'

Helen was grateful to have someone other than her aunt and two friends to confide in. She knew, too, how lucky she was to have a job where she could occasionally take Bobby with her, and didn't like to bother Mrs Jeune with her personal problems.

Insisting she was fine, Helen returned to her work, but was glad when the end of the day finally arrived. She removed her apron and dressed Bobby in his hat, woolly mittens and a coat that she realised with dismay was becoming rather too small for him. She had no idea where she might find another, and by the look of things he wasn't going to be able to wear this one for very much longer.

'I'll be off now, Mrs Jeune,' she said, taking hold of the pram and pushing it towards the kitchen door. 'Hopefully my aunt or Mrs Hamel will be able to look after Bobby for me tomorrow.'

'Don't you fret about him, my girl. He's a dear little soul and no trouble at all. He brightens up the place. I had noticed he's getting a little big for that pram of his.'

Helen had been thinking the same thing. 'I need to find him a pushchair, but I've no idea where to look.' She didn't add that she couldn't afford to buy one.

'I'm sure he'll be fine for now.'

Helen smiled gratefully. She never used to feel guilty about things before having Bobby, but it amazed her how kind some people could be. She was pushing the pram out of the back door to leave the house when a deep voice called out to her.

'Frau Bowman.'

She tensed. It was Leutnant Müller. His voice was quiet. Sensing that he had been waiting for her, she felt a chill pass through her.

She turned slowly. 'Y-Yes?'

She noticed he was holding something wrapped in newspaper.

'Please,' he said, his voice hushed. 'Take this.' He glanced to his side to check they were still alone.

Helen's grip on the pram handle tightened. Unsure what to do but aware she daren't make a scene and draw attention to herself, she waited for him to continue. She looked down at the package he was holding. 'I don't think—'

'Please. Take it.'

'What is it?'

'Meat.'

She gasped. 'I can't take this, it's stealing.' It was her turn to check they weren't being watched.

'*Nein*. No. It is not. This is my food. I asked for it not to be cooked.'

She felt cornered and wished he would leave her alone. He was trying to be kind, but his familiarity intimidated her 'I don't understand.'

He looked shamefaced. 'I hear you speaking to the cook before. About your aunt who is ill,' he added when she didn't react.

Helen grimaced. So she had been right to suspect he had overheard her conversation with Mrs Jeune. She struggled to explain her reason for refusing his kind gesture. 'It doesn't feel right to take it from you.' She pictured her aunt, so frail now, and wanted more than anything to grab the package from him and run home with it.

'I assure you it is acceptable. Your aunt needs this. I have a mother in Germany. I would not wish her to starve.' He held it out towards her. 'I must go. Take it. Please.'

She took a deep breath, hoping she wasn't about to make a stupid mistake by following her emotions rather than her instincts. 'I will, but only this time.'

Taking it from him, she tried to think where she might hide it.

He pointed to Bobby's pram. Then, hearing Hauptmann Schneider shouting at someone from the front door, and not daring to waste any more time, Helen lifted the thin mattress near her son's feet and quickly shoved the package underneath. With the blankets tucked back in, it was neatly covered. Helen quietly thanked him. 'I'd better go.'

He seemed as relieved as she was that their covert conversation had ended.

Helen felt as if everyone could tell she was sneaking meat off the property. As she neared the guard at the gate, she hoped she didn't look as guilty as she felt. She might not have stolen the meat, but would a soldier believe that if she was caught with it? Even worse, she mused, as the guard waved for her to pass the raised barrier, would be if one of the islanders discovered her with it. Would they accuse her of collaborating for favours? She shuddered at the prospect. She couldn't bear people thinking her capable of horizontal collaboration.

She hurried along St Aubin's Road, glad to be away from the villa, and was about halfway home when she spotted Babs coming towards her.

'Hello, there,' Babs chirped, clearly in a cheerful mood. 'Isn't it lovely to see the sunshine?'

Helen was about to agree when she noticed Babs's expression change to one of horror. Unsure why, Helen tensed and glanced behind her in case she was being followed. She looked back at her friend, who pointed discreetly at the pram.

'What?' Helen asked before following her friend's gaze. To her horror she saw that small drops of blood were pooling at her feet. She was barely able to breathe. The meat. She should have wrapped it in something else, but she hadn't had time.

Two soldiers appeared at the entrance of Hansford Lane. They seemed to be deciding which direction they should go. Unsure what to do, Helen focused on trying not to panic. She reached forward and, desperate to stop the blood leaking from the pram, took Bobby's blanket from him and stuffed it under the mattress, hoping it would soak up any liquid.

As the breeze came in contact with his legs, Bobby's face crumpled, and he let out a bellow. She didn't blame him but wished he would calm down and not draw attention to them. She froze when the soldiers looked over in her direction, alerted by Bobby's infuriated cries as they increased in pitch. Helen knew she was about to be stopped.

She was bracing herself for being arrested for theft as soon as they spotted the blood, when Babs cried out. The soldiers immediately turned their attention to her pretty blonde friend.

'Go!' Babs hissed. 'Now, and don't look back.' Realising this was Babs's way of distracting them to let her escape, Helen increased her pace, grateful to her friend for her quick thinking.

As Helen strode away from the scene, she heard the soldiers asking Babs if she was all right and her replying that she had dropped a couple of Reichsmarks down the drain near her feet. Not daring to slow down and check on the meat, Helen hoped she would be able to reach home before any more blood began to drip. Bobby's cries were causing people to look at them and reminding her that his legs were exposed. Without slowing down she hurriedly unwound her scarf from her neck and draped it over them.

'That's better, isn't it?' she soothed. 'We'll soon be home.'

He pulled the edge of the silky scarf up to his face and covered it, calming immediately now he had something soft to cuddle.

She pulled his pram up the front steps, adrenalin helping her manage it more quickly than usual. As soon as the front door closed with a satisfying clunk, Helen leant her bottom against it, trying to catch her breath, and promised herself she would never take a chance like this again.

'Is everything all right?' Sylvia asked, joining her from the kitchen. 'Helen?'

She smiled, not wanting to concern her aunt. 'I'm fine. We both are. But I've smuggled something back for our supper and almost got caught doing it.'

Aunt Sylvia scowled. 'Smuggled? Helen, what have you done?'

'I'll tell you as soon as I've gathered myself,' she replied, unbuttoning her coat and hanging it up. She took her scarf from Bobby's grip, setting his crying off again. Then, unclipping him from his harness, Helen lifted him and carried him through to his highchair, relieved his clothes hadn't been soiled by the liquid under his mattress.

When she returned to the hallway, she noticed her aunt peering in the pram. 'Is that—'

'It's blood,' Helen said, shaking her head when her aunt looked at her aghast. 'From a piece of meat I was given.'

Her aunt's mouth dropped open. 'You have meat hidden in Bobby's pram?'

'Why don't you make us a cup of tea while I clean this up, Aunty?' She lifted the mattress and removed the dripping paper package, trying not to retch at the iron smell of the blood.

Her aunt grimaced. 'Wait a minute while I fetch a plate for that.' She disappeared into the kitchen. 'We don't need a mess on the floor.' She returned and Helen placed the soggy parcel on the plate for her aunt to take back with her to the kitchen.

A few minutes later, after cutting the fillet into two, having determined to give half to Babs as a thank you for her help,

Helen divided the rest between her and her aunt. Sylvia had refused to eat it unless they shared it.

'I'm not sure how to cook it to make the most of it.'

Sylvia sipped her tea. 'I think we should make a nourishing stew,' she said eventually. 'We have a few vegetables past their best, but they'll be disguised well enough in a stew.' She focused her attention on Helen, who struggled not to look away under her aunt's scrutiny. 'You never mentioned who gave this to you. And more to the point, why?'

Recalling their previous cross words over the hard-boiled egg, Helen explained about the soldier overhearing her conversation with Mrs Jeune and wanting to help. 'I wasn't comfortable accepting it, but we heard someone calling him and neither of us wanted to be caught. I know it was nicely meant. I just wish I had been able to wrap the bundle up a little better to contain the drips.'

'You were incredibly lucky not to be caught,' her aunt said, after Helen explained what Babs had done. 'Thank heavens that dear girl appeared when she did and reacted so quickly.'

'I agree. That's why I thought we should share the meat with her. I know it'll mean we have less, and there won't be much at all for Babs once she's shared it with her mum and sister, but at least we all have benefit from it.'

A knock on the front door made them jump. Sylvia put her hand to her chest, and Helen worried that the two soldiers had been suspicious of her after all and followed her home.

'You see who that is,' her aunt said. 'I'll hide this lot.'

Leaving her aunt to find somewhere to hide the meat, Helen rushed to the front door, relieved that she had thought to clean the pram before doing anything else.

She smoothed down her hair, hoping she didn't look as

flustered as she felt, before turning the door handle and opening the door.

'Babs, it's you.' She exhaled sharply, unable to hide her relief.

'I thought I'd better come and check you're all right,' Babs said, lowering her voice as two women walked past the house.

'Yes, thanks to you.' Helen gave the nosy women a pointed look when they glanced up in her direction. 'You'd better come inside.' She stood back to let her friend in. Closing the door, she pulled Babs into a hug. 'I can't thank you enough for what you did back there,' she said, her voice tightening with emotion.

'Don't be silly.' Babs patted her on the shoulder. 'I was happy to do it. Mind you,' Babs said widening her eyes, 'I wasn't sure it would work.'

Helen recalled how promptly the two soldiers had responded, spotting her pretty friend in distress and running to help her. 'Well, I'm eternally grateful for your quick thinking. Come through to the kitchen, I have a little thank-you gift for you.'

As she walked through, Helen decided there and then that she needed to get rid of the pram. Bobby was too big for it, anyway, and with nowhere to hide parcels in a pushchair she would have the perfect excuse to refuse any further offers of meat.

Chapter Fourteen

RICHARD

It took a while before Richard was able to recall the name of the aunt Helen had mentioned whom she and her family stayed with each summer, but he was determined to find a way of contacting her. After all, if he hadn't waited to finish with Felicity and had been open about his engagement from the start of his relationship with Helen, she never would have left to go to Jersey. It was his fault entirely that she was in this predicament now and he needed to let her know he was there for her.

It was Sylvia, Sylvia Bowman. He remembered Helen talking about the house and where it was on the island, and after looking at a map he hoped he was right in concluding that she lived on St Aubin's Road. He had cobbled together an address of sorts. It wasn't perfect but, preferring not to upset her mother and brother by visiting them again to press them for details, he decided to send a telegram and hope for the best.

'Twenty-five words only?' he asked, astonished, at the

92

telegraph office. What could he say with so few words? He stepped aside to let the next person in the queue take his place, then took a pencil and piece of paper and began to draft his message.

Rereading it for the fourth time, Richard knew it didn't say exactly what he wanted but hoped Helen would understand his meaning behind it – if it ever reached her.

No longer engaged. Sorry you left without knowing.
Desperately hoping you are safe and well with Aunt Sylvia.
Please send word. Fondest love always, Richard

He queued again and, handing his message over the counter to be transmitted, paid and thanked the woman.

All he could do now was pray Helen received his message and took it in the way that was meant. He loved her – had always done – and ever since he'd discovered she was being held captive on the island by those damn Nazis, he'd realised even more how deeply.

For once he was grateful that he only had a brief leave and was due to return to base in the morning. He needed to be busy so his thoughts had little chance to torment him.

What would he do if she didn't reply? The thought that she might choose not to worried him, then it occurred to him that there might be some reason why she wouldn't be able to. His heart raced as he thought about her and what she might be suffering at the hands of those Nazis. He clenched his fists, knowing there wasn't anything he wouldn't do to protect her. If he was ever given the chance to see her again, he would find a way to make up for all that she had gone through. He prayed he would be able to.

Chapter Fifteen

HELEN

November 1941

The afternoon dragged and it was a relief to have an excuse to pop into the Hamels' home on her way back from work. Ida had been looking after Bobby again because her aunt had needed to go to the doctor's surgery for another check-up. Despite her prayers it was clear to them both that her aunt's health was declining by the week. She pushed the troubling thought aside and knocked on number 3's front door.

She hated the early nightfall of the winter, especially now the streets were filled with uniformed soldiers who always seemed to be watching them from under their caps. Hearing German voices she looked up to see three of them coming in her direction. Aware she had to pass them, and not wishing to do so, she picked up her pace and crossed the road, taking care not to catch their eye.

'Hello, love,' Ida said waving her in. 'Hurry up and get

inside, we're trying to keep the worst of the cold air out of the house.' Once the door was closed behind Helen, she added, 'You sound slightly out of breath. You all right?'

'Yes, thanks.' She didn't add that she was in a rush to share what she had discovered with Peggy. 'Is Peggy home yet?'

'She is, love. You'll find her and Tony in there with the little one,' she said indicating the living room door before making her way to the kitchen.

'Thank you.' Helen was relieved she would be able to speak to Peggy and Tony alone, excited not to have to wait to share her news with the pair of them.

'Hello,' Peggy said smiling at her as she walked in. 'Come and sit down with us for a bit.'

Helen sat on the chair opposite the sofa where the couple were seated, aware that Peggy assumed she would be in a rush to get Bobby home. She leant down to ruffle Bobby's hair. 'Obviously too happy playing with his toys to bother with his mummy,' she joked.

'How's your day been?' Peggy asked.

Tony nodded.

'We've just been talking about these poor enforced workers being made to build all the fortifications springing up around the island.'

Helen pictured the rows of badly treated men and women she had seen being marched through town on various occasions when she had walked to Westmount to visit her aunt at Overdale. 'I have some news about that,' she said, excited to share what she had heard.

'It infuriates me to see how badly treated they are,' Tony said scowling, a fierce look in his dark brown eyes.

'Strangely enough, that's what I wanted to speak to you about.'

She saw her friends sit up a little straighter and hoped she wasn't about to disappoint them with what she had to share. Seeing their eager faces, Helen hurriedly explained what had happened. 'I'm not sure if I've remembered that word correctly,' she said, 'but it sounded something like *Hohlgangsanlage acht*. I don't know if it means anything to you, but I tried to remember it in case it did.'

Tony's mouth opened for a second and she could see he was clearly intrigued. 'Was there anything else, do you recall?'

Helen felt her excitement rise, hoping she did have something that the pair of them could use to help someone. 'Yes. They also said *untermenschen*.'

'Are you sure?' Peggy asked, taking hold of Tony's hand as she stared at Helen.

'Yes, definitely. The were referring to an enforced worker, weren't they? I could tell they were angry about it.'

Tony turned to Peggy, rubbing his chin. 'One of the workers has escaped, I imagine. I've heard about these tunnels being worked on. They're down past Meadowbank, along Les Charrières de Malorey.' His voice petered out and he sat back thoughtfully.

'This is very useful information, Helen,' Peggy said reaching forward and taking Helen's hand.

'Really?'

'Yes.' Tony clasped his hands together. 'Either the worker escaped from there, or that's where they're focusing their search for him. With this information we can make a plan to try and track him down before the Jerries do.' He smiled at her. 'This is a great help, Helen. Well done.'

Helen realised hours had been wasted since she came across this news. 'I overheard them earlier this morning, so they might have already found the poor guy.'

Tony stood. 'That's true. But if they haven't, then we still have a chance to help him.' He bent to kiss Peggy. 'I'm going to have to go and see what I can do.'

Peggy took his hand in hers. 'Please be careful, Tony.'

'I will.' He looked at Helen, his eyes gleaming with excitement. 'You've done well.'

As soon as he'd left, Peggy wrapped her arms around her chest. 'I worry about him when he dashes off like that but I know he needs to feel useful.' She sighed. 'Tony's right, though, you have done very well.'

It was what she needed to hear. 'I'm pleased. Now, I'd better get this little one home. I shouldn't leave Aunt Sylvia alone for any longer.'

Helen left satisfied to have finally done something useful. It was a wonderful feeling.

Chapter Sixteen

HELEN

'Good morning,' Helen said, happier than usual, mostly because her aunt's health seemed to have improved slightly. She was hopeful that the prognosis, about the virus damaging her aunt's heart, had been wrong. Sylvia even seemed fit enough now to look after Bobby for the day. Helen was beginning to believe that somehow things were going to be all right.

Mrs Jeune seemed happier than usual, too.

She realised she hadn't heard any news from Peggy about whether her information had proved to be useful. Why would she? she reasoned finally. Everyone had to be careful to keep quiet about information they came across. Her role had just been to pass on to her friends anything she had heard. She wished she had discovered something more since then, but either the officers were being more careful in front of the household staff, or she had simply missed hearing anything.

'You're on time,' Dulcie teased as she entered the kitchen

from the scullery, a smile on her thin face. 'You're chirpier than usual, too.'

'I am, I—' Helen began, but Dulcie interrupted her.

'Did you receive one, too, then?'

She wasn't sure what Dulcie meant. 'I'm sorry?'

'A Red Cross telegram. Cook got one and I was wondering if you did, too.'

Helen shook her head, her good mood fading fast. 'No, I didn't.'

Cook walked in through the back door. She had a scowl on her face, but her voice was light, and Helen wondered why she was the only one of the three of them not to have received a valuable telegram. Then again, she mused, who was going to send her one? She had no idea how her brother or parents had taken the news of her abrupt departure when they read the letter she had left for them on her pillow the night she had snuck out. She doubted any of them would bother sending a telegram to someone who had let them all down so badly.

Forcing her disappointment aside, Helen asked her about the telegram and who it was from. She listened with a determined smile on her face as Cook relayed the message she had received that morning from her sister.

'She's on the mainland staying with our cousin,' Mrs Jeune explained. 'I was hoping to accompany her, but our cousin's home isn't big. She offered us all a place, but with my sister, her daughter and two grandchildren going, I thought I should stay here and keep an eye on my home instead.'

'I suppose you're right,' Helen said, thinking that Cook probably felt she had little choice. She was sad that the woman who had been so kind to her and Bobby was separated from her own family. 'Do you have any relations left on the island?'

Cook shook her head. 'Not anymore.'

How many people were in that position? Helen wondered.

Mrs Jeune looked sternly at her. 'Now, Miss, you can wipe that look off your face. I'm fine. I might miss them, but it's reassuring to have a message in my sister's own words and more than anything to know they're doing well.'

Helen supposed she was right. She was glad for her but wished now more than ever that she had someone to send a telegram to or receive one from. Her aunt had asked, a few months before, if she wanted to send a message to her family but Helen was too nervous to do so in case they didn't reply and she would be sure that they had turned their backs on her permanently. Maybe it was better not to know.

Still, despite the situation she had found herself in, she hoped to one day return to her family home and introduce Bobby to her parents and brother.

Maybe Aunty Sylvia could travel with them to the mainland when the war was over? Helen doubted her mother would ever do anything to upset her sister. And as for her father, hadn't he always professed that Sylvia was the wisest of them all? Happy with her plan, Helen decided that was what she would do. The thought cheered her, and she was only vaguely aware of Mrs Jeune chatting with Dulcie about her telegram and the reply she was planning to send.

As soon as she arrived home that evening Helen could sense excitement in the air and wondered what had happened.

'I'm home, Aunty,' she called, entering the kitchen as soon as she had hung up her coat. She saw her aunt sitting at the table holding what looked like a telegram.

'Mum and Dad?' she asked, barely able to contain her delight.

'I can't think who else it might be from,' her aunt replied happily. 'Well, don't just stand there, open it. I've been dying to know what it says.'

Helen took a deep breath and sat as Sylvia slid the envelope towards her. She stared at it, nervous about reading their message. She looked at her aunt.

'For pity's sake just open it.'

Helen braced herself as she withdrew the flimsy sheet of paper with the Red Cross emblem on the top of the page. Her eyes caught the final word, and she began to tremble.

'What is it?'

She couldn't speak for a second. 'It's—' She swallowed. 'It's not from Mum and Dad. It's from Richard,' she whispered, her voice quavering.

'Bobby's father?'

Helen barely heard her as she read the message. *No longer engaged. Sorry you left without knowing. Desperately hoping you are safe and well with Aunt Sylvia. Please send word. Fondest love always, Richard.* He said 'fondest love', she mused, feeling as if she was having some sort of out-of-body experience. She handed it to her aunt to look at.

'It's a bit late for him to tell you this now,' her aunt snapped, clearly furious on Helen's behalf. 'Silly, silly man.'

Her aunt had every right to be furious with him. 'It's fine, Aunty.'

'It is not,' her aunt argued. 'If he hadn't behaved like a cad then you and your darling boy would not be having to cope in this place. I truly despair of young men sometimes.'

Helen couldn't think straight.

'Will you reply to him?' Sylvia reached out and took

Helen's hand in hers. Then, after a few seconds, she asked, 'Does he even know about Bobby?'

Helen forced herself to look at her aunt. 'No,' she admitted.

Her aunt didn't hide her shock. She stared at Helen thoughtfully. 'I see. What will you do?'

'Nothing, for now. I need to come to terms with what he's told me.' She sighed. 'It's not as if anything I say can make a difference to either of our situations anyway. Bobby and I are stuck here and he's there, and that's all there is to it.'

Her aunt's eyes filled with sadness. 'I suppose you're right.'

Helen replaced the message in its envelope and slipped it into her pocket. So much for wanting a telegram. Hearing from Richard had upset her. She had been coping before, mostly. Now she had to make decisions: about Richard, and of course about Bobby.

'I don't think I'll reply,' she said, but took out the envelope again and looked at the date it had been sent. 'It's taken three months to get here,' she sighed. 'So much might have changed in that time.'

She couldn't bring herself to say, 'Richard could be dead,' but it was a possibility. Or he could have reconsidered his feelings for her. 'Maybe he's met someone else by now.'

She knew it was an unfair thing to say but she couldn't help herself. This message had torn open the wound his engagement had caused and the pain stung deeply.

Damn it, Richard, she thought. Why couldn't you have just left me alone after all this time?

Chapter Seventeen

PEGGY

December 1941

I t was almost Christmas. Another year was over and the war's ending was still no closer. Peggy anxiously wondered what 1942 had in store for them. There was little news to be cheerful about as far as she was concerned, although Tony, who she now suspected must have a radio hidden somewhere, insisted that now the Americans had entered the war, hundreds of thousands of men, women and children's lives could possibly be saved and the war might be brought to an earlier conclusion than it would without them.

Any pleasure she might have found in that was diminished when she thought of the men and women who had been killed at the US Navy's Pearl Harbor base in Hawaii. It was strange to think how familiar that name was now; when the news was first reported, she had needed to look it up in their world atlas.

Right now, though, she needed to get ready to accompany Tony into town to find a gift for his father. She also needed one for her mother and sister, and Bobby for his first birthday a few days before Christmas. Unfortunately there was little left in the shops and she had no idea what to buy.

'I suppose we should be focusing on useful gifts,' she suggested thoughtfully. 'Soaps, that sort of thing.'

Tony took her hand in his and pulled a face. 'That doesn't sound very exciting.'

'It's necessities we need now,' she said recalling some of the beautifully scented soaps she had enjoyed only the year before. 'Anyway, that's what I'll be hoping to find for my mum.'

'I suppose the best place for that sort of thing is Boots, then?'

'That's where I was planning on stopping first. Babs was saying there are a few scented soaps left that would make perfect gifts, but not many.'

'Well, I'm sure she'll be able to steer us in the right direction. She must have lots of customers needing her assistance at this time of year.'

Peggy supposed she must do. 'Good, then that's agreed.'

She spotted Babs as they walked into the shop from Queen Street. She was serving a customer but noticed them and gave a discreet wave, which Peggy returned with a smile.

'We'll have a look around this area,' Peggy suggested quietly to Tony. 'As soon as Babs has finished serving that lady, we'll nip over to her and see what she can do for us.' Then she noticed a middle-aged woman watching her and Tony, and she let go of his hand.

'What's the matter?' he asked.

She told him about the woman staring at them. 'It might look odd if we're seen holding hands when I work for your father.'

'I'm not sure why.' He looked over her shoulder in the woman's direction and gave her a courteous nod. 'Then again, I know her. She's one of my father's oldest clients and is a bit of a busybody. She'd love nothing better than to stir gossip, so maybe you're right. Do you think she saw us?'

'I've no idea.'

'Ah, well, it's too late now if she did. Let's not worry about it.'

'Good afternoon, Madam. Sir,' Babs said. Despite sounding formal, she was clearly pleased to be serving them. 'How may I help you today?'

'We've come for suggestions for Christmas presents.' She looked at Tony. 'What exactly are you looking for?' Enjoying herself, too, Peggy spoke loudly enough for the staring woman to hear, since she could tell she was eavesdropping.

'Something for my father and also my mother,' Tony said. 'My father has his birthday a few days before Christmas, too, and I was hoping to find a couple of small gifts for him. He said not to bother this year, but it feels wrong not finding something to give him to mark both occasions, don't you agree?'

'I do,' Babs confirmed. 'Let me see.' She gave his request a little thought and then, raising a finger, smiled. 'I think I might have just the thing.' She bent down behind the counter and opened a cupboard. Straightening up, she placed two small boxes on the counter and pointed to one. 'We still have one of these beautiful shaving brushes left.' She took the other box and opened it, lifting out a small metal contraption: a mirror with a small folding stand.

'What's that?' Peggy asked, intrigued.

'Let me guess,' Tony said, as Babs hid the box underneath the counter. 'May I pick it up to have a better look?'

'Of course.' Babs smiled at the two women who had been hovering nearby trying to listen in to their conversation. 'May I assist you, ladies?'

'Not at the moment,' the woman who recognised Tony snapped. Peggy realised she was with a friend. The two of them seemed rather unimpressed by her, which was odd, seeing that they didn't know her at all. 'We were just on our way.'

Peggy gave her sister a conspiratorial smile. 'That was clever. I thought they'd never go away.'

Babs grinned. 'It was rather, wasn't it? Actually, I'm used to nosy parkers trying to snoop on other customers. Really gets on my pip and I'm always happy to see them on their way.' She looked over Peggy's shoulder. 'They've left the shop. Thank heavens for that.'

Peggy couldn't agree more. What was wrong with some people?

'I bet I know what this is,' said Tony.

'Tell us, then.' Babs said.

Peggy suspected he was trying to distract them and, knowing Tony was good at working things out, nudged him. 'Go on, tell us what you're thinking.' She peered at it. 'I haven't a clue.'

'Is it a little night light?' He held up the small metal object and opened one side to show Peggy the circular holder. 'I think a candle is placed in there. And this mirror is to reflect the light as much as possible.'

Peggy thought he might be right. 'But why does it fold up? What's the point of that?'

'For travelling,' Babs said.

Peggy looked from one to the other of them, unsure whether it would be rude of her to point out the obvious flaw in this gift idea.

Tony smiled. 'I know none of us are going anywhere very soon,' he said. 'But my father will love this. He's always trying to persuade my mother to stay positive and hope that this war will end at some point. He'll like having something to keep for when we're all able to travel again.'

Peggy didn't dare admit that she often thought that time might never come.

'It's also something he can easily store away,' he said, handing the object back to Babs. 'I'll have it, please,' he said. 'And the shaving brush. Thank you, they're perfect suggestions and I know he'll be happy with them.'

Peggy waited while Tony paid for the items and Babs put the boxes in a paper bag. She was glad that her sister had been able to help resolve his gift quandary. 'Would you be able to make any suggestions for something for Mum?'

Babs nodded. 'I have just the thing. One minute.'

Peggy was unsure whether to buy something her mother would deem necessary and practical, or a gift that would be more of a luxury. She hoped that whatever it was Babs had in mind would solve her indecision.

'Here,' Babs declared, lifting a box that was larger than either of those Tony was carrying. 'Again, this is the last one we have.' She lowered her voice. 'I know we're probably expected to purchase items that have a more practical use, but I think that while we still have things like these in stock, we may as well give them to those we love to enjoy. Don't you agree?

And I know Mum will love this. I thought we could buy this for her together.'

Babs turned the box to face her and Tony. Peggy studied the three glass tubs.

'The fragrance is heavenly,' Babs said, taking out one of them. 'Lavender. This one is hand cream, this is for the face and this,' she said proudly, 'is for your feet.'

'Feet?' Tony shot Peggy an astonished glance. 'Feet?' he whispered, obviously not understanding why anyone might spend good money for cream for their feet.

Peggy noticed Babs's amusement at his reaction, glad she wasn't upset by his surprise.

'She'll love this. Although you don't think she might be a bit cross with us for buying something frivolous?'

Babs frowned. 'There's nothing frivolous about looking after yourself,' she said.

Her sister had a point. 'Still, it is a time for cutting back and taking care, isn't it?' Peggy said doubtfully.

'Nonsense,' Tony said. 'If you think your mother will appreciate this, then buy it for her. Who knows when you'll have another opportunity to give her a gift this lovely.'

'It is the last one, don't forget,' Babs reminded her. 'I would buy it myself, but it's a little more than I can afford to spend. Anyway, she can always keep it for special occasions, or as a treat to cheer her up over the coming months…'

Peggy noticed her sister's smile slip, and realised that Babs had stopped herself adding 'or years'. It was what they all dreaded: years of life as it was now, or worse. She took a calming breath. 'You're right. She deserves something special after all she's been through. We'll buy it for her and if she isn't happy, which I'm sure she will be, then we can use the creams.'

'Leave this with me, then,' Babs said. 'I have a little discount, so I'll pay for it later.' Aware she still had to find something for her sister, Peggy thanked her and she and Tony left Boots.

'I'm glad you suggested we go there,' Tony said. He passed his packet from one hand to the other and touched the back of her hand with his as they walked. 'I wish we could hold hands like other couples.'

Peggy nodded. 'Me, too.'

'You don't sound very happy,' he said frowning. 'What's the matter?'

She explained about it soon being Bobby's birthday and that she wanted to buy him something from her family for both then and Christmas. 'But even if I did know what to get for him, I'm not sure where I'd find it.'

Tony beamed at her. 'Now this I can help with.'

'You can?'

He pulled a face. 'I was a little boy once, you know. Leave it with me.'

'All right, then, I will.' She looked forward to discovering what Tony came up with and smiled happily.

'Good,' he said taking hold of her hand briefly before letting it go again. 'One of these days we won't have to hide our feelings for each other in public.'

'But not yet,' she said, desperate not to lose her job when she needed it most. It wasn't only that she needed to earn a living now that her father had passed away and her mother was struggling to come to terms with life without him. Going out to work enabled her to support her mother, as well as tiring her out enough to be able to fall asleep at night. Working and thinking about Tony kept her from dwelling too deeply on their miserable situation. She had no intention of giving up either if she could possibly help it.

Chapter Eighteen

HELEN

'We can't keep forcing this coat onto the poor little mite,' Aunt Sylvia said, trying her best to button up Bobby's coat, which Helen thought must now be almost two sizes too small for him.

Bobby stuck out his lower lip, his face crumpled and he burst into noisy tears. Helen sighed deeply. 'I've no idea where to find another coat for him,' she admitted, as she desperately tried to comfort him. 'If only it wasn't so cold, and I could get away with dressing him in a second sweater.'

There was a knock at the door and, frustrated, both women swapped glances.

'I'll see who it is,' Helen said, hurrying to the door. She opened it to find Babs standing there, her arms wrapped around herself as she shifted from one foot to the other. Helen waved her inside. 'Quick, it's freezing out there.'

'Thanks.' Babs's smile disappeared as Bobby let out another furious bellow. 'I didn't bother putting a coat on because I was only coming from next door. Oh dear, have I come at a difficult moment?'

'It's fine. Come through.' Helen lowered her head to her son's level and pointed at Babs. 'Look who's come to visit us, Bobby.'

He looked up at her. Ordinarily, the sight of Babs's pretty face never failed to make him smile, but this time he just continued crying.

'What's the matter, little man?' Babs frowned, chucking him under his chin. When that didn't make any difference she gave Helen a questioning look. 'Why is he so upset?'

'He's feeling restricted in his winter coat.'

Babs pulled a face. 'I'm not surprised. It does look a bit too small for him.'

Helen groaned guiltily. 'That's it. I'm taking it off. I can't expect him to wear this, but what else can I do?' she asked, only just holding back her own tears. 'There aren't any children's clothes anywhere as far as I can tell.'

'Have you tried Summerland?'

Helen had heard of the factory. 'Is that the place next to the orphanage?'

'Yes, Sacre Coeur. I've heard they unravel knitted items at Summerland and make them into something else. They also do the same thing with discarded fabric from blankets or curtains, that sort of thing. Their opening hours are reduced but I can find out what they are, if you like? Maybe they might have something you can buy for Bobby.'

It was a good idea and Helen appreciated Babs's suggestion. 'Thank you.'

'Maybe you could ask someone at Boots if they're in need

of a coat this size?' Aunt Sylvia suggested. 'What with money being so tight.'

'That's a good idea,' Babs agreed. 'I will. I know Mum has bartered a few things over the past year.' She looked thoughtful. 'Leave it with me. I'll see what I can come up with.'

Helen thanked her friend, then realised she hadn't asked why she'd come over. 'Sorry, I forgot to ask – is there something we can do for you?'

Babs seemed at a loss for a moment, then nodded. 'I'd forgotten all about that in the excitement.' She pressed her palms together. 'Please don't feel you have to accept, it's just a suggestion.'

'Go on, lovey,' Aunt Sylvia encouraged. 'What is it?'

'Mum and Peggy were discussing Christmas Day. I don't know what food you've managed to get hold of for the day, if anything much, but they were wondering if you'd like to come to our house and we'll all share our food. It would be fun celebrating the day together. Making an event of it. Mum will be going to church early in the morning, but you'd be welcome any time that suits the two of you.' She ruffled Bobby's hair. 'And you, of course. You'll be the most important guest.'

Helen loved the idea and looked at her aunt for her reaction. She was smiling.

'I think it's a wonderful idea,' Aunt Sylvia said. 'Don't you, Helen?'

'I do.' She thought about how they should go about the cooking. 'As we only live next door, why don't we cook our food here and carry it over at a pre-arranged time?'

'I like that idea.' Babs's eyes sparkled in amusement. 'It will save me doing extra washing up too.'

Helen and Sylvia laughed.

'And we can take our dirty plates home with us,' Sylvia pointed out with a smile.

It cheered Helen to see her aunt looking so happy for once. Even Bobby seemed happier, probably because their jollity had taken his mind off himself.

'And if the little one becomes tetchy or tired,' Helen said thoughtfully, 'I can simply bring him home and put him to bed.' The more she thought about it the happier she was with the idea. 'I'm getting a little excited about Christmas now we have something planned.'

'So am I,' her aunt agreed.

It would be Christmas in two days and Helen couldn't wait. Then a thought struck her. 'Oh!'

'What is it?' Babs asked.

'Um, it's nothing,' she stalled, not wishing to mention that she would now have to find a gift for Babs and her family if they were to spend the day together. She had very little money and most of what she did have she would need to pay for a coat for Bobby, if she could find one that fitted him.

As if she had realised what was on Helen's mind, Babs said, 'Mum insists none of us think about bringing presents.'

'She does?'

'Yes. Everything is scarce now, and we'd all be hard pushed to find anything, even if we could afford it.' Babs clasped her hands together. 'The most important thing is for all of us to spend time with each other.'

Helen was extremely relieved. 'As long as we're all agreed, then that's what we'll do.'

'Perfect.' Babs turned to leave. 'At least we're allowed our radios at the moment, so we can listen to music.' She did a little jig, making them laugh. 'I should be going now. Mum and

Peggy will be delighted you're joining us.' She raised an eyebrow. 'Although I have a feeling they'll mostly be excited about Bobby spending the day with us.'

They followed her to the front door. Babs turned before leaving. 'I won't forget to ask about coats for Bobby.'

'Thank you. I appreciate your help.'

Helen watched her friend run down the steps and up the ones leading to her home next door, giving a quick wave before disappearing inside.

How lucky she was to live next door to such a kind family. Her mother used to say that angels come into our lives in various guises just when we need them, and Helen couldn't help thinking that Babs, Peggy and her mum were her own personal angels. And Aunt Sylvia, too.

Chapter Nineteen

PEGGY

Christmas Day 1941

S he read the note that had been popped in through the letterbox earlier, which her mother had placed on the hall table. What could Tony be writing to her about? She had seen him at work earlier in the day and he hadn't mentioned sending her a letter. She opened it and unfolded the single sheet of paper.

Dear Peggy,

I forgot ask you something earlier and didn't like to trouble your mother by calling in this evening. Please meet me at the bus shelter along from your house at ten-thirty, if possible. I have a little something for you and would love to be able to give it to you in person. I'll wait for an hour but will then need to return home to be with my family. I hope to see you.

Tony x

She checked her watch. It was ten-fifteen already and she was only halfway through peeling the few potatoes her mother had queued over an hour for at the greengrocers the previous day. Their lunch was going to be meagre, to say the least, but if they were spending the day together, Peggy didn't care what they ate. It wasn't going to be as tasty as the chicken they had eaten for their first Occupation Christmas the previous year, but that couldn't be helped.

Today wouldn't be special like her childhood Christmases – and not only because celebrating without her father seemed odd. At least they had baby Bobby to distract them and cheer them up.

She hurriedly finished the potatoes and popped them into a small pan of water, placing the lid on top before drying her hands.

'I'm just running out quickly, Mum,' she shouted as she put on her coat, scarf, hat and gloves. 'I shan't be long.'

'Make sure you're not,' her mother replied from upstairs.

She had to run most of the way to the bus stop, not wanting to keep Tony waiting in the cold any longer than necessary. As it was she wouldn't have long to talk to him if she wasn't to upset her mother. As she neared the stop, two soldiers walked towards her.

'You're just my kind of girl,' the taller one said in German, a sneer on his face. 'How about coming out with me tonight?'

Desperate to say something to him but aware they probably assumed she couldn't understand them, Peggy pretended not to understand and focused on the way ahead.

'I don't think she likes you very much,' the other one mocked. 'Maybe I'm more her type.'

Peggy wondered how they would react if they discovered

she did understand. Would they be embarrassed, or frightened she might report them? Either way, she decided, they weren't going to know. Anyway, she had Tony to see and that was far more important than two silly German privates showing off to each other.

She spotted Tony waiting, his coat collar turned up against the brisk wind, arms folded across his chest. He saw her and smiled, opening his arms.

Peggy ran to him, relishing being enveloped in his strong embrace. She rested her head against the rough tweed of his winter coat, breathing in the scent of the cold sea air and the brand of tobacco his father smoked. He led her further into the bus shelter to keep them out of the worst of the wind.

'I'm sorry to ask you to meet me out here when it's barely above freezing.'

She stifled a shiver. 'I was happy to come.'

He lowered his head and kissed her. 'I have a little something for you. It's not much, and when this is all over, I intend to rectify the lack of choice here.'

'That's not necessary.'

He handed her the small package. 'I'm sorry it isn't wrapped nicely, but I couldn't find any Christmas paper.'

She stared at it, wondering what it might be. She knew she would love whatever he had given her.

Tony put his arm around her shoulder 'Are you going to open it, or just look at it?'

She unfolded the paper bag and withdrew a silver brooch in the shape of a daisy. 'Tony, it's beautiful,' she gasped, unbuttoning her coat.

'What are you doing?' he asked, looking shocked. 'It's too cold to take your coat off.'

'I wasn't. I want you to fasten it to my cardigan, so I know it's properly pinned on.'

She waited while he did as she asked, watching his hands.

'You like it, then?' He gazed at her and Peggy was surprised to see how unsure he seemed. Before she had got to know him better she had always assumed this strong, handsome man was briming with confidence.

'I love it.' She studied it, loving him even more for his thoughtfulness. 'It's such a treat having something this pretty.'

'It reminded me of you.'

'That's so sweet!' She flung her arms around his neck, happy they were in the relative privacy of the shelter.

She felt Tony's lips draw back into a smile and loved that he was enjoying himself as much as she was.

'I could become used to this,' he said, his voice gentle. 'In fact, I'm already smitten.'

Her heart pounded to hear him say that. She already knew she loved him but had never shared her feelings with him, or even with her sister. The thought of any of the staff at the firm discovering their closeness sent a pang of panic through her.

'What's wrong?' he asked, holding her tightly.

'We must be careful no one sees us, remember? We both know we aren't allowed to have relationships with other members of staff.'

'Stupid rule,' he whispered before kissing her again. 'But I know you're right. As much as I want everyone to know how we feel about each other, I'm aware the directors would insist you left if they found out about us, and that wouldn't be fair to you. Or to the firm.' He smiled. 'Or to me. Seriously though, your translations are very useful, helping us stay one step ahead.'

She realised she hadn't given him his gift and pushed her hand into her pocket. 'I have a little something for you, too.'

She saw excitement register on his face. 'It isn't nearly as perfect as your present,' she said, handing him the gift she had kept in her pocket for the past few days, waiting for the right time to give it to him.

He stared at it as if she had given him something worth hundreds of pounds. 'A Christmas present. Thank you.'

He was so sweet. 'You don't know what it is yet. I'd open it first before complimenting me.' She was teasing him and he knew it.

'It could be an old dishcloth and I'd love it because it was from you.'

'Who knows,' she teased. 'Maybe that's what it is.'

He opened it and withdrew a white cotton handkerchief. She had spent hours over the embroidery, so that Tony's initials in one corner, in an elaborate font, looked perfect. She hoped it was to his taste. 'You see, it *is* almost an old dishcloth,' she joked to cover her nerves.

He pulled her into his arms and kissed her tenderly. 'It's nothing of the sort. It's the most perfect present I've ever received.' He studied her handiwork again. 'You're very accomplished.'

'I'm so pleased you like it.'

'I love it. It's something from you that I can always carry around with me.'

She liked that idea. Then, remembering the time, she gave him a quick peck on the lips. 'I'm afraid I have to run, otherwise Mum will be furious. Happy Christmas, Tony,' she said. As their eyes locked, she saw something else in his expression.

'Happy Christmas, my sweet Peggy.' He held her tightly for a moment, wrapping his coat around her before whispering in her ear, 'Who knows, maybe next year this nightmare will all be over, and we'll be able to celebrate properly.'

Not wishing to tempt fate, she gave him another kiss. 'Let's just focus on right now and this Christmas. We've got each other, and I feel extremely lucky to have you in my life.'

'And I you.' He kissed the top of her head.

Unable to help herself, she asked him if something was wrong.

He frowned. 'Why would you ask?'

She sensed he was keeping something from her. 'I'm not sure. There's something about the way you looked at me just then. I'd like to think you felt you could confide in me about anything.'

He took her by the shoulders. 'I promise it's nothing for you to worry about. Now, we'd better be on our way. I'll see you after Christmas.'

Wanting to press him further, but aware she didn't have time to do so without annoying her mother, Peggy relented. 'Just be careful with whatever it is that's on your mind.'

'You know me.' He grinned. 'I always am.'

She hoped so. With one last quick kiss, she wished him a happy Christmas and ran back home to spend the festivities with her family.

Chapter Twenty

HELEN

Helen was surprised she felt as excited as she did. This wasn't a perfect way to spend Christmas but it was her little boy's second Christmas and she intended to make it special for him and her aunt in whatever way she could. Aunt Sylvia and she had exchanged gifts earlier, amused to discover they had chosen matching bars of soap.

'At least we know we like our gifts,' Aunt Sylvia had exclaimed, sniffing the fresh lavender scent. 'Where did you find this? Boots?'

Helen nodded. 'Babs helped me.'

Her aunt laughed. 'The dear girl did the same for me.'

Helen was grateful to Babs for her cleverness. She thought of the wooden train Peggy had given Bobby on his birthday two days before, explaining that a friend of Tony's had made it for him. How kind people were. She had given Bobby a small teddy that Mrs Edwards had brought into work to sell for a friend who was hoping to make a few pfennigs to spend on their family Christmas. 'She's a very particular woman,' Mrs

Edwards had explained. 'And I know the bear will have been well looked after, otherwise I would never have suggested it.'

Helen had thanked her profusely, delighted to have something Bobby could cuddle when she wasn't around. She found a new ribbon in her aunt's sewing basket and tied it neatly around the bear's neck. Bobby had been playing with it ever since that morning and now they were having to take it with them to the Hamels' home.

She knew that however difficult her circumstances might be, she was luckier than a lot of people. At least she and Bobby shared a home with someone who loved them, and never made Helen feel as if they were imposing.

'I wanted to ask you something,' Aunt Sylvia said, interrupting Helen's thoughts as they covered the plates of food they were taking next door with clean tea towels.

Helen had a feeling she might know what was worrying her aunt. 'Yes?'

'You haven't replied to Richard's telegram yet, have you?'

She hadn't, and despite everything couldn't help feeling a little guilty. He was fighting for his country, after all. 'Not yet, no.'

'Do you think you will?'

Helen shrugged. 'I'm not sure. Part of me wants to, but then I think about what happened and can't help being angry towards him all over again.'

Her aunt rested a hand on Helen's shoulder. 'You must do what feels right for you, lovey. Shall we go next door? We don't want to delay lunch by being late.'

'You're here,' Ida Hamel announced cheerfully as she opened her front door with a welcoming smile. 'We've been dying to see this little one. Here, let me take those plates from you,' she said, relieving them of their offerings and stepping back to let them pass. She beamed at Bobby. 'Look at you, all wrapped up.'

Helen hoped her face wasn't showing how embarrassed she was to have put a blanket around Bobby to bring him the few steps from their home. She had attempted to put his coat on again, but he had protested loudly and she had given up, not wishing to upset him.

She couldn't imagine ever wearing anything too small again. Unlike Bobby, the few clothes she possessed were now several sizes too big. Even her aunt looked as if her clothes were borrowed from someone larger than her. Helen felt a pang in her heart, remembering the immaculately dressed woman she had known before the war changed everything. It couldn't be helped, though, not with the scanty food they were all having to survive on these days.

Helen carried Bobby through to the parlour and smiled at the sound of Babs's familiar voice as she walked in. 'This looks festive.'

'I'm glad you think so,' Babs said cheerfully. 'It's not as we would ordinarily have it, but we've replaced the holly we usually have over our pictures with ivy.'

Mrs Hamel entered the room and motioned for Sylvia to hand her her coat. 'Babs found the ivy on a wall on her way home the other day. An old disused house along a back street, wasn't it, Babs love?''

'That's right. On a side wall.' She grinned. 'I checked no

one could see me before taking a length of it. Thankfully I had little else in my shopping bag so could slip it in there.'

'It looks very festive,' Aunt Sylvia said, reaching to take Bobby from Helen. 'Let me take the little one so you can take off your coat.'

Helen passed her son to her aunt and unwrapped him carefully as soon as she saw that he was firmly in Sylvia's arms. She hurriedly folded the blanket and, unsure where to put it, held onto it. She noticed an amused look pass between Ida and her daughter and embarrassment surged through her. Helen opened her mouth to explain why she had used a blanket but before she could speak, Babs left the room and Ida motioned them towards the square table set up in the middle of the front room. She pulled out one of the chairs. 'Take a seat here, Sylvia. We're going to be a little squashed together, I'm afraid.'

'It'll be cosy,' Sylvia assured her. 'The table looks beautiful.'

Helen noticed the flower-patterned plates and white napkins that someone had embroidered with forget-me-nots to match the ones on the crockery. 'It does.'

'We don't often use this set,' Peggy said, who had joined them, 'but Mum thought today was the perfect day to do it.'

Ida grinned. 'What I actually said was I thought we all needed reminding that however dreadful these times are, one day the world will be a happier, more cheerful place again. I thought making the table pretty and sharing our food with close friends was the perfect way to do it.'

Helen swallowed the lump in her throat at her neighbour's words. 'What a wonderful idea,' she whispered, her voice hoarse from the tightness in her throat.

'I agree,' Sylvia said, wiping away a tear.

Peggy rubbed her mother's upper arm. 'You're a clever soul, aren't you, Mum?'

'I'm not so sure about that.' She stroked Bobby's cheek. 'And how's my favourite boy today?'

Bobby answered by holding out his teddy for her to see. 'That's a lovely present. Did Mummy get that for you?'

Helen decided to go and see if she could help Babs in the kitchen. 'I'll just pop through and see if Babs needs me for anything.'

'Good idea,' Ida said. 'I'll fetch some drinks and we'll get started with that food. We don't want to ruin our meal by letting it go cold.'

'This is delicious,' Aunt Sylvia said half an hour later as she dabbed at her mouth with her napkin. 'You must let me know how you make these potatoes so tasty. Mine always seem rather bland, especially now.'

'Your potatoes are fine, Aunty,' Helen argued. 'Although you're right, these really are wonderful.'

'They're all Mum's doing,' Babs said proudly. 'She won't tell us what she adds to them, though. You can try and find out, but I doubt you'll succeed.'

'You're not going to tell us?' Sylvia asked.

Ida shook her head. 'I can't.'

'Can't, or won't, Mum?' Babs said, before addressing Helen and her aunt. 'If you can find out I'll be over the moon. I've been trying for ages.'

After the washing up was completed and the table and chairs pushed against a wall to give them more room, Helen relaxed on the sofa, staring into the fire and listening to the chatter of the other women. Sylvia pointed to Bobby asleep in Ida's arms and Helen's heart filled with love for her little boy. He was so precious and she was grateful that these four women also loved him. She was lucky in so many ways and having this adopted family around the two of them meant everything.

She reflected that even though they hadn't been able to enjoy the usual Christmas fare, there had been no Christmas tree and they'd had to make paperchains out of old newspapers, it had still been a special day.

Helen felt a yawn coming and covered her mouth. She had been up since six that morning looking after Bobby and then helping prepare the meal with her aunt, and her tiredness had caught up with her.

A moment later Babs whispered something to her mother, got up and left the room.

'I think it's time we made a move,' Sylvia suggested.

'Just a moment,' Babs said, returning. 'I want to give Helen something before you go.'

Helen saw she was holding a bag out for her. She took it and opened it. 'I thought we weren't to buy each other gifts,' she said, concerned not to have bought the Hamels anything.

'This isn't for you, it's for Bobby.'

Helen pulled the item of clothing out of the bag and held it up, gasping. It was a navy blue, double-breasted woollen coat which she guessed must be a couple of sizes larger than his current one, if not more.

She wasn't sure what to say. 'This is far too much.'

Babs shook her head. 'It isn't. Anyway it's not just from me but also from Mum and Peggy.'

Helen wasn't sure she could accept such a generous gift, especially when none of them had very much to live on as it was. 'I don't think—'

'Let me stop you right there,' Ida insisted. 'I don't think you realise how fond we all are of this little chap.' She pursed her lips at Bobby, making him giggle. 'He's a much-needed light in these dark days and one of the few things that make us smile. One of the women at Boots told Babs she had this coat and what she wanted for it.' She cocked her head to one side. 'A pair of winter boots. We knew it wasn't any bother for us to give her those.'

'Winter boots?' Sylvia said, and Helen heard the shock in her aunt's voice. 'We can't possibly allow you to be out of pocket. I'm sure we'll think of some way to find him a coat.'

'You misunderstand.' It was Ida's turn to argue. 'We had already given Babs a short list of items none of us wear anymore. One of those things that had been sitting uselessly in a cupboard for a couple of years was a pair of ankle boots. My husband bought them for me as a surprise and they pinched horribly. I never had the heart to tell him and always found an excuse not to wear them. Now someone has them to keep her feet warm and Bobby has a coat that fits. Everyone is happy.'

'We must give you something in return,' Helen said. uncomfortable at being beholden to anyone, even friends.

'Letting me look after a little one is payment enough,' Ida said.

'But you're the one helping me out by doing that.'

She tried to continue, but Ida shook her head. 'I don't think you realise how much I value my time with him.' She looked down at her hands. 'It's been a long while since I've found much to cheer me up, isn't it, girls?'

Her daughters looked at each other sombrely and Helen presumed they were thinking about their late father. 'Yes, Mum.'

'Please let us do this one thing for him.'

Helen felt her resolve weakening. 'All right, then. Thank you very much, all of you. I really appreciate your kindness, and I know Bobby will be much happier wearing this instead of me cramming his arms into the other one.' She had an idea. 'I'll bring his old coat to you tomorrow if you like, Babs. Then you can take it to Boots and see if any of the other employees has a child who might benefit from it.'

'That's a great idea.' Babs said smiling. 'I'll do that.'

'If the woman has given her son's coat to you,' Aunt Sylvia said thoughtfully, 'won't that mean that her son is now without one?'

Babs shook her head. 'She has three sons. I mentioned that you might have a smaller one for her baby. The middle son will now wear a hand-me-down from the oldest one.'

'I see,' Sylvia said.

'Maybe when Bobby has outgrown this coat, I can swap it back to her for something else?' Helen was beginning to warm to the idea of bartering. They might not have any money but knowing she might have items that others could benefit from made her feel useful.

'That's exactly what I was thinking,' Babs said, grinning. 'Now that the shops have run out of most things, we all need to be creative with our thinking.'

Taking Bobby from Ida, Helen placed him onto the sofa and crouched down in front of him. Picking up the coat, she slipped his arms into the sleeves and fastened the four front buttons. 'He looks very smart,' she said proudly.

Bobby took hold of one of the buttons and stared at it before looking up at her and giving her a wide grin.

'I think he approves,' Peggy said with a laugh.

'As he should do.' Helen got up and hugged her and Babs.

'He's such a treasure,' Ida said. 'Doesn't he look adorable? Like a proper little Lord Fauntleroy.'

Helen wouldn't go quite that far, but even she had to admit her son did look especially sweet in his new coat. And he was smiling. It was an enormous relief. 'I think we can all safely say that Bobby is very happy with his new coat.' She smiled at each of them. 'Thank you for a lovely day, I've thoroughly enjoyed it.'

Peggy fetched their coats, and when they were ready, Sylvia led the way to the front door. 'Merry Christmas and thank you again for sharing your day with us.'

'We've enjoyed every moment,' Ida said.

Back at home, as she took off her son's coat, Helen couldn't help thinking how much better Christmas Day had turned out than she had expected.

She wondered where Richard had spent the day.

Chapter Twenty-One

PEGGY

January 1942

L ying on her bed staring up at the ceiling on the first day of the new year, Peggy thought of Tony and the beautiful brooch and reminded herself how lucky she was to have someone who cared so much about her. Someone she was falling more deeply in love with each day. She hoped he had enjoyed his family Christmas.

She thought of poor Helen, with a little boy to care for and distanced from her parents and brother, and was comforted to know that she at least had her Aunt Sylvia for company. Would Helen's life be any easier if she had a husband away fighting? Probably not. So many women were struggling to care for families on their own these days. It was soothing to know she herself had family to look out for her, just as she looked out for them. How difficult it must be for those without someone close to lean on, she mused.

'Peggy, what are you doing up there?' her mother bellowed. 'You'll be late to work if you don't move yourself soon.'

Peggy jumped off the bed, quickly pinned her new brooch onto the lapel of her jacket, then lifted the material to gaze at it. She slipped on her shoes, picked up her handbag and ran downstairs.

'I'm here.' She took the sandwich her mother was holding out for her. It was neatly wrapped in greaseproof paper, as always. 'Thanks, Mum,' she said, kissing her on the cheek as she pushed her lunch into her bag. 'I won't be back late tonight. Have a lovely day.'

'I will if I manage to find something decent for our supper,' Ida grumbled. Then, frowning, she turned Peggy round and pushed her gently towards the door. 'Go. Your sister left ten minutes ago.'

She hadn't seen Tony all day but presumed he was being kept busy in meetings. It wasn't until after three that afternoon that her boss summoned her to his office. She had felt tension in the building for most of the day and dreaded what might have caused it.

'Good afternoon, Miss Hamel,' Advocate Le Gresley said when she walked in holding her notepad and pencil. He didn't seem his usual cheerful self and a feeling of dread swept through her.

'Is everything all right, Advocate Le Gresley?'

'Please sit down, Peggy.' He sighed deeply. 'I'm afraid something terrible has happened and I know I can trust you to keep the matter confidential until it's somehow resolved.'

She sensed by the gravity in his expression that it was about Tony.

He placed his elbows on his desk, his hands clasped together, and exhaled sharply. 'I'm afraid my son has been arrested.'

Remembering her boss's insistence that employees do not forge personal relationships, Peggy struggled not to show her horror. She swallowed and focused on remaining calm. 'What's he supposed to have done?' she asked, her mind racing about the risks they never discussed but she suspected he took on some nights when they weren't together.

'I gather he was caught out after curfew.'

'I see.' Peggy knew some soldiers, intent on showing their superiority to locals, liked to arrest people for minor infractions. 'Surely they'll let him go with a warning for that, though?'

He pulled a framed photo towards him and studied it. Peggy knew it was a picture of Anthony and his mother. 'If only that was all he had been doing.'

Her dread increased. 'May I ask what?' She recalled their conversation on Christmas Eve and knew she had been right to sense he was planning something then. Why hadn't he been more careful? Why hadn't she pushed him to tell her more? But even if he had, she doubted she could have dissuaded him from doing what he felt was right.

'He was caught with a couple of others near to where one of the workers had gone missing. I've discovered he's been questioned, but as he had the sense not to have anything incriminating on him, I'm hoping they don't take things further.'

'Do you think they'll let him go soon?' she asked. She knew

that if he was found guilty and sentenced to longer than three months, he would probably be transported to a camp in Germany. He shook his head slowly. 'I doubt it. He's in Newgate Street jail now.'

She pictured the ominous Napoleonic prison just off Gloucester Street and suppressed a shudder.

He lowered his face into his hands for a second then looked up at her again. 'I've requested permission to visit him as his lawyer.'

'They don't know you're his father? Won't they become suspicious when they see you have the same last name?'

'I had thought of that, but what else can I do? I need to do something.'

Peggy wondered why he didn't ask one of the other partners in the firm, but reasoned that to question him might be seen as overstepping her place. She needed to help in some way, though. She pushed aside thoughts of her mother and how angry she would be to discover Peggy had come to the attention of German authorities. She knew she would never forgive herself if she didn't do something to help the man she loved. 'I could go to the prison for you.'

He stared at her in disbelief. 'I'm not certain they would agree to let you see him.'

'I'm your secretary, aren't I? And if they look up my name they might realise that I translate documents for them.' She saw his expression brighten slightly. It felt good to give him some hope. 'We won't know if we don't try. It might work, then I could speak to him on your behalf.'

'I'm not sure.' He stared at her as he mulled over her suggestion and Peggy willed him to agree.

She struggled to hide her desperation. 'Please, let me do this. I want to help.'

'It's Friday and I'm not sure we'll be able to do much for him until Monday anyway, but if we can secure his release sooner rather than later, I suppose it's worth a try.' He seemed to perk up slightly. 'I'll draft a note for the Prison Governor. I need to speak to one of my colleagues first about how best to word the letter, so if you can come in tomorrow morning for a short while, I will have something ready for you then.'

Peggy left his office, nervous but relieved. Had she done the right thing volunteering to go? She had never been to the jail before, but this was for Tony. As the reality of what she was about to do sank in, though, Peggy's bravado began to weaken slightly. She only hoped she wasn't too late to help him.

Chapter Twenty-Two

HELEN

Helen hated the cold weather. The shorter, miserable days seemed to make everything gloomier. It was bitterly cold and had been snowing on and off for a few days. Each time she ventured outside she needed to cover her mouth with her scarf and by the time she got into the building she could barely feel her toes, fingers or cheeks.

It didn't help that Aunt Sylvia had been unwell since Boxing Day and had needed to spend a few unhappy days in her bed. Today was the first day she felt well enough to look after Bobby while Helen went to work.

Helen was lost in thought, rubbing her frozen hands together to try and warm them, when Leutnant Müller greeted her in the corridor as she neared the kitchen door. She repressed a groan. She had thankfully seen little of him since the meat incident and wished she had been a minute earlier and missed him.

'*Guten Morgen*, Frau Bowman.'

'Good morning,' she replied, having no intention of using

his language to acknowledge him. He seemed a kind enough man, but there was still something a little creepy about him and she was careful not to be anything other than socially polite to him.

The kitchen door opened and Cook frowned, reading the situation instantly. 'What are you doing skulking out there, young lady?' she snapped at Helen. 'You have work to do.' She acknowledged the officer. 'Good morning.'

He nodded at her greeting, his cheeks reddening as he turned and walked away. Helen was shocked at Mrs Jeune's tone and ran into the kitchen, hurriedly removing her outer wear before she was told off again.

'Don't fret none,' Cook said in her usual tone. 'I only said that to get rid of him.'

Helen relaxed, almost dropping the apron she was about to put on. 'That's a relief. Thank you for rescuing me.'

'You can make us both a cuppa to pay me back. I've been here for an hour already and I'm parched. Have a look over on the table there,' she said, pointing to a Red Cross telegram. 'Received that yesterday, I did. It was sent a couple of months ago from my sister, so it's taken its time getting here, but it's better than nothing.'

Helen went over to the table and picked up the precious piece of paper with the red emblem. 'You must be delighted to have heard from them again.'

'I am. It's a relief to know she and the grandkids are all fine. It's in reply to one that I sent her.'

The older woman washed and dried her hands and sat at the table while Helen made their drinks. 'You heard from your folks in England yet?'

Helen shook her head. She still hadn't replied to Richard

and felt guilty about it, but couldn't think what to say. She wished she knew if her parents were safe and well. She swallowed the lump in her throat. How had their Christmas been? Had her brother been given leave to spend time with them over the festivities?

She wondered if Aunt Sylvia could have tried to send word to the family without telling her. It was something she might possibly do, but Helen would only know for certain if she asked her. She wasn't ready to broach the subject yet, though.

'Sorry, Helen,' she heard Cook say. 'I didn't mean to say anything insensitive.'

'You didn't.'

'You sure? Your face is telling me otherwise.'

Helen realised she must have been frowning. 'I'm fine. A little tired, maybe. My aunt's been a bit under the weather for a few days.' When Mrs Jeune frowned, too, Helen added, 'She insists she's fine today and she does appear to be much better. So much so in fact that she insisted on babysitting for me.'

She decided to change the subject. She didn't like to bother others with her troubles and certainly didn't want to bring down Cook's mood. She pointed to the telegram.

'Are you going to send a reply straight away?' she asked.

Mrs Jeune talked about her sister, and her concerns for her niece and the grandchildren. 'I worry sometimes that I won't live to see them again and give them hugs.' The woman's eyes filled with tears.

'I'm sure you will,' Helen said, trying to sound positive.

'Did you see any of those leaflets the RAF dropped on the island last week?' Dulcie asked, joining them in the kitchen.

Helen shook her head. 'I heard about them but haven't seen any.'

'My dad was outside in the garden when he spotted one under the hedge. It was written in French.'

'I'm told they all were,' Cook said.

'Maybe. My dad speaks French and said he thinks they were meant for the Jerries, but dropping them shows us we haven't been completely forgotten.'

'That's something, I suppose.' Curious about the leaflets, Helen asked, 'Did your father happen to say what the message was about?'

'He did.' Dulcie gave the question some thought. 'It was something like, "when our planes come over, take cover".'

'I'm not sure I like the sound of that,' Mrs Jeune said, frowning.

Neither did Helen. What if she wasn't somewhere where there was cover? And what if her aunt and Bobby weren't able to get somewhere safe? She shuddered.

'At least,' Cook was saying, 'we'll feel a little less isolated from the rest of the world, having the RAF fly over and drop leaflets.'

Helen supposed she was right and felt slightly better at the thought.

The snow showers eventually stopped after a few days but instead of temperatures rising they continued to drop, turning the melting snow to ice and the pavements very slippery.

Helen couldn't wait for spring to arrive and bring some warmth with it. Maybe some decent weather might help cheer them all up. She hadn't been home long when Babs came to see them. She and her aunt were sitting, each with a blanket around them, next to the cold, empty grate. Her aunt knitted and Helen watched Bobby playing with his wooden train and his teddy. They were too fed up to bother talking.

'I just wanted to ask if you heard that the RAF bombed Guernsey harbour earlier.' Babs refused a seat, excitement in her voice as she told them the reason for her visit. 'I have to get back. Mum wants me to go up to the attic and see if we've missed anything we've stored up there that might be useful.'

'Like what?' Helen asked, unsure what this could have to do with her and her aunt.

'We're tired of being cold and are hoping to find anything made of wood. Old picture frames none of us want any more, that sort of thing.'

'To burn them?' Aunt Sylvia lowered her knitting onto her lap and stared thoughtfully at Babs.

'That's right. We've run out of almost everything else. I was worried about keeping something to use for firewood next winter, but Mum insisted that without heat she doubted she would last until then.'

Helen knew Ida must be desperate to burden the girls with something so worrying. Seeing how thoughtful Sylvia seemed, Helen worried that she might be thinking about her own worsening health. 'What about the bombing though, Babs?' she asked, wanting to change the subject.

Babs bit her lower lip before replying. 'There was a terrible kerfuffle. I wanted to let you know about the RAF, just in case you hadn't heard.'

'I hope no one was hurt in the bombing,' Sylvia said.

'Mum said the same thing, but we don't know. At least it shows us, as with those leaflets, that we haven't been entirely forgotten here.'

'Poor Guernsey.' Sylvia picked up where she had left off with her knitting. 'This awful war is interminable.'

'It is,' Helen agreed feeling sombre.

For someone who was supposed to be hurrying home, Babs didn't seem as if she was in any rush to leave. Helen sensed something was troubling her and was about to ask what, when her friend spoke. 'I'd better go before Mum sends Peggy to fetch me. I'm not looking forward to going up into that attic again,' she scowled. 'It's full of dust and creepy-crawlies, and it's dark. Not to mention horribly cold.'

Helen tried to find something encouraging to say. 'But if you do find a few useful things it will be worth it.'

Babs pulled a face. 'I suppose you're right. Bye, then.' She hesitated before leaving the room and, wanting to check she was all right, Helen followed her into the hallway.

'Is something wrong?' Helen whispered, checking over her shoulder that they were alone.

Babs thought for a second then shook her head.

Helen didn't like to pry. 'You can tell me anything, I hope you know that, Babs. I promise I wouldn't tell a soul.'

Babs seemed to contemplate something. 'It's Tony,' she said staring down at her hands. 'He's been arrested.'

Helen covered her mouth to stifle her shock. 'That's terrible. How's Peggy?'

'Distraught.' She sniffed. 'I went into her room without knocking earlier and found her sobbing. It was awful, Helen. I sat next to her on her bed and asked her what was wrong. She didn't want to tell me and I don't know what he's supposed to have done. She made me promise to keep it to myself.' She looked up at Helen again and winced.

'It's fine. I promise I'll keep it to myself.'

'Thank you. I just wish I could do something to help but she insists there's nothing.'

Helen hugged her. 'Just being there for her is probably a great help.'

'I hope so.'

'You'd better get going,' Helen said, quietly relieved to have comforted Babs, if only a little.

When Babs had left, Helen thought about Peggy and how frightened she must be to know her boyfriend was in jail. What would happen to him? she wondered anxiously.

'Is everything all right, Helen?'

Hearing her aunt's voice, Helen returned to the living room. 'I was thinking I should go up into your attic and see if can find anything useful.'

Her aunt lowered her knitting. 'I've been trying to recall what's up there. The ladder attached to the trapdoor in the ceiling is rickety and I haven't dared use it for over a decade.' She gave Helen an unsure look. 'I'm not sure I'm happy with you going up there. Who knows what state everything will be in by now?'

Helen wasn't worried. She promised to take care with every step. 'There must be something and if you've lived without what's up there for this long, you probably don't need much of it now. It's worth a look.'

'I suppose you're right,' Sylvia said after a brief hesitation. 'You want to go up there straight away, don't you?'

'You know me well.' Helen laughed, relieved she hadn't had any objection from her aunt. 'I want to light a fire tonight if we possibly can.'

'No, dear. You've had a long day today and you're tired.

That's when accidents happen,' her aunt argued. 'It can wait until tomorrow when it's your day off.'

Her aunt had made up her mind, and Helen didn't try to change it.

Chapter Twenty-Three

PEGGY

Peggy woke up after another cold night. She tucked her arm under the covers, making the most of the slight heat, and closed her eyes. For a moment she wondered why everything seemed quieter than usual. She couldn't hear the usual car sounds passing their home, or any voices coming from the pavement outside. Something wasn't right. She realised it must have snowed again and groaned.

It took a moment for her to remember that Tony had been arrested. Her heart dropped and a feeling of nausea flowed through her. Unable to lie down any longer she sat up and rubbed her tired eyes. She had only slept for a couple of hours, what with worrying about what might happen to him.

She got up and decided to make her way to the office. She needed to know if there was any news, and the only way that would happen was through Advocate Le Gresley. Knowing him, Peggy thought, he would already be there.

She threw back her bedclothes, swung her legs over the side and slipped her feet into her slippers so that they didn't connect with the cold wooden floorboards. She grabbed her dressing gown and put it on as she walked over to the window. Pulling back the curtains she was stunned to see that everything was white. Again. It must have been snowing for hours and by the looks of the thick flakes drifting past her window there was little chance of it stopping soon. No wonder everything appeared quieter with all the sounds being muffled by the thick blanket of snow.

Though she only lived about fifteen minutes away from the prison, she would need to walk past the turn-off and on to her boss's office near the Royal Square. That meant it would take another ten to fifteen minutes before she could collect the letter from her boss and then double back on herself to the prison, hopefully to see Tony. She hoped he was being well treated.

Dressing and not bothering with any food, Peggy put on her ankle boots, unsure how long they would remain watertight. Freezing toes were no trouble, though, if it meant she could spend even a couple of minutes with the man she loved.

'You're not going out in that blizzard, surely?' her mother fretted. 'You'll catch pneumonia.'

Peggy had little choice. 'Mum, I'd much rather stay here, I can assure you, but I have to go in today. Advocate Le Gresley has something very important for me to do and it won't wait.'

Her mother didn't look convinced, but Peggy couldn't worry about that, not today.

She had barely walked several feet before her woollen tights were soaked through by the deep snow slipping in over the top of her boots. She looked behind her to check if there was a bus on its way, but the snow was falling too hard for her to see very far. Peggy decided to stop worrying about catching a bus and just get a move on. She would find a way to dry her tights and boots later.

'Good grief,' Advocate Le Gresley exclaimed, holding the front door open for her when she came gingerly up the front steps of the building. 'You look frozen.'

'It's perishing out there,' she said, shivering, her voice sounding strange through her chattering teeth. Almost biting her tongue, she closed her mouth and pointed upstairs to their offices. She was desperate to collect the letter for the governor and leave to see Tony. 'I'll make your coffee and bring it to your office, then we can get started.'

'You'll go and warm up first,' he insisted. 'Come to my office when you're ready.'

She ran up to her office, tired from wading through the deep snow, and closed the door with relief. Dropping her bag onto her chair, she went to feel if the radiator was on. It was, but only just. Peggy wasn't sure if the temperature was hot enough to dry anything, let alone woolly tights, but didn't fancy wearing wet things on her legs for the rest of the day. That surely would lead to a chill, if not something worse. Why hadn't she thought to bring a second pair to change into?

A short while later she heard a knock at the door. Expecting it to be one of the German messengers, she checked to make sure any view of her tights hanging over the radiator was obscured by her chair. Satisfied, she called for the person to enter.

It was one of the other secretaries. 'Advocate Le Gresley has been called away, but asked me to bring you this.' She placed a cup of tea on Peggy's desk. 'And this letter. He said you'd know what to do with it.'

'Thank you…' Peggy couldn't recall her name. 'Sorry, I…'

'It's Marie-Therese.'

'Thank you, Marie-Therese. Is the Advocate in a meeting?'

The secretary, whom she had only met once before, nodded. 'All the senior chaps have been called into the boardroom. I'd better go,' she added. 'I have mountains of dictation to type up.'

'Thanks again for the tea,' Peggy said, lifting the cup and relishing the warmth in her hands. Wondering if the reason for the meeting had anything to do with Tony's arrest, she picked up the envelope and saw it was addressed to the prison governor. Her heart raced. She was eager to get going, but looking at her watch realised it wasn't even nine o'clock, so there was little point in leaving just yet. Unsure what to do, Peggy decided to make the most of the hot drink.

Ten minutes later, her tights were still cold, itchy and clammy against her skin, but Peggy didn't care. She had held back from leaving for long enough and decided that even if it was too early to be let into the prison, then she would simply find somewhere to wait.

Chapter Twenty-Four

HELEN

T he following day Helen refused her aunt's suggestion to put off going up into the attic. 'We need a fire if we're to sit in here,' she insisted. 'And I won't forgive myself if you come down with another cold.'

'Suit yourself, but we'll need to put the little one somewhere safe while we're going through the bits you bring down.'

Relieved her aunt wasn't going to argue, Helen said, 'I'll carry Bobby upstairs and pop him in his cot, then if you wait at the bottom of the ladder, I'll hand what I find down to you. You can have a good look at it all and decide what to keep and what to use. I can put back anything you want to save until after the war.'

She saw a fleeting moment of doubt cross her aunt's face but didn't acknowledge it. Her mind went to Tony in jail and then to Richard still waiting for her reply. Where was he stationed? she wondered. An icy feeling washed through her. Was he even still alive? Helen's heart raced. With all that was going on, was she right not to reply to him? How would she feel to discover he had been killed and then have to live with the knowledge that he died never knowing about their son? As hard as it had been for her, she needed to do what she believed to be right. She would try to send a telegram to him tomorrow.

'Is something the matter, Helen? You've been quiet since Babs left. Is she all right?'

Her aunt was very perceptive and would sense if she was lying, but Babs's secret wasn't hers to share. 'She's just worried about something, Aunty.' Determined to remain as positive as possible, Helen added, 'I'm excited to see what's stored up there.'

'I suppose I am, too, now that you mention it.'

Twenty minutes later, after a sneezing fit and hysterics when a large spider ran across one of the rafters in front of her, the last of the boxes had been carried into her aunt's bedroom. They decided not to waste time and energy carrying the boxes downstairs to the living room only to have to bring some of them back up again to store away.

Helen hoped her aunt wasn't too attached to items that might keep their fire going for a while.

'Let's see what we have in here, shall we?' Sylvia said, when Helen placed the first box in front of the dressing-table stool where she was sitting. 'There's nothing wooden in here,' she reported, handing folded sheets and sweaters for Helen to take. 'But these moth-eaten sheets will make smaller ones for Bobby's cot and for dusters.'

Helen added, 'And I can unravel these sweaters and try to knit a few things for us. Some hats and scarves,' she said when her aunt gave her a doubtful smile. 'You can make the more intricate items.'

The second box was more rewarding. 'Look.' Her aunt held up several photo frames, then a pair of wooden candlesticks. 'These are perfect for the fire.'

'Take these for us to look through one evening.' She handed Helen three photo albums.

Helen took them, unsure whether she was ready to reminisce about happy summer holidays with her family. The prospect of seeing photographs of their smiling faces, her parents smartly dressed on the beach, she and her brother enjoying cornets topped with creamy Jersey ice cream, made her miss them terribly.

'These old books have been half eaten by something, so we may as well burn them too.

It wasn't perfect, but at least they had found some useful items, Helen thought with satisfaction.

Her aunt began coughing.

'I think we have enough for now,' Helen said, wanting to close everything up and get her aunt away from the dust and chill coming down from the attic. 'I'll take the boxes we've looked through back up and close the trapdoor.' When her aunt began to protest, she added, 'And you need to get to bed. I can see you're tired and you need to rest.'

Helen was surprised when her aunt didn't argue and suspected it was because she had been hiding how unwell she was feeling. The thought troubled Helen and she hoped she was wrong.

Chapter Twenty-Five

PEGGY

Peggy barely noticed how wet and achingly cold her feet and ankles were as she made her way to Newgate Street prison. She focused on what she intended to say to keep her mind off her discomfort. She probably had one chance to speak to someone in authority and try to either secure Tony's release or find out more about how long he might be kept there. She dismissed the possibility that he could be sent away to a camp, because the prospect was too terrible to contemplate. She struggled to remain calm, but she was supposed to be going there as Advocate Le Gresley's secretary, not as Tony's girlfriend. She needed to remain as professional as possible.

Slamming into something, Peggy's feet slid from under her, causing her to land heavily on her bottom on the pavement. There was a shout in German as she struggled to climb to her feet, her efforts hampered by the icy conditions. Slipping over a second time, Peggy fell onto her hands and knees, making them sting.

'Here, let me help you,' a kindly person said, taking her by the arms and helping her carefully to her feet.

'Thank you.' Peggy looked into the sad eyes of a dark-haired middle-aged man.

'I hadn't banked on it being this icy.' She peered past him to see the soldier striding away, not caring whether she was hurt. 'I must have bumped into him.'

'Nasty piece of work, that one,' he said. Peggy assumed he had had a run-in with the man before. 'He should have been looking where he was going. He was too busy sneering at me to notice you before it was too late.'

'I should have been a little more careful, too,' she said, doing her best to brush snow off the seat of her coat and her knees. 'I must look a mess.'

'You'll soon dry when you're somewhere warmer.' He considered something for a moment. 'Would you like me to accompany you to wherever it is you're going?'

Peggy didn't think that wise. 'There's no need. I'm on my way to Newgate.'

He looked aghast. 'The prison?'

She nodded. 'I have a letter to deliver.' When the man eyed her suspiciously, she thought it best to elaborate further. 'I work for an advocate and one of his clients has been arrested. We're hoping to secure his release.'

'I see.' He looked around, seeming uncomfortable. 'I really should be on my way. My son will worry if I'm late.'

'Thank you again for helping me, it was very kind of you.'

Determined to be more careful, Peggy set off again and shortly afterwards reached the junction where Seaton Place met Gloucester Street. She was about to cross the road when she spotted someone she thought she recognised, walking with head bowed and his hands deep in his coat pockets.

'Tony?' She breathed his name, barely daring to hope he had been released. Realising he wasn't coming in her direction but heading towards the Esplanade, she picked up speed until, slipping slightly, she had to grab the wall beside her to keep her balance. She slowed her pace, hoping not to lose him. She was about to call out to him when she saw two officers coming in her direction from Newgate Street.

She crossed Gloucester Street, doing her best to follow Tony, wishing he would slow down and allow her to catch up. Damn this ice, she fumed. If only she could run, she would catch up to him in no time. Where was he going, anyway? His father's office was in the opposite direction.

Eventually, seeing the road was clear of soldiers, Peggy called out to him. She kept her voice fairly low, not wishing to draw attention to herself, but when he didn't hear she shouted again, this time a little louder.

'Tony, wait.'

He stopped and turned, looking surprised to see her there and immediately hurried to join her.

'Where were you going?' she asked as he slipped his arms around her in a brief hug. 'Your father will be waiting to hear from you.'

'I was going straight to see him but changed my mind.' He smiled, looking a little sheepish. 'I wanted to let you know what had happened.' He took her hands in his. 'I knew you'd be worried.'

'I was.' She slipped her arms around his waist and clung to him for as long as she dared until a military vehicle passed and she let go, not wanting to draw any unnecessary attention.

'Never mind me, what are you doing here?'

She quickly explained about taking a letter from his father to the prison governor. 'Well, that was the plan, but it doesn't matter now you're free.' She brushed away a tear. 'We never dared expect you to be out this quickly.' She saw him studying her.

'You're trembling.' He noticed her damp skirt. 'And you're soaking. Did you fall?' He took her arms and held her away from him as he inspected her knees. 'Your tights are ripped.' He took her hand and began leading her along the road.

'Where are we going?'

'I'm taking you home. You need to change into something dry before you catch a chill.'

She tugged at his hand trying to stop him. 'I must go to the office first,' she explained, her voice rising when he didn't slow down. 'Your father will be waiting to hear from me.'

'That can wait. He won't be expecting you to be very quick, anyway.' He held her tightly to his side. 'It's because of me and my actions that you're out here in the freezing cold wearing wet clothes. I'm not going to have you falling ill and on my conscience.' He led her towards St Aubin's Road. 'And before you argue, I can assure you my father would expect me to do this.'

She gave in, aware that he was right and grateful to be going home. Her head ached with the cold and her knee throbbed. She looked up at him as they walked and, sensing her gaze on him, Tony smiled at her. 'When you're changed, you can tell me what you intended saying to the jail Kommandant.'

'Happily,' she agreed. 'And you can tell me what you were doing to cause your arrest.'

They reached her home and Peggy opened the front door, beckoning him inside.

'Are you certain your mother won't mind?' he asked looking past her towards the kitchen.

Peggy loved that her tiny mother barely five feet in height intimidated a man as big as Tony. She was about to tease him when Ida marched through from the kitchen, a wooden spoon in one hand and a towel draped over her other arm. 'Won't mind what?'

'Tony, you're out?' Babs cheered from halfway up the stairs. She ran down to join them.

Tony widened his eyes at Peggy and she could tell he was embarrassed.

'What are you doing back home so early?' Ida noticed Peggy's ripped tights and bedraggled appearance, moved forward and touched her daughter's leg. 'Are you hurt?'

Peggy shook her head. 'I slipped, Mum. I'm fine. Tony spotted me and insisted on walking me home.' She didn't elaborate, and was glad when her mother didn't ask questions.

'That's very gentlemanly of you, Tony.' Ida gave him a grateful smile then, turning her attention to Peggy, raised her eyebrows. 'Go to your room and change before you catch your death.'

Not wishing him to leave before she was back down again, Peggy said, 'Maybe Tony would like a warm drink before he sets off to work?'

Her mother winced. 'Where's my manners? Babs, show Tony through to the living room.'

'Please, it's fine,' he argued. 'I really should speak to my father without delay.' He caught Peggy's eye and that usual flutter in her stomach increased. 'I'll see you on Monday, then?'

'It's all right, Mum, I'll see Tony out.'

Her mother gave a resigned sigh. 'Fine, but be quick about it. I want you in dry clothes in the next couple of minutes.'

She waited for her mother to return to the kitchen. Babs gave her a cheeky grin then said goodbye to him and joined Ida.

When they were alone, Peggy hugged him. 'Thanks again for bringing me home.'

'Thank you for trying to rescue me.' He looked over her head, then lowered his voice. 'We'll speak at the office on Monday. I doubt your mother will be happy with you going out in this weather tonight and I assume my parents will have a lot to say to me.'

'Could we meet tomorrow?'

He didn't catch her eye for a second then sighed. 'I would love to, but I have a meeting.'

Peggy mood dipped and her head ached with worry. 'Oh, no, Tony—'

He put a finger to her lips and shook his head. 'I'll be fine, I promise.' He checked they were alone then pulled her into his arms and kissed her. 'I really must go now.'

She held onto his hand, hoping that whatever he was doing wouldn't get him into more trouble. 'You're not going to tell me what you were doing when they arrested you, are you?'

'It's safer if you don't know.' He gave her a searching look and she knew he was trying to gauge whether she trusted him.

'It's fine. I understand, but please be more careful in future.'

He stared at her thoughtfully for a moment and Peggy hoped he was about to confide in her about something. 'I will,' he said, kissing her. 'I promise never to get caught again.'

'I don't see how you can say that.'

'Peggy,' her mother's voice boomed from the kitchen. 'You'd better not still be in those wet clothes.'

'Go and change.' He kissed her quickly and was out of the door before she had a chance to say anything else.

'I'm changing now, Mum,' she shouted, running upstairs to her room praying Tony would keep safe.

Chapter Twenty-Six

HELEN

Helen sat opposite her aunt in front of the small fire that had gone a little way to heating the front room. If only the ceilings weren't so high in these Victorian houses, she thought, watching as her aunt snoozed, a knitted shawl around her shoulders and two blankets covering her from her chest to her feet. It was peaceful with only the occasional voice passing their front window.

Bobby was asleep on the sofa snuggled in blankets, his toy train clutched in his tiny hand. Helen thought how perfect this scenario would be if it wasn't wartime and her aunt wasn't unwell. Sylvia had developed another chest cough and there was a greyish pallor to her skin and purplish circles under her eyes. Helen had pleaded with her to let her go for the doctor, but Sylvia had refused to allow it, telling her she was fine and there was little he could do anyhow.

As she watched the closest person to her after Bobby, fear shot though her at the realisation that one day she might be staring at an empty seat. Her aunt might do her best to reassure her but Helen wasn't fooled. Aunt Sylvia was dying, and there was little she could do about it.

Helen's throat constricted and she wiped away a stray tear just as her aunt opened her eyes.

Sitting up straighter with some effort, Sylvia frowned. 'Whatever's the matter, dear?'

Irritated with herself for not being more careful, Helen shook her head. 'It's nothing,' she fibbed, frantically trying to think of something to say. 'I was, er, just thinking about Richard.'

'You've decided to reply to his telegram then?' her aunt asked, appearing happy at the thought. Helen suspected her aunt wanted her to reply more than she would like to admit and she couldn't help thinking that it was the right thing to do.

'Yes, I think I will.'

Sylvia pulled her shawl tighter round her chest. 'I'm pleased, though curious to know what made you change your mind.'

'I think it was discovering Tony had been arrested. It made me consider how I'd feel if something happened to Richard and I hadn't bothered to reply to him when I had the chance.' She couldn't bring herself to say the words

'I know, dear. And for what it's worth, I think you're being sensible.'

'You do?'

'Yes. It's one thing sticking to your principles during peacetime, but this is war and everything is a bit topsy-turvy, especially when it comes to relationships, and especially love.'

She wasn't sure why she was surprised to hear her aunt's opinion. 'Now I need to think what to say. I don't want to give him false hope and I don't think it's right that I tell him about

Bobby. Something like that should be done face-to-face.' She noticed the doubt on her aunt's face. 'What do you think?'

'I believe the most important thing is to know you've done the right thing by Bobby.' Sylvia looked down at her hands briefly. 'I'm sorry, but I believe that would be to tell Richard about him. Everything else will sort itself out somehow.'

Her aunt was right. She had already wasted too much time, and if she couldn't do what she believed to be the right thing during these dark times, then there was something lacking in her.

'You're right. I'll do it during my lunch break tomorrow.'

'Good girl.' Sylvia smiled. It dawned on Helen that her aunt had been waiting for her to come to this conclusion for a while.

'It matters to you that I do this, doesn't it?'

Sylvia nodded slowly. 'I worry that when this war ends – because we have to believe that it will – your parents might not accept that dear little boy.' She took a deep breath. 'I'm concerned that if I'm not around, you'll need someone to turn to.' She reached out and took Helen's trembling hand in hers. 'Sweetheart, none of us should be alone, especially not a young mother, and even if the only relationship you have with Richard is as friends, at least I'll know there's another adult who loves Bobby almost as much as I do.'

Helen cleared her throat, not wishing to cry. 'Almost as much?' she teased, desperate to divert her aunt's attention from the seriousness of what she was saying.

Sylvia stared at her before her face relaxed into a smile. 'All seriousness aside, I believe his father couldn't fail to love Bobby.'

Unable to contain her tears any longer, Helen began to sob.

Her aunt went to her and gave her a hug. 'Whatever happens, promise me you'll never give up hoping that everything will work out in the end.'

How could she make a promise about something she didn't know she had the strength to do?

'You mustn't despair, Helen. It never helped anyone. Bobby needs you to be strong.'

Seeing the concern on her aunt's face, Helen knew she needed to reassure her. 'I promise I'll stay strong for him.'

She helped her aunt upstairs, promising to tell her what she would write in her telegram to Richard the following morning, then kissed her goodnight.

Her aunt hugged her tightly. 'Don't fret too much about what you'll say. The most important thing he needs is a reply. Anything else will be a bonus.'

'I'll bear that in mind.'

Helen closed her aunt's bedroom door quietly and went to her room where Bobby was sleeping soundly. As she washed and changed, she thought about what her aunt had said. It was a relief to have the pressure taken away, not having to struggle to find the perfect reply. She slid between her freezing sheets and shivered. She still hadn't decided whether to mention Bobby.

By the morning, she was no less agitated. The dawn was breaking and after only a couple of hours' sleep she sat on her bed with a pencil and piece of paper determined to come up with a message for him.

Finally, she had something. It wasn't perfect but it would do.

Should have spoken before leaving. Bobby (your son), Aunt

Sylvia and I are well. Have job and friends. Keep safe. Please send word again. Helen

Deciding she couldn't improve it any further, Helen dressed, folded the piece of paper and tucked it in her skirt pocket to show her aunt.

She carried Bobby downstairs, raising his chubby hand and kissing it. 'You're such a handsome boy,' she cooed, noticing that his eyes were the image of Richard's and wondering why she hadn't seen it before. Probably, she thought, because she hadn't wanted to. Now that she had prepared the telegram, she was eager to send it and decided to leave early for work to give her time to do it.

'Good morning, Aunty,' she said, smiling as her aunt waited for her to put Bobby into his highchair before kissing the top of his head.

'You're looking pleased with yourself,' her aunt said a twinkle in her tired eyes. 'You've written it, haven't you?'

'I have.' She took the piece of paper from her pocket and handed it to her aunt. 'Sit down and read it, then you can tell me what you think while I put the kettle on.'

Helen didn't mind not eating breakfast, especially as Cook usually had something tasty when she arrived at work, but she wasn't comfortable with her aunt going without.

'I'll bring some food home for our supper,' she promised, dropping the tea leaves they had left out to dry the previous evening into the teapot and watching as her aunt read her words. 'What do you think?'

'You've managed to convey a lot in twenty-five words.'

'I'm happy to change anything you think might give the wrong impression.'

'If you mean the bit where you let him know he has a son, then I think that's well done.' She held the note out for Helen to take. 'This is good. Well done. Make sure you send it today.'

'You needn't worry about me changing my mind.' Helen laughed. She was looking forward to sending it, now that she had worked out what to say.

Chapter Twenty-Seven

HELEN

March 1942

Helen sensed a different atmosphere in the house as soon as she woke. Her aunt's health had continued to deteriorate, and the cool spring weather hadn't helped alleviate her symptoms. She knew without checking on her that something dreadful had happened. Not wishing to take Bobby to Sylvia's room, she lowered him into his playpen, ignoring his protests, and ran upstairs to her aunt's room. Standing outside the door Helen struggled to find the strength to enter, her fear at what she might discover making her feel lightheaded.

Knowing she couldn't delay going inside any longer, Helen took a steadying breath and, without allowing herself to think, put her hand on the doorknob and turned it. She pushed the door open slowly and stepped inside.

Even with the curtains closed Helen couldn't mistake her aunt's slightly opened eyes staring ahead, unseeing. It was clear she had passed away.

Helen dropped to her knees by the bed and took Sylvia's cool, lifeless hand in hers. 'Please don't leave me,' she sobbed, unable to bear the thought that this woman who had been everything to her and Bobby had gone.

Struggling to control her grief, she knew she had to do something. Had to tell someone.

Remembering her aunt's words about staying strong for Bobby, she knew she had to keep her promise. Fresh tears flowed down her face. She couldn't move away from the bed, certain she couldn't take any more heartache.

'Come along now,' she cried, repeating words her aunt had said to her when she was finding things difficult. 'You can do this. You must do this for Bobby, and for Aunt Sylvia.'

Saying her aunt's name brought on a fresh wave of grief. She struggled to regain her composure, but hearing Bobby's yells from downstairs knew she needed to pull herself together somehow. Unable to cover her aunt's face, she straightened the bedclothes, ensuring they were over her aunt's shoulders. 'Thank you for everything you've done for us, Aunty. I'll make sure Bobby never forgets you.'

She stood and went over to the window and drew the curtains, then carried her aunt's full glass of water down to the kitchen. Forcing herself to think, Helen realised she needed someone to sit with Bobby while she went to phone the doctor. She picked him up and carried him next door, only knocking once before Babs opened the door.

'Helen? You look... Whatever's happened?' She looked past Helen before taking her arm and leading her inside. 'Mum?' She pushed the door closed. 'Mum!'

Unable to form any words, Helen stood in the hallway.

She was vaguely aware of Babs taking Bobby from her arms and being led trembling into the living room, then Peggy was crouching in front of her, a hand on each arm of Helen's chair.

'Put this around her shoulders. She needs something warm to drink.'

Helen looked up to see Mrs Hamel standing in front of her.

'What's happened, Helen?' Peggy asked, her voice gentle.

Helen tried to clear her thoughts, then remembered and started to cry. 'Aunt Sylvia. She's…'

'I think I know,' Ida said her voice gentle. 'I'll go next door. Babs, you make that tea and find food for the little one to eat. Peggy, you stay here with Helen.'

It wasn't until later, when Helen woke in a strange room, that she remembered what had happened. Where was Bobby? She sat bolt upright and went to get up, but Peggy appeared from somewhere and sat on the edge of the bed, gently pushing her back down.

'Everything's fine,' she said, her voice calm but determined. 'The doctor has been called and he arranged for your aunt to be taken to the hospital.'

Thinking she must have been mistaken earlier, Helen sat up again. 'She's alive?'

Peggy shook her head slowly. 'I'm afraid not. It's where they take people who've passed on.'

Helen let out a sob and squeezed her eyes closed. Then, lying on her side, she brought her knees up into a foetal position, wishing she could go back in time.

Peggy pulled a light, lacy cover over her and stroked her back. 'I'm so sorry, Helen.'

'You mustn't think you're alone,' Ida's voice came from the

doorway. 'We're here for you. We'll look out for you and Bobby.'

'Thank you,' Helen said, desperately trying to stop crying. 'Where's Bobby?'

'He's downstairs with Babs.'

Helen wondered why her teeth where chattering when it wasn't that cold, then supposed it must be from shock. 'I should go home,' she said eventually. 'I don't want to be any trouble.'

'You're not,' Peggy said. 'But if you wish to I'll come with you and help you pack up your aunt's things, if that's what you want to do.'

Helen had no idea what she wanted.

The following couple of weeks passed in a heartbroken, stunned haze. Helen couldn't face returning to work and sent a message to Cook to let her know what had happened. Not long afterwards, she received a visit from her, and was touched when Mrs Jeune handed her a small package of food for her and Bobby.

'I want you to know I'm here, if ever you need me,' she said. 'And please call me Pearl.'

Helen wasn't sure why she was surprised that Cook, or Mrs Jeune as she knew her, was called Pearl. She looked at this woman who had only ever shown her kindness, if sometimes in a gruff way, and her heart filled with gratitude.

'Thank you, Pearl.'

Pearl looked around the neat living room. 'I know it's a difficult thing to do but if you need me to come and help you sort through your aunt's belongings or find a home for them you only need ask.'

'That's very kind of you.'

She stared thoughtfully at Helen. 'Your aunt and I were friends since our first day at the parish school we attended. She was a good woman. Always kind. And I know she loved having you and Bobby living here with her.'

Helen was only aware she was crying when Pearl's expression changed, and she delved in her handbag and pulled out a neatly pressed handkerchief. Shaking it out she held it to Helen. 'I'm sorry. I didn't mean to upset you.'

Helen wiped her eyes and blew her nose. 'You didn't. I'm a bit of a mess and many things set me off. I... I just don't know how I'm going to face the future without her.'

Pearl patted her hand. 'You're not alone. You have me and Mrs Edwards.' She gave a tight smile. 'She asked to be remembered to you.' She sighed. 'You must keep busy, and vigilant.' She shifted in her chair. 'Please don't think I'm overstepping our friendship when I say I think you must consider what you're going to do, now that your aunt is no longer here.'

'I don't understand.'

'This is a big house for you and Bobby, and a young girl like you should think before deciding to stay here with only the little one for company.'

Helen realised she was suggesting she and Bobby move, but didn't think she could cope with doing something like that. 'I can barely stand being in this house without her,' she admitted. She hesitated and continued, 'But this place is my only connection to Aunt Sylvia now and I can't cope with the thought of leaving.'

Pearl Jeune rested her forearms on the table and lowered her voice, as if there was anyone nearby to overhear what she was about to say. 'I understand, really I do. And I don't want to worry you but I believe you really must consider moving somewhere where you won't be by yourself. Will you try to do that for me?'

Fear felt like a lead weight in the pit of her stomach. 'But where would I go? There's not many people who'd take a spinster with a child, Mrs Jeune.'

'I told you you're not alone, and I meant it. You might not know many people, but I do. When you decide you want to move, let me know and I'll do my best to find somewhere that suits you.'

Helen saw the hope in her friend's eyes. 'Thank you.'

'I don't mean to put pressure on you, but I feel a sense of responsibility for you and this little one.'

'And I really do appreciate it.'

When Pearl left, Helen decided she needed to keep busy and settled on rearranging her home slightly. She was unable to face packing away her aunt's belongings. Instead, she tidied Sylvia's bedroom and put everything neatly away in the wardrobe, hoping it would feel as if Sylvia had gone out for the day but would be returning soon. Helen knew they weren't the sort of changes Pearl had meant, but it was all she could cope with.

After her initial sobbing, for the last week a strange numbness had come over her. Helen assumed she was in shock. She much preferred it to the agonising heartache she had been feeling. She hoped this phase of her grief would last.

Chapter Twenty-Eight

PEGGY

13 September 1942

'You look serious,' Tony said, making Peggy jump. She hadn't heard him knock or enter her office and now he was standing on the other side of her desk smiling sympathetically at her.

She tapped her fountain pen against the edict on her desk that she had just translated and was now typing up.

'What's worrying you?'

She rubbed her tired eyes and groaned. 'Apart from Helen, you mean?'

'Have you seen much of her since her aunt passed away? How is she coping without her?'

Peggy shook her head sadly. 'Not as much as I would have liked. I've usually left for work by the time she brings Bobby round for Mum to babysit. I do pop round most afternoons, but although she's always polite, the spark has gone out of her. I can tell she's still struggling to come to terms with her loss.

It's been months now, and I worry that she's so withdrawn, but at least she's back at work.'

Tony pushed his hands into his pockets and looked slightly awkward for a moment. 'I hate to ask, but I don't suppose she's reported back about hearing any further information at work we might find useful?'

Peggy shook her head. 'No, unfortunately not.' A chilling thought occurred to her. 'I hope she doesn't get despondent about that and start taking unnecessary risks.' She pictured Bobby and felt slightly reassured. 'Hopefully, with Bobby to care for, she won't be tempted to.'

'I hope not. We must not do anything to draw attention to ourselves and neither should she.'

'We definitely don't want that happening,' she said, terrified of being arrested by the German Secret Field Police.

'If you're worrying about the Geheime Feldpolizei,' Tony asked, as if reading her thoughts, and giving them their German name, 'Then don't. The GFP have more than enough on their hands right now worrying about people helping escaped enforced workers. They won't focus much on anything we're doing.'

Peggy glanced at the closed office door, thinking about the many rumours she had heard about prisoners being taken to a house in Havre des Pas called Silvertide. She felt sick at the thought of being interrogated. 'I hope not. I'm not sure how brave I'd be if I was arrested.'

He leant against her desk and gave her a reassuring smile. 'You won't be arrested if I have anything to do with it.'

'You never did tell me why you ended up in prison,' she said intrigued to know what he had done. 'Or why you were released.'

He sighed. 'I think it's better you know as little as possible about what I was doing. As far as why they released me, all I was told is that there wasn't enough evidence against me to prove my involvement.'

'Thank heavens for that.'

He pointed to the papers on her desk. 'I presume there's more bad news in that document?'

She nodded. 'It's an order being announced in the *Evening Post* either tomorrow or the next day, this time about British subjects being deported to Germany.' She didn't think she had been this angry since her father died. 'What's worse is that the order has come straight from German headquarters. From Berlin, no less.'

He groaned. 'Probably from Hitler himself, then. That is bad news.'

'It is.' She thought back to the census that had been taken the previous year and how she had hoped it was just a tactic to frighten everyone when the deportations had been postponed. 'It looks like this time there'll be no delays. No one is going to ignore an order from him, unfortunately.'

Tony pulled out a chair and sat. 'This sounds like he's found out about the deportation order that wasn't carried out last year.'

She closed her eyes in frustration. 'It does. I can't see these deportations not happening now. I suppose we should have known they couldn't be put off for ever.' She slid a piece of paper over to him to see for himself, then, remembering he couldn't read German, translated it for him. 'It says people have no choice. They must go. It doesn't even take into account people's age or their health.'

'But why now? I don't understand.'

She looked at his face, seeing her fury mirrored in his eyes. 'Apparently, it's because the British authorities have interned all the German people in Persia. Some of them have supposedly been caught spying.' She realised she was crying and put her hand into her pocket looking for her handkerchief, but Tony gave her his. 'Thank you.'

Her thoughts turned to Helen, aware that her friend's grieving would have little effect on Nazi officers determined to carry out orders from their Führer. 'I must warn Helen.'

Tony's face paled. 'Yes, and as soon as possible. Unfortunately the Jerries keep meticulous records and she'll be on their lists as not being local.'

The enormity of what this would mean to Helen's life dawned on Peggy and her heart raced, making her slightly breathless. 'She'll need to go into hiding now. There's nothing else for it as far as I can see.' She decided to speak to her mother about Helen's predicament as soon as she got home.

He rested his hand on hers. 'Try not to panic.' He cocked his head towards the door. 'You don't want someone noticing you acting differently, and they will do if they see you upset. We'll come up with a plan,' he said quietly, a determined look on his face.

Peggy took a steadying breath. 'You're right, I need to calm down,' she agreed, trying to regain her composure. 'I think my family can sort something out for her. We'll certainly try.'

He didn't seem convinced. 'Are you sure? If you're caught you'll all face prison.' He hesitated, fixing her with his gaze. 'Or worse.'

She was past caring. The world was a terrifying and dark place and as much as she didn't like the prospect of putting herself or her beloved mother and sister's lives into jeopardy,

Peggy was certain that they could no more live with the knowledge that they had stood by while their neighbour and her dear little boy were deported than she could. 'It's a chance we'll have to take.'

'And you're sure your mum and Babs will agree with you?'

Peggy stared into his eyes. 'What do you think?' Before he had a chance to answer, they heard heavy footsteps coming along the corridor towards her office. Peggy waved for him to leave. 'You should go.'

Tony leant forward and kissed her. 'If there's anything I can do to help, promise to let me know.'

'I will.'

'Good,' he whispered, 'and if for any reason your mother is concerned about hiding them, then I'll find somewhere else for them to go. Don't feel you're on your own with this, Peggy. Promise me.'

'I know you're always there for me.'

He went to the door, then turned, a thoughtful look on his face. 'Tell me exactly who they're planning to deport this time.'

She reread her translation. 'People and their families whose permanent residence is not on any of the islands. So any who were on the island when the war broke out, and non-islander English males between the ages of sixteen to seventy.'

'That sounds like quite a lot of people.'

'Feldkommandant Knackfuss has instructed that they want at least twelve-hundred people sent away, but I can't see how they can make that happen. Not quickly, anyway.'

'Neither can I, but we all have enough experience of them to know if that's their orders, then they will do their utmost to make it happen. And soon.'

He was right. Helen had to move as soon as possible. Peggy

covered her face with her hands and tried to steady herself. 'I'd better get this work done,' she said. 'So I can leave a little early and start putting everything in place for Helen.'

He blew her a kiss. 'We'll sort this out, somehow, Peggy.'

As Peggy hurried home she thought how, with all that had happened in the past two years, this surely was the lowest point so far for them all. Poor Helen had dealt with far too much already in her life and now this. It was too tragic.

Her mother was walking out of the living room when Peggy arrived home.

'What's happened?' Ida asked, a look of dread on her tired face.

'Let me take these things off and I'll join you and Babs in the kitchen.'

Her mother knew her well enough to guess the gravity of whatever was bothering her. 'I'll go and put the kettle on,' she said from the bottom of the stairs. With one hand on the banister, Peggy called up to her sister. 'Babs, come down here.'

A few minutes later Peggy had explained to her mother and sister what had happened and her plans for Helen and Bobby and she sat waiting for them to speak.

'I understand if either of you don't agree with my suggestion.' She didn't want them to feel guilty in any way. 'Tony knows and has offered to help find somewhere for them if you think it safer for us not to have them here.'

Her mother folded her cardigan over her chest and leant back in her chair looking grim. 'I'm aware we would be putting ourselves in danger,' she said thoughtfully. 'But that dear girl has already been through enough. It would be unfair of us not to have them here. At least they know us and it's only next door to number 2, so she might be comforted to be close to where she lived with her aunt.'

'I agree, Mum,' Babs said. 'They can't go to be with strangers, it would be too cruel. And it's less frightening for them here.'

Peggy relaxed slightly. 'I told Tony you'd think the same way as me.'

'When will you speak to her about it?' her mother asked as she looked at her watch. 'It's probably best if they have one last night in their home before you break this news to them.'

'I agree,' Peggy said. 'We can't do too much this evening now, anyway. I'll go next door on my way to work and break the news to her about the new ruling. At least then she'll have the day to pack a few things and try to come to terms with moving here.'

'Never mind that,' Babs said. 'We need to work out where to hide her. There's no point in them coming if we don't have anything prepared.'

She was right. 'I suppose it wouldn't be safe for them to sleep in one of the bedrooms.'

Their mother stood up. 'Don't you worry about that. Babs and I will sort something out in the attic, while you go and speak to her. Then the pair of you can help Helen pack up and bring over hers and Bobby's things when it's dark.' She stared past them thoughtfully. 'She'll need to bring the odd thing of Sylvia's, too, no doubt. We've all heard of empty houses being looted, and although we can keep an eye on the place, there's not much we can do if we don't want to draw attention to ourselves.'

'Good point, Mum.' Peggy thought through her mother's

suggestions. 'We're going to have to do this secretly in the middle of the night.'

'What about curfew?' Babs asked, looking frightened. 'I don't mind hiding them here but I'm really scared about being arrested.'

Peggy didn't look at her sister, worried that she might see the guilt in her eyes. Expecting her mother and sister to hide their neighbours was a lot to ask, and exceptionally dangerous. She pushed the thought aside. Each of them had agreed to commit to the plan and that's what they would do.

'We're going to have to be extremely careful,' her mother insisted. 'We can't afford for people to see Helen bringing things here. As it is, the authorities are bound to come looking for her at number 2 and will automatically come here to ask us if we know anything. We don't need people seeing us acting oddly and tipping the Nazis off.'

'No, we don't,' Peggy agreed. 'I'll go and speak to her in the morning on my way to work. The announcement won't be in the newspaper yet, so we can give her one more night in her home.'

Chapter Twenty-Nine

HELEN

Helen slouched in front of the living room grate until the last remnants of the wooden stool she had found earlier in the eaves were little more than cool cinders. She didn't think she had ever understood how true loneliness felt before losing her aunt.

Helen shivered and looked up at the photo on the mantelpiece of Aunt Sylvia and her husband. She struggled to believe her aunt had been gone now for over half a year, and the effort of having to be strong for Bobby continued to be exhausting. All Helen wanted to do was lie in her bed with the curtains drawn and cry.

'Who will I reminisce with now, Aunty?' she asked, staring at the photo of the happy couple so clearly in love. 'Why didn't I ask you all the practical questions I need answers to?' She had been too busy refusing to acknowledge that her aunt was extremely unwell despite the proof being in front of her eyes.

Helen wasn't sure what would happen to her aunt's home

now Sylvia was no longer there. Would she and Bobby be allowed to keep living here?

The thought of going anywhere else unsettled her further. It was wartime, she reasoned. Aunt Sylvia had welcomed her and Bobby into her home and she would stay until she was told otherwise.

Feeling a little calmer, Helen knew she should finally do something about her aunt's possessions. But, looking at the photos displayed in the living room, she decided to leave things as they were. Although her aunt was no longer in the house, Helen still felt her presence. In the first weeks after her death she had treasured the wafts of Shalimar, her aunt's favourite perfume, which filled her senses whenever she plumped the cushion on Sylvia's favourite armchair. And breathing in the delicate scent of roses and jasmine with a hint of sandalwood whenever she brushed against her Sylvia's coat, still hanging in the hallway, soothed her and allowed her to believe for a few precious seconds that she was still alive. She had looked forward to these sensory treats, but they'd long since faded.

Later, Helen was halfway up the stairs on her way to bed, when a loud banging on the front door startled her. She heard Bobby cry out from their bedroom and gritted her teeth in irritation. It had taken her almost an hour to settle him, and she had been hoping to enjoy a reasonable night's sleep for once.

There was another bang and a German accent ordered her to open the front door at once. Helen's breath caught in her throat and her heart raced as she grabbed the banister to steady herself.

Hearing them shout once again, Helen forced her feet to

move. She reached the front door and turned the key with trembling fingers. She opened the door to find two German officers standing on her step glaring at her.

They walked in without any pleasantries, forcing her to step aside. Bobby began crying noisily, no doubt terrified by the loud noises.

'You've woken my baby,' she snapped, her motherly instinct to protect her son making her forget who she was addressing for a moment. 'I need to fetch him.'

They seemed taken aback by her cheek, then the shorter of the two nodded. 'We will wait.'

She ran up the stairs needing to comfort her sobbing toddler. Wait for what? she wondered. Why were they here, and at this time of night? Gripped with fear about what she was about to face, Helen went to placate her sobbing child.

Chapter Thirty

PEGGY

'Good grief, who can that be?' Ida gasped when someone knocked on the front door just after eight the following morning. 'Go and see who it is. Quickly, Peggy.'

Peggy was about to put down her piece of bread when Babs bellowed from the hallway, 'I'll get it, Mum.'

Peggy heard voices and smiled. 'It's Helen and Bobby.' Peggy exchanged a curious glance with her mother.

'Something must have happened,' her mother whispered. 'She's never usually out this early.'

The two of them hurried to the hall.

Peggy saw Helen's puffy eyes and ashen face, and knew that whatever it was must be bad. Hadn't the poor girl already suffered enough?

Ida stood in front of Helen looking at Bobby. 'Is there something wrong with the little one?'

Helen sniffed and shook her head. 'He's fine.'

'That's a relief.' She took Bobby from Helen's trembling

arms and handed him to Babs. 'Take him through to the living room while your sister and I chat with Helen.'

Peggy could tell Babs was disappointed not to be included in the conversation, but she knew Helen needed to have the freedom to show her emotions without worrying about frightening her little boy.

'Let's sit down,' Ida said. 'Peggy, fetch this lamb a cup of tea.'

Helen raised a hand. 'No, please. I don't want to take your rations. I've had a cup already this morning. Water will be fine, thank you.'

'Tell us what's happened,' Peggy heard her mother say, as she held a glass under the tap and half filled it with cool water. 'You clearly haven't slept a wink.'

'I've been up all night fretting about what I should do.'

Peggy couldn't understand how Helen had heard about the deportations when she knew Tony wouldn't have told anyone, and she certainly hadn't shared the information with anyone other than him. She joined them at the table and listened miserably as Helen relayed all that had happened the evening before. 'I can't understand why we didn't hear them banging.'

So that's what had happened, she mused, wishing Helen could have come to them the previous evening but knowing she would have been unable to because of the strict curfew.

'I'm at my wits' end,' Helen said before taking a sip of water. 'They said that the house is too big for just me and Bobby.' She began to cry, and Peggy wished she didn't have to tell Helen about having to leave the house, anyway. She listened as Helen continued. 'They're moving us elsewhere but wouldn't say where. Apparently Aunt Sylvia's house has been requisitioned to house officers.' She sobbed into a hanky before looking up at Peggy, then Ida, her large eyes bloodshot. 'Nazis sleeping in my aunt's house. She would be horrified.'

Peggy gritted her teeth. 'How dare they do this, and to a grieving woman, too.'

'Never mind that,' Ida snapped. 'We can waste time going on about how dreadful it is later.'

'What do you mean?' Helen asked, clearly thrown by Ida's reaction.

Peggy watched as her mother took Helen's hand in both of hers. 'Helen, dear, the most important thing to your aunt, and to me, is yours and Bobby's safety. She spoke to me a few weeks before she died and asked me to promise to look out for you both, which I have done and will continue to do. I always keep my promises.'

It was the first Peggy had heard of her mother speaking with Sylvia.

'I don't understand,' Helen said, looking from Ida to Peggy.

Peggy sensed exactly what her mother was about to say. She was glad that the three of them had already worked out a plan.

'You're going to move in here,' Ida insisted in a voice that Peggy recognised as one that didn't invite argument.

'Pardon?' Helen looked startled. 'I don't understand.'

Ida sat back and focused on Helen. 'Peggy was coming over to see you shortly to explain about everything.' She reached out and rested a hand on Helen's arm. 'Peggy's learned there's to be deportations from the island.'

Helen turned to Peggy. 'When?'

Peggy felt deeply sorry for her friend and willed her to find the strength to cope with this unexpected turn of events. 'Imminently, I'm afraid,' she said in the gentlest voice she could muster. 'I was translating the order yesterday and the three of us decided then that the best thing for you and Bobby would be to move in here.'

'Here? But you don't have room for the two of us.' A look of hope crossed her face. 'Do you?'

Ida smiled. 'We'll make room. It will be safer for you and Bobby to hide in the attic, especially now those parasites are moving in next door.'

They watched as Helen thought about their offer. She didn't seem convinced.

'Don't you like the idea?' Peggy asked, wondering if it was the prospect of living in the attic that had put Helen off. 'I promise it'll be fine when we clean it up.'

Helen shook her head. 'It's not that. I love the idea of being here with you. I'd feel much safer than anywhere else, and it'll be,' she thought for a moment, 'comforting to be in a family environment again.'

'Then what's worrying you?' Peggy asked, confused.

'What if Bobby cries or misbehaves and they overhear him next door? I can't risk your safety,' she explained, her voice cracking with emotion. 'And have your lives, most probably, on my conscience.'

'We hadn't thought about the noise side of things, Mum.' Peggy turned to her mother for an answer.

Ida waved the comment away. 'Nonsense. These walls are thick enough not to let any sound travel through them. Well, not too much. The only difficulty I can see is having to keep the window closed in the summer when Bobby is awake or upset, but that's something we can worry about when we need to.'

Helen bit her lower lip and closed her eyes briefly. 'Thank

you all ever so much. I'd rather come here than go anywhere else. I admit I'm terrified of being deported to one of those camps in Germany.'

Relieved that Helen hadn't turned down their offer, Peggy went to comfort her and put an arm around Helen's shoulders. 'I promise you we'll do our best to make sure that never happens.'

'We will.' Ida rested her palms on the table and stood. 'I doubt we have much time before those devils return. We need to start moving you in here as soon as we can.'

Peggy listened as her mother began instructing Helen about what to do next.

'You need to pack up any essentials for you and Bobby. I'll send my girls over to you shortly and they'll bring your bits back here.' She turned her attention to Peggy. 'You'll have to be careful none of the neighbours or other passersby spot you bringing things here.'

Peggy wasn't sure how they could manage that and said so. 'It's daytime, Mum.'

'We can't help that. I'm worried about how soon those soldiers may return. We can't move Helen and Bobby once they're back there, so we have little choice but to bring them here as soon as we can.'

'I'm afraid I'm a little stunned by everything that's happened in the past few hours.' Helen gave a weak smile. 'But I'm very grateful to you all for helping us in this way.'

Ida rested her hands on her hips. 'I know you and Sylvia would have done the same if things were the other way round.'

'What about Aunt Sylvia's belongings?' Helen asked her as the enormity of what she was about to do began to register.

'I can't leave her things there. Not for those...those men to take.'

Ida leant forward and Peggy sensed her mother was getting impatient. 'You listen to me, my girl. Now is not the time for sentiment. We're talking about saving your lives. You need to be brave and move fast. Choose the most precious of your aunt's belongings – jewellery, favourite family photos – that sort of thing.' She thought for a moment. 'And maybe a scarf of hers, or a warm coat you might find useful for next winter. Some meaningful and some useful things.' She chewed her lower lip briefly. 'And anything that Bobby can make use of over the next few months.'

Peggy thought of the meagre stock in their pantry. 'And bring whatever food you have. Also don't forget your identity card.'

'They're good suggestions, Peggy,' her mother said, her voice softening as she turned her attention back to Helen. 'I don't mean to be harsh, my dear. All I want is for you both to be here and safe.'

'Yes.' Peggy immediately backed up her mother's words. 'Leave the house looking as if you've hurriedly packed up and run away. Maybe leave a few drawers open that sort of thing. Hopefully then they'll assume you've gone into hiding elsewhere.'

Ida agreed. 'We need them to be too busy rounding up the poor souls who won't be able to hide from them to spend too much time worrying about you two.'

Helen wiped her eyes and got to her feet. 'I know you're taking a chance helping us and I really am grateful. I'll take Bobby home now and start putting our things together.'

'You have too much to do already without having the little

one with you. Babs can watch him while you go and pack.' Ida tapped her lips thoughtfully. 'I'll send my girls over in an hour to help bring back some of your things. We'll have to make it look as if you're not doing anything suspicious,' she said. 'Pack things under your coat, that sort of thing. I'll expect you whenever you're ready, but,' she said, pulling Helen into a hug, 'don't take too long, dear. You don't want to still be there when they return.'

Chapter Thirty-One

HELEN

Her legs shook as she stepped into her hallway for the last time. Leaning back against the door, Helen studied the familiar area with its tiled floor leading to the kitchen, and doors to the living room and back parlour. As she stared at the highly polished mahogany banister her aunt must have run her hands along hundreds of times as she walked up or down the stairs, it dawned on her that her decision to leave the house that held so many memories for her was now not one she had the luxury of making.

Helen could barely comprehend that she might never again enter this house that had always meant so much to her.

There wasn't any time to spend reminiscing though; she needed to sort out her and Bobby's things and return to him as soon as possible. She decided to pack necessary items first and have them ready for Babs and Peggy to collect in case the Germans returned earlier than she expected. Deciding to start in the bedrooms, she ran upstairs.

She tried to picture what they would need for summer and for winter. For the first time, she was grateful that she didn't own many clothes and that it would be easy to move everything to number 3. She pulled her case from the top of her wardrobe and placed it on her bed. She opened her chest of drawers, scooped up her underwear and night clothes and dropped them into the open case. The ridiculousness of what was she doing occurred to her. Hadn't Ida explained the need for discretion? She quickly tipped the clothes from the case, closed it and pushed it back on top of the wardrobe. No, she needed to be cleverer than that.

Unsure how much bedlinen the Hamels had, she decided to pack some for her and Bobby. Going to the linen cupboard, Helen took several sheets and pillowcases, ensuring she left enough so that it wasn't obvious she had taken any, then packed what she and Bobby needed into them, tying the sheets carefully so she could then tie them around her waist under her coat and give them to the Hamel sisters to do the same. The thought of imposing on the Hamels troubled her but she had little choice now, and if she had to be hidden by anyone Helen welcomed it being her lovely neighbours.

Pleased with her ingenuity, she ran into her aunt's room, bracing herself for the usual slap of emotion that hit her each time she entered it. She opened her aunt's wardrobe, the bedside cupboards, dressing-table drawers and the chest of drawers, carefully taking things she knew to be most valuable to her aunt, not wanting to leave them behind. She chose photos her aunt always had around her, most of her jewellery, several scarves and a half-empty bottle of perfume, wanting to keep the scent of her darling aunt with her for as long as possible and placed them on the dressing table ready to collect after she had taken the other items downstairs for the Hamel sisters to take.

Satisfied that she had done all she could, Helen checked she had her own and Bobby's identity papers and ran downstairs to the kitchen to look for food and whatever else she thought necessary to take.

In the living room she spotted the photo on the mantelpiece and a small painting her aunt particularly loved and always had nearby. It had been a gift from her husband that he had bought for her in St Malo on their honeymoon and Helen knew she must try to save it. She lifted the small painting from the wall, then studied the room for another picture to replace it with. Finding a framed photo of some of Sylvia's friends whom Helen hadn't known in one of the drawers of her aunt's desk, she hung it on the nail where the painting had been.

Her heart ached as she looked at all the things her aunt had treasured. The book Aunt Sylvia had been reading each evening when she had fallen ill was still on the small table next to her armchair. Slipping on her coat, Helen decided to make the most of the deep pockets and picked up the book, along with another that she remembered her aunt reading. It comforted her a little to own some things her aunt had held.

A gentle tap at the front door snapped her back to the present. Helen ran to answer it, praying it wasn't the officers testing her, pulled the door open slowly and peered around it. She was relieved to see her two friends.

As soon as they were inside the house, Babs took several cloth bags from inside her coat. 'Mum said to bring these in case you needed them. How are you doing?' She leant to one side and peered into the living room. 'Are you anywhere near ready?'

Their sympathy nearly dissolved her determination to stay strong. She had to think rationally and focus on not forgetting anything she might need later. 'I'm not sure I've packed everything I should, but I've done my best. What if I leave something valuable behind?'

'Mum said we mustn't let you be very long,' Peggy said apologetically. 'She also said to remember that yours and Bobby's safety is far more important than trinkets or photos.'

It was exactly what she needed to hear. 'She's right,' Helen agreed, straightening her shoulders, knowing she daren't allow emotions to overcome her common sense. 'I have one or two things I need to fetch from my aunt's room first, but I think I'm almost ready.'

'That's good.' Peggy gave her an encouraging smile. 'You're doing really well, Helen. Truly you are. We know this is hard for you.'

Helen smiled, grateful to Peggy for her understanding, but she didn't want to delay them in case the officers returned. She couldn't bear to be the one to get these sweet friends into trouble.

'I'll be two minutes,' she said, running upstairs, terrified she could be the cause of Peggy being sent to a prison camp if the authorities discovered that the confidentiality she had sworn to work by had been breached.

She pushed open her aunt's bedroom door, and scanning the room, quickly opened her dressing-table drawer and took out a powder compact. Then, taking her silver-backed hairbrush, comb and mirror set that her aunt had received as a wedding present from her husband, removed the books from her coat pocket deciding to carry them instead. No one would think it odd to see someone carrying books. Helen then slipped everything she had collected from her aunt's bedroom into her coat pocket. They were far too personal to her aunt to leave behind.

'Bye, Aunty Sylvia,' she whispered kissing her fingertips and touching her aunt's headboard, feeling as if her heart was being ripped from her chest and she was losing her aunt all over again.

'Helen? Are you coming?'

Hearing the tremble in Babs's voice, Helen gathered herself and ran back downstairs. 'I'm ready,' she said aware that if they let her she would be tempted to spend the next few hours trying to choose other items to take with her.

Peggy glanced upstairs. 'Where are the things you want us to carry next door?'

Helen pointed into the living room. 'I've put everything in there.'

When the girls had gone to retrieve them, she finished putting the food and Bobby's mug and small spoon and fork together in a basket. She hoped anyone seeing it might think it was just some shopping.

'Ready?' Babs asked from the kitchen door.

'I think so.' Helen held up the house keys. 'Should I take these? There's another pair I've left on the kitchen table for them to use. They were Aunt Sylvia's.'

Peggy nodded. 'I'd leave the front door unlocked, so there's no need for them to break down the door, but keep one set so that you can let yourself in when this war ends.'

'If it ends,' Babs grumbled angrily.

The thought of the war ending and being able to move back in gave Helen hope. 'You think I'll be able to live here again?'

'I hope so,' Peggy said, motioning for them to leave.

'Come along, you two,' Babs said. 'We don't want to be here when they come back.'

No, Helen thought, terrified at the prospect, they didn't.

Chapter Thirty-Two

PEGGY

Peggy was astonished to find her mother up in the attic, sweeping the floor. She stood at the top of the narrow staircase her mother always hated using and stared into the large room that covered the entire width and length of the house. 'You've been working hard up here, Mum. You must be shattered.'

Her mother went to reply but was consumed by a sneezing fit. 'The ruddy cobwebs are everywhere.' Ida brushed her hand over the scarf she had tied around her head to cover her hair and shuddered. 'You and Babs can finish off this cleaning, while I go and find something for Helen and that little boy to sleep on. Then we can sort out those bits of furniture in that corner. We need to make this place as cosy as possible for them.'

It was going to take some doing, Peggy realised. It was only September, but it was a cool day and already felt colder up here than it did downstairs. Peggy wondered how the pair of them would cope during the depths of winter but pushed her concerns aside. There was plenty of time in the coming months to find solutions. It wasn't as if Helen had anywhere better to hide.

She stepped into the attic and took the broom and dustpan from her mother. 'Maybe ask Babs to bring up a mop and bucket with some hot water in it. Then we can wash the floors, too.' As her mother went down to the next landing, Peggy had another thought. 'You can ask her to bring up the rug from my room and the one from hers too. They'll help make this place a bit more comfortable.'

By the time she and her sister had finished, Peggy thought they had done a decent job.

'How's it going up here?' Helen asked joining them. Her mouth opened in surprise. 'Gosh, it's much nicer than our attic next door. We have to climb through a hatch. And it's dusty and full of boxes, bits of furniture and old paintings.'

Peggy laughed. 'This one wasn't much better a few hours ago.' She leant on the mop handle. 'How are you doing?'

'I'm a bit overwhelmed, to be honest, and trying not to think too deeply about everything.' She smiled. 'You've all been incredibly generous and kind.'

Peggy shook her head. 'You're our friend, Helen. And we're only doing the neighbourly thing.'

'I'd like to think that was true of all neighbours,' Helen said. 'But I suspect it's not the case. Anyhow, I've unpacked the small amount of food we managed to bring from next door and your mum has hidden some of it in her basement. She seemed happy with what I've brought, which makes me feel a bit better about everything.'

'You need to stop feeling badly about all this,' Peggy said, hoping to reassure her. 'It's not your doing that led you here and I don't want you to forget that. I'd already come up with the idea last night, actually, before those officers forced us to move a little quicker on it.'

She could see by Helen's concerned expression that she wasn't convinced.

'It's true, Helen. These are exceptional times. We can only do the best with what we have.'

'I know you're right, but I already felt guilty about Aunt Sylvia taking me in, and how drastically her life must have changed when I turned up on her doorstep. I feel such a burden.'

Peggy leant the mop against the sloping roof. 'Now you listen to me. We all know you and Bobby meant the world to your aunt. Imagine how frightening it would have been for her to live alone for the past year. Then, when she became ill, having you there to help her meant an awful lot, and Bobby kept her company. It was plain for us all to see how much joy you both brought into Sylvia's life. You should never feel guilty about that.'

Helen was about to argue, but Peggy raised her hand to stop her, clearly having no intention of letting her continue until she had finished having her say. 'Babs and I are so grateful for your friendship. We've loved seeing your aunt happy, and I know Mum loves Bobby. Spending time with him has given her a new lease of life.' She smiled, sadly. 'She struggled for a long time to come to terms with losing Dad, and she dotes on that little boy, so please forget any concerns you have.'

'I'll do my best.'

'Good, that's settled then. Now, as soon as this floor has dried you can help me make up a bed for you both.'

Chapter Thirty-Three

HELEN

That night, as Helen lay on the mattress cuddling Bobby, she stared out of the window at the stars in the inky black sky and wondered at how quickly everything had changed. The day had passed in a blur. Her mind was still spinning from the drama of having to pack essentials and sneak them over to this house, which was so similar in layout to number 2.

It helped to know her aunt's home was on the other side of the stone wall separating the properties. Although, she mused, it was also painful to think that it was within touching distance and yet permanently separated from her.

She looked around the attic space, which now held a small table and a clean leather suitcase with her and Bobby's clothes folded neatly inside. Babs was going to help her make it more homely the following day, and Ida had promised to cut down a pair of old curtains, so that Helen could shut out the night whenever she wanted to. Now, though, she was happy to be able to lie here as the rest of the house slept and watch the same stars that she had always seen from her own window.

Bobby stirred in her arms and Helen realised she needed to try and sleep. There was still a lot to do if she and her little boy were to make this cavernous room their home for the foreseeable future.

She woke to Bobby giggling and poking her gently in the eye.

'Ouch,' she said, pretending to be shocked and making him curl up in amusement. 'Cheeky boy!' She laughed, tickling him and wishing he would stay like this, unfazed by all that was going to happen to them over the coming months and, she thought, feeling sick, possibly years. She shook her head to banish the troublesome thought and tickled him again.

Bobby jumped out of bed and ran off across the wooden floor. It occurred to Helen how noisy his footsteps might become as he grew. She would have to find slippers or footwear with a soft sole if she was to ensure he wasn't heard downstairs. Thoughts raced through her mind as she realised that the two of them would need to make many adjustments if they were to remain hidden from the Nazis.

Helen sighed and wondered if she was doing the right thing, putting Bobby into this prison, albeit one looked over by friends.

'What's that sigh for?' came a voice behind her. She turned to see Babs at the attic door carrying a jug of water. 'Mum sent this up so you can wash.' She opened her arms for Bobby to run into them. 'How's my favourite boy?'

Helen took the jug and set it down on the deep windowsill, where Peggy had left a bowl, two facecloths and neatly folded towels.

'How did you sleep?' Babs asked, giving Bobby a cuddle before letting him go and watching him run off to find his toy bunny.

'Well, actually. The mattress is comfortable.'

Babs frowned thoughtfully. 'Something's wrong, though, I can tell.'

'I'm still concerned about the three of you taking us on and the risk that goes with it, but I'm also worried about him.' She indicated Bobby with a tilt of her head. 'Am I doing the right thing by taking him into hiding?'

Babs gave her a sympathetic smile. 'I can't see you have much choice. If you're not here, you'll have to hide somewhere else on the island or be deported, and surely you can't think that would be a better option.'

Helen shook her head. 'I don't.' She pressed the heels of her hands against her tired eyes. 'I just wish there was a third option.'

'What, like the war had never happened?' Babs teased, giving her a sympathetic look.

'Something like that, yes.'

'If only that was the case.' Babs took Bunny from Bobby and pretended to hide it in her cardigan. He squealed and tugged open one side, laughing when Babs pulled the toy out and waved it in his face before handing it to him. 'Anyway, Mum said you're both to come down to the kitchen and eat something. I think she's worried they'll come searching for you both sometime today and wants to be certain you've eaten.'

'That's kind of her.'

'I'll leave you both to get dressed.'

Helen watched her friend leave, closing the attic door

behind her. 'Come along, poppet. Let's get you ready for breakfast.'

Peggy poured Helen a cup of weak tea and placed a couple of toasted bread soldiers for Bobby to eat on the table in front of where he was sitting on Ida's lap. 'I was thinking we need to set up an area for you both to hide in when you're in the attic,' Peggy said.

'A hiding place within their hiding place?' Babs said in between sips of her tea. 'Is that necessary?'

'I agree with Peggy,' Ida said, handing Bobby the next piece of toast. 'We can't be too careful.'

Peggy continued, 'I thought we could block off part of the eaves on one side and make a small section at one end into a cubby hole for the pair of you to go if any soldiers do go up there searching for you. That might work.'

Helen tried to picture what she meant. 'But who will make it? I don't have any carpentry skills.'

'I'm sure I could, with help,' Peggy said, 'and we have enough pieces of wood and boarding stacked up there to be able to do it. What do you think?'

Helen shrugged. 'If you think it's necessary, then I'm happy to go along with it.'

'It only needs to be somewhere small that you two can fit into. We can arrange the room so that it won't be obvious when they do come.'

'Don't you mean if they come?' Babs asked.

'No, it'll be when,' Peggy said with an assurance that frightened Helen. 'Don't think we won't be the first place they look, Babs. I've had enough dealings with these men to know they are clever, thorough and above all determined. We will need to be prepared for any eventuality and must never underestimate them. I have had an idea what to do and I'll get started as soon as we finish eating.'

'I'll help you,' Helen said, wanting everything ready as soon as possible. She hated small spaces but if it meant keeping Bobby safe then she would hide wherever Peggy thought best. 'I'm going to need to clear everything away each morning too, just in case they do come unexpectedly, and we don't have time to make the room look uninhabited.'

Peggy gave her a reassuring smile. 'I can see I've frightened you and I don't mean to. I promise we'll make a good job of it. I have no intention of letting them find you.'

If only that was all it took, Helen thought, sipping her tea and struggling to swallow.

Chapter Thirty-Four

PEGGY

Peggy pulled the paper from her typewriter with such vigour the page tore in half. 'Damn it,' she grumbled, crumpling it up, before realising she would need to keep it to copy if she didn't want to start the translation from scratch.

She was halfway through retyping it, when there was a single knock on her office door and a German officer walked in. He locked eyes with her and didn't move for a few seconds. Unsure why he was acting so oddly, Peggy tore her eyes from his gaze and straightened the pile of papers on her desk.

He still didn't speak and, not seeing anything in his hands, she forced herself to address him. 'Is there something you wanted?'

'*Ich*, er, I must fetch a document.'

She frowned, trying to work out which one. Most of the Germans she came in contact with seemed confident but this one didn't and was acting strangely.

'Do you know which document?'

He considered her question before shaking his head.

Why on earth was he acting so oddly? 'Is something the matter?'

'The matter?'

'Wrong. Is something wrong?'

He frowned then shook his head.

Realising she should speak German to him, Peggy asked what he wanted from her in his own language. Finally understanding her, he mentioned the Order about the deportations. The tone and look of sadness on his face led her to assume he was upset about what the islanders were soon to discover. Aware he might have been sent to test her level of secrecy and whether she would be vocal about her feelings, she decided to hurry up and get rid of him. Quickly looking through her work, she gathered several completed transcripts and put them into an envelope.

'These need to be taken today, so maybe one of them is what you're looking for.' She held out the envelope, waiting for him to take it, feeling more uncomfortable as the seconds passed and he didn't move.

She heard footsteps outside her office door, and a knock she recognised. 'Come in,' she called, delighted that Tony had chosen that moment to visit her.

He walked in, noticed the officer and stepped back out of the doorway. 'I'm sorry, I didn't realise you were busy.' He looked from her to the officer, who was now staring intently at Tony, eyes narrowed. He was clearly interested in who Tony was, and not wishing him to stay any longer than was necessary, Peggy decided to introduce them. 'Captain – er, I'm sorry, I didn't catch your name.'

Without taking his eyes from Tony, he said, 'Captain Heinrich Engel.'

'Captain Engel, this is Advocate Le Gresley. His father is the senior partner at this firm.'

The captain clicked his heels together and gave a curt nod but seemed pleased to discover that Tony had a reason for coming to her office.

'Would you rather I came back later?' Tony asked, sounding as if that was the last thing he hoped to hear.

'No,' she said forcing a smile. 'The captain has what he came for.' Turning to the officer, she added, 'Is that correct?'

He thought for a moment before giving a curt nod. 'Goodbye, Miss Hamel.'

Tony waited for him to go, then closed the door. 'Well, he was a bit odd, don't you think?'

'Very.' She shivered. 'I can't tell you how relieved I was when you arrived.'

He walked towards her and opened his arms. Feeling them around her as he held her calmed her slightly. 'He gave me the strangest feeling. There was something about him.'

She felt Tony tense. 'What did he say to you?'

She thought back. 'Nothing untoward.'

'Did he do something?'

She sighed. 'Nothing I can put my finger on.'

'I'll try and keep an eye out for him,' he said. Then, after a moment's thought, he added, 'Would you like me to wait for you after work and walk you home?'

'But you go the other way.' She hoped he would argue with her and insist on accompanying her. She felt him kiss the top of her head.

'When has that ever worried me? I'll wait for you if I leave first. But if you do, please wait by the front door for me. Agreed?'

'Thank you. That makes me feel much better.' She realised he hadn't told her why he was there. 'Did you want me for something?'

'Only this,' he said putting his finger under her chin and gently lifting it and kissing her.

Peggy slipped her arms around his neck and gave in to Tony's kisses, forgetting all about the strange officer she hoped never to see again.

On their way to her home, Tony slowed as they neared the newsagents. 'My father asked me to fetch an *Evening Post*.'

She accompanied him inside the small shop, noticing how bare the shelves were, now that there was no confectionery or British magazines. She wondered whether the deportation order she had translated might be in the local newspaper and decided to buy one to take home to her mother in case it was.

They paid for their papers and went outside. Both stared at the headline.

'There it is,' Tony said as Peggy gazed at the upsetting words. 'Some of the people being made to leave have probably lived here for decades,' he said, his voice solemn. 'Their children will have been born here.'

'And their grandchildren, in some cases,' Peggy said miserably.

She felt his hand take hers. 'Stop that.'

'What?'

'Blaming yourself.'

'I can't help it.' She began walking, embarrassed in case anyone coming out of the shop might hear them.

Tony caught up with her and took her by the wrist, slowing her. 'Peggy, all you've done is translate the words, nothing more.'

He was right, but she still found it difficult to come to terms with having any part in it.

'You need to warn your friend Helen about this, too.'

Peggy realised she hadn't told him about Helen's visit the previous morning and what had happened since then. 'I already have,' she said taking his hand and walking on again. 'In fact, there's something I should probably tell you.'

Chapter Thirty-Five

HELEN

They decided between them that one of the Hamels would bring up something for Bobby's lunch, and that if Ida thought it safe, she and Bobby should join the Hamels for their evening meal. Then, when he had been asleep for a few hours during the evening, Helen could go down to sit with the family for a while.

'We'll keep the hall light off,' Ida said. 'If we're disturbed, no one will see you running upstairs while we stall them to give you and Bobby time to hide in the secret place.'

Helen felt slightly more settled, having spent her second day in their new home. Bobby hadn't minded being there at all and seemed to think it was all a game, which was an enormous relief. He had played happily with his toys for most of the day and, deciding it would help them both to cope if they kept to a routine, Helen put him down for his nap at the usual time.

She heard the front door close and knew one of the sisters had arrived home. When it closed for the second time, she waited before taking Bobby downstairs, stopping on the top landing to listen in case she heard unfamiliar voices.

She heard the three women talking and could tell they were upset about something. Hoping it was nothing to do with her and Bobby, Helen nervously came downstairs and stood by the kitchen door.

Babs noticed her there. 'They've published the order Peggy told us about. I hadn't realised how severe it would be,' she said, pointing to the headline on the newspaper lying on the kitchen table. 'They're sending all Englishmen aged between sixteen and seventy, as well as their poor families. Imagine that?'

'But that's a lot of people, surely?' Helen asked breathlessly. 'Men and women, too?'

'And children,' Ida said without looking up, her hand flying to her chest as she read on.

'Children?' Helen's vision dimmed and she grabbed the back of Peggy's chair, frightened she was about to pass out with fear.

'Mum, really,' Babs said, taking Helen's elbow. 'Here, come and sit down.'

Helen felt a glass of water being pressed into her hand. 'Have a drink of this,' Peggy said before sitting down again. 'I thought I told you about this.'

'You probably did, but the full scale of it can't have sunk in. When do they have to leave?' Helen began shivering, despite it not being cold.

'Tomorrow,' Ida said. 'But lovey, you won't have to go. Not now.'

Ida was right, Helen reminded herself. 'Thanks to the three of you. Although I can't help feeling dreadful for all these people.' Something occurred to her. 'They're definitely going to come looking for me, aren't they?'

Ida shrugged. 'Maybe not. Hopefully they'll be kept busy with this dreadful deportation and might forget about you.'

'Yes,' Babs agreed. 'They might even think you've been sent away in all the confusion.'

Helen hoped she was right, then saw doubt in Peggy's eyes. 'You don't agree?'

Peggy seemed to wrestle with her conscience, then shook her head. 'They're too well organised for that. I can't imagine they'd ever let anyone slip through their tightly planned net.'

She almost spat the words and Helen saw for the first time how difficult it was for her friend to have to deal with the Germans at work.

Helen covered her mouth to stop crying out. 'Thanks to the three of you, Bobby and I still have the chance of a future. I only hope they don't come looking for me here. I couldn't bear it if anything happened to any of you because of what you've done for us.'

Ida looked at Peggy. 'You need to stop feeling guilty for the work you do and remember the lives you have saved by sharing information.'

'Mum's right,' Babs agreed. 'You can't save everyone, Peggy, as much as you might wish to.'

Peggy sighed then smiled at Helen. 'I have to admit I'm relieved you and Bobby came here when you did.'

'We all are,' Babs agreed.

'As we're on the subject,' Ida began, and Helen felt the older woman's gaze fall upon her. 'I don't want any more talk about you being grateful to us, Helen. We feel honoured to be able to help you and that sweet little boy. Your aunt would do the same thing for my girls if the roles were reversed.'

Helen started to thank her again then, seeing her piercing look, stopped herself. 'Fine. I'll say nothing more about it. But I want you to promise that if it ever becomes too much, or too dangerous for us to be here, you will tell me and I'll make other plans. I won't have you taking even more chances than you are already.'

Ida would have argued, but Peggy interrupted. 'We promise we'll tell you.'

Helen doubted they would but felt slightly reassured by Peggy's reply.

The following evening when Babs returned from work, Helen noticed she had been crying. 'Whatever's the matter?' she asked when they were alone in the kitchen preparing their meagre supper.

Babs blew her nose and sniffed. 'Mum said I wasn't to tell you.'

Confused, Helen said, 'I had hoped you could tell me anything.'

Babs thought for a few seconds then her shoulders slumped. 'It's my manager. She was deported today. I hadn't realised she was going.' She blew her nose. 'I didn't even know she was English until I asked where she was and one of the girls who lives near her told me that her husband moved over here with her about thirty-six years ago. They could only take one suitcase each. A small one at that. I mean, how can you pack up decades' worth of belongings into a small case? It was like the evacuation, but going to a rotten camp somewhere in Germany rather than to England.' She sniffed. 'I gather the constable of her parish visited them late last night to let them know they had to go.' She burst into tears again. 'She's ever such a lovely woman, too. Loved her life here. She'd been working at Boots since she arrived on the island in 1906.'

Helen was unable to stop crying. 'Oh, Babs, that's heartbreaking.'

'I know. A bus collected them and took them to the ferry. They must have left a few hours ago.'

Helen couldn't imagine how shocking it must be for those poor people, forced to leave everything and everyone they knew. Fuelled by hatred for the Germans, she clenched her teeth. She couldn't help blurting out her feelings. 'They are unbelievably cruel to do this to innocent people. It's despicable.'

'I agree. There were a lot of us in tears at work today. We were told to put on a brave face by another manager. He went with a couple of others to see her off at the harbour and told us later how brave the English people were despite what they were facing.'

'Oh, lovey,' Ida said entering the kitchen and hugging her daughter. 'I see that you told Helen then.' She gave a minute shake of her head. 'It's only natural to be sad for those poor souls. I was talking to Mr Vibert down at the greengrocers and he was telling me about a couple only four doors down from here who've had to go with their three small children.' She wiped her eye with the back of her hand. 'He said the deportations will carry on for the best part of another week yet.' Her voice trembled as she added, 'It breaks my heart to hear of people having to leave everything they've worked hard for, but it's worse to think of children being taken to heaven knows where.' She turned away, her shoulders shaking as she tried to stifle her sobs.

Helen wasn't sure what to do and was somewhat relieved when Peggy appeared.

'Mum, I wish we could do something to help them.' Peggy stood behind her mother, her arms around her as she wept.

Helen, feeling as if she was imposing, decided she should go and find comfort in holding her little boy. The thought that chance had played such an enormous part in all their futures, saving her when so many others had been forced to leave, was humbling. She knew that without the generosity of her neighbours she and Bobby might also now be on a ferry to Germany.

Chapter Thirty-Six

PEGGY

The following day all anyone could talk about was the continuing deportations.

'They're nothing more than animals,' one of the secretaries grumbled in the kitchen as Peggy made Advocate Le Gresley's morning cup of coffee.

'Animals wouldn't be that cruel,' her friend argued, and Peggy had to agree. It was unthinkable that innocent families could be treated so cruelly. She hadn't said so to her family or Helen, but it had shaken her badly.

'I heard those bastards had bayonets and were threatening the poor souls queuing to leave. How could they? And with children there to witness such behaviour.'

Peggy wrapped her arms around herself in a vain attempt at comfort.

'Mind you,' the secretary continued, 'I heard about one man who had recently had an operation on his stomach who was turned back. Didn't want the effort of taking him with them, I suppose.'

'Did they let his family stay behind, too?'

'I think so.' She shivered. 'Imagine having such a close call as that. Poor things.'

'They're better off than those who had to go, though, aren't they?'

Unable to bear any more, Peggy finished making her boss's coffee and left the kitchen. Happy though she was for the family who had been allowed to stay, imagining the fear of the deportees was too much for her. She returned to her work hoping to keep busy enough to stop thinking about what was happening at the harbour.

Focusing on what she could do, instead of what she couldn't, Peggy decided to speak to Tony and invite him to number 3 to check her handiwork in the attic. It would be useful having a fresh eye survey the room and see how well hidden Helen and Bobby were. There would only be one chance to save them if the Germans did decide to search their home.

Her thoughts were distracted by more documents being delivered. After the messenger left, she sat and stared at the folder, nausea surging through her as she tried to pluck up the courage to look at the paperwork. She wasn't sure how much longer she could go on doing this job. As much as she wanted to help others and knew that having prior knowledge of bad news before it was imparted helped some people, there was something to be said for blissful ignorance.

She took a deep breath and pulled the file towards her. Slowly opening it, she looked down at the top document and began to read. When she finished, she closed her eyes. 'Thank God,' she said, her heart pounding with relief to be able to translate good news for a change.

Tony was unable to accompany her home, having been called into a late meeting with his father and a couple of the directors, so Peggy left by herself. A few times on her way home, she sensed she was being watched. Hoping to see who it was, she stopped in front of a shop pretending to look in the window while studying the reflection. She noticed two German officers, but they were far enough away for her not to be concerned about them. Telling herself that feeling watched was expected at times like these and that she was being oversensitive, she continued her walk home.

'The rest of the deportations are postponed, you say?' Ida asked, clutching Peggy's hand. 'Due to bad weather? But how long can that be expected to last before they start again?

'I don't know if it even is the true reason, or if maybe this is their way of bringing the deportations to an end. Not all these soldiers are dreadful people,' she reminded her mother. 'Some are as fed up at being stuck here as we are having them on the island. I also think there's quite a bit of embarrassment about sending people away against their will.' She lowered her voice. 'Some English people will still be going in a few days, but only because they've been jailed for various offences.' She thought of Tony, relieved that nothing else had cropped up about his arrest. 'I'm not sure why they're sending them to Germany, but I presume they're making an example of them as a warning to the rest of us.'

'What offences will they have committed to be punished so severely?' Her mother's face paled, and Peggy wondered if she too was thinking about youngsters who had been caught

215

carrying out small acts of resistance against the German authorities.

'Sabotage, breaking curfew, that sort of thing.'

Ida shook her head slowly. 'That's ridiculous. I can't stand much more of this, I really can't.' She pointed at the ceiling and lowered her voice. 'I was told when I was at the bakery this morning that they were planning to send English women now, even those without husbands. Will they still do that, do you think?'

Peggy wished she knew. 'I've no idea. I haven't been given those documents. Maybe they were sent straight to the Constables of each parish where those women live, but hopefully now they're blaming the bad weather for the delay, those women might also be spared.' She thought of Helen and Bobby. 'At least we know of two people who are safe for now.'

Her mother closed her eyes and rested a hand on her chest. 'Let's hope they stay that way.'

Peggy opened her mouth to respond when a heavy knock on the door made them both jump. 'Who can that be?' She knew it wasn't Tony by the knock. Something told her that whoever it was would be in uniform. Her heart dropped.

'I'll get it, Mum.'

She stepped into the hallway as Babs hissed at her from the first-floor landing, 'Keep them busy. I'll go and warn Helen, she's just out of the bath.'

Peggy waited for her sister to run up the next flight of stairs and open the attic door, before taking a deep breath and slowly opening the front door. Surprised to see the officer standing on her doorstep, she froze. 'Captain—' She couldn't recall his name.

'Captain Heinrich Engel of the Wehrmacht,' he said proudly, clicking his heels together.

'Good evening, Captain Engel,' she said as loudly as she dared without drawing his attention to her behaving oddly. 'Did I forget something at work?'

He seemed pleased with himself for some reason. 'No. I. We are—' He indicated Sylvia Bowman's house next door, and it took a moment for Peggy to understand what he was trying to convey. Her mouth dropped open before she managed to gather herself. 'You're billeted in that house?'

He beamed at her. 'Ah, yes.'

An icy sensation trickled through her nerves. It was all she could do to refrain from shivering. 'I see.' She didn't at all. Struggling to calm her rapid breathing, Peggy forced herself to remain professional.

'You live here with your family?' he asked in German, looking over her shoulder at the hallway and kitchen beyond.

'I do,' she replied in English but gave a nod in case he didn't understand what she said.

Hoping he wasn't going to offer to walk her to work, or even back home again, she tried but failed to think of a way to bring Tony into the conversation without voicing her thoughts. She stared at him waiting for him to fill the silence.

His face reddened and he stepped from one foot to the other. Peggy was relieved to see him look uncomfortable but said nothing, hoping he would leave.

Eventually he gave a nod and a tight smile. 'Goodnight, Miss Hamel,' he said again in his native tongue. 'I hope to see you again in your office.'

Not wishing to encourage him, she said, 'Goodnight, Captain,' and closed the door.

She watched through the mottled glass panel in the door as he hesitated before turning and walking down the steps. Seconds later the front door slammed in the next house. Peggy let out a groan, and it was only then that she realised she'd been holding her breath.

The kitchen door opened a touch, then fully as her mother came out to join her. 'I couldn't hear much,' she said. 'Especially as he spoke German, but I didn't like the tone of his voice.' She narrowed her eyes and crossed her arms over her chest. 'I have a horrible feeling Peggy, my girl, that the captain has taking a fancy to you.'

Peggy was thinking the same thing. 'I wish I could disagree with you, Mum,' she said miserably. Why was it that just when it seemed as if things might be getting a little better, some other torture was foisted on them?

'Has he gone?' Babs whispered from the landing.

'Yes,' Ida answered. 'But I have a nasty feeling he'll find an excuse to come back soon.'

Chapter Thirty-Seven

HELEN

December 1942

The next couple of months dragged for Helen. So far no one had come to inspect the house, but each of them was on constant alert, especially when Captain Engel made one of his impromptu visits. Helen hoped that the Jerries' attention had been diverted from her disappearance, what with everything else that had happened. Whatever the reason she was relieved to have been left in relative peace with Bobby.

But Peggy had seemed troubled recently. Helen had tried to broach the subject with her friend but Peggy had brushed off her concerns, insisting there was nothing wrong.

She decided to ask Babs if she knew anything. Babs agreed. 'I've noticed how distracted Peggy's seemed for weeks now, but she insists she's fine, just tired from long hours at work.'

'Do you believe that's all it is?'

Babs had shrugged. 'No, but I know my big sister well enough to know when to drop the subject.'

Helen assumed it probably had something to do with the German officer who kept coming to the house under different pretexts, but he had never asked to come in, as far as she was aware, and Peggy always spoke to him on the doorstep.

Helen felt a little better discovering that Peggy had given the same amount of information to her as she had to Babs. She had suspected for weeks that the Hamel women were trying their best to keep any bad news from her and, although she appreciated their efforts, she would rather they treated her as they did each other.

Her thoughts were interrupted when Bobby dropped his wooden train on his toe. She saw his face crumple in pain, and, scared he might be about to scream, Helen dashed over to him and took him in her arms, hugging him to her to muffle his cries.

When he calmed down, she gently lifted his foot and, slipping off his sock, inspected his big toe. It was red and would probably have a bruise by the following day. Her heart ached for him and that he was spending most of each day cooped up in an attic with only her for company. She gently blew on his toe to soothe it, unintentionally making him laugh. Delighted to have amused him, she did it again. Their game lasted for several minutes and by the time he grew bored and returned to playing with his train, Helen felt a lot better.

They might be cooped up in here, but they were together and relatively comfortable.

That evening, soon after Bobby had fallen asleep, the attic door opened and Babs appeared. She scanned the room, then, seeing him sleeping, smiled and rested her hand over her heart. 'He is angelic,' she whispered. 'I hope if I have children one of them is just like Bobby.'

Helen didn't like to point out that with Babs's naturally pale blonde hair rather than her own auburn and Richard's almost black, that wasn't very likely. 'I'm sure you will.' She noticed a glint of excitement in her friend. 'Has something happened today?'

Babs grinned. 'It has. Mum said to come down if you can. She received a Red Cross telegram with news from her cousin.'

Helen thought of the one she had sent to Richard so many months before, telling him about Bobby and letting him know she was happy for him to respond. She pushed the thought aside, not wanting to think about why he had chosen not to reply.

'I'll be down in a couple of minutes,' Helen said, needing a little time to calm her emotions before joining them.

'Don't be too long or Mum will think you don't want any supper.'

Supper. Helen hated that the Hamels had to share their meagre rations with her and Bobby, but not wanting to keep them waiting, she pulled her son's covers up so that he wouldn't be cold now the temperature had dropped, and went downstairs.

'There she is,' Ida said, holding up her telegram. 'Look what came today. It's from my cousin in Wimbledon.' She beamed at Helen.

'Is it the first time you've heard from her?' Helen asked, feeling Ida's excitement.

Ida reread her cousin's words. 'It is, and it's such a surprise, and a huge relief. I'd heard on the radio that Wimbledon has been bombed quite a bit, like so many other places. I've been concerned about her and her family.'

'How wonderful that she's put your mind at rest.'

'Yes,' Peggy said. 'Although they've moved to a new place, so they might have had bomb damage at some point.'

Ida nodded. 'Mavis and her husband Bill had lived in their previous home their entire married life. They would never leave there unless they had little choice.'

Helen noticed the growing concern on Ida's face and tried to reassure her. 'But now you know they're all safe and well.'

'I do.' Ida poured them all a weak tea. 'Maybe you'll receive a telegram from your family at some point, Helen.'

Helen noticed Peggy and Babs glance at each other.

'Mum, I can't see how that will happen,' Peggy said quietly.

'Why ever not?

Helen didn't like to think of Ida being embarrassed when she hadn't meant anything by her question. 'I think Peggy is referring to me being here now,' she said, smiling to ensure her words were taken at face value. 'No one would know where to deliver it.'

Ida gasped. 'Oh, lovey. That was insensitive of me. Here's me showing off about my news while you haven't heard from your family. Really, I could kick myself.'

Helen shook her head. 'Please, don't worry. It's fine.' She sighed. 'I'd like to hear from them, but my mother never made any effort to contact me before the invasion and I have no reason to expect she'll try now.'

'But what about—?' Babs stopped. 'Sorry. None of my business.'

Helen saw her cheeks redden and supposed Babs was referring to Bobby's father. 'I did telegram Richard before Aunt Sylvia died, but never received a response.'

'These things take months to reach the addressee,' Ida said, looking embarrassed. 'Then another few months for their reply to come back, so maybe it's been delayed.'

'Thank you, but now I think about it, even if he did reply he would have sent it to the wrong address.' She stared miserably at her short fingernails and the dry skin on the back of her hands. Realising no one was speaking, she looked up at her friends, who were all staring at her miserably. 'Please, don't feel badly for me. I have a lot to be grateful for, thanks to you three taking me and Bobby into your home.' When they still didn't speak, she added, 'Tell me more about your cousin. It'll be good to hear about England again. I do miss it rather a lot.'

Later, when she was lying on the mattress she shared with Bobby, Helen's thoughts returned to Richard. Had he replied to her? And if so, what might he have said?

Chapter Thirty-Eight

RICHARD

Richard barely noticed how uncomfortable his bed was after another exhausting shift coast-watching for enemy attacks. Not that there had been many lately, now the Jerries were focusing their attention elsewhere, he thought.

If only news was coming from the islands, and he could at least know she and Bobby were safe.

He took his book from his nightstand and opened it. Helen's telegram lay between two pages to preserve the flimsy paper for as long as possible. He reread it. Not that he needed to, having memorised the words, but it was comforting to know Helen had written them herself. He ran his fingertips lightly across the precious twenty-five words in pencilled capitals. Helen had touched this piece of paper, he reminded himself. It was the closest he had been to her since early 1940 when they had become intimate that one special time.

Should have spoken before leaving. Bobby (your son), Aunt

Sylvia and I are well. Have job and friends. Keep safe. Please
send word again. Helen

He murmured the words so as not to disturb any of the
others trying to catch some sleep between their shifts. He
needed to hear them as well as look at and touch them.
Anything to bring her closer to him.

He wondered what his son looked like. Bobby must have
been born sometime in December 1940, he guessed. He tried to
picture his son playing. It was hard to believe he was two years
old and they hadn't ever met. It had been nine months since
Helen had sent her telegram, and though he had replied as
soon as he could, there had been nothing since. Could she have
changed her mind and decided she no longer wished to have
contact with him? No, Helen wasn't cruel. She would never
have begun communicating with him only to stop for no
reason. Perhaps his had never reached her.

He sat up. Yes, that's what could have happened. He
needed to send another one and hope it got to her.

Satisfied with his plan, Richard tried to recall what he had
said in his previous message. Then, taking his notepad and
pencil, he began drafting a telegram, to send that afternoon.

Happiest message about Bobby. Thank you. Also you and
aunt being well. Wish was with you both. Am fine but sorry
for damage caused. Richard

Later, at the telegraph office, having carefully rewritten the
message, he added Helen's address and sent a silent prayer
that this one would reach her and that her reply wouldn't be
too long coming. His exhaustion meant nothing if he had word

---

from Helen and their little boy. He slid the telegram across the counter to be checked and paid for it. As he left the office, he looked up at the cloudless blue sky and tried to imagine what the weather must be like in Jersey.

The south coast of England was only eighty-five miles from the island at its nearest, although in Sheerness he was further away than that, and the thought of their closeness helped him. He wasn't the only man missing the woman and child he loved, but most of the other men had met their children and, he thought miserably, married the women who had given birth to them. Another dreadful error on his part. He had behaved unbelievably carelessly towards Helen. Not that he had meant to, nor would he have done if he had thought for a moment that she was carrying his child. What a fool he had been. He groaned and closed his eyes, wishing desperately that he could go back in time and change the way he had behaved.

There was no going back though, he thought as he started walking to his base. At least she was with her aunt who loved her. Hopefully they would have a future after this tiresome war ended. All he wanted was to be given the chance to make amends. If he was lucky enough to be given a second chance, he intended making the most of every second with her and Bobby.

He pushed his hand through his hair and shook his head, frustrated that the two people he loved most were imprisoned at the mercy of the damn Nazis. And all because he hadn't thought to tell her earlier that he had broken things off with his fiancée. Richard didn't think anyone could feel as much regret as he did now.

Chapter Thirty-Nine

HELEN

Christmas Eve 1942

Helen covered her ears, desperate to block out the din coming from her aunt's home. It had been going on for hours now and if she heard them singing 'O Tannenbaum' one more time she was certain she would lose her mind and bang on the wall dividing them.

O Tannenbaum, O Tannenbaum,
Wie treu sind deine Blätter!
Du grünst nicht nur zur Sommerzeit…

She gritted her teeth and held her pillow across her mouth, screaming into it as loudly as she dared without waking Bobby. As if this Christmas wasn't awful enough, being the first without her aunt. It was also the first when she and Bobby were in hiding, and just like his birthday a few days before, she didn't have any presents for him. What two-year-old doesn't receive presents? she mused miserably. She tried to remind herself that there was little she could do about any of it. At least he was too young to have any memories of previous Christmases and what they were like, she reasoned.

She gazed at his angelic face, eyelids moving as he dreamed about something. Poor little boy, Helen thought. What experiences did he have to give him anything to dream about? It wasn't fair that such a vibrant child, any child, should be cooped up in a house month after month having to keep quiet most of the time.

She had taken to keeping the curtains open as soon as it was daylight, not closing them until dusk, determined that he should have as much sun on his skin as possible. It wasn't healthy being inside all the time, but what could she do?

Helen rested her head on her arm. Noticing her skin was wet she realised she was crying. She missed Aunt Sylvia terribly. It felt as if she had last spoken to her only the previous day, but at the same time the past few months had been interminable.

'I can't do this,' she sobbed. 'It's too difficult.' Bobby stirred, snuggling back against her stomach. She cuddled him, breathing in his scent and calming slightly. She could go on. She had no choice but to do so. Bobby deserved the best life she could give him and although their circumstances were less than perfect, it was all they had.

Another chorus of cheers rang out in the night air from the officers next door. 'I'm glad you're having a fun Christmas,' she murmured sarcastically. Then, hearing a voice she thought she recognised, she silently got out of bed, ensuring Bobby's shoulders were covered with their blankets so that he didn't get cold and wake up. She crept to the window and opened it, needing to be certain.

Another drunken voice shouted something, several people laughed, then she heard the voice and her heart plummeted. 'Hauptmann Wilhelm Schneider,' she whispered, shuddering as she pictured the formidable man. How unfair was it that he was billeted in her aunt's home? She needed to tell the others to keep an eye out for him, she decided, recalling the way he had studied her with his piercing, unnerving gaze that first time she had met him at Villa Millbrook.

'Mama,' Bobby's voice interrupted her thoughts.

'Yes, poppet?' She quickly closed the window so they couldn't be heard and went to him. She kissed his cheek. He didn't stir and she realised he was talking in his sleep.

Sleep. It was what she needed right now. Time away from her reality of grief, restriction and longing to be living a different life somewhere else. She gave a shuddering breath and closed her eyes, willing her mind to settle enough for her to drift off.

Helen was woken an hour later having dreamt that the Hauptmann had broken into the attic through the window. Unsettled by the memory, she sat up trying to calm her breathing. She thought of the German soldier who was pestering Peggy and wondered if it might be him. She hoped not. If while she was downstairs someone came unexpectedly to the house, someone who knew that there were supposed to be only three women living there, she might avoid being caught, but not if that person was the Hauptmann. He would recognise her immediately, she had no doubt about that.

Troubled by her thoughts, Helen concentrated on breathing

in slowly, then exhaling, several times, hoping to calm her racing pulse before lying down and trying to get back to sleep.

She was woken a few hours later by Bobby pulling her nose. Her eyes flicked open, and she made a face at him, taking his hand and gently removing it. 'Ouch.'

Bobby giggled and, getting up from their mattress on the floor, ran across the room to his toys, seeming very happy.

It was Christmas Day. Helen wondered how many more they would be forced to celebrate in this way, and hoped not many. 'No,' she said, determined to make the most of her day, regardless of how different it was for her this year. Like the Hamels would no doubt do, she would put on a brave face and at least try to appear happy even if she felt like sobbing into her pillow. It's what her aunt would have wanted, that much she did know.

'Come along, Bobby,' she said. 'Let's wash and dress so that we're ready for when Babs comes to give us the all-clear.'

He clapped his hands together, no doubt because of the excitement in her voice rather than understanding what she had said. Seeing his reaction made her determined to give him the best Christmas she possibly could.

Chapter Forty

PEGGY

Babs was upstairs letting Helen know it was safe to come down for lunch. They had decided to eat early and agreed that only Bobby would have breakfast today, to help stretch their rations. Peggy went through to the living room to light a fire as a treat to cheer them up. As she entered she smiled to see the hard work her mother and sister had done the previous evening putting up Christmas decorations.

They had used the ones they had put up every year for as long as she could remember. The familiar scene cheered her slightly. The pine cones she and Babs had collected many years before when walking with their parents up at Noirmont were her favourites. Her mother had given her and Babs paints and glitter to decorate the cones There had initially been eight but only four remained today and, although most of the glitter had been rubbed off over the years, they had pride of place on the mantelpiece.

There was no real tree this year but a small handmade one

standing on a side table. She walked over to it and on closer inspection saw that it used a triangular cushion that she vaguely recalled seeing amongst all the junk in the attic before they had tidied it up for Helen and Bobby. Pins were inserted into the material, holding coloured glass baubles against it. It was imaginative and pretty and made Peggy smile.

'What do you think?' her mother asked behind her.

Peggy turned, her arms outstretched. 'It's inspired, Mum. I always love seeing those.' She pointed to the pinecones. 'And I think we should always have this as our Christmas tree.'

The smile on Ida's face slipped slightly. 'I'm hoping this is the one and only year we don't have a real tree.'

Peggy hoped for the same thing but having picked up Allied news – until private radios had been confiscated in mid-June – she doubted it. Until then the news had been grim and seemed to worsen with each passing day. It would take a miracle for the war to end in the next twelve months, but Peggy had no intention of dampening her mother's spirits by saying so.

She spotted their tatty angel made of a ping-pong ball with a face drawn on it, strands of yellow wool for her hair and a body made of a cardboard tube covered in slightly torn crepe paper. They had used the same one for a long time, and although her father used to moan about it whenever it was brought out, none of them had the heart to throw it away. She was about to remind her mother about their father when there was a knock at the front door.

'Who can that be?' her mother asked clasping her hands together.

Seeing Ida's panicked expression, Peggy rubbed her upper arm. 'It's fine, Mum. You stay here and I'll go and see.'

She opened the door expecting to see one of their neighbours and instead saw the captain standing stiffly waiting to speak to her. She noticed he was holding a bottle of wine in his right hand. He looked uncomfortable but determined as he raised the bottle and held it out to her.

'For your family.'

Why was he bothering her this way? she wondered, wishing his attention could be paid elsewhere. 'I can't accept this, Captain. You must know that.'

'I do not understand.'

Not wishing to antagonise him, she changed the subject. 'Your English has improved.' She decided a few visits ago to try and discourage him by whatever means she could, including not conversing with him in German. If he was living in Jersey and wished to speak to her then he could speak English. It seemed that he had taken note and had been practising the language.

He smiled at her proudly. 'I am happy you think this is so.'

How was she going to make him leave? She knew it would be good manners to invite him inside but she had already noticed someone she recognised vaguely, walking along the opposite pavement, who kept looking in her direction, no doubt wondering why there was a German officer on her doorstep talking to her and holding out a gift.

'Who's that you're talking to, Peggy?' her mother asked from the hallway.

Peggy suspected her mother knew full well who it was and was trying to get rid of him. The door opened further, and her mother came and stood next to her, her arms crossed over her chest. 'Oh, it's you again, Captain. We heard your celebrations last night.'

His eyes turned finally from Peggy as he cleared his throat. 'I hope we do not…' He struggled to find the words.

'Interrupt our sleep?' Ida snapped. 'You did, as a matter of fact, but I suppose it is Christmas.'

He lifted his gaze from the floor to Ida. 'I am sorry for this, Frau Hamel. I shall report to my *Kameraden*. It will not happen again.'

Not happen again? Peggy gave her mother a sideways glance, staggered that her petite mother had shamed this tall, imposing officer. Unsure what to say next, she kept quiet, enjoying her mother's control of the situation and seeing a hint of the woman she had been before she had retreated into herself, trying not to be noticed by the Germans.

'Was there something you wanted, Captain?' Ida asked pleasantly.

He hesitated then held out the bottle towards her. 'I wish for you to have this. It is French wine,' he added as if knowing that her mother might either refuse a bottle of German wine or take it and pour it down the sink.

Her mother thought for a moment then took the wine. 'If this is by way of an apology for last night, then I shall accept it.'

Peggy held her breath. Her mother was pushing her luck now, she thought anxiously. But when she looked at the captain's face, instead of seeming angry with her, there was a fondness in his expression that took her by surprise.

'I wish you a good Christmas,' he said. Then added, 'Mrs Hamel, forgive me, but you remind me of my mother.' Without another word, he clicked his heels together, gave them a curt nod, turned and walked down the steps, then up the steps on the other side of the metal handrail and into number 2.

Ida pulled Peggy backwards into the house and closed the front door. Neither spoke for a few seconds.

'Mum, what were you thinking, speaking to him like that?' Peggy didn't know whether to be impressed or concerned.

Her mother shrugged. 'He didn't seem to take offence. Anyway, they did keep us awake last night and it's not right.'

'Maybe not, but you really shouldn't do that again. Who knows how he might react next time?'

'Are you insinuating I was impertinent?' Ida asked with an amused glint in her eyes.

Worried that her mother might get into trouble if she continued to act this way, Peggy grimaced. 'I wouldn't put it quite like that, but we both know it's not the way these soldiers expect to be addressed.' She placed a hand on her mother's shoulder. 'I couldn't bear it if something happened to you.'

She hadn't meant to worry her mother, only to try to warn her before she confronted the wrong officer, who might take umbrage and retaliate in a less friendly way.

'Don't worry, lovey. I enjoyed that exchange, but I'm not silly enough to try it a second time. I saw the shock in his face before he thought of his mother. He's probably still a bit hungover from last night, and even I know his reactions could be different if he was in a less convivial mood.'

Relieved, Peggy smiled. 'That's good to hear. Now, let me have a look at that wine. I think we're going to enjoy drinking it while we toast our absent friends.' She couldn't bear to mention her father, aware that it might be too much for her mother when she was doing her best to make sure they had the best Christmas possible.

'That's a wonderful idea, Peggy. We'll do that.'

They had only been in the kitchen for a few minutes,

looking at the unappetising meat that was to be their Christmas lunch, when there was another knock on the door.

'For pity's sake.' Ida pushed the sleeves of her cardigan up to her elbows and went to leave the kitchen. Horrified to think her mother might be about to do something reckless, despite her protestations a few minutes before, Peggy grabbed her arm.

'No, Mum. Let me get this.'

They stared at each other for a moment before her mother relented. 'Fine. You go but don't get drawn into another conversation with that man.'

Drained by the thought of yet another awkward conversation on their doorstep, Peggy braced herself before opening the front door. Her forced greeting died on her lips when she saw Tony standing there holding something wrapped in newspaper.

'May I come in?' he asked eagerly.

Peggy immediately stepped back and ushered him inside, closing the door behind him. 'Of course. I wasn't expecting you.' She leant forward and kissed him lightly on his lips. She looked at the item he was holding. 'What's that?'

'A chicken.'

'A real one?' Babs asked, running downstairs to join them. 'For us?'

'Yes.' Tony laughed. 'A real one. It's fresh, too, and I'm hoping you'll accept it for your Christmas meal.'

'We haven't had such a treat for ages.' Babs pressed her hands to her cheeks. 'This is so kind of you.'

'I also have a small gift under my arm for you, Peggy, if you want to take it,' he said, turning sideways to her so she could remove the brown paper bag with something soft inside. 'It's not much but my mother knitted it when I said I wanted to give you something to keep you warm.'

'That's kind of her.' Peggy was about to have a look inside when her mother interrupted.

'Bring that chicken through to the kitchen, will you, son?' She led the way while Peggy took out a pretty red and blue knitted hat with matching scarf and gloves. 'The wool is lovely and soft. Please thank your mother for me,' she said, following them into the kitchen.

'She'll be thrilled you like them.'

She could tell by the look on his face that it meant a lot to him that she liked his gift. 'I have a little something for you. I'll just fetch it.' She ran through to the living room where she had left his gift and returned to the kitchen and handed it to him. 'It's only a book that I found in the attic and thought you might like it. Don't worry if you don't.'

He took the book out of the newspaper wrapping and beamed at it. 'Thank you,' he said, smiling as he looked at the detective novel she recalled him saying he wanted to read. 'I look forward to reading this.'

'I'm pleased.'

'Well, I can't wait to have lunch, now that I know we're going to be treated to something delicious,' Babs said.

'Me, too.' Ida motioned for them all to leave the kitchen. 'Why don't you join the girls in the living room?' she suggested to Tony.

'I'm afraid I can't stop for more than a couple of minutes,' he said. 'My parents are expecting me home soon.'

'That's a shame.' Ida held up the bottle for him to see. 'Do you have time to join us for a glass of wine?'

'French? Where did you get that?'

Ida tapped the side of her nose. 'Ask no questions and I'll tell you no lies.'

'This is turning out to be a far better day than I expected,' Babs said before glancing up at the ceiling.

Peggy realised she was asking if it was safe to let Helen join them. 'Yes, it's all right for them to come down now.'

'This is so exciting,' Babs enthused, immediately running back upstairs to fetch their friends.

Helen walked into the room holding Bobby's hand. 'Merry Christmas, everyone.'

'Tony's brought us a chicken,' Babs announced.

Helen beamed at him. 'Did you hear that, Bobby? That's so kind of you.'

'I hope you enjoy it.' He stood. 'I'd better dash. Mum will be expecting me for our Christmas meal, and she'll never forgive me if I'm late.'

'But where did you get it from?' Ida asked.

He tapped the side of his nose, a wide grin on his face. 'Don't ask me questions and I won't have to lie to you, Mrs Hamel.'

'You didn't pinch this from somewhere, I hope?'

Peggy knew her mother was teasing but saw by the look of shock on Tony's face that he didn't realise it.

'It was one of Dad's clients, a farmer who gave him the chicken in payment for helping his family.'

Peggy hated to think they were taking good food from Tony's family. 'But why are you giving it to us?'

He smiled. 'Because another patient gave him a goose and that's what we're having for our lunch. I thought it greedy for us to enjoy both so I asked if I could bring the chicken to you. Dad was thrilled to give your family something for Christmas.'

She thought of her boss and what a kind-hearted man he was. 'I'm so lucky to work for your father, Tony. Please thank him from us, and your mother, too. We're very grateful and it will make all the difference to our day.'

'It certainly will,' Ida assured him.

Chapter Forty-One

HELEN

That evening Helen helped Babs with the washing up while Ida and Peggy watched over Bobby as he played on the floor with the teddy Ida had made for him out of an old felt skirt and stockings for stuffing. The day had been far better than she had expected, thanks to Bobby receiving a present and the delicious meal provided by Tony's family. She didn't recall her stomach feeling this comfortably full for months now and it was such a treat.

'It wasn't such a bad Christmas, all things considered,' Babs said, placing a clean wet plate onto the wooden drainer for Helen to dry.

Helen agreed. 'It cheered me up watching Bobby eat so well and he had so much fun. I worry that he isn't getting enough nutritious food, but today helped.'

She wondered why Babs had stopped washing crockery and turned her head to look at her. She was surprised to find her friend studying her. 'What is it?'

'You seem a little down today.' Babs shook her head. 'Or

rather troubled. Yes, that's what it is. Has something happened?'

'I wasn't sure whether to mention it.'

Babs placed her hands on her hips. 'Go on. Tell me.'

Helen explained about the Hauptmann making her feel uncomfortable at Villa Millbrook and hearing his voice coming from her aunt's house the previous night. 'There's something vicious about him,' she said thoughtfully. 'You can see it in his eyes. I don't mind admitting it shook me up.'

'I'm not surprised.' Babs rested a wet hand on Helen's forearm. She gave a sharp intake of breath. 'You don't think he's the one who's taken to calling on Peggy?' she asked. 'I was hoping he was more annoying than dangerous. Do you know his name?'

Helen thought for a moment. 'I do. He's called Hauptmann Schneider.' She shuddered. Then, continuing with the drying up, she added, 'Try not to worry too much.'

'I'll try not to, but we'll let Mum and Peggy know what's happened, and we'll all be more vigilant about keeping you and Bobby out of sight.'

Helen thanked her but wasn't very reassured. The thought of spending even more time stuck in the attic was wearing. She was beginning to feel like a discarded ragdoll that rarely saw the light of day. She gave herself a mental shake. Feeling sorry for herself wasn't going to get her anywhere.

They finished their chores and took cups of weak tea through to Ida and Peggy. Helen wondered how many times the tea leaves had been reused. She was glad not to need milk any longer, now that there was so little to share among them.

'Helen has something to tell you both,' Babs announced, after picking up Bobby's teddy and pretending to make it walk along the floor before handing it back to the giggling child. She took a seat next to Helen on the small two-seater sofa that had seen better days.

'Go on, lovey,' Ida said.

Ida and Peggy listened intently as Helen explained about recognising one of the voices the previous night. 'He has black hair and a deep scar on his right cheek from here to here,' she told them, running a fingertip from the right side of her mouth almost to her right ear. 'Does that sound like the same man who comes to see you, Peggy?'

Peggy shook her head. 'No. Anyway the soldier pestering me is called Captain Heinrich Engel.'

Helen closed her eyes with relief. 'I'm glad about that. Although knowing Hauptmann Schneider is living next door is worrying.'

'Do you recognise any of the others?' Peggy asked, leaning forward and resting her elbows on her knees.

Helen sighed. 'Unfortunately, I do. His name is Leutnant Klaus Müller. He has fair hair and seems rather gentle, if a little creepy. I think he's lonely rather than dangerous, though, unlike Hauptmann Schneider. They're often together for some reason and both spent time at Villa Millbrook.'

'I have to admit it unnerves me having them next door.' Peggy thought for a moment. 'What was the leutnant like with you? I mean, how did you find him?'

Helen thought back to the hard-boiled egg and meat he had given to her. 'He was kind. In fact, he went out of his way to give me food to bring home for Aunt Sylvia.' Helen felt the colour rise in her cheeks, hoping they didn't jump to the wrong conclusion. 'He had intended it for Bobby but obviously had no idea he couldn't eat it. I think he's quite young, and inexperienced about life.'

'Hmm.' Peggy nodded. 'Good to know he wasn't troubling you. And what about the Hauptmann?'

Helen groaned. 'I just always felt there was some sort of underlying threat in whatever he said. It was never anything I could put my finger on, more how he leered at me and blocked my way so that I had no choice but to listen to what he wanted to say.' She thought back to the other times she had seen him in the dining room. 'I was always anxious in his presence, even when he didn't speak to me.'

'Pop some more wood on the fire, will you Peggy?' Ida asked. 'I think we need to be extra careful with them next door. We won't be able to pretend you're one of my daughters, Helen, not if they already know you.' She frowned. 'It's rotten luck having them living at Sylvia's.'

Helen couldn't agree more. 'I'm sorry to add to your worries,' she said feeling a lump constricting her throat. 'You're all so kind and I've been an endless source of trouble for you all. Maybe I should let Tony find me somewhere else to move to?'

'You'll do nothing of the sort,' Ida snapped, glaring at her. 'And I'll have no more of that talk. You'll both stay here where I can watch over you for Sylvia. I've told you before we're glad to be able to take care of you, and I meant it.'

Helen didn't know how much longer she could stand the weight of her guilt, putting these gracious women's lives at risk. Maybe she should take it upon herself to speak to Tony when he next came to the house? If she got the chance to talk to him alone, which she doubted would happen.

Chapter Forty-Two

PEGGY

March 1943

M arch arrived with little ceremony and overcast weather. Peggy would have welcomed sunshine to brighten the days, but the thought of 1943 being as bad as the previous year was depressing. She thought back over the previous twelve months. Little had improved; in fact quite the opposite. From what she heard islanders saying, there wasn't much to be cheerful about as far as the Allied forces were concerned, either. Morale on the island had been at an all-time low since the deportations the previous September.

Peggy discovered from her boss that there had been a massive bombing raid on Berlin by the British and US forces on the first of the month with heavy casualties. She hated to think of innocent people being killed regardless of which side they were on, but seeing less exuberance in the German soldiers on the island did make her feel slightly encouraged that maybe the year might not be all that bad after all.

Hope was what they needed, and this had given them a taste of it. They just needed more. Much more.

She sat in Advocate Le Gresley's office with her pencil and notepad waiting for him to dictate a couple of letters, but he seemed more thoughtful than usual.

'Is everything all right, Advocate Le Gresley?' she asked.

He sighed. 'I'm concerned about the increasing shortage of food and now medicines. I've also noticed the petty crime on the island, too. There seems to be so much more of it now and it worries me.' He shrugged. 'I understand the frustration people are dealing with, and the desperation for medicine in some cases, but stealing from others, especially Nazis, really isn't the answer. All it will do is bring bigger trouble to our doorsteps.'

'It will.' Peggy wished there was something she could do about it, and said so.

'We all probably feel that way, Peggy,' he said. 'I know I do. Tony, his mother and I were talking about this only the other night and saying how much luckier we are to have a garden and somewhere to grow a few extra vegetables than those without an outside space.' He gave an apologetic grimace. Peggy realised it must have shown on her face that she wished she was one of those with a garden. 'I don't mean to speak out of turn.'

'You didn't. Although I would love to have somewhere to grow things. Even a window box.' She thought of Helen and Bobby and how much it could brighten their day to see something colourful on their windowsill.

His expression changed and he seemed rather pleased with himself. 'Leave it with me. I'll ask Tony to help me make a couple for you. I'm sure we have some wood somewhere and we certainly have soil to plant them up. I'll be certain to let you have seeds, too.'

Peggy saw his shoulders relax slightly and was glad he seemed more cheerful. 'It's very kind of you. My mother and sister, and…' she hesitated, stopping herself just in time from adding Helen's name '…me, of course, will be very grateful. It will be exciting to be able to grow a few things for ourselves.'

'I'm glad to help in any way I can.' He stopped pacing and sat at his desk. 'I find watching plants grow gives me hope somehow.'

'I can see why.' Peggy couldn't wait to go home and tell the rest of her household that they could soon expect to be able to plant some vegetables of their own. It would be a new experience for little Bobby, and would give him and Helen something to do.

'Shall we begin?' he asked smiling.

It took Peggy a moment to realise he was talking about the dictation.

'Yes, of course.'

Chapter Forty-Three

HELEN

April 1943

'Come and see how they're doing,' Helen said, leading Peggy, Babs and Ida up to the attic, with Bobby on her hip. He had a wide grin on his cherubic face. 'Bobby's been helping me water them a little each day. Haven't you, Bobby?'

He nodded over her shoulder at the three women she had come to love like sisters and an adoptive mother. It was a joy to be able to give them something to smile about. The success of her tiny patch of vegetables in the two window boxes they kept up in the attic had given them all a fresh interest.

Helen was taking charge of one of the window boxes and Bobby the other, though really Helen was doing most of the work. He might only be two and a half, but he was used to being part of an older household. It troubled her sometimes how he might cope when the war ended and he had to mix with children his own age for the first time.

The boxes stood on the wooden floorboards in the place

where they received most sunlight. 'Here we are,' Helen said. 'Show them, Bobby.'

'Cawwots, beans and—' He looked up at her. 'What's this one, Mummy?'

They had attached lengths of wool to tiny hooks on the back of the box and looped them over tacks they had driven into the wall. Helen saw that one of them had come undone. A shoot from one of the beans had fallen over, and she carefully strung it up again. 'It's beans. There, that's better.'

'They're doing ever so well,' Ida said, ruffling Bobby's hair. 'You're a clever boy.'

'I am,' he announced proudly, making them laugh. Helen wished there were more moments like this. 'It was very kind of Tony to do this for us.'

'It was his father's idea,' Peggy reminded them. 'I think he enjoyed making up the boxes.'

Babs sighed happily. 'It's like having our own tiny gardens.'

'I agree.' Peggy reached down and brushed the tips of her fingers over the tiny fronds which Helen hoped meant carrots were growing underneath.

Bobby took her hand and moved it away. 'Not to touch.'

Peggy widened her eyes at Helen. 'Sorry, I wasn't thinking.'

Helen wished they had more things for Bobby to do. He was a placid child, rarely naughty. She wondered if it was because he was naturally well-behaved or just that he hadn't any experience of running around in a park or on the beach. The thought saddened her.

'What's wrong?' Ida whispered, drawing Helen back so that they were standing away from the others. 'If you're worried about the little one, try not to be.'

'I was,' she admitted, glad to share her concerns with the

older woman. 'What if this time hidden away affects him when he's older?'

Ida stared at her for a second. 'Now you listen to me, lovey. There's little point in you worrying when there's nothing you can do to change your circumstances, is there?'

Helen supposed not. 'But—'

'But nothing. All we can do is make the most of what we have. Worrying about things beyond our control leads to madness.'

'You're right,' Helen conceded. She heard Peggy gasp. 'What's the matter?'

'Did you hear that?'

They looked at each other. Ida, Helen and Babs shook their heads.

'What did you think you heard?' Ida asked anxiously, her voice low.

Helen noticed the pallor of Peggy's face. 'What?'

'Shush.' Peggy held up her hand. 'There it is again.'

Helen heard it that time.

'There's someone at the door,' Babs hissed looking as terrified as her sister. 'And by the sound of that banging, it isn't friendly.'

Helen's breath caught in her throat. Panic coursed through her and she grabbed Bobby as Ida hurried out of the room.

'You'd better hide,' Peggy insisted before following her mother. 'Stay up here, Babs, until they're hidden, then go to your room and pretend to be reading.'

'Will do,' Babs replied before hurrying over to pull back the pile of boxes and old chairs blocking the hidden door in the eaves. 'Quickly, get in.'

'Mummy?' Bobby's eyes filled with tears, their recent

excitement gone. He was frightened and seeing fear in his sweet face devastated Helen.

She ushered him into the small space. 'Come and sit on Mummy's lap,' she said, wishing they had practised hiding in here before now to help it seem less traumatic. He sat facing her, his arms wrapped around her neck and legs around her waist. She pulled the door closed with the neat little handle Tony had fixed inside when he had come to check on Peggy's handiwork.

'Scared, Mummy.'

'Don't be,' she whispered. 'Cuddle Mummy and don't be frightened. Close your eyes and pretend we're in a fort.'

'A fort?'

'Shush, you must be very quiet.' She held him closer to her chest. 'Yes, this is our fort. It'll keep us safe.'

'From Nasties?'

'Nasties?' What did he mean?

'The men?'

Two and a half and he knew far more about their circumstances than she would have liked. 'Do you mean Nazis?' she whispered, keeping her voice as low as possible.

'Yes, Mummy. Nasties.'

Helen flinched. He must have overheard her speaking to the other women despite the four of them taking care not to let him hear anything that might worry him. She sighed miserably. 'Yes, we're hiding but it's not scary, it's fun.'

She wasn't sure he believed her, but if he was safe that was all that mattered.

Her bottom was becoming numb, and Helen decided that if they weren't discovered today she would be sure to make their hidey-hole far more comfortable. There wasn't space to lie down, only to sit cross-legged. Bobby would be able to lie across her if he fell asleep, which Helen now realised would be preferable if they had to be here for any length of time.

Hearing heavy footsteps coming up the stairs, she concentrated on not tensing and frightening Bobby.

'Will you at least tell us what you're looking for?' she heard Peggy ask. 'This isn't right, coming in here unannounced.'

The man laughed, a mocking noise that she sensed would infuriate her friend. Not that she would let herself show her disdain for him. Peggy was far too professional for that.

'We have every right, Miss Hamel.'

It was the Hauptmann's voice. Damn him, Helen thought. Of all people to come searching for her and Bobby. Even Leutnant Müller would be better. He, at least, had some compassion.

The footsteps neared. 'What is up there?'

'It's just a messy attic,' she heard Peggy insist.

'Open it.'

Helen heard the all too familiar jackboots stamping on each of the wooden steps and wondered if he wanted her to hear him coming, wanted to increase her fear as much as possible. The atmosphere in the attic changed. He was in there with them. Helen raised her hand ready to cover Bobby's mouth in case he made a sound.

The footsteps made their way, ominously slowly, around the room. Helen listened as chairs were dragged out of the way, then a couple of old trunks. He was near. Too near. She was relieved they had always rolled up the mattress and put it away in one of the trunks each morning, just in case this very thing happened. It was tiresome having to hide all traces of herself and Bobby each day, but clearly Peggy had been right to insist they do it.

'You have vegetables growing?'

'The sun comes in up here and we thought it a good place to grow them,' Peggy explained. She had told Helen once that the most important thing was to have a believable answer for any question that might be asked. Helen wondered if her friend had always been this wise or had learnt things from working for the advocate these past few years.

A kick against one of the panels behind her made her jump. She covered Bobby's mouth and bit her lower lip to stop crying out. Her eyes had become accustomed to the darkness now and she could make out her son's tightly closed eyes. She kissed him lightly on his cheek, barely daring to breathe.

'Vot is in here?' He kicked the panel further back from her.

'It's the eaves. There's nothing in there.'

'No cupboards?'

Peggy must have shaken her head. 'Not enough room for them,' she replied. 'My father must have boarded them up years ago. I don't think I've ever seen behind there.'

No one spoke for a few seconds and Helen worried she might pass out from fear.

She heard another familiar voice. 'Hauptmann, we must leave now.'

The Hauptmann shouted his reply, clearly angry to have been disturbed by Leutnant Müller. She held her breath, willing him to leave, and almost collapsed with relief when she heard his footsteps stamping down the stairs and someone, possibly Peggy, slamming the attic door. Helen sensed Peggy was indicating that she and Bobby were alone and could relax.

'Are the Nasties gone?' Bobby whispered so quietly it was barely a breath.

'I think so, but we won't go out until Babs or Peggy lets us know for sure.'

He hugged her tightly. 'Love you, Mummy.'

'I love you, too, sweetheart. You were very brave and Mummy is very proud of you.'

Helen's knees were aching from sitting still for so long and she hoped one of the girls would come and give them the all-clear soon. It was a struggle not to fidget but she didn't want to give Bobby any reason to move so she fought her instincts and remained still.

A few minutes later, the attic door opened and lighter footsteps walked across the floorboards towards their hiding place. Trunks were moved again, and the small door pressed to let the catch open. Light shone in, making Bobby press his face against Helen's cardigan. Helen shaded her eyes from the sudden brightness.

'They've gone?' she asked, realising instantly that it was a silly question and noticing for the first time how cold she was.

'They have. I've never been so pleased to see an officer before as I was when Leutnant Müller appeared. The Hauptmann was very close to finding you both at one point.'

'I heard him and thought he was going to break the boarding and discover us sitting here.'

Peggy reached out and lifted Bobby from Helen's arms, then put him down and held out her hand to help Helen to her feet.

She stood up slowly, groaning at the ache in her numb bottom and knees.

'Uncomfortable?' Peggy winced sympathetically.

'Very, and cold. I'm going to spend the next few days arranging cushions and putting a blanket in there and maybe a small torch, if you have one spare.'

'Good idea. Maybe keep a flask of water in there, too, and a couple of biscuits in case you're hiding for longer next time.'

Helen agreed, hoping there wouldn't be another time, but realised that this was probably the first of many. She didn't relish the prospect of repeating her recent experience but it was part of her life now and there was little she could do about it, if she was determined to keep them free. Or as free as they could be, hiding in an attic.

Chapter Forty-Four

PEGGY

1 May 1943

Peggy loved Saturdays and was looking forward to this one especially because it was her birthday. She had told her mother, sister and Helen that the only present she wanted was to have a calm, pleasant day with no visits from the Nasties, as they had now taken to calling their next-door neighbours.

The only visitor she wanted today was Tony. She looked at her watch, happy to know he would be arriving in the next couple of minutes.

She brushed her hair. It needed a trim as it was now below her shoulders and too long for her liking. She wished she had thought to ask Babs to cut it the previous evening but it was too late now, and in any case her sister was working her Saturday shift. She would ask her later.

She went to the living-room window and saw Tony crossing the road. He looked up at her and beamed when she waved. Excited to see him, Peggy ran to the hall and pulled open the front door before he had a chance to knock, just as she heard the door close at number 2, and Captain Engel's voice calling to her.

'Good morning, Miss Hamel,' he said with a quick tilt of his head. He spotted Tony and she could see by the change in his expression that he recognised him from work. Now he would know there was something between them, Peggy thought.

'Good morning, Advocate,' the captain said.

'Good morning,' Tony replied politely.

Peggy wasn't sure if Tony could place him, but she could tell by his set expression that he sensed something was not quite right.

'Shall we go in?' Peggy said trying to keep her tone light. 'Goodbye, Captain,' she said with a half-smile before shutting the front door. She closed her eyes and gathered herself for a moment.

'I know where I've seen him before,' Tony said quietly as they heard the soldier's footsteps passing her home. 'Didn't he come to deliver documents to you once?'

'A few times, unfortunately.'

'Does he make you feel uncomfortable? If you like I could arrange for the documents to be left at reception and brought up to you.'

Peggy loved him wanting to protect her. 'He's always behaved like a gentleman,' she admitted.

'What does Captain Engel talk to you about?'

'That's the thing. Nothing much. I think he just likes talking to me. It's always when I'm in,' she added thoughtfully. 'Mum said he's never called while I'm out. I've never invited him in and he's never seemed fazed by the lack of an invitation.' She remembered one of his remarks. 'He did mention that Mum reminded him of his mother. He's probably just homesick.'

'Maybe.'

She realised he didn't know about the attic being searched and Helen and Bobby almost being discovered. She told him what had happened.

He narrowed his eyes. 'I sense there's something else worrying you.'

'I was thinking about another officer who could be a problem. Hauptmann Schneider,' she explained. 'Helen recognised his voice when her window was open one evening and she heard him talking in Sylvia's house. She knew him from the where she used to work. Thankfully a Leutnant she also knew from there came in and distracted the Hauptmann and saved her and Bobby from being found when Hauptmann Schneider searched the attic. Unfortunately now we're aware they would both recognise Helen, we know we can never pass her off as being my sister if either of them returns while she's downstairs.'

'Hmm, that's not good.' He thought for a moment. 'I can't see what can be done about it unless Helen and Bobby move to another safe house.'

Peggy sensed she wasn't going to like what he was about to say. 'Go on. I can tell you've had an idea.'

'Only that I'm happy to find somewhere for them to move to and will make arrangements if Helen is worried about being here with them next door.'

'I'll keep that in mind. I know she was unsettled by them coming so suddenly, but I don't think she's ready to move. We're being extra vigilant.'

'I'm glad. You know I'll always be here for you, Peggy.' He

pulled her into his arms and kissed her. 'Please don't hesitate to ask me anything. If I don't have an answer, I'll do my best to find one.'

'I will.'

He cupped her cheeks in his hands and gazed into her eyes. 'Happy birthday, my sweet Peggy.'

She studied his handsome face, his dark eyes full of love. She didn't think she could love him more as she wrapped her arms around him and kissed him again.

'Would you like my gift now, or after our walk?'

Peggy pulled him into the living room, sat him down on the sofa and sat next to him. 'I'd like it now, please.'

Tony laughed. He put his hand into his pocket without taking his eyes off her and took out a rectangular flat package wrapped in newspaper and tied with string. 'Sorry about the unexciting wrapping.'

She took it from him and ran her hands over it. 'What is it?'

He pulled a face. 'Maybe you should open it and find out. I hope you like it. I had no idea what to buy you and there's so little in the shops.'

She carefully untied the string, wrapping it around two fingers neatly before setting it down on the small table at the end of the sofa. Then, unfolding the newspaper which she planned to use to start the fire in the living room later, she unwrapped the present lying in her lap. It was an oak photo frame with daisies engraved on it. Inside was a photo of the two of them. 'So that's why your father insisted on taking a photo of the pair of us. How kind he is.' She beamed at Tony. 'I couldn't love it more.' Or you, she thought.

The photograph had been taken by his father the month before when she was invited to spend the afternoon at their home. Peggy had been surprised so see her boss with a camera, Only people with a permit were allowed to use them.

'That was such a lovely afternoon.' She kissed his cheek, then studied the photo again. 'Did you ask him to take this especially?'

'Yes.' He raised his eyebrows. 'He was reluctant at first but when I told him it was for your birthday, he insisted that if anyone asks about it, we say it was taken in '39.' He sighed. 'If you ever take the photo out of the frame you'll see Dad has written that date on the back in pencil in case anyone ever checks.'

'How typical of your father to think of everything,' she said, impressed but not surprised. 'Don't worry, I'll remember.'

She carried the frame over to the mantelpiece. 'I'll leave it here until we come back then I'll take it up to my room. I can't believe I'll have you with me all the time now.'

He kissed her check. 'I asked him to make a print for me, too, for that very reason.'

Peggy giggled. 'What, so you have a photo of yourself?'

He tickled her making her squeal in protest. 'No. Right, shall we go for our walk now? It's such a lovely day.'

She glanced at the photo one more time before leading him to the hallway. As she straightened the permit hanging next to the front door – a document every household was required to have, declaring who was in the house in case of an inspection – her thoughts turned once again to Helen and Bobby, whose names were of course not on it.

'When this is all over, I'll be glad not to have one of these things reminding us that we're doing something illegal by giving our friends a home,' she said, trying to quell the anger she felt every time she saw it. Today was her birthday and she was going to do her best to enjoy it.

'You're not the only one,' Tony said, helping her on with her jacket and taking her hand. 'Let's go and enjoy some fresh air.'

As they passed number 2, out of the corner of her eye Peggy saw the curtains twitch. She didn't react, determined not to let whoever was spying on them know they had been spotted. She had thought having nosy neighbours was bad but that was nothing compared to being watched by Nazis.

They had walked most of the way to town when Tony's hand gripped hers more tightly.

'What is it?' Peggy asked, anxiously.

He was looking up at the sky, then pointed. 'A plane. My God,' he gasped. 'It's American. A bomber. Look.'

She followed the direction of his gaze. Then machine guns began firing. She shrieked and clung to Tony in fright.

'It's fine,' he said calmly, though there was excitement in his voice. 'Whoever the pilot is he's making a point to the Germans by flying that low.'

Anti-aircraft guns began pounding as the Germans tried to hit the plane. Peggy covered her ears to block out the noise, then noticed that the bomber was accompanied by two fighters.

Tony stepped backwards instinctively, pulling Peggy with him and holding her protectively as two bombs dropped from the plane and landed in the harbour. 'This is incredible.'

He sounded like a child on Christmas Day, clearly enjoying every moment.

The sound of the planes faded. 'Why weren't you frightened?' she asked, her heart pounding.

'It gives me hope, seeing things like that,' he said cheerfully. 'Confirms to me that we haven't been completely forgotten.' His smile slipped. 'Are you all right?'

'Just about,' she said, forcing a smile to reassure him.

They resumed their walk. 'Did you hear about the RAF planes that flew over the island at the beginning of the week?'

She shook her head. 'I heard the foghorn so I knew something was happening. They bombed German ships in the Channel, didn't they?'

'They did. Dad was ecstatic and I must admit to feeling the same way.'

Peggy was glad there had been some retaliation on their behalf but still didn't like to think of men being killed. Even enemy men. Not all of them were evil, she knew that much. She thought of Captain Engel. As much as it unnerved her to have him appearing on her doorstep every so often, she still wouldn't like to think of his mother having to grieve for him.

'What a birthday treat,' Tony said giving her hand a gentle squeeze. 'Maybe the Americans put on the display just for you.'

Peggy laughed. 'Somehow I doubt it.'

'But you don't know for certain,' he teased.

She nudged him, catching him off-guard and making him stumble. 'Sorry,' she laughed, biting her lower lip.

'You're a bit of a toughie on the quiet, aren't you, Peggy Hamel?'

'I certainly am.' She liked to think she was strong, in determination, even if physically she wasn't as tough as most men would be. 'I'll always stand up for myself.'

'I think I've worked that out already,' he said, and grinned.

Chapter Forty-Five

HELEN

Helen continued to stare out of the window across St Aubin's Bay, still trembling from the roar of the huge plane that had appeared and flown off with two smaller ones a short time earlier. The sound had been tremendous and had initially scared Bobby, so she had lifted him up and held him high enough to be able to see the planes for himself.

Lowering him to his feet again, she crouched so she was level with him. 'Wasn't that exciting?'

'We saw big planes, Mummy.' He spread his arms as wide as they would go. 'They were that big.'

'Bigger, even,' she said. 'And they were here to let us know we will be all right, weren't they?' She had no idea what they had flown over for, but wanted to make sure Bobby hadn't been frightened by the incident. Who knew if more might fly over soon? If one large and two small planes were that loud, she could only imagine how noisy several might be.

She pictured Richard. He would have definitely signed up but she had no idea where, or in which force. Was he flying bombers, too? She hoped he was safe wherever he might be stationed. Her positive mood vanished. How was she going to get word to him that she no longer lived at number 2? She desperately needed to hear from him, from anyone outside the island. This claustrophobic feeling of living in a bubble could be made more bearable if she received word from someone outside it. If only she could go out and send her own telegram. She could send one to her parents, maybe.

'Mummy, water?' Bobby was holding up the small, tin watering can Ida had found for him somewhere. He knew he needed to ask before pouring water over the plants.

'Yes, good idea.' She watched her little boy taking care not to pour too much and wondered if he was behaving like other children his age. She only had an older brother and no cousins and didn't have any experience of toddlers. Not wishing to fall into another guilt-ridden mood, Helen decided she needed to find something, a hobby maybe, to keep her mind busy. She had little to write about when their days had no variation, and she was hopeless at knitting or sewing.

Helen noticed Bobby's trousers were above his ankles. Not that anyone outside their tiny circle would see him but that didn't mean she should let her standards slip. She thought of Ida and how she enjoyed spending her evenings knitting or sewing. Helen decided that if she was going to keep her son in clothes, she should ask Ida to teach her how to do these things.

Helen thought of all the things the two of them needed and, impatient to start, rummaged through the trunk holding their clothes. She took out a sweater of Bobby's that was now too small for him and sat down to unravel it. If she was going to ask for Ida's help, she needed materials for them to work with.

As she pulled gently at the wool, winding it round her left

hand, her thoughts returned to Richard and how to send a message to him. She would speak to Peggy later and ask if she had any ideas. Yes, she decided, feeling slightly more settled, that's what she would do.

Later that evening she sat with the family in the living room. Tony had been invited, and to ensure he was home for curfew they ate their meal earlier than usual. She gave Peggy the birthday card she had made for her, and Bobby had drawn what could have been almost anything, but which she suspected might be a flower.

'This is beautiful, thank you.' Peggy beamed at them both and ruffled Bobby's hair.

'I wish we had something to give you,' Helen admitted, hating not being able to shop for her good friend.

'There's no need. All I want is for everyone to be safe. There's nothing more important to me.'

'That reminds me,' Ida said happily. 'I received this from the Red Cross today.'

They all looked at the flimsy telegram with the now familiar Red Cross logo printed onto it.

'Is it from your cousin?' Babs asked, excitement in her voice.

Helen had seen photos of their cousin, who Babs had said had left Jersey to join the Royal Navy as soon as war was declared. She wondered how he must feel, unable to come home on leave.

'It is.' Ida proudly read the telegram. 'He's a good lad. His parents would have been proud of him if they were still with us.' She wiped a tear from her eye.

Fit, well and missing you all. Hope all coping and safe. To be

married. Know you will love Wendy. Hugs and love to all,
Martin

Ida held up the telegram. 'I'd like to meet this Wendy of his.' She frowned. 'It comes to something when your nephew gets married and you can't be there to witness such an important event in his life.'

Helen saw Peggy and Babs exchange looks.

'Yes, Mum,' Babs said, going to sit on the arm of her chair. 'But we now know he's healthy and in love and that although he doesn't have us nearby, he does have someone.'

Peggy nodded. 'He sounds happy.'

Ida stared at the telegram. 'You're right. That's the most important thing to remember. Martin is well and happy. We'll meet his Wendy after this is all over, won't we?'

'I'm sure we will, Mum,' Peggy agreed.

Helen wondered if now was the right time to mention her telegram dilemma. 'I hope you don't mind me asking for your help about something?'

Four faces turned to her expectantly. 'What is it?' Tony asked. 'Please let me know if there's anything I can do.'

'I'm not sure.'

'Why don't you go ahead and tell us what's on your mind,' Peggy suggested.

Helen told her about the telegram she had sent to Richard. 'I was upset when he didn't reply then I realised that if he did send me one he would have addressed it to number 2. And obviously there's no way I can go there and ask if they've received one.'

Peggy groaned. 'And we can hardly go and ask on your

behalf, either. Not if we don't want them to know you're here. What a shame.'

'There must be something we can do,' Babs said, resting an arm on the back of her mother's chair.

'I could send one to him,' Tony suggested.

Helen was grateful for the offer but couldn't see how that might work. 'But he won't know who you are, and you only have twenty-five words to get your message across.'

Tony shifted slightly in his seat and rubbed his chin as he gave the matter some thought. His face brightened after a few seconds. 'I know. You can tell me the name of his school, or where he worked. Something familiar. He'll see it's come from Jersey and will be able to work out that you're unable to send it for some reason. The difficulty is going to be saying all you need me to.'

She wasn't sure it would work. 'Maybe I should leave it for now.'

'I think you should try. There's no point in delaying something during wartime, Helen,' he added, his voice gentle.

Helen wasn't sure what difference it would make if the chances of Richard receiving the telegram were already slim.

Tony continued, 'My point is that we never know from one week to the next what new changes or restrictions these Jerries will enforce. Who knows, they might find a way to stop us receiving or sending telegrams next. And imagine how you'll feel if you leave it too late to send one.'

Helen hated to think that might happen and knew her aunt would have given her the same advice. 'I can tell you're a lawyer,' she said smiling. 'You make a very good argument. Thank you. I will take you up on your offer.'

'I think you've made the right decision,' Peggy said. 'Now

all we need to do is work out what to say to convey the message in the best way.'

Helen was relieved when Tony read through the final draft of her message and promised to send it to Richard first thing on Monday morning.

'Read it to us one more time,' Peggy suggested. 'Just in case we notice something missing.'

Helen lifted her notepad and began reading to herself.

Our friends next-door well. Send best. Missing loved ones and waiting for news. Hoping all fine. Please respond soonest to Ida Hamel. Your schoolfriend, Tony

She reread it aloud. Ida's knitting needles clicked away as she nodded her approval. 'I can't see what else you might say.' She looked over at Helen. 'And you think Richard will work this out, do you?'

'He'll have to, Mum.' Babs patted her mother's shoulder.

'He will,' Peggy said. 'It's not as if we can mention little Bobby, when there's not supposed to be a child living here.'

Helen was relieved Richard would receive something. 'Thank you so much, Tony. It's very kind of you to do this for me.'

He shook his head and took the piece of paper from her as soon as she tore it out of the pad. He slipped it into his trouser pocket. 'I'll burn this as soon as I'm done with it.' He indicated the scraps of paper with discarded messages that she had torn out of the pad. 'Those should go in the fire. You don't want anyone finding them if they decide to inspect this place again.'

He was right. She bent to retrieve the pieces she had dropped onto the floor and threw them into the small fire, watching them flare up and burn into ash. 'Now I just need to wait and hope Richard replies.'

'This has been such a lovely birthday,' Peggy said, leaning back in her seat. I'm sure you'll hear from him soon. We must keep hoping for the best, it's the only way we're going to survive this mess.'

She was right, and Helen decided that from now on she would do her best to be positive.

Chapter Forty-Six

RICHARD

June 1943

I t had been months and still no news from Helen. He was almost certain she would have tried to reply and he wondered what could have happened to stop her. He hated imagining her and Bobby being stuck on the island with no hope of escape. If only there was something he could do about it. Maybe he could try and find out if raids were being planned and volunteer to go. Almost as soon as he had the thought, he realised it was impossible. What chance did he have of finding out about anything secret? He wasn't in a position to know much at all, he reasoned miserably.

If only he knew they were still alive. He had heard about deportations from the island the previous year and it terrified him to think that Helen and Bobby might now be held in a squalid German camp. Just knowing they were somewhere on the island would be better than nothing.

He was on leave, staying at his mother's home for the first time in months. It felt strange being back here in the neat,1930s terraced house, with paper crosses stuck onto the windows and blackout blinds put up each evening.

It was his final day before returning to his ship and Richard was in the kitchen peeling the couple of potatoes his mother had managed to buy for their supper when the doorbell rang.

'I'll get it,' his mother shouted, immediately going to the front door.

'Who is it, Mum?' he asked. Sensing something had happened, he stopped what he was doing and waited for her to reply.

Her footsteps came towards the kitchen. She stood at the door holding up an envelope with the Red Cross emblem on it. His heart raced as he dared hope it might be from Helen. 'Is that for me?'

She frowned and held it out to him. 'It is. But it's from a Tony Le Gresley. Unusual name.'

His excitement instantly evaporated. Not from Helen then. The disappointment felt like a punch to his gut. 'Tony Le Gresley?' He had never heard of him.

'Who is he, son?'

'I've no idea.' He opened the envelope and read.

Our friends next-door well. Send best. Missing loved ones and waiting for news. Hoping all fine. Please respond soonest to Ida Hamel. Your schoolfriend, Tony

He read the words several times. It didn't make any sense. Who was this guy and why was he pretending to be an old schoolfriend? Who was Ida Hamel? Could the telegram have been mixed up with someone else's?

He reread it another few times. Then it dawned on him. 'The message is in a kind of code.' He laughed, excited and relieved.

'Why would it be in code?' his mother asked, picking up a tea towel and drying a plate.

'Because they have to be careful on the island.' When she shook her head in confusion, he added. 'The Germans, Mum?'

'I see.'

He wasn't sure she did, but the explanation satisfied her.

Richard sat at the small kitchen table and studied the message trying to work out exactly what it was meant to convey. 'Our friends', he presumed, must be Helen and Bobby. Ida Hamel? He thought he recognised the name. Maybe he had heard Helen mentioning the Hamels in the past? He supposed she might have done if they were her aunt Sylvia's next-door neighbours. Next door. That was it: he needed to address his reply to Ida Hamel who lived next door.

But which side? Did the Hamels live at number 1 or number 3? Richard rubbed his throbbing temples lightly. He had no way of knowing and would have to take a chance, hoping that whoever delivered the telegram would hand it to the addressee regardless of whether he used the correct house number or not. If she didn't reply then he would address his next telegram to the house on the other side of number 2.

Richard's heart seemed to skip a beat as it dawned on him what must have happened. 'This chap has contacted me on Helen's behalf,' he said, needing to say it out loud. He felt rather than saw his mother stiffen, but was in no mood to hear what she thought of his situation with the woman he loved. 'That must have been what's happened.'

'It all sounds very complicated to me.'

'I've been sending messages to her aunt's home, but she's moved to the house next door by the looks of things.' Anxious to work out why, he looked at his mother. 'I wonder why she moved, though.' Sensing it must have been something serious, he hoped nothing too dreadful had happened to her aunt. Helen adored her. She had reminisced about summer holidays staying with her Aunt Sylvia many times.

He felt his mother's hand on his sleeved arm. 'I'm happy for you, son. Now you can contact her and let her know you're all right.'

'I'm going to do it right now,' he said, patting his trouser pocket to check he had his wallet on him. 'Sorry to run off like this, Mum. I'll try not to be too long.'

She pushed him gently towards the door. 'You take all the time you need. I'm relieved to see you looking cheerful again.'

He rushed out into the street, his mind racing as he thought over the message he had just received. They were alive and, he hoped, well. Now he had a way to contact her thanks to this Tony chap, which must also mean Helen wanted to hear from him. Richard didn't think he could be happier.

He wished he had time to think of a perfect response, but having seen the date Tony had sent his telegram, Richard realised it had taken the best part of a couple of months to reach him. He wanted to reply immediately so that Helen heard from him as soon as possible, certain that hearing from him was more important than his actual message. He just hoped it wouldn't take too long to reach her.

As he hurried to the telegraph office all he could think of

was what might have happened if the telegram had arrived the following day, after he had returned to base. Forcing himself not to dwell on what might have been, he struggled to come up with the most eloquent way to show his love for Helen and Bobby in a message that would be received by a supposed schoolfriend.

Chapter Forty-Seven

HELEN

3 September 1943

Helen lay on her mattress resting her head on one hand as she watched Bobby colouring in the book Babs had found for him. She didn't think she could be more miserable. She still hadn't heard back from Richard, the attic was airless and muggy, despite the window being wide open, and today marked the first day of their fifth year at war. Even the Great War only lasted four years, she thought, covering her mouth so Bobby couldn't hear her sobs.

She wasn't sure how much longer she could keep living in this purgatory. Even people in prison had a break walking around a yard outside for an hour, or so she believed. All she and Bobby had to look forward to was going downstairs for a couple of hours.

The thought of not being able even to step outside was driving her mad. An hour outside. Just one. Surely that wasn't too much to ask? She wiped her eyes with the backs of her hands. Unfortunately, it was too big a risk to take with the soldiers living next door. If they weren't there then maybe she could take a brief walk when darkness fell, but in summer, when it didn't become dark much before nine o'clock, she wouldn't have much time to go anywhere and be back inside before the eleven o'clock curfew. Maybe she could persuade the sisters to let her borrow Babs's coat and hat so she could join Peggy for a walk some winter evenings when it was darker.

She decided she would broach the subject that evening. She needed something to look forward to, because it didn't look like there was much else in her life to give her hope.

There was a gentle tug at her sleeve and she opened her eyes to see Bobby holding his colouring book near her face. She took it from him and sat up, impressed with his attempt to keep most of the colouring between the lines of the farm animals printed on the page.

'Clever boy,' she said, putting the book down and clapping, sad to think he had never seen a cow, or even a dog close up.

Bobby jumped up and down and gave her a cheeky smile. If only that was all it took to cheer her up. She might feel endlessly guilty about him being stuck in the house but it helped that it didn't seem to faze him. 'Does Mummy's clever boy want to give her a hug?'

He stepped into her arms, wrapping his own tightly around her neck and making her laugh. He might spend his life within the walls of the house, but he was certainly strong. Another thing she should be grateful for, she decided.

'Shall we look out of the window and see what birds we

can find?' He nodded. 'Remember, we must whisper.' She lowered her voice to remind him how quiet he must be. 'We don't want the Nasties to hear us, do we?'

His eyes widened and he shook his head. 'No, Mummy.'

She lifted him and sat him on the wide window ledge, taking care to hold onto him. They both enjoyed these times each day, when they watched for birds. Helen reminded herself that she might be stuck up in the attic most of the time but at least she had a changing view of the sea in St Aubin's Bay. She wasn't sure which view she preferred: like this, with the sea so calm it was almost mirror-like, reflecting the azure of the sky, or on stormier days. Stormy days had always been her aunt's favourite. One summer day, when Helen and her family were holidaying with her, Sylvia had come to Helen's room and pointed out of the window at the view. It wasn't as clear as this because they were a floor below, but Helen could still see the sea. On this particularly dismal day, her aunt had commented that the sea was the colour of her favourite jade ornament.

Helen thought of the small jade netsuke her aunt had treasured and wondered what might have happened to it. If only she hadn't been in such a rush she might have thought to bring it with her to number 3. She sighed cross with herself for not picking it up when she was packing her aunt's precious things. Maybe it would still be in the house after all this was over, she thought, doubting it but hoping for the best.

Bobby's small hands rested on her cheeks and turned her face towards him.

'Mummy, are you crying?' he whispered, his eyes welling with unshed tears.

She forced a smile, angry with herself for letting her emotions get the better of her when she needed to stay strong for him. 'No,' she whispered. 'Mummy was thinking, but not of bad things.' She spotted a bird and was glad of the distraction. 'Look, Bobby, there's one.'

He forgot his concerns and immediately pressed his palms together with excitement. 'Birds, Mummy. In the sky.'

Hearing voices coming from her aunt's house, Helen put a finger to her lips, then lifted Bobby from the windowsill and lowered him quietly to the floor. She pulled the windows closed, careful not to make a sound. She hated having to shut out what breeze there was, especially on a day as warm as this one, but had little choice. She kissed the top of Bobby's head, thinking how good he was not to make any fuss.

'Shall we have your afternoon nap?' she asked. She should have put their mattress and bedding away when they got up that morning but had little energy to do much these days.

He looked at her as if he was trying to make up his mind then went to join her, and they both lay down on the mattress.

'If you close your eyes, Mummy will tell you a story.' She wasn't sure what to tell him but watched as his eyelids fluttered shut, a smile on his sweet face. She loved him so much her heart ached. She took a long, deep breath. He was the most precious child and all she needed in her life. So what if she was stuck in this room? She had Bobby with her, and they were safe. They wouldn't always be here, she was sure of it.

She gazed at him and made a silent promise that when they escaped the confines of the house once and for all, she would make up for all the times they had missed running on the beach, playing in the woods or with kites, swimming in the sea. And if they couldn't do all the things she wanted them to do, she would help him imagine how it would feel to push his feet into warm sand and run into cool waves.

'Are you ready for Mummy to begin?'

'Yes,' he whispered.

'This is the story of a little boy called Bobby,' she began, and his cherubic lips drew back in a smile. 'And his first trip to the rock pools on a magical beach.'

Chapter Forty-Eight

PEGGY

Peggy finished her final translation, removed the two sheets of paper with carbon paper between them and placed them neatly on her desk. She rubbed the muscles on either side of her neck. She wasn't sure if it was the heat in the airless office or tension that caused her neck to ache so badly. Maybe it was knowing that they had completed four years of war. It was all too depressing.

Nothing seemed to be improving, only dragging endlessly on with more restrictions and tightening of rations. For the last couple of months there had been less bread for each person – and they were already struggling to have enough to eat, having committed to share what they had with Helen and Bobby.

Her office door opened and she heard someone come in. Before she looked up, Tony spoke. 'Want a massage?'

She smiled at him. 'Yes, please.' She rubbed her right shoulder. 'I'm all achy today, worse than usual.'

He walked around to stand behind her and began massaging her neck muscles. 'How's this? Too much?'

'No,' she groaned. 'Keep going. This is heavenly.'

'You sound a bit down,' he said, kissing her right shoulder. 'What's the matter? Other than the usual.'

She heard the smile in his voice. 'I was just pondering.'

'About anything in particular?'

'Just about how nothing ever seems to get better.'

His fingers worked on her muscles for a few more seconds before he stopped and moved in front of her to sit on the edge of the desk.

She looked up at him and saw a hint of – what? Amusement? 'Has something happened?'

He raised his eyebrows and nodded slowly. 'Two things.'

Two? When he didn't elaborate, she poked him in the chest. 'Well, tell me, then.'

'The first one is exciting for all of us.'

A feeling she wasn't used to flowed through her and it dawned on her that it must be excitement. She hadn't felt it for so long that she had almost forgotten how it felt. 'Go on.'

'The allies landed on the Italian mainland today.'

That could only be a good thing, that much she knew. 'Really?'

'Yes. The Canadian and British forces. It will hopefully lead to more good news in time.'

Her heart raced. 'That is exciting. I can't wait to tell them at home. We need something to hang on to right now. We're all struggling to remain upbeat, and I suspect Helen is finding it the most difficult. She's been very stoic and brave since losing her aunt, her home and, let's face it, her freedom, but the dark circles under her eyes are more apparent every week.'

'Then I think this might be exactly what she needs.' He slid his fingers into his trouser pocket and withdrew an envelope.

Peggy immediately recognised what it was. 'Please tell me that's from Richard?' She wasn't sure why she was whispering. Her office door was closed.

'It is.' He handed it to her. 'I've not read it, but it has his name there.' He pointed.

Peggy clasped it to her chest, closing her eyes, near to tears. 'This is the best news.'

'You don't know what it says yet.'

'No, but he's still alive if he can send a telegram, and he cares enough to reply.' She leapt up and flung her arms around Tony's neck. 'You're so clever to have thought of this. I know Helen is going to be over the moon. Thank you.' She kissed him again and again. 'Thank you so much, clever, clever Tony.'

He laughed. 'Hey, steady on.' He pulled her into his arms and kissed her slowly and Peggy lost herself in his love for her.

Hearing footsteps they leapt apart and, remembering she was holding the telegram, Peggy quickly pushed it into her pocket, not wishing anyone to see.

'It must be time to leave,' she said, hearing more footsteps coming down the stairs.

'I'll fetch my jacket and meet you downstairs. I'd like to see Helen's face when you hand her Richard's telegram.'

Chapter Forty-Nine

HELEN

Helen was surprised when Babs came to fetch her earlier than usual, insisting she join Peggy and Tony downstairs. She followed Bobby down the narrow attic staircase and down to the kitchen, where Peggy and Tony were sitting chatting to Ida as she filled the kettle.

Everyone seemed in high spirits for some reason, and she wondered what could have happened to cheer them up so much.

'Good afternoon, everyone,' she said as they all took it in turns to look at the toy Bobby was waving in the air.

She realised they were all staring at her; Peggy with a strange look on her face.

'You're all looking very cheerful,' she said, as Peggy took something from her pocket. It took a couple of seconds for Helen to see that it was a telegram.

'For me?' she whispered, hardly daring to believe what she was seeing. 'Is it from Richard?'

Tony nodded.

'It is, Helen,' Peggy said handing her the buff-coloured envelope and hugging her.

Ida stepped forward. 'There's this one, too.' She held it out for her.

Helen gasped, unable to take in that she had not one but two messages from Richard to read. 'But I don't understand.'

'I presume the one addressed to me,' Tony said, 'was in case you didn't receive the one he sent here.'

Babs started to cry. 'This is so romantic.'

'Hush, foolish girl,' Ida said. 'We don't know what they say yet.'

Helen stared at the envelopes in her trembling hands, unsure what to do for a moment. 'I hope you don't mind if I take these to the living room to read?' she said. She would prefer not to be watched while she read his words, at least for the first time.

'You do that, lovey.' Ida smiled. Then, addressing Babs, she said, 'The blackouts are up everywhere, I hope? I don't want those buggers next door walking past and spotting Helen in there.'

'Yes, Mum. No one can see inside.' She grinned at Helen. 'I'm ever so happy for you.'

'We all are,' Peggy agreed.

'Thank you. May I leave Bobby in here?'

'Yes, of course,' Peggy said with a laugh. 'Now go and see what he's got to say.'

As soon as she was in the living room, Helen closed the door. She took a deep breath to steady herself, determined not to cry, then read the twenty-five words Richard had written to Tony, wanting to save the one to her for last.

Thank you for excellent news. Missing all. Please send
fondest love to all. Am fit and well but longing to see
everyone. Your friend, Richard

Helen reread his message, conscious that Richard's
fingertips had touched this piece of paper. It was far more than
she had ever hoped for, or expected to need, especially from
the man she had promised never to bother with again.

She folded the piece of paper and slipped it neatly into its
envelope and set it down on the table next to her. Then, her
legs feeling like they might give way beneath her, she sat on
the nearest chair and took a steadying breath as she opened the
next envelope and unfolded the single sheet of paper it had
been holding.

Ecstatic to know you are both well. Missing you dreadfully.
Sorry for everything. Determined to make amends to you
both. Deepest love and hugs, Richard

Helen read it several times before flattening the telegram
against her chest and closing her eyes. 'Oh, Richard, why
didn't you let me know you weren't getting married before I
ran away?' she whispered. They could have been married by
now. Bobby wouldn't be hidden away and, she thought
tearfully, he'd have a father to spend time with and learn from.

She sat trying to absorb the sentiments Richard had
attempted to convey. Maybe things might be all right in the
end. Whenever that end might come. If they came. No, she
thought, angry with herself, this wasn't the time to overthink.
She needed to take the good things as they came and make the

most of them. Relish them. There were so few things to be excited about these days, and receiving these messages from Richard was like getting all her birthday and Christmas presents at the same time.

Chapter Fifty

PEGGY

December 1943

Another Christmas was on its way but, like everyone she knew, Peggy had little enthusiasm for it. What was there to be cheerful about? And it must be worse for poor Helen, not being able to go outside. Peggy could tell her friend was finding each day more difficult, despite the respite of receiving the two telegrams from Richard. That had been three months ago now, though. She wondered when another one might arrive.

She was looking forward to spending the day with Tony. They planned to walk to his parents' house and cycle to Grouville together to deliver a birthday present to his aunt. His mother had offered Peggy the use of her bicycle when Tony suggested she join him for the ride and she had been delighted to accept. She had something she wanted to talk to him about. She wasn't sure if it was a silly idea or not.

She arrived at his home and sat with his parents enjoying a

glass of water before they set off. She let Tony lead the way, glad she had wrapped up warm. The weather was much cooler lately and she wasn't sure if snow was on its way. As long as it didn't arrive while they were out, she would be happy.

'I think we could have chosen a better day to do this,' she said with a laugh as they rode along St Clement's Coast Road, his aunt's present wrapped in a cloth bag sitting in the basket attached to Peggy's handlebars. 'It would have been more fun in the summer.'

'Certainly would be,' he agreed, waving at a friend who was coming in the opposite direction.

Several German military cars passed them going towards the town and Peggy wondered if there would ever be a day when they could go out and not see these stark reminders of their unfortunate circumstances.

They arrived at Gorey Village in good time, no doubt because they were too cold to want to stop for a break.

'It's this way,' Tony said, getting off his bike in front of a sweet little cottage and wheeling it through the small gate before propping it up next to the front door. 'We don't have to stay long,' he said, lifting the gift out of Peggy's basket and giving her a quick peck on the lips.

Forgetting the cold and happy to be spending this time alone with the man she loved, Peggy said, 'It's fine. She's your aunt and it's her birthday. We'll stay for as long as you like.'

'I suppose you're right. She's a sweet lady, although she can be a little over the top sometimes.'

He knocked on the door and soon afterwards a woman who looked almost exactly like his mother but with grey hair opened the door and pulled Tony into a tight hug. 'It's marvellous to see you, young man.' She noticed Peggy standing behind him. 'And who is this pretty girl?' She let go of him and waved them inside. 'Come inside, it's perishing out there, and I'd rather not let the cold in.'

Peggy followed them into the living room, which was only slightly warmer than outside, and was glad she had raised her body temperature with the cycle ride.

Not wishing to use up any of his aunt's rations, they both insisted they were happy with a glass of water.

When they were seated in the pretty, floral living room, he passed the present to his aunt.

'This is for you. Mum said to make sure you open it when we're with you so that she knows for certain you like it. Apparently you'll know what it is.' He grinned. 'I'm interested to see it.'

'As am I,' his aunt said, placing the gift on her lap and slowly withdrawing it from the cotton bag. It was wrapped in brown paper and tied with string and Peggy noted how carefully she untied the string and paper and put them aside before looking at her gift.

Perched on the edge of their seats, Peggy and Tony exchanged amused looks, wishing his aunt would hurry up and let them see what his mother had given her.

'It's a wooden box,' Tony said, forced enthusiasm in his voice. 'How nice.'

It was a mahogany box, well polished and beautifully cared for, with exquisite mother-of-pearl inlay in a flower pattern on the top. Peggy didn't think she had ever seen anything quite so lovely. 'It's beautiful,' she said, fascinated.

'You have good taste,' his aunt said, then pursed her lips. 'It's more than a box, dear boy, as I think your friend already realises. Let me show you.'

They sat watching in silence as she made a production of slowly turning the box to face them then gradually lifted the lid.

'A sewing box,' Peggy said, delighted. 'My mum would love something that beautiful.'

'It was my grandmother's,' the older woman explained. 'I was away when she died and our mother gave it to your mother, Tony. She loves it but knew I'd always adored it and told me that one day she would pass it on to me.' She sighed and smiled at them. 'And now she has.' She sighed again. 'Please, wait here while I write her a thank-you note for you to give her, if you don't mind.'

'I'll be happy to take it, Aunty.'

Peggy was enjoying herself. It was a joy to watch someone as happy as his aunt was at that moment. But it reminded her of her friend's troubles and she was determined to speak to Tony and put forward her idea to help pull Helen out the rut she was sliding further into.

As they pushed their bikes through the village back to the main road, she decided to broach the subject. 'May I ask you something?'

He stopped walking, concern crossing his face. 'Of course, anything.'

'It's about Helen.'

'What about her?'

'I think we need to find a way for her to spend some time outside the house.'

He stared at her. 'You do?'

'Yes.' She saw the anxiety on his face. 'I know it's probably a silly idea.'

'It's a dangerous one,' he said. 'But I understand why you're suggesting it. I just can't think how to make it happen.'

Peggy had spent days devising different scenarios and trying to find one that had a chance of working. 'I thought we could try to do something with her hair so it resembles mine. Then, if I gave her my papers and she wore my clothes, you could come to the house and take her, and maybe Babs, out for a walk. Nothing too much. I just want her to have some freedom outside.'

He frowned and stared thoughtfully at her. 'Why not dress her in Babs's clothes? Why yours?'

Peggy took his hand in hers, aware he would rather spend time with her than her sister. 'Because Babs is very fair, whereas Helen's hair is auburn.'

'Yours is darker than hers.'

Peggy had expected him to use this argument. 'It is but in the dark it will be harder to notice the difference.'

'I suppose you're right.'

'I'm glad you agree with me.'

He nodded thoughtfully. 'I think it's a brave and clever idea. We must be careful not to be caught, though, especially by those two officers from next door. We can't risk them recognising her.'

She dreaded the thought. 'I know, and I can't deny I'm anxious about even suggesting this.' She rested her hand on his arm. 'I haven't mentioned anything to Helen yet, so I don't even know if she'll agree to go along with it, but I wanted to run it by you first.' She frowned. 'Especially as you will be accompanying them both, so you would be taking an enormous risk, too.'

'Sweetheart, I'll do whatever it takes to make you happy,

and if your sister and Helen are willing to give it a try, then I'm happy to accompany them.'

'I love that I can always rely on you.'

They mounted their bikes, and as they set off Peggy knew the easiest part of the plan had been completed. She still needed to approach Helen with her idea and, if she agreed, to arrange everything and hope for the best outcome. It was a risk, but in her eyes it was one that was worth taking.

Chapter Fifty-One

HELEN

The stormy weather that had blighted their days in October and November made Helen yearn for longer days and warmer nights. It was miserable not having blue sky to look out at for weeks on end. The rain had been depressing enough but now it was colder and she doubted her mood could sink any lower.

The only brightness in her day was her darling Bobby. It amazed her how he managed to stay content in his small world. If only she could do the same.

'Do you mind if I come and join you both for a bit?' Peggy asked from the doorway.

Helen was surprised to see her friend standing there. She must have been deep in thought not to have heard Peggy's footsteps on the creaky floorboards on the stairs up to the attic.

'Not at all,' she said, hoping to hear how her friend's cycle ride to Gorey had gone. 'Come and tell me everything.'

She opened the trunk and Peggy helped her pull out the mattress and bedding and set them down on the floor so they had somewhere comfortable to sit. Peggy was rubbing her arms to warm up so Helen picked up one of the blankets and handed it to her. 'You'd better wrap this around your shoulders, it's pretty chilly up here.'

'It's more than chilly,' Peggy said giving her a sympathetic look. 'I thought it was cold downstairs, but this is perishing.'

'Which is why Bobby is wearing three layers of clothes and the woolly hat your mum knitted for him – and also why we go to bed earlier when it's colder like this.'

'You sound down,' Peggy said. 'Not that I'm surprised with what you have to deal with each day.'

'I am a bit.' Not wanting her friend to think her ungrateful, she added. 'I always find the winters more difficult, although sunny winter days are fine.' She noticed Peggy studying her hands thoughtfully. 'Is something up?'

Her friend looked at her. 'I've had an idea but I'm not sure what you'll think about it.'

Intrigued, Helen widened her eyes. 'Well, are you going to tell me or keep it to yourself?' she teased, desperate to hear something interesting.

'You'll need to hear me out before deciding.'

Helen raised her hands. 'You have my undivided attention.'

She listened in stunned silence as Peggy explained her plan, excitement mounting with every word.

'What do you think?' Peggy asked when she had finished.

Helen wasn't sure. 'I want to go out, desperately. Although I can't help worrying that if I do and something happens, your family and Tony will be in terrible trouble. You could be imprisoned or even sent away. Tony in particular. He's already spent time in prison, and he's known to the authorities – and he's already been extremely kind to Bobby and me.'

'I know, and if I'm honest it worries me, too. However, it bothers me seeing you become more withdrawn, and it's not healthy for you to be stuck inside all day. It's not right. I'm sure that even if you only have one evening outside it will do you the world of good.'

Helen loved the idea of a change of scenery. 'Never mind an evening, an hour would be heavenly.' She pictured herself walking along the pavement, breathing in the night air, as most people had the freedom to do. 'But what if I'm caught and separated from Bobby? Who would look after him?' A sob caught in her throat at the prospect and her enthusiasm for the idea dissipated.

They turned to Bobby and watched him playing quietly.

'He's such a lovely child,' Peggy said quietly before addressing her again. 'I hope it goes without saying that Mum, Babs and I would always make sure Bobby was cared for. We love him almost as much as you do, and he feels like family to us. We would never allow anything to happen to him, I promise you that from the bottom of my heart.'

Helen reached out, took her friend's hand and gave it a squeeze. 'I know you would. You three are closer to me than my actual family now.'

She saw how her words touched Peggy, who wiped away a stray tear. 'Babs and I see you as a sister and Mum definitely sees Bobby as her grandchild.'

Reassured, Helen pictured her two friends. 'I could certainly pass as you from a distance,' she said. 'I might not be as dark-haired as you but I'm almost as tall.'

'And a similar shape,' Peggy said. 'Unlike Babs, who's several inches shorter and fairer like Mum.'

Helen watched Bobby for a little longer. Should she not rather remain in the safety of the house with him?

Peggy patted her knee. 'If you're worried about going out—'

'Am I being selfish wanting to do this when Bobby can't go anywhere?'

Peggy shook her head and frowned. 'No. He's sensitive to your feelings and if you're happy and content then he will be, too. Don't you think that if I've picked up on your sadness, he's bound to have, given that he's with you all the time?'

She had a point. 'Now you're making me feel guilty.'

'That's not what I meant. Anyway, you mustn't think that way. These are terrible times, especially for people in hiding. I think you should go out. It will give you something different to think about when you're stuck up here.'

'I'll do it,' Helen said, realising her longing to be outside was increasing by the second. 'Tell me what to do.'

'I'm so pleased.' Peggy stood up. 'And I know the others will be, too. I'll go and tell Tony and Babs now.'

'Now?' Helen asked, shocked at the immediacy. 'You mean he's waiting downstairs to go out tonight?'

Peggy shrugged. 'Why wait another day? It's freezing cold now that the sun has set and everyone will be wrapped up in hats and scarves. It will be easier to hide in all that clothing and far less likely that you'll be recognised.'

'I suppose you're right.' Her confidence waned slightly.

'You'll be out there and back in here before you know it.' Peggy thought for a moment 'Your accent is different to mine, so maybe try not to speak to anyone.' Helen nodded feeling her nerves getting the better of her. 'I'll go and speak to the others, and you follow me down with Bobby when you're

ready. Better put on a couple of layers now, and then I'll lend you my coat, boots and hat.' Peggy stopped at the door and raised a finger. 'And don't think about it too much.'

Half an hour later, Helen was waiting for Ida to open the front door, her heart racing so fast she wasn't sure she could make her legs work properly. Peggy's navy beret was pulled low over her hair and ears, and a thick woollen scarf wound around her neck covered her lower face. She looked down at Peggy's coat, wishing she had one as beautiful. Even her friend's boots were more comfortable than her own.

'You ready?' Babs asked coming to stand next to her.

'It's a bit slippery out there,' Tony warned, doing up his coat and putting on his hat. 'You'd better slip your arm through mine because that's what Peggy would do.'

She did as he asked, feeling a little awkward at first, but relaxing slightly when Peggy gave her an encouraging smile. 'I'll go into the kitchen and take Bobby, in case anyone comes past,' she said. 'It would ruin everything if either of us were seen.'

'Shall we go?' Tony asked.

Helen took a deep breath before exhaling slowly. 'Yes, let's do this.'

Ida smiled and opened the door. 'Off you go then, lovey. And remember, enjoy every moment.'

'I will, thank you.'

She stepped out onto the front steps and faltered as her courage began to fail. She hadn't been outside for so long and the shock of being exposed to danger hit her like a slap. 'I...I'm not sure I can do this.'

Babs followed them out. 'You have to. There's one of the officers near the window next door and if he sees you acting oddly, he'll suspect something.'

Helen took in a slow deep breath, closing her eyes briefly and remembering herself standing at her attic window each day, wishing she was outside like everyone else. Now she was.

'Let's go this way, shall we?' Tony suggested, leading her away from number 2 so they had their backs to anyone watching. He patted her hand that rested on his arm. 'You're doing well,' he said, leaning his head closer to hers and keeping his voice low.

As she walked, her discomfort lessened, and when Babs came up next to her and gave an excited squeak, Helen relaxed enough to laugh.

'Having fun yet?' Babs asked.

'I think so.' Helen was enjoying the cold night breeze brushing past her legs. 'This is wonderful.' She took care not to be over enthusiastic about gazing up at the stars. She could do that from inside her attic room. Instead she focused on taking in all the sights and smells she had missed while being in hiding for so many months. It was a joy to pass houses she recognised from her walks to and from work. How oblivious she had been then, unaware that the simple act of walking down the road could be taken from her for so long.

'Evening,' a man and his wife said, giving them a nod as they passed.

'Good evening,' Tony said, squeezing her arm to his side slightly when she didn't react.

Recalling Peggy's warning not to speak, Helen nodded feeling as if they could see straight through this act of hers. It occurred to her that this was the first time she had been addressed by anyone other than Tony or the Hamel family since going into hiding.

Most people they passed huddled into their clothes and kept to themselves, and when they walked all the way to Millbrook, Helen was shocked at how much her legs ached. It wasn't surprising that she was tired, she mused, realising how unfit she must be through lack of exercise and food.

'I hope your feet aren't becoming sore in Peggy's boots,' Babs whispered.

'I hadn't noticed if they were,' Helen said with a laugh. She didn't care about blisters. This was far too exciting and special to have it dampened by those little blighters.

'Good.'

'I thought we'd pop into the shop for something,' Tony suggested. 'Give us a reason to come this far. Would that be all right?'

Helen tensed, then, wanting to make the most of her outing, agreed. 'Good idea.'

'How do you feel?' Babs asked, her excitement clear in her voice.

'I'm loving every moment,' Helen assured them. 'Thank you both from the bottom of my heart. This is something I'll never forget.'

Tony patted her hand in reply.

Babs nudged her gently. 'Maybe it won't be too long until you're able to do this freely.'

Wouldn't that be nice, Helen thought, hoping her friend could be right.

Chapter Fifty-Two

PEGGY

P eggy leapt to her feet.

'What are you doing, lovey?' her mother said, frowning as she turned from chopping the few carrots she had managed to buy that day. 'Sit down and stop acting edgy. You're making me nervous.'

'Sorry, I thought I heard them coming back.'

'It was them rotters going out from next door.' Ida waved the knife at their small ration of French meat. 'If you need a distraction you can chop that lot up. I'm making a stew. There's not much else I can think to do with meat this stringy.' She pulled a face. 'I miss decent beef.'

So do I, Peggy thought. She disliked eating the only food they could buy now but knew she needed to force herself.

She found a sharp knife in the drawer and began cutting the meat into small pieces. As she worked she glanced at her mother and noticed how much weight she had lost over the past few months. She had grown up listening to her mother complaining about being too curvy for her liking, and how difficult she found it to lose those extra pounds. Peggy herself had taken in her own skirt waistband twice recently and she hadn't had any pounds to lose in the first place.

The front door closed. 'They're home,' she said, dropping the knife onto the chopping board and following her mother into the hall, relieved to have them back safely. She was eager to hear how Helen's venture had gone but refrained from asking until they had removed their outer clothes and hung them on the coat stand.

'Your cheeks are all flushed from the cold,' Peggy said, delighted by Helen's happy expression. 'Did you enjoy yourself?'

'It was incredible,' Helen gushed, clearly happier than she had been in months. 'How was Bobby while I was out? Did he ask for me?'

'He was fine,' Ida said, pointing up the stairs. 'Fell asleep down here about half an hour ago so Peggy took him up to his bed.'

'That's good.'

'Come through while I finish preparing supper and you can tell us all about it.'

'I'd better go,' Tony said. 'My mother will be wondering where I am.'

Peggy went to follow him out, but he pressed his hand against the door. 'No, it might look odd if you come out with me when we've only just returned.'

He had a point, she thought, anxious not to slip up.

'Babs, why don't we go through to the kitchen with your mum and leave Peggy and Tony to have a moment together.' Helen rubbed her hands together. 'Thank you both so much. This evening has been very special. It really is very kind of you, especially when I know you have both given up time you'd otherwise have spent together to do this for me.'

'It was my pleasure,' Tony said. 'I'd be happy to do it again whenever you like.'

'Yes,' Peggy agreed, stroking her friend's arm. 'I think we've all probably felt as much enjoyment as you have, being able to do this for you.'

Peggy watched Helen and Babs go into the kitchen and then stepped into Tony's arms. 'I'm so happy this worked,' she said. 'I don't think I'll ever meet anyone as kind as you.'

'Nonsense,' he said kissing her. 'It was your idea, don't forget.'

It was and she was glad it had occurred to her. 'I think this will make all the difference to Helen. At least she now knows she can go outside, if only occasionally.'

The following morning when Peggy entered the kitchen Helen was already there, cutting up a slice of toast for Bobby and chattering to him. It cheered Peggy to hear her friend sounding much happier than she had in months.

'Good morning,' Peggy said. 'How are you today?'

Helen smiled and Peggy noticed how bright her eyes looked, the dark circles less obvious.

'I slept more soundly than I've done since before the invasion. It must have been all that fresh air.'

'And exercise,' Babs said, bringing a pot of tea over to the table. 'It was fun to be out together, wasn't it?'

'It was. I really can't thank you all enough.'

Ida walked in from the scullery drying her hands on her

pinny. 'I think we're all more cheerful this morning. It was a good idea of yours, Peggy. Well done, love.'

'Thanks, Mum.'

They ate their breakfast of toast and a scraping of margarine, each lost in her own thoughts.

'I know you'll probably think me silly,' Helen said eventually. 'But I wish he could have a run around somewhere.' She sighed deeply. 'Don't get me wrong, I'm aware there's no way that could possibly happen.'

Peggy looked at the little boy. She realised her friend hadn't used his name so he wasn't aware they were talking about him. 'I must admit I'd love to see that, too.'

'Is there no way?' Babs gave Peggy a questioning look before turning to her mother.

'Don't look at me,' Ida said. 'Your sister's the clever one when it comes to making plans.'

Peggy didn't want to give Helen false hope after such a successful outing. 'I don't see how that can happen when we're not supposed to have a child in the house. We don't want nosy neighbours reporting us.'

'Yes, I've heard of some people grassing on people they know, to pay them back for silly grievances.' Babs scowled in disgust. 'We already have those neighbours at number 2 and they'd be delighted to catch us out.' She rolled her eyes. 'It is a shame, though.'

'It is,' Helen agreed. 'I shouldn't have said anything.' Her muscles still ached after walking so far, and that made her think about how Bobby was missing out on valuable exercise while his body was growing. She didn't know what she could do about it. She just hoped that it wouldn't have a lasting effect on her little boy.

Chapter Fifty-Three

HELEN

I t was just after seven-thirty a few evenings later when someone knocked on the door. Helen was sitting with the family after supper and the unexpected sound made them tense. They stared at each other for a second before Helen and Babs stood up.

'Quick, get upstairs,' Ida hissed at Helen. Then, pointing at Babs, she added, 'You answer the door but wait until the coast is clear.'

Helen quickly carried Bobby to the first landing and gave Babs a nod when she glanced up at her from the front door. She heard Babs speaking to Tony and then to a woman. She froze when she recognised the voice. Why was Mrs Edwards visiting Ida's home?

'Please, do come in,' Babs was saying.

Unsure what to do, Helen stayed where she was on the first floor, deciding it was safer to wait until one of the Hamels came to fetch her, as they usually did to let her know when it was safe to join them again. She heard Ida asking probing questions and smiled. Her fondness for the woman who had taken her and Bobby in was increasing all the time. If only her own mother had been as approachable and put others' needs before her own like Ida had done, then she wouldn't have felt compelled to run away and Bobby would be living in relative safety with her family in East London.

Hearing footsteps, Helen moved further back into the shadows.

'Helen,' Babs called to her quietly. 'Mum said for you to come down. You have a visitor.'

Unsettled by the unusual event, she smoothed down her skirt and pushed her fingers through her hair, wanting to look her best before going down. She entered the living room wondering why the woman who had employed her at Villa Millbrook had come to number 3.

'Mrs Edwards. How nice to see you.'

The housekeeper got to her feet and held out her hand. 'Hello, Helen. You're looking well.'

Helen knew she was much thinner than when they had worked together, but then so was everyone else. She noticed more lines around the housekeeper's eyes and streaks of grey in her neat hair and wondered what the upright but kind woman had gone through in the time since they had last met.

'It's lovely to see you,' Helen said honestly.

Ida motioned for them to sit.

'I'm sure you're surprised to see me here,' said Mrs Edwards.

'I am a bit,' Helen answered.

Mrs Edwards folded her hands in her lap. 'Tony came to see me,' she began. 'And I have a suggestion to put to you.'

Helen and Peggy swapped glances and Ida frowned suspiciously. 'And what might that be?'

Mrs Edwards gave her a tight smile before continuing. 'I have a bungalow, Mrs Hamel. It's up Mont Cochon, so not too far from here. It has a mature garden with lots of trees.' Her voice was gentle. 'Most importantly, I don't have neighbours close enough to overlook either house or garden.'

Helen heard Ida mumble something. She wasn't sure why Ida seemed unhappy with what Mrs Edwards was telling them. Come to that, she herself didn't know what Mrs Edwards was getting at. Then it dawned on her. 'You're inviting me and Bobby to stay with you?'

Mrs Edwards nodded. 'I am. I appreciate it might not suit you and it is only a suggestion. Tony is aware that I am alone and have space for two more people, also that my home is relatively private.'

'I didn't realise you knew each other,' Helen said surprised.

'It's a small island,' Mrs Edwards said. She breathed in deeply before exhaling slowly, then added, 'We met though my personal circumstances. You see, my mother lived with me until earlier this year when she passed away.'

'I'm so sorry,' Ida and Helen said at the same time.

'Thank you. Soon afterwards Tony delivered paperwork for his father, who has always looked after my mother's affairs, which is how we know each other.'

Helen couldn't think what to say. On the one hand she loved living with the Hamels. She sensed it must have been her comment about Bobby that had caused Peggy to speak to Tony, and then Tony to speak to Mrs Edwards. Whether she liked it or not, she needed to put her son's health first. She was going to have to be brave and not let the gratitude she felt towards the Hamels cause her to turn down this offer.

As if aware of her thoughts, Mrs Edwards said, 'Naturally you will all be welcome at my home at any time.'

Helen turned to Ida. 'What do you think?' she asked, wanting her to feel involved.

Ida stared at her silently for a few seconds. Then she lowered her gaze to her fingers. 'It's a generous offer. And –' she sighed, turning her attention back to Helen, '– although I haven't seen Mrs Edwards' home, it does sound exactly the right place for Bobby.'

Peggy gave Ida a surprised look. 'Tony wouldn't have approached Mrs Edwards if he hadn't thought it the best option.'

'I understand he's done what he thinks best,' Ida said, her tone resigned.

'But we'll miss you and Bobby,' Babs said miserably. She sat back in her chair and folded her arms. 'Ignore me, I'm being selfish,' she said when everyone looked at her. 'It is a good idea.'

Ida turned to Helen. 'We will all miss you and the little one,' she said. 'But this isn't about us. It's about what's best for the pair of you.' She wrung her hands. 'I've also been concerned that Leutnant Müller has come here a couple of times. I've worried that he might spot either one of you.'

'Don't you mean Captain Engel, Mum?' Peggy asked, looking stunned.

'No, dear. This was that younger one who came that time Hauptmann Shneider was here searching the attic.'

Helen couldn't understand why Ida hadn't told them before now. 'I never heard him.'

Ida raised her hands. 'I didn't like to worry you. You've all got more than enough to contend with and I wasn't going to add to your concerns.'

'But Mum, we need to know,' Peggy argued.

'Leutnant Müller?' Mrs Edwards turned to Helen and gave her a thoughtful look. 'He was at the house when you worked there, wasn't he?'

Helen nodded slowly. 'He was. He moved in next door when they took the place over after my aunt died. That was when the Hamels kindly took Bobby and me into their home.'

Mrs Edwards puffed out her cheeks. 'I always thought him a rather kindly young man, but there was something about him.'

'He's a Nazi,' Tony said.

'Tony, stop.' Peggy smiled, probably to soften her words, Helen supposed. 'I don't like him coming here for any reason.' She narrowed her eyes. 'There's more, isn't there, Mum?'

Ida hung her head. 'I'm afraid there is.'

Babs knelt at her mother's feet and took her clasped hands in hers. 'Tell us, Mum. What's been going on?'

'That other one, the nasty one. Hauptmann Schneider, he came once in the day when you girls were at work.'

Helen felt sick. He had been in the house while she and Bobby hid upstairs? What if they had made a noise when he was there? She swallowed bile as it rose in her throat. 'When?'

Ida turned to her. 'I didn't like to frighten you and I couldn't warn you. It was all so unexpected. Anyway, you're two flights up and you and Bobby are always quiet, walking in your stockinged feet.'

It was true, Helen thought, calming slightly. She was always careful not to drag one of the trunks across the floor during the day, and Bobby never wore shoes anymore, although that was mostly because he didn't possess any that fitted. Another thing her son went without.

'Why was he here?' Tony asked. 'Did he give a reason?'

Ida shrugged. 'I think it was to frighten me. He didn't stay long, or say much, just came into the house and through to the kitchen, had a look around and left.'

Helen had heard enough. 'We'll go,' she said, without giving Mrs Edwards' offer another thought. She might be slightly intimidated by the housekeeper, but clearly she and Bobby were in more danger than she had imagined. They needed to get away from the soldiers next door and not have to worry each time Bobby made a sound. Also, he needed to be able to play outside as any child should have the chance to do.

'Are you certain, Helen?' Mrs Edwards asked. 'Please don't feel obliged.'

'I don't,' she said honestly. 'I'm very grateful for your kind offer. Although I am slightly concerned that, as well-behaved as Bobby is now, he might become rowdier when he discovers your garden and is allowed to run around freely.'

The woman's face broke into a smile. 'I know I come across as rather staid.' Helen was about to argue, but she raised her hand to stop her. 'I'm aware how I appear to others. And to a certain extent that has been my aim, both to gain respect as housekeeper of an important house and because it helps keep people, especially soldiers, at arms' length.'

It made perfect sense to Helen. 'I can imagine why you'd want to do that. However, I worry that after living quietly with your mother, you might find Bobby more boisterous than you expect. I'd hate there to be any bad feeling between us.'

'Helen,' she said looking amused. 'I'm the youngest of six

children and the only girl. I've grown up with noisy, unruly boys.' She looked at Bobby. 'I think I'll be able to cope with this little one, so please don't worry on that score.'

Tony stood up. 'I'm afraid I'm going to have to accompany Mrs Edwards home now. I have somewhere I need to be straight afterwards. Can I assume a decision has been made?'

'You can,' Helen confirmed, avoiding looking at any of the Hamels. 'Please let me know when you want us.'

'That's settled, then. I have some ideas about how we might get you both to Mrs Edwards' house,' Tony said. 'I'll let you know more tomorrow.' He looked at the wall dividing their house from number 2. 'I don't think we have any time to lose, especially now we know that both officers have been back to the house. I'll let Peggy know what I need you to do in preparation.' He gave Ida an apologetic look. 'I'm afraid I think that we have little choice but to move Helen from here tomorrow night as soon as it's dark.'

No one answered. Helen couldn't imagine how Tony was going to slip Bobby away right under the Germans' noses. She would just have to trust he would manage it, somehow.

Chapter Fifty-Four

RICHARD

He hadn't heard anything from Tony for a while and presumed life must be getting more complicated for everyone on the island. If only he could be there with them. Deciding to let Helen know he was thinking about her and Bobby, he made the most of his brief leave and sent another telegram.

He forced himself to focus, aware he was addressing his message to Ida. If only he could share his feelings...but he needed to ensure that the message wouldn't seem suspicious if it was intercepted. He would make it seem as if he was addressing the entire Hamel family.

All well here. Sending Christmas wishes to you all. Hope to celebrate with you next year. Always in my thoughts and prayers. Sending love, Richard

As he strolled back to his mother's home Richard tried to picture how Bobby might look, saddened to think he had never met his own child, let alone hugged him. Was Bobby tall for his age, like he had been? He wished he had a photo of the pair of them.

He reminded himself that he wasn't the only one in this situation. How many other soldiers must have had children born after they were sent away? The most important thing to do was try to make contact and let them know they were in his thoughts and that as soon as he could he would come to them.

He smiled, imagining the day when he would be able to hold Helen in his arms again and cuddle his son. He vowed silently to spend the rest of his life making up for the trouble he had caused by his stupidity. He wasn't sure how, but he was determined he would find a way.

Chapter Fifty-Five

HELEN

Helen tried to remain calm as she listened to Peggy's instructions.

'Tony said to dress Bobby in as many of his clothes as you can manage. You must also take everything you'll need with you. Mum, Babs and I intend visiting you as much as possible and can always bring bits along with us, so no need to panic.'

'Thank you,' Helen said, wishing she could control her trembling fingers and button up Bobby's pyjamas more quickly.

'Here, let me,' Peggy said. 'You sit and try to calm down. You'll need all your energy when you go out with Tony. It's still cold out there and you have quite a walk ahead of you, some of it uphill.'

Helen ran through all the things she had packed into her small bag and Peggy's large coat pockets. 'I feel terrible taking your coat. How will you get it back?'

Peggy shrugged. 'Mum or Babs can fetch it for me. Or Tony. That's the least of our worries.' She finished doing up Bobby's pyjamas and put two sweaters over them, then pulled on his coat. 'There. You look very cosy in that lot,' she said, taking his woolly hat from Helen and putting it on his head. 'It won't be for long, Bobby.'

He went to stand in front of Helen. 'When are we going, Mummy?' he asked excitedly.

She had explained that they were going on an adventure and that he must be sure not to speak until they got to where they were going, in case the Nasties heard him. 'When Uncle Tony arrives. Remember, you must hold on to him tightly. He'll carry you all the way.'

Peggy knelt in front of him. 'There's no need to be frightened. Mummy and Uncle Tony want you to see how long you can stay very still and not speak. Do you think you can do that?'

He nodded slowly but Helen didn't miss the doubt on his sweet face. She reached out and pulled him into a cuddle. 'There's nothing to worry about, sweetheart,' she soothed. 'I'll be with you the whole time. I'll be walking next to Tony and will talk to him sometimes so you can hear my voice and know I'm with you. All right?'

Peggy kissed his cheek. 'Do you have your two best toys?'

He patted the pockets on either side of his jacket.

'Good boy,' she said. 'Babs, Nana Ida and I will bring your other things when we come to visit.'

He lurched forward and gave Peggy a hug, holding tightly around her neck. Helen saw tears spring to Peggy's eyes and knew how much the three women were going to miss having him in the house.

'Can I come back here?' he asked his lower lip quivering.

How strange was his life, Helen mused. He was going to

miss the place that had essentially been his prison since he was a toddler.

'If you want to, of course you can,' Peggy said kissing his cheek. 'But like Mummy said, you're both going on an adventure and we'll visit you very soon, so you mustn't worry.'

Helen heard distant voices followed by Babs's footsteps outside the attic.

'Tony's here,' Babs said. Her eyes were suspiciously red. 'He said to come down so you can leave as soon as possible.'

Helen had caught Ida blowing her nose earlier and was determined not to let her own emotions get the better of her. Her pulse raced. She had expected to have a little more time saying her goodbyes, but she didn't want to keep Tony waiting. He must be as nervous as she was.

When they joined Tony, Ida looked away and wiped her eyes, before turning back to them, a forced smile on her face. She patted Bobby's cheek and kissed Helen's. 'We'll see you both very soon,' she said, her voice cracking. She cleared her throat. 'I'd, er, better get back to the kitchen and wash those pots.'

Helen knew it was an excuse so she didn't have to watch them make their final arrangements and leave the house, possibly for the last time.

'Thanks for everything, Ida,' Helen said.

Ida turned away and waved her hand in the air, too emotional to speak.

'We need to hurry,' Tony said. 'I saw four of them going out as I was on my way here. The fewer of them in that house when we leave the better. Right, let's be having you, Bobby.'

He lifted her son and wrapped round him a sling-type

contraption he must have made for the purpose. 'This goes under your bottom,' he said as he manoeuvred it into place. 'That's right. Peggy, will you strap this behind my back and connect it to the straps over my shoulder? It'll help keep Bobby in place and hopefully won't be too uncomfortable for him.'

'It's a good thing it's cold out there,' Peggy said, doing as he asked.

'We probably couldn't get away with this if it wasn't,' he said. 'As it is I've borrowed my father's old tweed coat from when he was larger. I thought if I bulked up with a thick hat and my largest scarf it might hide Bobby better and just look as if I've wrapped up well.'

'It's a good idea,' Helen said, checking Bobby was comfortable. 'Good boy,' she said. 'Now remember, cuddle Tony and say nothing until Mummy asks you to.'

'Yes, Mummy.'

She was relieved he seemed excited rather than frightened, and hoped nothing would happen to change that.

Helen fastened Peggy's coat. She was wearing her own thinner one underneath. She tucked her hair under the scarf Peggy had loaned her, pulled on the hat and gloves and checked the coat pockets to make sure her toothbrush and personal items were there. Then, taking the larger handbag Ida had lent her for the occasion, she patted it. Inside were her most important belongings, including underwear and her aunt's photo.

'We'll keep your Aunt Sylvia's belongings safe here until we can get them to you.' Babs leant forward and kissed her on the cheek, wiping a tear from her own with the back of her hand. 'I wish we had longer to say goodbye.'

'There's no need for that, Babs. We'll be seeing them soon.'

Ida said. 'You'd better get going before those lot next door return. Good luck, all of you.'

'Thank you,' Helen said, her voice little more than a squeak.

'Open the door please, Peggy,' Tony said, leaning forward awkwardly and kissing her quickly. 'I'll come back with your ID card as soon as I've dropped Helen and Bobby with Mrs Edwards.'

'Thank you, but only do it if you possibly can. Don't take any risks on my account.'

Helen knew they were all taking risks using Peggy's identity card, and that she needed it in case she was stopped.

Peggy opened the door. Tony gave Helen a solemn nod and stepped forward. 'Let's get this over with.'

Chapter Fifty-Six

HELEN

Helen let Tony go first, then stepped outside and immediately noticed movement behind the curtains at number 2. Her step faltered. If it was Captain Engel she assumed he had watched Peggy enough to know how she walked. Would he realise it wasn't her with Tony now?

'Keep going,' Tony hissed through gritted teeth. She forced her feet to move and keep up with him and Bobby.

Tony took her hand, which calmed her slightly. She needed to pull herself together. Acting suspiciously in any way would draw attention to them. She felt short of breath but realised it was through fear rather than anything else.

'Keep your head down,' he said. 'No one will find that odd now it's snowing again. At least the weather's working in our favour tonight.'

Helen took a long, slow, steadying breath. She needed to dig deep and find the courage to get her son to safety. She focused on the garden she had yet to see and the thought of spending time in it each day with her little boy.

They passed quite a few people as they made their way towards First Tower. Helen was beginning to think it wasn't going to be such a difficult journey after all.

'We cross over here,' Tony said when they reached First Tower. He gave her hand a gentle squeeze, indicating the start to Mont Cochon, the hill on the opposite side of the road.

Helen walked next to him, wishing she could talk to Bobby, but kept quiet, suspecting that if she did he might become restless and want her to carry him. She knew she could do that for a while, but no longer. She simply wouldn't have the strength. Already her muscles felt tired, after less than ten minutes' walking.

The incline was gentle to start with but soon became steeper. Helen slipped several times, each time grabbing Tony's arm to regain her balance. When she did it for the third time and made him almost lose his footing, she realised she needed to be more careful if she wasn't to make him fall over on top of Bobby. 'I'm sorry. I'm not used to walking on such a slippery surface.'

'It's fine. We'll go more slowly. It's my fault for wanting to hurry and reach the house.'

She heard the fear in his voice and realised he was as frightened as her. 'You're incredibly brave doing this for us,' she said, taking care to keep her voice low, even though there was no one around that she could see.

'I'm only doing what's right.' He took her hand again and helped her along.

'I hadn't realised it would be this icy,' she said by way of apology. 'Or that I'd be this clumsy.'

They continued walking, slower now, their progress hampered by her breathlessness.

'Would you like to stop for a while?'

Helen would have loved to but daren't waste any time. 'No, let's keep going. I'm just unfit, that's all.'

They walked on in silence and the next time Helen slipped she grabbed hold of a tree root on the bank next to her. She was glad Tony had thought to bring a torch.

'I hadn't realised this was where we were going,' she admitted. 'I don't think I've ever been up this way.' She tried to imagine where they were.'

'We're on Ruelle Vaucluse.'

She was none the wiser. 'It's certainly rural here.'

'Which will be much better than living next door to those soldiers.'

He was right. Once she and Bobby were at Mrs Edwards', all this would be behind her. 'I'm not sure how Ida will make it up this way,' she said. She hadn't meant to voice her thoughts.

'It's much easier in better weather and in daylight.'

'I suppose so.' She tapped his arm lightly. 'Everything all right in there?'

'Sleeping, I suspect,' Tony said when Bobby didn't answer.

She hoped he was. She would hate to think of Bobby being anywhere near as frightened as she was at that moment.

'What's that?' Tony hissed.

Helen tensed. 'What?'

'It's a military engine.' He grabbed her sleeve and without saying anything else pulled her into an entrance and switched off his torch. 'Don't move, or speak,' he whispered as they slunk back into what she assumed must be a hedge.

She was too terrified to utter a word. She hoped Bobby wouldn't be woken by them suddenly stopping. She held her breath as headlights lit up the lane. A vehicle was making its way past where they were hiding. The two soldiers inside were arguing about something she couldn't understand.

They waited for about thirty seconds until the danger had passed and Tony took her hand to help her out of their hiding place. Helen realised she had dropped her bag in her panic. 'Oh no.'

'What is it?'

'My bag. I must have dropped it somewhere.'

He muttered something under his breath, turned on his torch and waved it back and forth slowly until its beam rested on her bag lying just inside the entrance, thankfully out of the soldiers' line of vision.

'There it is,' he said, keeping the light on it so Helen could pick it up.

'I'm sorry,' she said. 'I just panicked.'

'It's fine,' he said, his voice gentle. 'I think we're nearly there now. Only a bit longer.'

She caught sight of his face in the torchlight and saw him wince. Bobby wasn't heavy but carrying him under all those clothes for over half an hour now must be tiring. 'Are you all right?'

'I'm fine. Come along, there's no time to waste. We don't know if that vehicle will come back up this way and it's too cold out here to wait to find out.'

After another few exhausting minutes, Tony shone the torch on a sign on a gatepost. It was the first house they had come across since the driveway they had taken refuge in.

'This is it.' He sounded as relieved as she felt.

Helen read the house name. 'Sans Souci.' She wondered what it might mean.

'"Without worries",' he said, reading her thoughts. 'Very apt for a place of sanctuary, don't you think?'

'I do.'

She followed him up to the front door, desperate to be safely inside. Tony gave a single knock. Seconds later the door opened and Helen followed him in, waiting for Mrs Edwards to lock the door after them and draw across a thick velvet curtain to block out the light.

'You made it,' she said, pressing her hands together in front of her chest. 'I was worried when I heard that vehicle go past a while ago.'

'We hid in someone's drive. Thankfully we were right next to it.'

Her eyes moved to Tony's front. 'Better come into the living room. I have a small fire in there and it's the warmest room in the house. There's a tray of something for the three of you.'

They thanked her and followed her into the prettiest living room Helen had ever seen. Even if it hadn't been lovely, she would have thought it her favourite place, she was so relieved to finally be out of the cold and somewhere safe.

Tony pulled off his hat and scarf and unbuttoned his coat. Helen stepped forward, ready to help free her little boy. He stirred and opened his eyes. He'd been in darkness ever since they left number 3, but now he could see in the firelight. He looked around him, his gaze settling on her.

'Are we there, Mummy?'

'We are, sweetheart. Hold on while I help undo these straps.'

'I'll do that,' Mrs Edwards instructed. 'You take hold of Bobby.'

Relieved to finally have her small son in her arms once again, Helen kissed the top of his head, forgetting it was pressed to Tony's chest and her action might not be entirely appropriate.

'Sorry,' she mouthed, looking up at the man who had carried her child to safety.

His lips drew back in a weary smile. 'Please don't worry.'

Helen sat on the sofa cuddling Bobby. He was warm and seemed unfazed by his ordeal.

'Here you go,' Mrs Edwards said, placing bowls of steaming soup and a slice of bread each in front of Tony and Helen, and a piece of toast cut into strips, each covered with what looked like a thin coating of jam, for Bobby.

'Look what Mrs Edwards has made for you.' She let him off her lap and he knelt in front of the coffee table and began eating.

'Do you need a cushion to sit on?' their hostess asked.

He shook his head, too engrossed in the tasty treat to reply.

'This is very kind of you, thank you.' Helen thought she would never get over the kindness of local people who had risked their freedom for her and her son. 'And I don't think I can ever thank you enough for all you've done for us, Tony,' she said, unable to hold back tears.

'I think Tony and I are simply relieved you're both here now.' She pointed to their bowls. 'It's only vegetable soup but it should warm you up.'

Helen picked up the bowl and her spoon and began eating the hot soup. 'It's delicious.'

'Good. You've got Cook to thank for it,' she said smiling. 'She wanted to do something for you both and she's promised to send whatever she can from the kitchen for you, because my rations won't stretch three ways too well.'

Helen swallowed the lump forming in her throat. 'Everyone is so kind.'

Tony lowered his spoon and turned slightly in his seat. 'Stop thanking us, Helen. We've all done this because we care about you and Bobby. It makes us feel better to know we've helped someone. Most of the time, I, for one, feel frustrated that there's so little I can do.'

Mrs Edwards sat down in an armchair near to the fire. 'I couldn't have put it better myself. You're not to thank us again. Just be safe here. Together we'll look after this little mite. Hopefully he'll benefit from my garden, and you can relax knowing you don't have soldiers living next door.'

'I'm sure I will. But I want to be helpful. I hope you'll give me jobs to do.'

Mrs Edwards thought for a moment. 'You can help me look after the vegetable patch. I have a feeling we're going to need whatever veg we can grow even more over the coming months.'

They ate in silence and Helen felt her hands and feet slowly warm up. She yawned and covered her mouth. It must be the effort of walking in the snow and her heightened fear during their journey, never mind her build-up of anxiety over the months, living with the constant fear of being discovered.

They were still at risk, she knew that much, but maybe not in such danger up here. She swallowed a mouthful of soup. 'We'll be fine here by ourselves. You could leave a list of anything you'd like me to do while you're out, that sort of thing.'

'I'll be out most of the day during the week and some Saturday mornings. I hope you won't be lonely up here.'

'We'll be fine. Please don't worry about us.'

Mrs Edwards nodded. 'I've put you up in my mother's room. I thought that if you and Bobby share a bed then at least if they come and inspect this place I'd be able to say I hadn't the heart to strip my mother's bed.'

Tony nodded, clearly approving of that idea. 'Clever.'

'Bobby and I slept on the same mattress at the Hamels' home so it's what we're both used to. I'll also make sure to put all his clothes and toys away in a box or trunk, if you have one. You could explain about them by saying they belonged to a nephew who visited before the war.'

'Yes,' Mrs Edwards nodded. 'I'll find something for you to store your belongings in.'

Helen continued eating. She noticed Mrs Edwards had become thoughtful. She was about to ask if anything was worrying her when Mrs Edwards spoke again.

'I usually leave before eight when I'm working, and I'll always be home by six-thirty. If there is a reason I'm not home by then I should know beforehand and will leave you a note so you don't wait to eat supper with me.' She folded her hands neatly on her lap. 'We can iron out any other things when we think of them. There is one thing, though. I'd rather you call me Daphne. It'll feel strange to act formally now we live together.'

Just hearing her suggestion helped Helen relax further. 'Then that's what I'll do, Daphne. Although maybe Bobby should refer to you as Aunty Daphne.'

She smiled. 'I'd like that.' They all turned their attention to the little boy, who had fallen asleep on the floor. 'Bless him.'

Tony placed his bowl and spoon on the table and stood up. 'Do you need me to carry him through to his bed?'

Helen shook her head. 'No, I can manage.'

'Then I'd better make a move.'

'Already?' Daphne asked. She looked at her mantel clock. 'It's later than I thought.'

'It is. I have an hour and a half to be at home and I'd like to return Peggy's things to her on my way so she has them for the morning. The Hamels will also want to know you're both safely ensconced and I'd like to do that for them.'

'Thanks again, Tony.'

He smiled. 'I thought you weren't going to do that anymore,' he teased.

Helen grinned. 'I forgot. Please give them our love.'

'I will.'

She picked up Peggy's coat, took out her things and folded it neatly so it would fit into the cloth bag she'd brought with her for that reason. Then, putting the hat and scarf neatly inside, she took out her friend's identity card and slipped it into Peggy's coat pocket. 'There you are.'

Daphne indicated Helen's half-finished supper. 'You finish eating your food, then I'll show you through to your room after I've shown Tony out.'

Helen lifted Bobby onto the sofa and sat down next to him. She carried on eating her soup, her eyelids becoming heavy in the cosy room. They were here, finally. She could hardly dare believe it.

Chapter Fifty-Seven

HELEN

6 June 1944

Bobby found it too difficult to say Daphne's name and insisted she was Aunty Daffy, so the name stuck. Helen was relieved Daphne seemed to be rather fond of his pet name for her.

It delighted Helen to see her little boy running around the garden, playing hide-and-seek with her and Daphne, his arms and legs growing stronger with each passing day. For the first time in his young life she was able to see his previously milky white skin turning a golden brown in the sunshine, as his hair lightened and became almost auburn like her own.

'I'll never tire of watching this sweet boy having fun,' Daphne said one morning as they sat in the garden enjoying the sunshine. 'He's brought so much joy into my life since his arrival.'

Helen was glad to hear it. It warmed her heart to know that

those who had risked so much to shelter her and Bobby found such pleasure in his company.

They had been lucky so far: no one had come to inspect Daphne's home. Maybe, she mused, that was because Daphne had worked with senior officers for the past four years and they trusted her, so didn't look too carefully at her life outside her job.

'We both love it here,' Helen confided, hoping Ida would never know how much happier they were, living at Sans Souci.

'I'm happy to hear you say so. You two arrived just as I was struggling to cope. I admit to feeling very lonely after losing my mother. I think that young Anthony Le Gresley helped us both enormously with his thoughtfulness.'

'Were you very close to your mother, then?' Helen asked, thinking of her own difficulties.

Daphne took a sip of water and placed the glass on the small wooden table between their chairs. They were sitting on the small terrace in front of the bungalow's open French doors. 'We always had a close relationship,' she said, gazing at her colourful garden, deep in thought. 'Especially after my husband died over a decade ago. I struggled without him and my mother suggested it was silly the pair of us keeping two homes and both being lonely. She moved here and we got along very well. When she died, I not only lost my mother, but the person I spent all my free time with. It was strange not to feel needed by anyone. It's a lonely place to be.'

Helen supposed it must be. 'In that case I'm glad for both of us that we are here, because I certainly needed your help, as does Bobby.'

Daphne smiled for the first time since they had come to sit outside. 'And I've been happier in these past months than I can remember being for a very long time.' She leant back slightly in her chair, still smiling. 'I know Bobby has to keep fairly quiet while he's playing out here, but having a child in the house lightens the mood somehow. Just watching his face light up with excitement whenever he's given permission to run around the garden and kick his ball on the grass cheers me up more than I can say.'

'I feel the same. As much as I loved living with the Hamels, and I did, I struggled more as time went on, seeing Bobby cooped up. Although it might sound strange, the fact that he was so well behaved and quiet concerned me. He wasn't like any other child I remembered, growing up.' She laughed. 'He's more boisterous now and has so much enthusiasm for everything out here.'

'It's a delight to watch him blossoming,' Daphne said. She picked up their empty glasses. 'I'll go and refill these.' Helen offered to go instead. 'No, you make the most of the sunshine.'

She returned a few minutes later and placed their glasses of water on the table. 'Did you manage to catch any sleep with all that bombing last night?' she asked, referring to the bombardment taking place in France.

Helen thought back to the distant thuds and sounds of planes roaring past the island, made far worse by the constant noise of anti-aircraft guns as the Germans did their best to shoot them down.

'Not really.' She yawned. 'What do you think is happening? It's obviously something going on in France.'

They heard someone calling and Helen leapt to her feet, her eyes immediately searching for Bobby. She was braced to run and hide him in the hedgerow at the bottom of the garden, which she had planned to use if they were caught unawares like now.

Daphne grabbed her arm to stop her. 'It's only Tony and Peggy,' she soothed. 'Maybe fetch a couple more chairs for them.'

Helen's heartbeat slowly returned to normal as she brought out two chairs and glasses of water for their guests.

'How delightful to see you both,' Daphne was saying as Helen joined them.

'We have wonderful news,' Tony announced, keeping his voice low even though the nearest neighbour wasn't very close.

'We do,' Peggy continued, obviously excited. Helen assumed it must be something to do with the noise that had disturbed them. 'The British army is in Normandy. Isn't that incredible?'

Helen covered her mouth, barely able to believe what she was hearing. 'It is. Do you think they'll be here soon?' She saw Tony's doubtful expression and her hope slipped. 'You don't think so?'

He shrugged. 'I've no idea but I think we need to be prepared in case they do come.'

Peggy took a sip of water. 'Gosh, I needed that.' She looked at Helen, then Daphne. 'There's going to be a proclamation in the *Evening Post* tonight.'

Helen realised Peggy had probably been asked to translate it.

'It's from Kommandant der Festung, warning us that whether the British forces arrive or not, now that they are on the French mainland he expects islanders to behave.'

'What a cheek,' Helen groaned.

'We do have to take note though,' Daphne said sagely.

'I agree. Sabotage or anything like that won't be tolerated and if there is any he will give the order to close all the streets.' She frowned. 'Even more frightening is that he's said he'll punish any unrest by death.'

Helen couldn't think what to say.

'That sounds a bit harsh. Do you think the Bailiff will make an announcement?' Daphne asked.

Tony shook his head. 'I think if he was going to he would have done it by now.'

Peggy nodded. 'I agree. Babs said that the Royal Square was packed with islanders earlier waiting in case he did.'

'Don't look so miserable,' Tony said, smiling. 'Whatever this means for us, it can only be good news for everyone eventually.'

'I hope you're right,' Helen said, wondering if they dared start hoping that the end of the war was in sight. 'It's been such a long time now and we all ran out of luxuries long ago.'

'Never mind luxuries,' Peggy grumbled. 'I'd be happy with the basics, although I wouldn't mind some scented soap.'

'Or shampoo,' Helen sighed, wishing she had taken care to use what she had more sparingly.

'For me, it's the thought of a long, deep, luxurious bubble bath,' Daphne added and they laughed.

'I wonder if we'll ever be able to enjoy those things again?' Peggy said dreamily.

'Aunty Peggy, Uncle Tony,' Bobby called, keeping his voice low as he ran to greet them.

'What a relief,' Tony said, standing up, catching him in his arms and spinning him round a couple of times before lowering the little boy to his feet. 'Someone cheerful to speak to.'

The women laughed.

Helen watched her son being hugged by Peggy, before being surprised by an apple from Tony. 'It's washed so you can eat it straightaway.'

He sat on a step and began munching happily.

'We do need to take care, though,' Tony continued, glancing at Bobby and seeming satisfied that he was too focused on his apple to listen. 'Now we've all been witness to so much Allied activity, I worry that the Germans will be more ready than ever to clamp down on us. If the Allies take France, then they'll lose their connection to their own country and will feel very much on their own here. And what happens when you corner a rat?'

His warning made sense. 'We need to take precautions even more now not to bring attention to ourselves' Helen said trying not to panic.

'Especially you and Bobby,' Peggy said sombrely.' And above all you, Daphne, now they live with you. Those rotters might be harsher towards someone they don't consider suspicious.'

'You're right,' Helen agreed. 'We'll take extra care and I'll be careful not to let Bobby play at the front of the house.'

Things were obviously changing, Helen mused, but in a way that none of them could predict just yet. The thought unnerved her even more.

Chapter Fifty-Eight

HELEN

The Germans didn't fire their anti-aircraft guns that night, despite the continued heavy Allied bombing in the distance. Helen was glad of the reprieve from the noise but sensed the tension in the air. She doubted she was alone wondering if the Allies might land on the more northern Channel Islands like Alderney – and if they did, what might happen to them all then?

Daphne went to work daily, coming home with snippets of news but mostly able to share the atmosphere at the Villa Millbrook. Whereas before she had managed to bulk up their rations with small amounts of food kept secretly from the officers by Mrs Jeune, now she hardly ever brought anything extra home in her bag.

'They've begun doing spot checks on staff when they leave for the day,' Daphne explained over their meagre supper of vegetables they had harvested from the garden. 'Poor Dulcie only just managed to get away with sneaking a bread roll in her pocket because the captain was distracted briefly.'

'It sounds extremely tense there now.'

'It is,' Daphne said, sadness in her brown eyes. 'It's not a pleasant place to be any more. It hasn't been since they came.'

Something occurred to Helen. 'Were you there before the occupation then?'

Daphne nodded. 'I've worked there for almost fourteen years now. Lady Trent, the owner, is a kind, decent person. She held parties for her birthday and loved being driven by her chauffeur each afternoon, stopping to speak to people and constantly handing out gifts. Her family insisted she went to live with their son up in the Scottish Highlands because he said they'd be safer there.' She sighed. 'It's still strange being in the house without her, but I'm glad she doesn't have to witness them in her home. She would hate it. I wish I didn't have to go there anymore, but I need a job and I tell myself that this way I'm keeping an eye on the place until she can return.'

'I hope you don't have to wait too long for that to happen.'

'As do I. The atmosphere there is changing, though,' Daphne said. 'Some of the soldiers seem withdrawn and more anxious than usual. The more outgoing ones appear happy and excited. I suppose their mood depends on whether they're looking forward to getting involved in the fighting after being stuck here for four years. They are trained soldiers, after all.'

It wasn't until the following Thursday that Helen heard machine guns. It was just after six in the morning and the sound woke her with a start. Daphne had already left for work but when she returned she explained that German ships had been sunk.

'There's been shots fired to the northwest of the island at a gun emplacement there. When I was walking to and from work I happened to notice fewer uniforms on the streets. It was surreal.'

'Dare we hope the Allies will rescue us?' Helen asked, absentmindedly crossing her fingers. It was tantalisingly knowing they were so close. 'Surely they'll come for us next?'

Daphne shook her head. 'I've no idea, but I worry that if they do, it could end up being a bloodbath here. After all, it's not as if we can leave the island while the two sides fight over it.'

Helen chewed her lower lip, unaware what she was doing until she tasted blood. 'Ouch.'

'Do be careful, dear,' Daphne said looking shocked.

As the next few days passed, some quieter than others, there was little opportunity of forgetting about the battle carrying on in France; planes were flying over and German artillery was firing at them. Helen did her best to keep her anxiety in check but was continually distracted by German fire and concern for the Allied planes, willing them not to be hit and to keep going.

She hated being left at the house alone with Bobby and eagerly awaited Daphne's return each evening, when she listened intently to the news she was able to bring.

'They're becoming nervous and snappy at work,' Daphne said. 'It hasn't been helped by the news that three of their minesweepers were hit yesterday, and some E-boats.' Helen noticed Daphne's hand trembling as she picked up the cup of weak tea she had placed in front of her. 'I don't mind admitting, I'm becoming increasingly concerned by the moods of some of these officers when I arrive at work.'

Helen felt sorry for her. 'If only you could take a few days off.' As she spoke, she noticed how pale Daphne seemed.

Sallow somehow, despite her usual healthy appearance. There were dark circles under her eyes and she had become very thin. Helen hated to think that her friend's weight loss had been made worse by her sharing her rations between the three of them. Daphne would never discuss it.

'I wish I could, too.' She pressed her hands together as if in prayer. 'We need to keep you two safe at all costs.' She reached out and rested her hand on top of Helen's. 'What else would I have to focus on without the pair of you? You've become family to me.'

Helen was taken aback. 'I, er, that's the loveliest thing anyone has ever said to me.' She had to swallow to clear her throat.

'It's true. I don't want you to worry about a thing. I'll do whatever I think best for all of us. You look after the little one and keep house here while I'm at work.'

Later that night, after Helen put Bobby to bed, she joined Daphne in the living room.

'This is such a lovely bungalow,' Helen said. 'You must have many happy memories here.

'I have,' Daphne said wistfully. 'I've been very lucky and I'm grateful to have been able to share it with you and Bobby these past six months.'

Helen settled back into the comfortable armchair. 'I'd love to enjoy this place in peacetime,' she said, thoughtfully. 'I can barely remember what the island was like back then.'

'Well, with all that's happening around us right now, hopefully we won't need to wait too much longer to find out what that's like.'

Helen prayed her friend was right. She opened her mouth

to speak when an enormous boom shook the house. She leapt up. 'What was that?'

Daphne seemed dazed, her hands gripping the arms of her chair. 'I've no idea,' she replied breathlessly.

'What should we do?' Helen asked. When her friend didn't reply she heard Bobby cry out. She wasn't surprised he had been woken by the terrible explosion. She ran through to him, relieved when the noise wasn't repeated, and sat down on the side of the bed, stroking his head to calm him.

'Everything's fine, darling. Try to go back to sleep. Mummy's here.'

He pulled her arm until he was cuddling it and Helen climbed on to the bed behind him and held him until he fell asleep again.

Chapter Fifty-Nine

RICHARD

15 June 1944

R ichard heard with horror about the V1 rocket exploding two days before in Grove Road in Bow, near the railway station where Helen's family lived. People had been killed and homes damaged, and, despite her family's refusal to speak to him, he decided to check they were safe. They were still Helen and Bobby's family and he wanted to offer them any help he could give.

He took the train as far as possible, then walked the rest of the way. As he turned into the road he was horrified to see the carnage in front of him. All the roofs were missing and the front of a row of several houses had been blown away. He ran to the property where her family had lived for as long as he had known Helen. It was plain that it was uninhabitable.

'Know 'em, did yer?' a boy asked, scratching his head before replacing his mucky cap.

Richard was nervous about asking but needed to know

what happened to them in case he ever managed to speak to Helen again. 'Did they…? Do you know where the family went?'

'No idea. I only came 'ere wiv me mate ter see it.'

'Right.' Richard tried asking a few more people and discovered that not only had people been killed or injured, hundreds in the area had been made homeless. It wasn't surprising. But no one was able to suggest anything other than trying the hospitals.

He spent the next two days asking at several hospitals whether the Bowman family had been admitted, but found no trace of them. He hoped they had survived. He struggled to recall the names of any relatives Helen might have mentioned, whom they could have gone to stay with, but couldn't think of anyone.

He decided to send her another telegram. He wished he could let her know that her family was safe but, as he didn't know, decided not to mention the matter at all. If only he knew how much information Helen was able to glean about ongoing events in England or France. He thought of everything that had been happening since D-day the previous week and suspected the islanders could possibly hear some of the commotion going on in Normandy. Either way, it was to be hoped that they knew France had been invaded by the British and American forces.

He wondered if the Channel Islands might be next to be liberated. At least then he could find a way to see Helen and meet his son for the first time. He still found it incredible that there was a little boy growing up on that beautiful but imprisoned island who had come from his and Helen's love. He thought back to the only time they had made love. It had been beautiful and something he could never forget. If only he had known then the repercussions of that magical afternoon. Feeling as if his emotions were choking him, Richard swallowed his pain and focused instead on what he would say to Helen this time.

Hearing news of all that's happening in France and praying freedom comes your way soon. Thinking of you all. Stay safe and strong. Love Richard

Chapter Sixty

PEGGY

Sunday 18 June

Peggy saw Helen's delight when she, Tony and Babs walked around the house to where they supposed Daphne and she would be enjoying the sunshine and watching Bobby play with his toys on the grass.

'What a wonderful surprise,' Daphne said, indicating chairs for them to sit on. 'I'll fetch us all something to drink.'

Tony immediately went to join Bobby, and Peggy couldn't miss the little boy's excitement at seeing his friend again. But she noticed a marked difference in Daphne's demeanour. She was much thinner than on their previous visit and seemed jittery – probably, Peggy thought, because of the constant noise of the bombardment. It had been going on for a week now and her own nerves were on edge.

'How's your mum?' Helen asked.

'She's struggling a bit with all that's been happening,' Babs explained. 'But she sends her love. She misses you and Bobby terribly even though it's been months now since the pair of you left.' She looked at Peggy. 'We miss you both, too, don't we?'

'We do, but you have more space here and more to do. And the garden, of course, and that's what matters.' She said the last few words pointedly to her sister, causing Babs's cheeks to redden slightly. Peggy loved her sister but she sometimes didn't think before speaking. Thankfully, Helen knew Babs well enough not to take offence at anything she said.

Helen tucked her auburn hair behind her ears. 'The garden has been wonderful. Bobby wants to come outside as soon as he's up each morning and it's a struggle to persuade him inside for supper. I love seeing grass stains on his knees and earth under his fingernails – something I'd never thought about before. We've been very happy here, although we have missed the three of you. Please don't think we haven't.'

'I'm sorry if I said the wrong thing,' Babs said.

'It's fine, you didn't.' Helen pressed her hand to her heart. 'I know what you meant, Babs.'

'I think I worry so much about Mum. She's always been there for us and it frightens me to see her changing almost in front of our eyes.'

'It must do.' Helen frowned.

'Babs.' Peggy shot her a warning look.

Ignoring her, Babs continued. 'You see, Mum's always been curvy,' she explained.

As she said it, Peggy noticed for the first time how much weight her sister had lost, too. She had been so focused on their mother and her work – how had she missed the change in Babs? She kept her thoughts to herself and listened as her sister continued.

'When we told Mum we were worried about her losing so much weight, she pointed out how we had all changed and joked that hopefully she would never have to worry about weight management again.'

Peggy saw Helen's happiness vanish and decided to change the topic of conversation before Babs became distressed about something none of them could do anything about.

'Mum has been trying to reduce her weight for as long as I can remember.' She crossed one leg over the other. 'I must admit I prefer her looking the way she did before, but as she said, we're all in the same boat and we will get through this.'

Helen indicated Daphne coming out through the French doors behind Tony. 'I'm worried about Daphne,' she whispered quickly. 'She's looking unwell but won't hear of us changing our share of the rations in any way.'

Peggy glanced at her.

'I see what you mean,' Babs said. 'I wish we could have brought something with us but...'

Helen shook her head. 'That's not what I meant. I'm just happy to see you and be able to share my concerns with someone.'

Peggy gave her a sympathetic smile. 'We know how you feel. This blasted war is slowly killing all of us. I'm beginning to think we'll all starve before this island is liberated.'

'I was thinking the same thing.'

'There are some very serious faces here,' Daphne said with forced cheerfulness. 'Now, who would like a glass of this delicious mint cocktail?'

They laughed as each took a cocktail glass of water with fresh mint in it from the tray that Tony had brought out for her.

'I'm impressed with Daphne's style,' Peggy said.

'This is so refreshing,' Helen said, taking a sip.

When they were seated, Tony said, 'I was telling Daphne about the British arriving in Carteret.'

'I've heard of that place. Isn't it quite close to the island?' Helen tried to recall what she had heard about it from conversations with her aunt. 'I believe Aunt Sylvia used to travel there each summer when my uncle was alive.'

'I used to love going there with my parents when I was younger,' Tony said. 'I'm planning on going again as soon as this nonsense is over and done with.'

'We should all plan to go,' Babs said, with more enthusiasm than Peggy had seen from any of them in a long time.

'We should,' Peggy nodded. 'I know. Let's promise that once this is all over, and I know in my heart it will be, we will all go away somewhere special together to celebrate.' And remember those who didn't make it, she thought, but decided to keep that to herself.

They looked up as another couple of planes passed and the firing began again in earnest.

'I can't wait to see the back of these rotten Jerries,' Tony snapped. 'I just hope it's sooner rather than later.'

Peggy agreed, knowing that they all were thinking the same thing. 'Let's talk about something else,' she suggested just as a fresh bout of firing began.

Chapter Sixty-One

RICHARD

August 1944

I t had taken Richard several weeks to track Helen's family down after their home had been hit by one of the doodlebugs, as people were now referring to the terror of the skies. He had only heard one once and his fear had been intense. He doubted he would ever forget the noise of the engine as it tore across the sky and the horror of hearing it cut out. Then of having to count as he ran for cover to the nearest doorway, covering his head and facing the wall as the bomb exploded several streets from where he was standing, making the ground shake violently beneath him.

Now he was on his way to see them. And to do his best to persuade them to speak to him. He needed to see for himself that they were fine before he sent another telegram to Helen. Although he had no way of knowing if his previous telegram had reached her, he suspected she must be desperate to hear news of her family after so long. Whether the Bowmans liked it or not, he intended to let them know that she and their grandson were doing their best to survive on the island.

Since discovering he had a child he had found his resentment towards the Bowmans increase. They might not like the fact that he and Helen weren't married, but he didn't understand why they hadn't told him about his son. He wasn't sure how well he might be able to keep hold of his temper, but he was determined not to let himself down. After all, he was going to see them for Helen's sake.

He checked the flat number again to make sure he was at the right place, then rang the doorbell and waited.

Helen's father opened the door and looked him up and down, not appearing to recognise him.

Richard didn't have long before he had to return to his base, so he introduced himself. Mr Bowman's expression changed immediately.

'I don't know why you've bothered coming here,' he snapped. 'We've nothing to say to you.'

He began to shut the door but Richard pressed his hand against it to stop it closing. 'I only wish to speak to you for a moment,' he explained. 'I thought you might like to know how your daughter is doing?'

Her father looked over his shoulder, then called over his shoulder.

'This chap of Helen's has news of her.'

'How so?' Mrs Bowman hurried towards the door wiping her hands on a tea towel.

Taken aback that they were giving him the chance to speak, Richard explained about the telegrams. 'Obviously I don't have much information, but I know Helen and Bobby were fine the last time I heard from her.'

'Bobby?' Mrs Bowman frowned and looked up at her husband for an answer.

'It seems you were right to suspect Helen was pregnant. So she had a boy then,' her husband scowled.

Richard felt his hackles rise at the cold description of his precious son. 'Our son,' he said, hoping to annoy them. 'He and Helen are being well cared for by neighbours since her aunt died—'

'Sylvia's dead?' Helen's mother cried, covering her mouth, her eyes wide with shock.

Richard tensed. Of course, they were sisters. How had he forgotten that? He was mortified to have made such a shocking announcement. 'I'm so sorry, I thought you knew.'

Mr Bowman shook his head. 'And how do you suppose that could have happened?'

Richard didn't like to remind him that people had been able to send and receive telegrams and that maybe, if they had bothered to contact their daughter or her aunt, they would have discovered this news for themselves.

'I think you should go,' Mr Bowman said putting his arm around his wife's shoulders.

This time it was she who stopped him closing the door. 'No, he's here now. I'd like to know how my daughter is doing. And the little one.'

Reassured to hear that Helen's mother still cared for her, Richard calmed slightly. 'All I know is what I've told you. The situation on the islands is dire, I think we all know that much, but Helen and Bobby are with people who care for them. They had to move after it became too dangerous for them where they were, but I've received a letter from a friend of the Hamels.'

He thought of the telegram he had received several weeks before, wishing it had been from Helen but grateful to receive any news about them. He hoped he would get the chance to meet Tony at some point and thank him personally for all he had done for his small family.

Both safe with friends and doing well. Try not to worry. Life bit of a struggle but all coping. No messages received for months. Tony

'Helen and Bobby are now at another house. I assume they're somewhere safer.'

Mrs Bowman gave him a grateful smile. 'I'm sorry for our unfriendliness. It's been difficult coming to terms with Helen leaving. I admit I have some responsibility for what she did and resented her for getting into trouble like she did.'

'What are you saying?' Mr Bowman asked, giving his wife a surprised look.

'Only that if I had been more understanding, then maybe Helen wouldn't have run to my sister.' She turned her attention back to Richard. 'We're relieved to know she's coping and with her little boy.' She cleared her throat. 'Your little boy.'

Unsure how to react, Richard decided it was time for him to go. 'I'm glad we've spoken and that I can tell Helen you're safe and well.'

Mrs Bowman drew in a sharp breath. 'You can do that?'

'It might take months but I'm hoping she'll receive my telegram.'

He left feeling as if he had achieved something worthwhile. Finally, he had reassuring news for Helen.

Chapter Sixty-Two

HELEN

August 1944

The next few weeks passed. Planes still flew by but there seemed to be fewer now, and shots had been fired at a few areas on the island. Instead of the islanders being rescued, life got worse and Helen felt more despondent than ever.

'How are we going to cope with even less food?' she asked Daphne as they sat in the garden making the most of the late summer sunshine. There was something different about her friend today, but she couldn't make out what it could be.

'I've no idea, but now the Germans' food supply chain has been broken by the Allies invading France, they'll be getting as hungry as we've been.'

Helen knew it also meant that the meagre rations they distributed to the islanders would end. She was frightened, not only for her and Bobby, but for everyone. What vegetables they could manage to grow were needed now more than ever.

'They're getting nastier, too,' Daphne moaned quietly so that Bobby couldn't hear.

Helen saw her glance to the right and wondered if she was expecting someone. She was about to ask, when there was another distant boom.

Helen flinched. 'And now they're bombing St Malo.' She had visited the beautiful walled town when she was a child and her parents had taken her and her brother over on the ferry from St Helier. She recalled the first time she had accompanied her father up onto the ramparts, enjoying seeing the tall, stone townhouses from the higher viewpoint.

'I spent my honeymoon in St Malo,' Daphne said wistfully. 'It's always held a special place in my heart. The Americans bombing the place to rid it of the Nazis is one thing, but I hope the townspeople have been able to get away to safety before this bombardment. Even if they survive the bombings, will they have anything left to return to?'

Helen couldn't imagine how anyone might survive so many bombs being dropped in such a small area. She pictured the top floors of the houses peeping over the ramparts as they arrived by ferry. It had been such a magical place. 'Poor St Malo.'

Each day Daphne had returned home it had been the same. Bad news. More and more of it, or so it seemed. Would this nightmare ever end? Was Bobby destined to only know a life like this one? Helen hoped not, with all her heart. She tried to imagine how different their lives would have been if she had found a way to stay in London, then pushed the pointless thought away.

Thinking about what-ifs was a waste of emotion. This was their life, whether they liked it or not. They had to find the best way to cope and hopefully survive the lack of food and medicines.

Stop it, Helen thought, irritated with herself for giving into negative thoughts. She needed to focus on the few things she did have the power to control, the most important being her resilience and keeping going, when all she wanted to do was draw the curtains, go to bed and cry.

She was about to call Bobby and put him to bed when Peggy arrived, out of breath and red in the face. Concerned, Helen leapt to her feet and rushed over to her friend, slipping her arms around her and leading her to one of the chairs.

'What is it?' Daphne asked.

Helen looked anxiously at Peggy. 'Sit down. I'll fetch you some water.'

Peggy shook her head and waved for her to stay. 'Sorry,' she panted. 'Out. Of. Breath.'

Helen sat and waited. 'Take your time,' she said, trying to ease the tension in her stomach. Studying her friend's face and not seeing distress, she calmed slightly.

Peggy put her hand in her jacket pocket and withdrew a buff envelope. 'For. You.'

Helen gasped at the sight of a telegram. 'From Richard?'

Peggy smiled as she nodded.

'That's so kind of you to bring it.'

'Let me fetch you a glass of water,' Daphne said, and didn't wait for either of them to stop her.

Helen held the precious telegram. It seemed so long since she had received one. She stared at it for a moment and then opened the envelope, removing the single sheet and unfolding it.

Visited your parents. Grove Street bombed. Now rehoused.
All safe and well.

Sent love to you and Bobby. Am well. Always in my
thoughts. Richard

Helen gasped then covered her mouth with her hand, hardly believing what she was reading.

'Please don't tell me it's bad news,' Peggy pleaded.

Helen felt Daphne's hand on her arm. 'What is it, Helen?'

Helen quickly reread Richard's message shaking her head to let them know that it wasn't bad news. She passed the telegram to Daphne. 'It's the most marvellous news.' She closed her eyes and took in a slow, deep breath. Exhaling gradually and trying to calm down, she opened her eyes and smiled.

Peggy leant across the table. 'Really, if you two won't tell me what this is all about, I'm going to have to find out for myself.' She took the message from Daphne and read it. Her mouth dropped open.

Helen saw her friend's joy and laughed. 'Isn't it the most exciting news? I never thought they would speak to Richard, let alone want to know about Bobby.' Emotion made her throat tight and her voice croaky. 'And did you see, they send their love to both of us.'

The tears she had been trying to contain began to fall. Unable to help herself, Helen began sobbing uncontrollably. She covered her face, not wanting to worry Bobby.

Seconds later she felt small arms wrapping around her legs. 'Mummy?'

Helen struggled to gather herself, relieved to hear Daphne's soothing voice. 'Mummy's fine, sweetheart. It's nothing to worry about. Those are happy tears.'

'Happy?'

'Yes, poppet,' Peggy said. 'Mummy has been sent a message from her mummy and daddy.'

Helen withdrew her handkerchief from her skirt pocket, wiped away her tears and blew her nose. She was desperate to comfort her little boy and hated that she had alarmed him with her outburst.

She opened her arms and Bobby ran into them and clung to her as she hugged him. 'I'm sorry, darling. Mummy didn't mean to frighten you. She's heard from your daddy.' She forced her lips back into a smile, still stunned by what Richard had told her.

Bobby frowned. 'My daddy?'

'Yes, darling. Your daddy.'

She needed to start telling Bobby about his father, she decided. She had been so angry with Richard, discovering he was engaged to someone his parents loved and were looking forward to calling their daughter-in-law. And then her mother's reaction to catching her being sick one morning had told Helen all she needed to know: that she was on her own and needed to be with someone who would love her no matter what. She pictured her kind, beautiful aunt and how she had welcomed her with open arms when Helen had arrived on her doorstep straight from the ferry. Not asking questions, never expecting explanations, her aunt had loved her unconditionally.

She felt her throat constricting with more tears and gave Peggy a pleading look.

Seeming to know instantly what Helen needed, Peggy got

up and held out her hand to Bobby. 'Why don't you show your Aunty Peggy where to find a glass of water?'

He immediately took her hand and led her into the house. Not having to contain her emotions any longer, Helen burst into fresh tears, wishing her aunt was with her now to know of her parents' change of heart.

'It's been a lot for you to deal with,' Daphne said, gently rubbing Helen's back. 'You let it all out.'

Unable to help herself, Helen sobbed into her friend's shoulder, trembling at the tumult of emotions carousing through her. She wasn't sure if she was happy, grief-stricken, or simply unhinged. 'I'm sorry.'

'Hush, now. You've had a lot to deal with and have been incredibly brave. It's not surprising your emotions are raw after such a message. It's perfectly natural.'

'Thank you, Daphne. I don't know what Bobby and I would have done without you taking us in like you have. You've made the world of difference to us, to me.'

'As both of you have done for me.'

Chapter Sixty-Three

HELEN

Helen had just finished washing Bobby's face before putting him to bed when she heard a sound. She stilled, holding her breath and listening to hear it again. Deciding she must have imagined it, she helped him into bed, handed him his teddy and pulled up the sheet to cover his shoulders. It was a warm night, and he didn't need anything more than that on the bed.

She bent to kiss him. 'Sleep well, poppet. Mummy will be back soon.'

She left the room, stopping when she heard whispered voices. One of them sounded like Tony's. Surprised, but happy at his visiting, she went through to the kitchen to join them. She opened the door and went to greet him, but stopped when she saw Tony wasn't alone. Sitting at the table, a glass of water in one hand and a slice of bread in the other, was a dishevelled man. It was obvious by his filthy state that he was one of the enforced workers who had been brought to the island to work on the many bunkers and gun emplacements that had been

built around the island over the past three years. She had
heard about these poor people but this was the first time she
had met one. He looked as if he'd been treated far worse than
she had imagined. Not wanting to frighten him, Helen kept
quiet.

He sensed her presence. His deep-set dark eyes stared at
her momentarily before he leapt up, knocking his chair
backwards so it crashed on the tiled kitchen floor.

'What the—?' Tony turned at the same time as Daphne,
both registering Helen standing there, while the man ran to the
back door desperate to escape. Tony took off after him.

'I'm so sorry,' she whispered, hating to have frightened the
stranger. 'I didn't mean to.'

'It's fine, dear,' Daphne soothed. 'I doubt he'll get far. He's
barely eaten for months, poor soul. Tony will bring him back.
At least I hope he does before anyone spots them both.'

They waited patiently and were relieved when they
returned. The man seemed less frightened and Helen gave
what she hoped was a friendly smile.

'I'm sorry I surprised you.' She made sure to keep her tone
gentle in case he didn't understand her.

He stared at her silently.

'Please,' Daphne said, indicating the food he had left when
he ran. 'Eat.'

He tore his eyes from Helen and looked at Tony, who
nodded.

Once he was seated, Tony sat opposite him. She and
Daphne did the same.

'We didn't mean to shock you, Helen,' Tony explained, his
tone gentle. 'This is Tomás.' Hearing his name, the man looked
up and gave her a brief nod before going on eating.

'It doesn't sound like a Russian name.'

'Not all the forced workers are from there,' Daphne explained. 'Some, like Tomás, are political prisoners from the Spanish Civil War.'

'That's right,' Tony said. 'Some are Dutch, or Belgian, and from various other places.'

Helen looked at his ragged clothes. 'We need to find something else for him to wear.'

'I was saying as much when you joined us,' Daphne said. 'I still have some of my husband's clothes in a trunk in the loft. I was wondering if you might seek them out for me before you go, Tony?'

'I'd be happy to.'

Helen saw the relief in his face and realised he must have been concerned about Tomás's clothes.

It dawned on her what her aunt had said. 'You're taking him tonight?'

Tony shook his head. 'No, I—'

'Mummy?'

Concerned that Bobby had walked in and seen their visitor, Helen went to him. 'What are you doing up? You're supposed to be asleep,' she said, trying to lead him away, but he tugged at her hand determined to stay. 'I'm Bobby.'

The man put down what he was eating, and his mouth drew back into a gentle smile, showing rotting teeth interspersed with gaps. His face lit up, making him appear very different. He pointed at his chest. 'Tomás.'

Bobby smiled at him. 'Goodnight, Tomás.'

Helen led him away, her mind racing. What if Bobby mentioned seeing him in the kitchen? Then it occurred to her that he never saw anyone other than them and occasionally

Peggy and Babs. Helen knew how secretive people needed to be. Maybe that was why Tony hadn't confided in either of them about this.

She returned to the kitchen and listened as Tony explained why he had needed to bring the escapee to Daphne's home. 'I was supposed to take him to another safe house.'

'Another?' She turned to Daphne. 'You mean, you've done this before?'

Daphne smiled. 'Quite a few times, yes. And I hope you know that this isn't something you should share with anyone, not even Ida and Babs Hamel, lovely as they are.'

'Of course.' Anxious about what would happen to Daphne, her and Bobby should they be caught with the man in the house, Helen struggled to push her fear to one side. These men had nowhere else to go and of course they must look after him. Helen gave Tony an apologetic look. 'Please carry on.'

'I'm aware how dangerous this is,' Tony said. 'And if I had anywhere else to take him I would.' He lowered his voice. 'Between you and me it was you tipping Peggy off in '41 after you overheard those Jerries discussing an enforced worker that enabled me to put in place the first safe house to take Pawel to.'

'Pawel?'

'The first man I helped hide.'

'What happened to him?'

'That's not something I can tell you.'

Helen wasn't sure if it was because he didn't know or because it wasn't her business. She assumed it was the latter. She was stunned. Had she really been the one to instigate Pawel's rescue? 'You really mean that I helped that man?'

He nodded. 'I promise you it's true.'

'I'm sure you have no idea how much of a difference the information we received from you and from Peggy has made to quite a few people. And because of my involvement this gentleman also has a chance of a future.'

She was staggered and happy to be able to put a human face to what she had done. 'I've done so little. It's people like you and your friends in the underground groups who've put their lives at risk.'

Tony gave her a pointed stare. 'Helen, information is key, and you've made the difference between life and death for Pawel. Hopefully, he'll continue to be safe until this nightmare is finally over and can have a chance of locating his family.' He hesitated for a moment. 'Or, probably, what's left of them.'

She wiped away tears she had only just realised were running down her face. 'This means so much to me.'

'To all of us.' He rested a hand on the back of one of the chairs.

She looked at the abused man sitting at the table. 'What about Tomás?'

'I'm planning to move him on somewhere else, but he'll need to stay here for a little while until that's possible. They have search parties out looking for him and, as you can see, we need to do all we can to change his appearance so that he'll have more chance to blend in. I'll be back tomorrow with whatever food I can find.'

'Come with me,' Daphne was saying to Tomás, mimicking washing her arms. 'I'll run the bath while you fetch those clothes, Tony.'

'I really hate putting the three of you in danger,' Tony said.

Daphne shook her head. 'We all need to help each other,'

she said. 'Now, shall I show you where to find the loft for those clothes?'

Helen guessed she might have slept for an hour or two but no more than that. She wasn't sure what had been worse, hearing imaginary footsteps and fearing that German soldiers were storming into the bungalow, or her nightmares that they had come. It was a relief to see daybreak. And now she was sitting in the living room, the curtains half drawn, with Tomás sitting to the side of the room in case unexpected visitors arrived to see Daphne. Thankfully, it was the weekend, and Daphne was at home with them – not that Helen didn't trust Tomás, but he was a stranger, and she couldn't be too careful where Bobby was concerned, despite the two of them getting on so well.

She watched as he played with Bobby's toys, making him laugh. She was amused that although neither of them understood the other they seemed to communicate well.

She was relieved when the sun set and they could sit in the relative darkness and it was less likely that anyone might call at Sans Souci, or even drive past and look in the window. Tony didn't come all day and she assumed he must have been detained elsewhere.

Hearing footsteps outside, the three adults tensed and stared at each other, but an agreed pattern of knocks at the back door told Helen that Tony had arrived.

He was out of breath and seemed more stressed than usual. 'I'm sorry,' he said, glancing at each one of them in turn. 'I was hoping to be able to move Tomás this evening, but the place I was taking him to was raided this morning.'

Helen saw Tomás had picked up on Tony's words despite not understanding English. She gave their guest a reassuring smile. 'You will be safe here,' she said hoping to help him feel a bit better.

After Tony left, Helen wished there was more she could do to help but being in hiding herself made going out too risky.

It was three days before Tony was able to arrange another safe house for Tomás and he moved on. Helen reflected that she would never forget the man who had spent five days with them. She hoped she might one day hear that he had been reunited with his family.

Half an hour after Tomás had left a sobbing Bobby, who had to be persuaded to let go of his hand, Helen and Daphne had cleared away any sign of him and sat in the living room, lost in their own thoughts.

'I almost feel as if we imagined Tomás being here,' Helen admitted eventually, wondering what would happen to him now.

'Me, too.' Daphne sighed. 'Poor man, I hope he eventually manages to get home.'

So do I, Helen thought, glad to have been able to help him in some small way.

Chapter Sixty-Four

PEGGY

Early September 1944

Tony and his father hadn't been to the office for several days and it worried Peggy that he hadn't called into number 3 to see her, either. She hoped he wasn't ill. It occurred to her that maybe something had happened to his mother, who, she had heard, struggled more and more with her nerves as the months passed. Peggy wasn't surprised. She herself was strong, as were her mother and Babs, but they were starting to bicker among themselves now, their patience stretched as their stomachs ached with hunger.

Life was miserable and, as far as she was concerned, made far worse knowing that Allied forces were so close yet continued not to liberate the islands. She had never felt this helpless before, and for the first time she worried whether she had the strength to see this through to the end.

Gossip was spreading from the country parishes about Germans stealing people's food – even ducks or chickens from those who still had them. People who had pets kept them under close scrutiny, not daring to leave them outside in case they were stolen to be eaten.

Peggy was nervous each time she ventured out of the house now. The atmosphere was far less friendly than it had been. There was a sense of desperation among the Germans now, and they were arresting people for more offences.

She was about to leave for work, her stomach rumbling because the only bread they had managed to find was mouldy. Despite her mother's insistence, Peggy was certain she had seen things moving in it. She was hungry, but not so much that she could eat something revolting. She put on her coat, picked up her handbag and stepped out of the house.

'Bye, Mum. I'll see you later.'

'Bye, lovey.'

Peggy closed the front door behind her thinking how much she missed Tony. He always managed to reassure her and she was struggling without the comfort of talking to him.

Hearing the distinctive sound of an aircraft engine, Peggy looked up to see a British plane. Immediately, artillery began firing, making her tense and wish she had stayed at home. Frightened that she might be caught by flying shrapnel, she ran for cover in a nearby doorway, and was relieved when the firing stopped and she was able to continue on her way.

As she walked along the road, something caught Peggy's eye in the trees to her left. She peered up at the pathways among rows of trees along Westmount that she recalled her mum saying used to be known as Gallows Hill, because there had been gallows there when prisoners were publicly executed. More recently, executions had been rare and private.

She spotted small patches of white in the grass and others

in the branches and stopped, trying to make out what they were. Intrigued and seeing no military vehicles, she ran across the road and up the steps, quickly reaching what she discovered was a leaflet. It was in German. Peggy smiled. She had heard RAF planes flying over the previous night and thought they were closer than usual.

'They must have been dropping these,' she said to herself. The leaflet was from the British Government, encouraging German soldiers to surrender. It wasn't much but it was a reminder that they hadn't been completely forgotten.

'Halt!'

Peggy tensed, instantly aware she was being addressed. She dropped the leaflet and turned to face the soldier. In English, she said, 'I'm sorry, I didn't know what it was.'

He narrowed his eyes at her and after staring at her for a few seconds cocked his head to one side. 'Move. Go.'

She didn't need telling twice. She was lucky that he hadn't known she understood what it said, or that he wasn't one of the more officious ones who took advantage of an opportunity to display their power.

She hurried back down the path to the road, crossed over to the other side and walked as quickly as she could all the way to work. She arrived at her office out of breath and weary. She had followed the same route, apart from her brief detour, that she took every workday morning and night, yet now she found it tiring and her legs ached. She knew it was due to the shortage of good food. Or any food at all, she thought miserably as she took off her coat and sat down at her desk.

She had only managed to remove the cover from her typewriter and take her notepad and pencil from her desk when the door opened and Tony entered, so quietly she barely heard him. Relief flooded through her. She leapt up and ran to him.

'Where have you been? I've been terribly worried about you.' She wrapped her arms around his waist and rested her head against his chest, feeling his bones against the side of her face where before had been muscles. When he didn't reply, she tensed. 'Are you all right? Your parents?'

He held her more tightly and she realised he was trembling. 'My mother,' he said, his voice tight with emotion. 'She's in the nursing home.'

'What happened?' she asked, knowing it must be something serious.

'She's had a breakdown. Dad is beside himself.' He exhaled sharply. 'As am I.'

She held him tighter against her, desperate to comfort him. 'I'm not surprised you're both upset. Do you know how long they expect her to be there?'

'They don't know. She was eating less than she was giving us but we didn't know. It can't have helped her health.' He sighed. 'I feel guilty not to have realised.'

Peggy moved back slightly and looked up at him, resting a hand against his cheek, until he lowered his eyes to hers. 'Listen to me. I've met your mother. It's obvious how much she adores you and your father. She only did what many mothers would do.' She thought of her own mother and decided to be more observant when Ida was serving meals in case she was doing something similar. 'She wouldn't have let you not eat that food, Tony. It's her way of showing her love for you.'

His eyes filled with tears. 'But how do I show my love for her?'

'By keeping going. By staying strong for her and your

father. She needs to know you'll both be fine.' It dawned on her then that whenever she and Babs got home from work and their mother insisted she had already eaten, she hadn't in fact done so. 'It's what I'd do,' she added, 'and I've just realised that my mother has been doing something similar.'

Tony's upper body seemed to sag. 'I'm not sure how long I can keep this up.'

She heard the despair in his voice and wanted to cry. Tony had always been the strong one, the one to encourage them all to keep going, the shoulder to cry on whenever they needed him. Her heart broke for him. She realised it was her turn to be the strong one now.

She grabbed hold of his upper arms, once so muscular and strong and now so thin. 'You have no choice,' she snapped. He gazed miserably into her eyes and she wanted to comfort him, not feign anger. 'You have too many people depending on you, Tony. Whether you want to do this for yourself doesn't matter any longer.' You have to help your family. Mine needs you, too, as do Helen, Bobby and now Daphne. None of us can survive if you don't keep going.'

It was cruel to add to the pressure on him, but she suspected it was the only way to persuade him or motivate him.

'We're starving and despondent, but we all need to dig deeper and find the resolve to do what's needed.'

He loosened his hold on her. 'You're right. We need help. The first thing I'm going to do is send a telegram to Richard, ask him to spread the word in England about our sorry state. If the British Government won't send forces to save us, then maybe someone will find a way to send us enough food and supplies to keep us alive until they do free us.'

Chapter Sixty-Five

HELEN

Late September 1944

H elen checked her watch for the third time that hour. It was eight in the evening and Daphne still wasn't home. She was always back by six-thirty at the latest and Helen wondered what could be keeping her. Maybe there had been an unexpected meeting and they had insisted she stay behind to look after the staff.

Helen tried to remain calm, hoping that was what had happened. But by midnight, she knew she couldn't lie to herself any longer. Daphne would never leave them alone to fend for themselves. If she couldn't make it home, she would have sent a message to Tony or Peggy asking them to come to Sans Souci and let Helen know not to worry.

After a sleepless night, Helen scraped the mould off the last of the bread and gave it to Bobby, cutting up one of the figs from the garden to bolster his breakfast. She took a deep breath, trying to quell the fear that something terrible had happened.

'Where's Aunty Daffy?' Bobby asked, tugging at her skirt.

Not wishing him to detect her distress, Helen steadied herself before crouching down in front of him. 'She's busy at work,' she fibbed. 'She said we must keep things nice and tidy while she's away. We can do that, can't we?'

'Yes, Mummy.' He looked around and ran from the kitchen. Intrigued, Helen followed him and found him tidying up his toys.

She needed to keep him busy and his mind off Daphne's absence. 'You don't have to put all your toys away.' She thought quickly. 'Come with me. I'll give you the dustpan and brush and you can sweep up our crumbs from this morning. Would you like that?'

He beamed at her, clearly delighted at the idea. Helen wished she felt the same way about housework. He followed her back to the kitchen and, as soon as he was holding brush and pan, began sweeping.

After washing their few dishes and wiping the worktop, Helen called for Bobby to follow her outside. 'Let's go and see if we can find any vegetables or maybe some fruit on the trees.'

He loved being in the garden so didn't need telling twice. She put on his sweater and her jacket and went outside with the trug Daphne liked to use to collect flowers and produce. Helen hadn't expected to find anything because they had only looked the day before.

'What's this?' she asked pointing down at green leaves.

He thought for a moment. 'It's mint, Mummy.'

'That's right. You're such a clever boy.' She ruffled his hair. 'You pick us a few leaves and Mummy will see what else we can find.' The mint wasn't going to keep them from starving but it would make the tap water taste nicer.

She found two tiny carrots. They would only make a mouthful and she should leave them to grow a little longer, but she decided that Bobby needed the nutrition now and asked him to pull them from the ground and place them in the trug.

'Look, Bobby.' There was a small tomato she must have missed the previous day. It was hidden under a leaf and was becoming rotten, but it was better than nothing. By the time they had finished their walk around Daphne's garden they also had an apple and two figs.

She crouched down to show him their haul. 'Aren't we clever?'

He jumped up and down clapping. 'We are, Mummy. Aunty Daffy will be happy.'

At the mention of her friend's name, Helen frowned. It was over twenty-four hours since she had last seen her. What could have happened to her?

'Mummy?'

Bobby had noticed her consternation and she was irritated with herself at not being more careful. She pulled a silly face. 'Let's go inside and you can help me wash these. Then later we'll eat them.'

He took hold of one side of the trug handle and together they went into the house.

By seven-thirty that night, Helen knew without doubt that something terrible had happened to her friend. She fed Bobby the fruit they hadn't eaten at lunchtime and was relieved when he fell asleep earlier than usual. She carried him through to their bed and, not wishing to wake him, slipped off the wooden clogs Tony had brought for him a few weeks before, and covered him so he was warm. She left him to sleep.

Returning to sit in the living room, Helen tried to think straight. If Daphne wasn't coming home, then she needed to take Bobby somewhere else. Daphne worked with senior German officers and if something had happened to her they would know about it. The way things were now, with all the shortages, those officers would probably come here to ransack the place and she had no intention of being at Sans Souci if they did. She had heard enough horror stories about the depths to which some of them would go.

Chapter Sixty-Six

PEGGY

2 October 1944

Peggy heard Tony's knock. She greeted him with a smile that disappeared the instant she saw his face. She stepped around her desk to reach him as quickly as possible and took his hands in hers. Her heart ached. 'It's not your mother, is it?' she asked, her voice barely above a whisper.

He shook his head. 'No, thank heavens, but it's not good.'

'Tell me.'

She listened, barely able to breathe, as he shared what he knew about Daphne. 'The poor woman died of a heart attack while at work.' Shocked, Peggy was about to ask what impact this would have on Helen and Bobby's safety, but he continued before she could. 'And that's not the worst of it,' he said, fear in his dark brown eyes. 'She died three days ago.'

'Three?' How must Helen be coping? 'Do you think Helen knows?'

'How could she? I only found out because my father was contacted as the executor of her will.'

Peggy covered her mouth with her hand, not wishing her anguish to be heard outside her office, as the implication of what he was telling her sank in. 'We have to go to Helen and let her know. Check that she and Bobby are all right.' She whimpered as her mind raced. 'She relies on Daphne for everything. They'll have no way to get food.' She began to panic. 'Tony, they must be terribly frightened.'

He put an arm around her shoulders. 'Which is why I'm here. I need you to go home straight away and ask your mother to prepare the attic for them.'

She stared at him, unable to grasp what he was saying for a moment. 'But surely they're safer where they are, as long as we take them food?'

'If only that was true. Maybe if Daphne hadn't worked where she did, then we might have time before they discover her home isn't empty.'

She wasn't sure what he was getting at. 'Are you worried the soldiers will go to Sans Souci searching for food?'

He groaned. 'I am, and whatever else they might hope to find there. Tools, bedding, who knows. The most important thing is that we make sure they don't find Helen and Bobby.'

Peggy's heart leapt to her throat. She had been frightened many times over the past four and a half years, but this really was a matter of life or death. 'We won't allow that to happen,' she said, determined to rescue her friend and the little boy they all loved.

She covered her typewriter and dumped her paperwork into the top drawer of her desk before slipping on her coat. Tony pulled her to him, kissing her hard on the mouth with an urgency she suspected was filled with love as well as fear that they might already be too late.

'You'd better hurry. I'll meet you at your house, then we'll go together.'

He left the room and Peggy followed, closing the door behind her and running down the stairs, desperate to get home as soon as possible. Tony would do quickly whatever he needed to do. She walked fast, trying not to look flustered and draw attention to herself. She arrived home in half the time she usually took and ran up the front steps, ignoring Leutnant Müller's figure standing at the front room window next door.

'Mum?' She didn't bother taking off her coat but ran through to the kitchen, then, when her mother wasn't there, called upstairs for her. She was relieved when her mother appeared at the top of the stairs.

'What's all the panic for?' Ida asked, scowling down at her. 'Please don't tell me something's happened, I've had enough of that already today.'

'What?'

Her mother shook her head. 'Only the usual. Friends being arrested for silly little mistakes.' She narrowed her eyes and began walking down to join Peggy. 'Something's badly wrong, though, isn't it?'

Peggy explained what had happened to Daphne and about her and Tony needing to rescue Helen and Bobby before it was too late. 'I just pray we get them out of there in time.'

'You will.' Her mother turned to go back upstairs, then, as a thought struck her, stopped, rested her hand on the banister and turned to Peggy. 'You must. But how do you expect to smuggle them back here? When Tony took them last time it was winter and Bobby was much smaller than he must be now.'

'That's what's worrying me,' Peggy admitted. 'Maybe we'll wait until it's dark because that's bound to be safer, but I don't know if that'll be too dangerous. We'll have to see.'

There was a knock at the front door.

'That'll be him.' She leant forward and kissed her mother's cheek. 'Try not to worry. We'll be as quick as we can and hopefully by tonight the pair of them will be safely back in the attic again.'

'I'd better get on and freshen it up then, hadn't I?'

Chapter Sixty-Seven

HELEN

It had been three days and still no news. Helen had already packed their most important belongings but didn't want to strip their bed in case they stayed for another night. The previous evening, she had come close to leaving and taking Bobby to the Hamels' but was anxious about being seen and putting them at risk. They could easily be stopped by a German and asked for their papers and she knew it wouldn't take them long to discover she had been missing for the past couple of years.

Helen thought she heard voices and tensed. 'Bobby,' she hissed, running to him and taking his hand. 'Come with Mummy, quickly.' She put a finger to her lips. After spending so long living in the attic at number 3, he thankfully knew how to keep quiet and only speak in a low whisper.

'Are we going to hide, Mummy?'

'We are. We must hurry.' She led him out of the back door to the garden where she had stored two bags of their things

behind a large bush. 'Here,' she said, pulling him gently so that
he knelt down next to her behind the bush.

It occurred to her that soldiers coming this far from First
Tower would probably have driven and she hadn't heard a
vehicle. Was that because she hadn't been listening? Or maybe
there wasn't any fuel left for them to use.

Or maybe they would want to surprise her? But for that to
happen they would need to know she and Bobby were at the
house and she was certain that Daphne would never have
given them up.

She heard a murmur of voices and for a second imagined one
might be female, but it was too hushed for her to be certain. She
put her arm around Bobby, pulling him closer and lower, as she
heard footsteps leaving the house and coming into the garden.

'Helen? Bobby? It's Tony,' he said, keeping his voice low.
'I'm with Peggy. We've come to fetch you.'

'Uncle Tony?' Bobby asked standing just before Helen
managed to do the same.

'Over here.' She picked up their two bags. 'We've packed a
few things, but we weren't sure whether to stay here where it's
safe, or leave.'

Tony pointed in the direction of the nearest neighbours a
short distance away. 'Let's go inside.'

Helen tried to grasp what Tony was telling her. 'How could
Daphne have died?' she sobbed. She was relieved that Peggy
had taken Bobby from the room before Tony broke the news
to her.

'I couldn't believe it when Dad told me,' he said.

'She was such a kind woman. Like my family, really. And she adored Bobby.'

'She did,' he soothed, hugging her. 'But the most important thing for her was that both of you were safe. Dad told me that as nothing can be done about contacting her cousin in England who's her next of kin, the Germans have told him they will be using her home for several officers.'

'But why? It's not close to town here, and it's only a bungalow,' she argued, hating to think of those men sleeping under Daphne's roof.

'It's the position of the house,' he explained. 'It's high and has far-reaching views over the bay. With all the Allied aircraft activity over the past few months this place will be useful to them.'

Dismissing thoughts of how distressed Daphne would have been to know this, Helen took a steadying breath. She needed to focus on Bobby and getting him to safety. 'We've already packed a few things, as you know,' she said. 'But where will we go? We can't go to the Hamels in broad daylight, can we?'

He shrugged. 'We'll wait until dusk, then begin walking down to St Aubin's Road.'

As terrified as Helen was to have to move, Tony insisted she complete her packing quickly, so that they could leave as soon the sun began to set. 'We'll take Bobby to the Hamels the same way we brought him here.'

Helen wasn't sure how that would work. 'But he's much taller and heavier now,' she argued. 'How will you manage to carry him that far?'

Tony stared at her for a moment. 'He was heavier, but

we've all lost a lot of weight in the past few months, maybe Bobby, too.'

He was right. 'But you won't be as strong as you once were, Tony.'

'Maybe not, but I can't see that we have much choice. You can't stay here. Bobby can walk some of the way but maybe not the last stretch along the main road or into the Hamels' house. The officers still live next door and we know that two of them may remember you and the fact that you had a son. We can't risk them recognising you.'

She loved the Hamels and had missed Ida, especially, as the older woman hadn't been able to make the walk up to Sans Souci. It would be lovely to see her again, but Helen couldn't help being upset that Bobby would no longer have the freedom to play outside and would once again be stuck indoors every day. At least when he was younger he hadn't had anything to compare his life to, but now he did and she worried about how he would cope.

She thought of the Hamels having to share their sparse food with her and Bobby.

Once again, Helen felt how much of a burden hers and Bobby's welfare was to their friends.

'We're all happy to help anyone who needs it, you know that,' Tony said, as though reading her mind.

'I do,' she said. 'But I don't know how much longer I can stand this way of life. It only ever seems to get worse.'

Chapter Sixty-Eight

PEGGY

Peggy left Bobby playing in the sunshine, wanting him to make the most of being outside before he was shut away again like a hothouse flower. She watched the little boy rolling on the grass and giggling. At least he has had this freedom for a while, she reasoned, trying to stay upbeat as she went inside to find how Tony was getting on with Helen.

It saddened her to think of everything her friend had gone through already. The last thing Helen needed was to lose her close friend and leave this comfortable home that she and Bobby clearly loved. Now wasn't the time for sentiment, though; not when their lives were once again at risk. Peggy braced herself to face Helen. They needed to get things done and she couldn't afford to lose her nerve.

She walked in and saw Helen's puffy eyes. It didn't surprise her that she had been crying. Tony gave her a pleading look and Peggy knew what she must do.

'I'm sorry, Helen, but we need to organise ourselves.'

Helen looked surprised to see her there. 'Sorry?'

Peggy repeated herself.

'I've...packed a couple of bags...with our necessities.' Helen pointed to two small bags by the wall to her right.

'Well done,' Peggy said encouragingly. 'Now we need to remove all trace of you and Bobby having been here.'

Helen seemed to become more alert. 'Yes,' she said standing. 'I wasn't sure what to do.'

'It's fine,' Peggy assured her, trying to think what they needed to do first. 'If we're going to leave at dusk then we only have a few hours to do everything. Leave Daphne's bed made, but yours must be stripped.'

'We won't be able to wash the bedding, though.'

Peggy had thought of that. 'Any dirty linen, towels and clothes of yours that could pass for Daphne's can be placed in her laundry basket. I presume she has one?'

'She does, but what about Bobby's things?' She sighed sadly. 'He doesn't have much but I couldn't pack everything.'

Peggy wasn't sure what to suggest.

Tony rubbed his chin. 'We can wrap them in a sheet and bury them with any toys he has to leave behind.'

'Bury them?' Helen and Peggy said in unison.

Tony shrugged. 'I can't think of a better suggestion, can you?'

'No,' Helen agreed. Seemingly galvanised, she pushed the chair she had been sitting on back under the table. 'Let's get started. I don't want to still be here when they arrive.' She stopped at the kitchen door and, without turning around, added. 'We'll leave Bobby playing outside until the last minute. I want him to have as much freedom as possible.'

Peggy heard the misery in her friend's voice and caught

Tony's eye. He was finding this as heartbreaking as she was. The sooner they got going the better, she decided.

Once it was dusk, they set off. 'I think when we reach the bottom of Mont Cochon you two girls should walk ahead and Bobby and I will follow a little way behind,' Tony said.

'What? No.' Helen looked horrified. 'If he's not going to be with me, I need to be able to see him at all times. You two walk in front of us, so that I can watch him.'

Tony nodded. 'Fine, but you follow my lead. If I'm stopped, do what Peggy says. Agreed?'

Helen still seemed unsure for a second, and Peggy was relieved when she finally consented.

'I also think,' Tony began, 'that it'll look odd if you're carrying too much. We can share the contents of the bags between us. Bobby can take two of his toys, which will help. He has pockets. We all do. Let's make the most of them. Then one of you girls can carry the other bag. The smaller one will draw less attention.'

Peggy was relieved when they finally got going. They managed to reach the bottom of the hill without seeing anyone apart from two elderly people who, Peggy noticed, had little energy to walk up the hill. She would have loved to offer them help but instead nodded a greeting and kept walking.

She and Helen pretended to look in the newsagent's window as Tony took Bobby's hand and led him further along the road. When they had almost reached The Overseas Trading Corporation frontage, where teas had been blended and packed since the early twenties for export across the world, Peggy linked arms with her friend. She could feel the tension in her.

'Remember not to look so concerned,' Peggy whispered.

'And stop staring at those two so intently, you're going to make any passersby wonder what's wrong with them.'

They passed the parish school, where she and Babs had been taught, and then the art deco garage. It wasn't far now. Only another few minutes and they would reach number 3.

'Oh, no,' Helen gasped, terror filling her voice.

'What?' Peggy asked, trying to see why she had reacted that way.

'Two soldiers have just come out of that shop.'

They watched as the uniformed men stopped, exchanged words and immediately began following Tony and Bobby. One of them shouted to Tony to stop just as he reached the entrance to Bellozanne Avenue. Peggy could barely breathe as the soldiers ran across the road to where Tony and Bobby were standing.

Why would they stop them? Peggy wondered, horrified.

'We have to do something,' Helen whispered, trying to snatch her arm from Peggy's grip.

Determined not to let Helen's panic catch the soldiers' attention, Peggy clung on to her. 'Stop it,' she snapped through gritted teeth. 'You're going to make things worse if you're not careful. Tony's no fool, he'll know how to deal with this.'

'And if he doesn't?'

Peggy knew that if anyone could remain calm and cope it was Tony. She and Helen had a role to play, and she was going to make sure they kept to it. 'We have to trust him. Keep walking.'

'If we pass them, I won't be able to see what's happening to Bobby.'

Peggy thought quickly. 'Tony will raise his voice so we can

hear him if there's anything to worry about. But we need to keep our distance in case Bobby calls out to you.'

She sensed Helen's reluctance, then something distracted her. Peggy followed Helen's gaze and saw a younger girl coming from the Avenue. She passed the soldiers with barely a glance and walked in their direction. She had a purposeful stride and Peggy wasn't sure what to make of her.

'Dulcie?' Helen said, as if she wasn't sure, either.

Peggy felt sick. Was this girl friendly? She had the power to alert the soldiers if she wanted to and Peggy was certain she had seen a look of recognition on Dulcie's face when she spotted Bobby. She hoped they weren't about to be caught.

The girl reached them. Peggy held her breath as she and Helen stared at each other in disbelief.

'Where have you been?' Dulcie whispered.

'I, er…It's a long story.'

Just when Peggy thought their plans were about to come crashing down around them, Dulcie hugged Helen. It clearly wasn't something Helen expected, from the stiff way she was standing. She stared at Peggy over the girl's bony shoulder, looking shocked.

Dulcie's arms dropped and she stepped back. 'No need to tell me now,' she said her voice low. 'Where are you headed?'

Peggy had a split second to decide whether to trust the girl. 'My house,' she said, hearing one of the soldiers questioning Tony. 'Over there. Number 3.'

'Link arms with me. We need to get away from here.' Helen did as Dulcie insisted and they began walking towards the Hamels' home.

'But Bobby – I can't just leave him out here,' Helen whimpered.

'Do not catch their eye,' Dulcie snapped. 'Anyway, I can't see you have much choice.'

Peggy's heart was in her mouth as the three of them neared Tony, Bobby and the soldiers. Deciding to try and distract Helen, she said, 'It's ever so good to see you again –' she hesitated, trying to recall what Helen had called the girl '– Dulcie.'

'You, too. How's your mum and dad?'

Peggy tensed at the sound of those two words together in one sentence. 'They're doing as well as can be expected.'

'What?' Helen glanced at her. 'Er, how's your family, Dulcie?'

Before the girl could reply, gunfire rang out, making Helen scream and instinctively lurch towards Tony and Bobby. Peggy clung to her friend. Tony would take care of the little boy. She daren't let Helen ruin their escape – not when they were almost home.

The soldiers yelled something as a man ran from a property followed by a third soldier. The two who had been questioning Tony instantly forgot about him and joined the chase towards West Park.

Tony turned to them. 'Quick.'

Peggy pulled Helen into following behind Tony. They were unable to keep up as he ran with Bobby, who was now crying loudly in his arms. Tony reached the front door of number 3 and quickly went inside. The three women ran across the road to the house and were a few doors down from the Hamels' when the front door of number 2 opened and three soldiers ran out.

Peggy tensed. They were too close for their venture to fail now, surely.

'Oh no,' Helen groaned tearfully. 'There's Hauptmann Schneider and Leutnant Müller coming out of Aunt Sylvia's house.'

'They mustn't see me either,' Dulcie hissed, keeping her head bowed. She put her arms around Peggy and Helen's shoulders, pulling them to her as if they were huddled together comforting each other as the drama unfolded. Peggy realised she must have worked with Helen and Daphne.

Peggy peered sideways, watching as Hauptmann Schneider's gaze passed over them. He didn't seem to recognise any of them, she noticed with relief. Just then gunfire echoed through the air again and the three men ran off to their right after the other three soldiers.

'Thank heavens for that,' Peggy whispered, barely able to breathe. 'Thank you, Dulcie. I think you've just probably saved us from being caught.'

'It's nothing,' she said but Peggy saw she was trembling. 'Helen was always kind to me when we worked together.' She looked over her shoulder as German voices screamed an order. 'I'd better be going home. It was good to see you, Helen. Maybe we can catch up when this is all over.'

'I'd like that.'

'Good luck,' Dulcie said before hurrying back towards Bellozanne Avenue.

'That was lucky,' Peggy said, feeling light-headed from their close brush with danger. 'Quickly, let's get inside.'

Her mother or sister must have been watching out for them because as soon as they reached the top step the front door opened. Peggy pushed Helen inside and seconds later leant against the closed front door, shaking. She tried to slow her breathing. Her legs were trembling with exertion and fear. She could barely believe they had made it.

Peggy was vaguely aware of her mother's voice and her sister's excitement, when strong arms enveloped her and Tony held her tightly against him.

'We made it,' he said, his deep voice quavering slightly.

'Only just.' She thought of the man who had run out of the property and diverted the soldiers' attention from them just when they had needed it. She hoped he had managed to escape.

'But we got them here.' He kissed her forehead. 'You were so brave.'

She looked up at him. 'I wasn't the one carrying Bobby, or being questioned.' She clung to him, her skin clammy from fear. 'We were all brave though, weren't we?'

'We were.'

Chapter Sixty-Nine

HELEN

31 December 1944

Helen woke, disappointed to see the small attic window instead of the larger one she had become used to in her bedroom at Daphne's home. She had been dreaming that she and Bobby were back at Sans Souci and it was an effort not to give into her grief. Losing Daphne had been an enormous shock and she missed her and their gentle life together. Each time Bobby asked if they would ever see Aunty Daffy again, her heart broke a little more.

Tony told her he had sent a couple of telegrams to Richard letting him know they were back at the Hamels but she was yet to hear from him. She ached with fear. She would be unable to bear it if anything happened to him. She had lost too many people already and needed Bobby to know his father.

She worried about whether she would ever recover from what she had experienced here. It was at times like these when she had too much time on her hands that her thoughts tormented her. She knew she must remain strong, although it was getting harder to keep her resolve as each day passed.

Instead of things getting better they were already so much worse than they had been the previous summer. There was barely any food, and soaps or detergents were things of the past, as was fuel. The house was cold now that they had run out of things to burn. But worst of all was their lack of hope. Helen suspected that if it wasn't for Bobby she would lie in a dark corner and simply spend her time sleeping. As it was they did sleep more, but only because there was little else for them to do and hunger sapped their energy.

Her feelings were irrelevant, though; she knew she was lucky to have Bobby to keep her despondency at bay. She was luckier than some to have such a precious reason to keep going, because, as difficult as she was finding it, she felt sure this war would end, especially since the Americans had taken back St Malo over three months before. Belgium had been liberated, too, and no doubt other battles would be won by the Allies.

She just hoped the islanders survived long enough to see it happen. She seemed to recall some excitement about a Canadian Red Cross boat bringing in food parcels, but since she and Bobby were in hiding they wouldn't be able to collect one.

Christmas had passed with little celebration, which she didn't mind. They had little to celebrate and nothing to celebrate with. All she wanted was for the days to pass and for them to somehow survive.

She heard excited voices. One of them was Babs's. The girl's enthusiasm for life was greatly diminished but she still managed to keep more upbeat than the rest of them.

'Mummy?'

Bobby's voice interrupted her thoughts. He pointed to the attic door, just as she heard footsteps. The door opened and Babs appeared. It took a moment for Helen to wonder what was different about her, then she remembered.

'Have you been out to collect your Red Cross parcel?' She asked, excited for her friends – and for herself and Bobby, because she knew without any doubt that the Hamels would insist on sharing with them.

'We have, and Mum said you're both to come down. We're not opening them until you two are present downstairs.'

Helen smiled at Bobby. 'Well then, we'd better go and see what's in the boxes.'

The happy faces that met her and Bobby as they entered the kitchen cheered her, reminding her that happy times were possible.

'Mummy, look,' Bobby shouted climbing onto a chair and kneeling so he could see what was on the table. He bounced up and down clapping his hands.

'Careful,' Helen said, trying to calm him. 'If you fall off that chair and hurt yourself you won't be able to watch.'

'You can help me open mine,' Ida said, going to stand on his other side. She pulled the box towards Bobby and opened the lid. 'Have a look inside and take each item out slowly.'

Helen watched proudly as her four-year-old son did as he was asked. He reached in, lifted out one item after another and set them down neatly on the table. Ida gave a running commentary as each box or tin was held up.

'Five ounces of chocolate. Twelve ounces of biscuits and three of sardines.'

'I love sardines,' Peggy sighed.

'I'm salivating over this chocolate,' Babs said, holding the package up to her nose and taking a long, slow sniff of the contents. 'Heavenly.'

'Yes, well if you've any sense you'll not wolf it all down in one go,' her mother teased. 'And don't forget we're to share all this with Helen and Bobby.'

Helen was about to speak, but Peggy put a hand up to her mouth. 'Don't say whatever it was you were about to, Helen. The three of us will be sharing these things with you. We've gone through this war together, the five of us, and we will continue to do so equally. I won't have any argument, so don't bother trying to persuade us otherwise.'

'Thank you,' Helen said, certain she would never find better friends than these women.

Ida pointed at the box. 'Come along, Bobby, what else do we have in there?'

They watched as he took out powdered milk, tins of prunes, salmon, Spam and corned beef. There was raisins, sugar, marmalade, butter, pepper and salt, but what made Helen's heart sing was seeing sugar, cheese and, especially, tea and soap.

'I've never seen anything so glorious,' she said, picking up the packet of tea and sniffing. 'Maybe this is the gold at the end of a rainbow.'

Ida was turning the wrapped block of soap in her hand. 'God bless those who packed these boxes and sent them to us.'

It dawned on Helen as she watched her adopted family enjoying their treats that these Canadian Red Cross parcels meant more to them than just their contents. It was the tangible confirmation that, despite everything they had endured in the past four and a half years, people they had never met cared about them.

Chapter Seventy

PEGGY

February 1945

The joy of receiving the Red Cross boxes lasted a while, but still their basic dietary needs weren't being met. They read a message in the *Evening Post* from the Bailiff telling them that if help didn't reach the island soon the bread ration would run out by the tenth of the month. That had been an especially dismal day as far as Peggy was concerned.

'If only we had a garden,' she said to Tony one evening, as they took a walk together, wanting to spend time with each other despite the cold. 'Or even lived out of town where we could go foraging.'

'I think you'll find everything there is to find has been picked. It doesn't help that the Germans are also starving, and don't forget they didn't have the benefit of receiving Red Cross parcels.' Tony groaned. 'If they had let the dockers unload the *Vega* in Guernsey we wouldn't now be waiting for the next parcels to arrive here. They really want us to suffer in any way possible, don't they?'

She agreed. 'It makes you wonder what makes some people act this cruelly.' She thought of the news her mother had heard a few days before. 'Maybe they're frightened.'

'How so?'

'Mum heard that a lot of the Jerries are suffering from malnutrition, and others have dysentery or TB. They're in a bad way, Tony.'

He kissed her cheek. 'I don't like to think of anyone suffering, Peggy, but have they bothered about us in all this time?'

She thought of Captain Engel and her relief when he had stopped calling on her the year before, although she had caught him watching her from the front window at number 2 on many an occasion and it unnerved her.

'Helen did tell us how Leutnant Müller saved food for her at the beginning of the war, which she fed to her aunt, don't forget. They're not all bad.'

Tony mumbled something she couldn't make out, then added, 'I suspect it was because he had ulterior motives.'

Peggy wasn't sure she agreed. She suspected he was just lonely. She decided to change the subject. 'How's your mother?' She gave his hand a gentle squeeze.

'She's back home now, which has cheered her up. She says she feels safer with Dad and me and he's happy to have her back with us.' He smiled. 'It's an enormous relief to know she's there.'

'I'm so pleased for all of you.' Peggy thought how distressed she would be if her mother had been taken to hospital or a home and realised how lucky she was not to have been separated from her family at any time.

Long may it last, she thought, crossing her fingers.

Chapter Seventy-One

HELEN

9 May 1945 – Liberation Day

So much had happened in the past few weeks that Helen could barely take it all in. She hadn't heard from Richard again and worried that something might have happened to him. Some news had given them hope though, which helped keep them going. Mussolini had been captured and killed, and then the Germans had finally surrendered.

Surrendered. She could scarcely believe it was true.

Yesterday had been Victory Day and the war in Europe was over at long last. Earlier, Peggy and Ida had tried their best to persuade her to take Bobby to the Royal Square with them to watch the island being formally liberated, just as Guernsey had been the previous day.

'I daren't,' she said, wishing she wasn't so scared of something going wrong. There were still thousands of German soldiers on the island and she was concerned that some might want revenge for losing the war. What if one of them came for her and Bobby? She had been in hiding far too long to chance being caught now.

'I'd rather wait until the British soldiers are here.'

'They'll soon be everywhere on the island, I imagine.' Ida took her hands as they sat in the kitchen. 'There's nothing to be fearful about. The Germans have surrendered and that's all there is to it.'

Helen wished she could believe that to be true. 'I know what you're saying, Ida but what if something goes wrong at the last minute? What if the British don't land here? What then? I can't risk them discovering our whereabouts. Not until I'm completely certain we're free from them at last.'

Like the other women, she had heard singing and laughter since the previous day and she realised she was possibly being overcautious, but she hadn't come this far or endured what she had, watching so much of her little boy's life being spent in hiding, to slip up before British forces arrived to liberate them properly.

'I know you think me silly, but I've made up my mind. I'll stay here with Bobby for now.' She thought of another reason to give them. 'He's only ever met a few people and might be frightened by the crowds that are bound to congregate in town.'

She saw Peggy's expression change as she accepted her reasoning. 'We'll come back and tell you everything. Then, if you're happy to, we can take Bobby for a walk somewhere. Not far, if it makes you uncomfortable. We'll see how you feel.'

Helen thanked her, grateful for Peggy's understanding. She wished her friends well.

They had only been gone a short while when someone knocked on the front door. She took hold of Bobby's hand.

'Come along, Bobby,' she said, leading him to the attic quietly and closing the door after them. 'Let's settle down and I can read you a story if you like.'

'We can't go with them?'

His sad eyes implored her to change her mind, but Helen had no intention of doing so. 'Not this time, but later, maybe. Would you like that?'

He nodded enthusiastically.

'Then that's what we'll do.'

She hoped the others wouldn't be too long because, regardless of what she had said, the thought of escaping this attic and never returning was something she had dreamed about almost every night. Freedom was coming and she was terrified something would go wrong before they could experience it properly.

Chapter Seventy-Two

PEGGY

'Come along Mum,' Peggy called, willing Ida to hurry. Tony was waiting impatiently, eager to go and celebrate.

As soon as they were outside, she noticed a strange look on her sister's face. 'What's the matter?'

'Um, there's a soldier.' Babs stared at the man in front of her.

A soldier? She stepped past her sister, surprised to see a British uniform. 'I didn't think they were disembarking until a bit later.' The man was staring at them. A lieutenant. Her heart raced.

'I'm sorry to interrupt you, when you're probably on your way to the celebrations,' he said.

He was looking at each of them in turn, clearly searching for someone. She barely dared to believe what she was thinking.

'I'm Lieutenant Richard Stanley.' None of them spoke, and his hopeful expression faded.

Finally, Tony reacted. 'I'm Tony Le Gresley.' He gave a wide smile. 'It's good to meet you finally, Richard.' He stepped forward and shook Richard's hand vigorously.

'I have so much to thank you for, Tony,' Richard replied, one hand on Tony's shoulder. 'So very much.'

'You can buy me a drink to celebrate one day, if you like.'

'I'd like that very much.'

Peggy couldn't believe it. Helen's Richard was standing in front of her. Outside their home.

Babs squealed, 'This really is the best day.'

Peggy studied the man's weary face. 'Bobby has your eyes,' she said almost to herself.

Realising what his presence would mean for Helen and Bobby, she turned to Tony. 'Why don't you accompany Mum and Babs to the Royal Square. I'll find you there as soon as I can.'

Tony hesitated. 'I'm not sure you'll be able to spot us in the crowds.'

Richard took off his cap. 'Please, if you don't mind me going into your home, I'm happy to find Helen and Bobby myself.'

Streams of islanders passed them on both sides of the road, singing and cheering and waving the Union Jacks and Jersey flags they had kept hidden since the island was occupied.

Peggy sensed Richard's desperation to see the two people he loved. 'Tony, take Mum and Babs. I promise I'll be a couple of minutes and will catch you up.'

They hesitated briefly and then left.

'Come along, Richard,' she said, beyond excited to imagine how much this would mean to Helen. 'I'll show you where to find them.' She ran back up the steps to the house. 'This way.'

She led him some way upstairs, then pointed upwards. 'You'll find them up there in the attic.'

He glanced up, then looked at her for a moment. 'Why are they still there?'

Peggy cleared her throat. 'I don't think Helen believed they were truly safe just yet.'

He nodded. 'I see.'

Not wanting to delay him a moment longer, she said, 'I'd better catch up with the others.'

She ran out of the house trying to take in all that was happening. She almost tripped as she struggled to pass islanders making their way to the town, intoxicated with excitement.

She didn't know whether to cheer, sing or cry as she hurried to catch up with Tony and her family. She thought she spotted the top of Tony's head, then the person turned and peered back through the hordes of people and waved. It was him. Ecstatic, she shouted her apologies and pushed her way past people until she ran into his arms.

'You found us,' he shouted, grabbing hold of her hand.

'I told you she would,' Babs said, laughing and rolling her eyes at Peggy.

'We should go to the harbour,' Tony insisted.

'Why?' Ida glared at him. 'Everyone's going to the Royal Square, or that's what I heard anyway.'

'Which is precisely why we shouldn't waste our time,' he argued. 'The British soldiers will be coming ashore at the harbour and if my contact there is right, then the place where we should wait to see them is the North Pier.'

'Come along, Mum,' Peggy said. 'It's closer to where we are

anyway.' Her mother didn't argue. Peggy could tell she was already slightly weary despite her excitement.

'Fine, we'll do that, then, but if you're wrong, Tony—'

He pulled a face at Peggy making her laugh. 'You'd better not be,' she teased.

They arrived and found a good place to stand just as the Tommies disembarked. An enormous cheer filled the air. Peggy didn't think she had ever cheered so loudly or with such delight. She clung to Tony's hand and waved wildly with her free one. Smiling soldiers made their way through the crowd, slowly because everyone was trying to shake their hands, thank them and welcome them to the island.

'I can't believe it really has happened.'

'It has, my darling. We made it.'

She saw the exhaustion in his eyes and pulled him down to kiss her. 'I always knew we would,' she fibbed.

———

'I'm going to take Mum home,' Babs said after almost an hour of excitement.

Peggy looked from her sister to her mother. 'Mum, are you unwell?'

Ida shook her head. 'Only footsore,' she said wincing. 'These shoes are pinching something terrible. I'm not used to walking this far anymore.'

'Would you like us to come with you?'

'You two stay here and have some fun. It's been a long time coming and you have the energy to enjoy it all.'

Tony slipped his arm around Peggy's shoulders. 'I'll look after her, Mrs Hamel.'

'I know you will, my love.'

Peggy put her arm around Tony's waist so that she didn't lose him in the crowds. 'I'll see you in a bit,' she shouted after them, though wasn't sure if her mother or sister heard.

His arm dropped and he took her hand in his. 'Come with me,' he said, leading her away from the crowds.

'Where are we going?' Peggy laughed as she ran next to him.

'Not far. I only want to take you somewhere quieter.' He glanced down at her, a twinkle in his eyes, and she suspected he wanted to kiss her.

She stumbled but he kept her from falling. Peggy laughed at the feeling of freedom. He led her past the crowds celebrating in front of the Pomme d'Or, down Mulcaster Street and into the Town Church garden, where fewer people were congregated.

'Here will have to do,' he said – looking a little nervous, she realised.

'Do for what?' They were out in the open – not really a place for a passionate kiss.

He let go of her hand and pushed his fingers through his hair, then straightened his jacket. Peggy was about to ask him what he was doing when he got down on one knee.

Her hands flew to her mouth and she gasped, barely able to take in what was happening.

From one of his pockets he withdrew a ring box and, after taking a deep breath, opened it.

'Peggy Hamel, I've loved you from the first moment I saw you. I told you when we first began courting that I wouldn't ask you to marry me until the war was over and we were liberated.' He beamed at her. 'Which we now are.'

'We are,' she whispered, delighted he hadn't wasted any time asking her.

He stared at her. 'You haven't answered me,' he said.

Peggy reached out and touched his cheek lightly. 'Because you haven't actually asked me anything yet.'

'No?' She shook her head. 'Peggy Hamel, will you do me the honour of becoming my wife?'

'Yes, Tony Le Gresley. I can't think of anything I'd rather do.'

He took the ring from the box and slipped it onto her finger. It was a little too big, so Peggy put it onto her middle finger for the time being. 'Just so I don't lose it,' she explained. She looked at the pretty sapphire with several small diamonds around it and didn't think she had ever seen anything quite so perfect before. 'It's exquisite.'

'It was my grandmother's. I hoped you'd like it.'

She pulled him to his feet and flung her arms around him, kissing him over and over. 'It's the most beautiful thing I've ever seen.'

Chapter Seventy-Three

HELEN

H elen heard another footstep on the stairs leading to the attic and covered her little boy's mouth with her hand. She forced a smile. 'Remember, Bobby,' she whispered, 'we mustn't make a sound.'

His small hand moved hers away. 'Because the Nasties are in the house?'

Helen nodded, her heart breaking to think that hiding in an attic from the Nazi officers who were billeted next door was part of his daily life. 'That's right.'

'We're safe in our fort though, aren't we, Mummy?'

She raised a finger to her lips, hearing heavy soles slowly making their way to their tiny hiding place, behind the secret cupboard under the eaves.

Seeing he was about to speak she covered his mouth again and pulled a silly face. 'We are safe in here, but we must shush now,' she said, hearing an unmistakable creak on the floorboard directly outside their attic room, followed by a squeak as the door was opened.

Desperate to clasp Bobby tightly against her, Helen resisted, aware that to do so might alert him to the seriousness of what was happening. He looked up at her, his large blue eyes so like his father's, and for the first time Helen saw fear.

Staring at the tiny shard of light piercing through a gap, Helen tensed as blackness enveloped them when the person entering the attic blocked the light as he passed their hiding place.

She felt Bobby's hands wrap around her arm and kissed the top of his head to comfort him. He began trembling almost as much as she was but didn't make a sound. He shouldn't have to be this brave at his age, she thought, struggling to control her emotions.

'Helen?'

She stilled. It was a man's voice. A deep one. One she thought she recognised. She closed her eyes tightly. She was imagining things. Opening her eyes again, she looked down into Bobby's. They were wide and staring up at her.

'Helen, are you up here somewhere? They said you would be.'

They? The only people who knew where she was were the Hamels and Tony, and Helen knew they wouldn't tell anyone about her and Bobby.

'Helen? Please. It's perfectly safe now, I promise you. The island has been liberated.'

Richard? It couldn't be him. Could it? She must have fallen asleep and was dreaming. Or she was delirious, that was it.

'Helen, I promise you everything will be fine now.' The voice she was hearing sounded so much like the one she had imagined time and again over the past five years, but how could he be here? She covered her mouth to stifle a whimper.

'It's Richard. Sweetheart, I'm here with the liberating forces,' he said gently. 'I promise you it's safe to come out now.' She heard his voice crack with emotion. 'I've come for you and Bobby. I promise no one will hurt either of you ever again.'

Bobby glanced at the low door then back at her. 'How does that Nasty know my name, Mummy?' he whispered trembling.

'He isn't a Nasty, Bobby.'

'Who is he?'

She felt a sob escape as she struggled to answer. 'He's your daddy.'

Light filled the tiny space as the door slowly opened and Richard, looking thinner and older, knelt on the attic floor. 'So this is where you've been hiding?'

His voice was gentle, and Helen knew he was trying not to frighten Bobby.

Helen opened her mouth to try and speak but Bobby interrupted her. 'Are you my daddy?'

She clasped her hand over her mouth, the sight of her son's sweet face blurred by her tears.

Richard wiped his right eye with the back of his hand and cleared his throat. He took a second to speak. 'Yes, Bobby. I'm your daddy. And I've come to fetch you and your mummy, so you'll never need to hide in this attic again.'

Richard reached in and held out his hand, waiting for Bobby to take it. The little boy looked up at Helen. 'Mummy?'

'It's all right, sweetheart.'

Bobby took Richard's hand and stepped out.

'Your turn now, Mummy.'

She took Richard's hand, too, remembering the feel of it

that last time on their walk in the park. She let him help her to her feet, her legs shaking.

'Are you all right?' His deep voice soothed her.

'I will be now.' She left her hand in his while she studied his face, aware he was doing the same to her. Then, feeling a tug on her skirt, she crouched to take Bobby in her arms. 'You were a very brave boy.'

Bobby pushed her gently away and she saw he was trying to appear grown up. He looked up at his father. 'I'm four and a half.'

Richard cleared his throat. 'I know.'

'Mummy and I play forts when the Nasties come.'

Richard frowned briefly, then smiled. 'Ah, the Nasties. They won't be coming for you anymore.'

'They won't?'

Richard shook his head. 'Never again.'

'Mummy, is that true?'

'If that's what your daddy says, then I suppose it must be,' Helen said. She was barely able to take in what was happening. 'We've definitely been liberated, then?'

'Well and truly. Can't you hear all the cheering and singing?'

She could. Going over to the window, Helen lifted the catch and pushed it open, letting in the sounds of pure joy she had almost given up hope of ever hearing. 'It's wonderful,' she said, crying.

'It is. There are massive crowds in front of the Pomme d'Or and by the harbour. I think the islanders will be celebrating for a long while yet.'

She didn't doubt it.

She saw Bobby pull at Richard's uniformed leg. 'Can we go and sing?'

'If your mummy agrees.'

Helen decided she needed to see for herself that the hated Nazi emblem had been replaced by the Union Jack. See British soldiers in charge, instead of those she had spent the past five years hiding from. That might persuade her brain that this was real. 'I do.'

'Do you mind if I give Bobby a cuddle first?' Richard asked, crouching down again in front of Bobby.

'I'd like it very much.'

She watched as Richard opened his arms and his son stepped into them. Richard's eyes closed for a few seconds before opening and looking directly at her. 'Thank you,' he mouthed.

If the past five years had taught her anything, it was that life was too short and precious to waste. She hoped there was a future for the three of them. Now they had their freedom, it was time to make the most of it.

'No, Richard,' she whispered. 'Thank you for coming for us.'

He took her in his arms and kissed her, startling her for a second. His kiss was familiar but different in some way. There was an urgency about it that hadn't been there before.

'There's no need to thank me, Helen. I should never have let you go. I promise to spend whatever time I have left making up for not being here for you both when you needed me most.'

She nestled into his arms, her head against his chest and her right hand on Bobby's back. After all they had gone through in the past five years Helen knew for certain that she and Bobby could be happy with this man.

'I'd like that, Richard,' she said, kissing him again. 'We both would.'

Author's Note

Dear Reader,

Thank you for choosing to read *Neighbors at War*. I loved writing this second book set during the occupation of Jersey and thought you might like to know about some of my inspirations behind the characters in this book.

It was after receiving an email from Robin Fredericks and his wife Heather in 2022 saying that they were researching his mother Laura's life that they visited the island and we met for coffee at the Pomme d'Or. This is the hotel where on May 9th 1945, British soldiers stepped out onto the balcony and hoisted the Union Jack onto the flagpole, bringing an end to five years of German occupation. Robin and Heather showed me letters and photos and told me about Laura's fascinating life during those dark years when she was trapped here, like my character Helen. The bit in the book about hiding the meat in the baby's pram happened to Laura. I thought Laura's life was fascinating and mentioned to Heather and Robin that they should write a book about it. They told me that was what they had hoped I might do but after explaining that I only write fiction, and after a lot of thought, I decided that I was happy to use this part of Laura's life as inspiration for my fictional character Helen Bowman in *Neighbors at War*. And that is what I've done. Helen's son Bobby's story was how I imagined Robin's young life to be.

Like Helen, Laura came from London and having been let down by the man she expected to marry and discovering she was pregnant with his baby, fled England to Jersey where her aunt took her in. Soon after Laura's arrival the German forces invaded the island and she was forced to spend the following five years moving from place to place with her little boy, Robin.

The second main female in the book, Peggy is loosely inspired by a linguist who worked on the island during the Occupation and married a local lawyer. Her name was Betty and although I knew very little about her story, it inspired me to write Peggy's character deciding she would make a great friend and neighbour for Helen.

In this book Helen's aunt, Sylvia came to the island in the twenties when she married her husband. My own grandmother, Mary Wood came to the island in the twenties with her mother (Marguerite Wood, the inspiration behind the grandmother Mrs Woods, in *An Island at War*). Mary Wood met my grandfather, George Troy, they married and she made the island her home until her death in 1992 leaving two sons and nine grandchildren.

The address I use in the book where Sylvia, Helen and Bobby live is inspired by the Victorian terraced house that was along St Aubin's Road during the war and where my great-grandmother lived. Number 2 Tynemouth Terrace housed, according to my research of Occupation Identity documents, six people in 1941. Two men, Claude Closs and David Owen were both born in England, they arrived at the property in June of that year but were unfortunately two of the people transported to Germany on 29 September 1942 - an incident covered in this book. I'm not sure why they were deported when another non-local man also living at number 2 at the same time wasn't. I hope they survived the war.

None of the people living in the property during the occupation were from Jersey, including my great grandmother who moved to the island in 1927 from Cardiff where she had been widowed and was living with my grandmother for several years. Granny Woods refused to be evacuated when her daughter left the island with her two sons and a nephew just before the invasion. My great-grandmother lied on her Occupation Registration Card (a photo of which you can see at the back of *An Island at War* courtesy of Jersey Heritage) about her maiden name and place of birth for some reason none of us can fathom.

The property no longer exists and was demolished and replaced by modern flats a couple of decades ago, but I was lucky enough to see it prior to that. Coincidentally, the house next door to Sylvia's where the Hamel family live, number 3 Tynemouth Terrace, was the home of one of my great aunts, Aileen Perkins (nee Troy). She was my grandfather George's older sister. She moved there in 1944 from her lodgings at the Public Prison in Gloucester Street where she was an assistant matron, and where my character, Tony Le Gresley was held after his arrest in the book.

As mentioned in my acknowledgements, Alison Barrington, Lord and Lady Trent's great-granddaughter told me several stories about their home during the Occupation when I was chatting to her during my research for my series on Florence Boot. It is thanks to her that I know about the silver being buried under the bonfire in the garden at Villa Millbrook (now known as Millbrook Manor) and Jesse Boot's portrait being damaged by one of the Nazi officers who defaced it by pushing a lit cigar into the painting.

I mention the Sacré Coeur Orphanage in the book and it's there that my late mother-in-law, Margaret Carr worked in the fifties and maybe sixties. She had many stories about her time there, some very sad ones about children she helped look after. When she died my husband found many photos of her with children from the orphanage.

Once again, thank you for choosing to read my book and for your continued support.

Until next time,

Deborah x

Sources:

As well as stories from family and friends, I have an enormous amount of documentation and telegrams held in two suitcases from my late mother-in-law, Margaret Carr.

Jersey Heritage was an excellent resource for my research on the island's history.

Jersey Occupation Diary by Nan Le Ruez, which I referred to for checking weather and dates at certain times during my book.

*Above: Occupation Registration Card for Laura Fredericks,
our Helen Bowman. (Courtesy of Jersey Heritage)*

*Above: Occupation Registration Card for Aileen Perkins, my
great-aunt who lived at Number 3, where the neighbours in
this book live. (Courtesy of Jersey Heritage)*

Acknowledgments

My late husband Robert was my greatest supporter. Like me, he was born in Jersey. He loved his island, its people and its history and enjoyed helping me with my research. I'm glad he knew about this book; I just wish he was here to read it.

My thanks too to Robin and Heather Fredericks, who I first met in 2022 when they told me about Robin's mother Laura's story and how Robin was born on the island during the Occupation. The Fredericks kindly shared photos of Laura and information from their research. This book is a work of fiction but it was inspired by Laura and Robin's experiences during the Occupation.

As ever, I want to thank my amazing editor, Charlotte Ledger. Charlotte is a huge supporter of her authors and I'm extremely grateful to be one of them. I'm also grateful to the rest of the wonderful One More Chapter team for all that they do. My thanks especially to Bonnie Macleod, and also to Tony Russell for his copy edits and Emily Thomas for proofreading this book, I appreciate your help enormously.

Jersey Heritage is an incredible source of information, and I would like to thank everyone there for their continued hard work bringing the island's history to the public and making research for my novels so much easier than it otherwise would be. I'm especially grateful to Stuart Nicolle, Senior Archivist at Jersey Heritage, who kindly agreed that I could use the

Occupation Registration Card photos for Laura Fredericks and Aileen Perkins in this book.

Thank you also to my niece, Amanda Goddard for answering my questions about having a small child. It's so long since I had babies that she became my go-to person to ask about Bobby for *Neighbors at War*, although any errors in this book are definitely mine.

Writing is a solitary job, but I'm lucky to have a great support network of close friends who also happen to be writers and who I chat to most days. They are Christina Jones, who along with her husband, Bob spent many happy times with Rob and I on their visits to the island; Gwyn Bennett and Kelly Clayton (my lovely fellow Blonde Plotters) also live here in Jersey. We meet up often and chat every day; Glynis Peters and Christie Barlow, fellow One More Chapter authors who will be coming to stay with me soon, and Laura Carter who also now lives on the island.

I'm also grateful to Alison Barrington, great-granddaughter of Florence Boot, Lady Trent who, when I was researching my Mrs Boots trilogy and asked her about where Lady Trent spent the Occupation, told me about Florence going to stay in Scotland and several other anecdotes about her home Villa Millbrook that was requisitioned by the Nazis during the Occupation.

To everyone who has shared stories with me over the years about their experiences during the Occupation from family to close friends, thank you.

Last but certainly not least, my thanks to you for choosing to read my book and follow Helen and Peggy's story through the Occupation.

ONE MORE CHAPTER

The author and One More Chapter would like to thank everyone who contributed to the publication of this story...

Analytics
Abigail Fryer
Maria Osa

Audio
Fionnuala Barrett
Ciara Briggs

Contracts
Sasha Duszynska
Lewis

Design
Lucy Bennett
Fiona Greenway
Liane Payne
Dean Russell

Digital Sales
Hannah Lismore
Emily Scorer

Editorial
Kate Elton
Arsalan Isa
Charlotte Ledger
Bonnie Macleod
Jennie Rothwell
Tony Russell
Emily Thomas

Harper360
Emily Gerbner
Jean Marie Kelly
emma sullivan
Sophia Walker

International Sales
Bethan Moore

Marketing & Publicity
Chloe Cummings
Emma Petfield

Operations
Melissa Okusanya
Hannah Stamp

Production
Emily Chan
Denis Manson
Simon Moore
Francesca Tuzzeo

Rights
Rachel McCarron
Hany Sheikh
Mohamed
Zoe Shine

**The HarperCollins
Distribution Team**

**The HarperCollins
Finance & Royalties
Team**

**The HarperCollins
Legal Team**

**The HarperCollins
Technology Team**

Trade Marketing
Ben Hurd

UK Sales
Laura Carpenter
Isabel Coburn
Jay Cochrane
Sabina Lewis
Holly Martin
Erin White
Harriet Williams
Leah Woods

**And every other
essential link in the
chain from delivery
drivers to booksellers
to librarians and
beyond!**

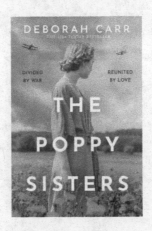

Divided by war. Reunited by courage.

Phoebe is a volunteer nurse at a Base Hospital in Étaples,
France, treating men who've served on the Western Front.
Their courage and resilience inspires her, and though she's
meant to keep her distance, Captain Archie Bailey soon
captivates her heart.

Her younger sister Celia is a nurse at a POW camp on the
island of Jersey. These men fight for the forces that bombed her
brother and parents, but long hours spent healing them shows
her they aren't the monsters she expected.

Despite the miles between them, both Celia and Phoebe come
to see the commonality in their experiences – the sense of
community and friendship, the unexpected moments of love
and laughter, and a bond so strong that even war can't
break it…

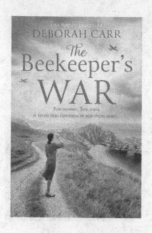

Two women
Two wars
A secret that threatens to tear them apart

1916

At the onset of war, Nurse Pru le Cuirot left her home in Jersey to care for injured soldiers at Ashbury Manor, Dorset. She wanted to do her bit but she never expected to meet American pilot, Jack Garland, so unlike any man she has ever met.

1940

Another lifetime, but another war and Pru's daughter Emma comes to Ashbury Manor. As Jersey falls to the Germans, Emma is fearful for her mother back home. And when she meets the mysterious beekeeper who lives in the grounds of the manor she finds herself caught up in a web of lies. As past and present collide, will the secrets of her mother's life finally be resolved?

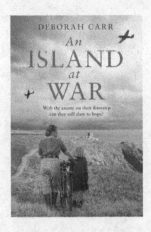

DEBORAH CARR
An
ISLAND
at
WAR
With the enemy on their doorstep,
can they still dare to hope?

This is a story of courage, resilience and everyday acts of defiance from ordinary people forced to live in an extraordinary time.

June 1940

While her little sister Rosie is sent to the UK to keep her safe from the invading German army, Estelle Le Maistre is left behind on Jersey to help her grandmother run the family farm. When the Germans occupy the island, everything changes and Estelle and the islanders must face the reality of life under Nazi rule.

Interspersed with diary entries from Rosie back on the mainland, the novel is also inspired by real life stories from the author's own family who were both on the island during the occupation and in London during the Blitz and is a true testament to the courage and bravery of the islanders.

ONE MORE CHAPTER

One More Chapter is an
award-winning global
division of HarperCollins.

Subscribe to our newsletter to get our
latest eBook deals and stay up to date
with all our new releases!

signup.harpercollins.co.uk/
join/signup-omc

Meet the team at
www.onemorechapter.com

Follow us!
 @OneMoreChapter_
@OneMoreChapter
@onemorechapterhc

Do you write unputdownable fiction?
We love to hear from new voices.
Find out how to submit your novel at
www.onemorechapter.com/submissions